KINGDOM OF REBELS

DEREK BIRKS

This is a work of fiction. Names, characters, places and incidents are either the product of the author's imagination or are used fictitiously, and any resemblance to any persons, living or dead, is entirely coincidental.

Derek Birks asserts the moral right to be identified as
the author of this book

Copyright © 2014 Derek Birks

All rights reserved.

ISBN-13: 978-1500841720
ISBN-10: 1500841722

To my son, Rob, who has been involved in this series from the start and whose encouragement and thoughtful advice have been a constant help.

ACKNOWLEDGMENTS

I would like to acknowledge the debt owed to Rob, for editing this book and in particular for his constructive suggestions and astute observations and also to Katie who, despite being on the other side of the world, was able to turn my rambling emails into a great cover design. Finally, as always, I must thank Janet for her long-suffering support and being the first to read the book.

DEREK BIRKS

CONTENTS

1	Part One: Exile	1
2	Part Two: House of Devils	73
3	Part Three: Brothers & Sisters	147
4	Part Four: Return	211
5	Part Five: Season of Good Will	275
6	Part Six: The Storm Breaks	349
7	Part Seven: Fathers & Sons	427
8	Author's Note	513
9	Historical Notes	514
10	About the Author	520

DEREK BIRKS

PART ONE: EXILE

DEREK BIRKS

1

24th June 1468, at Crag Tower in Northumberland

Eleanor woke up with a start. Across the other side of the room Maighread cried out in alarm. The chamber door lay open and Ragwulf stood in the doorway, a flaming torch in his hand.

"More trouble," he said. "Get dressed… if you will, ladies."

Eleanor slid out of her narrow bed in a hurry, only remembering her nakedness when she found Ragwulf staring at her. She snatched up a linen shift and her servant, Becky, scrambled up from her place on the floor to help her dress.

"Go on, I'll come after," Eleanor told Ragwulf.

He hesitated on the threshold. "You need not come at all, my lady. We have men enough to deal with it. Sir Stephen thought you should know, though… in case… it goes badly."

"Is it the same ones?" she asked.

"God alone knows. They're all thieves and murderers - every last one." His voice was gruff, dismissive.

"Go then," said Eleanor. Ragwulf left and the chamber was plunged into darkness with Becky still scouring the floor for clothing.

Once dressed, Eleanor bent down to rummage under her bed.

"Where's my sword?" she growled. When she stood up

and her eyes adjusted to the poor light she saw that Becky was holding it out to her. Without a word she snatched it and crossed the room to the other bed. Maighread was sitting up.

"Stay here, aunt," she said. "You need not be disturbed."

"And how in the name of Christ am I not to be disturbed," asked Maighread, "when there are raiders at our gates?"

Eleanor shrugged and then hurried after Ragwulf. She ran down the steps to the Hall where the young men had been rudely awoken and were only now arming themselves. Outside in the courtyard she found a short queue of men and women forming at the well. This night's struggle, like all the others, would be fought with water as much as steel. She could already see the glow of the flames snaking up the outside of the gates. Soon acrid smoke would spread across the yard and they would all be coughing in the midst of it.

Their captain, Sir Stephen, was on the wall rampart above the gate, bellowing orders into the night. Young Hal was there too with his bow trained on the ground below but on the fringes of the fire the attackers would be little more than wraiths.

A slight figure came to stand beside her and she gave him a smile. Fulk was the youngest of the men at arms and not really a man yet - just a boy. He had attached himself to her before and regularly pledged to protect her, should the gate be breached. Her smile dimmed and instead she gave him a solemn nod of encouragement - one warrior to another - his courage deserved that much.

Bales of burning straw thudded against the gate and the fire burned more fiercely. Her hand clenched and unclenched on the hilt of her sword. She did not expect to be using it much if the attack followed the same pattern as before. Whilst the defenders fought the fire, sporadic volleys of arrows fell upon them, usually harmlessly.

Wailing cries assailed them from beyond the walls and every so often a crudely-fashioned spear landed on the cobbled yard. Eventually the fire would be extinguished by pail upon pail of water and then, around dawn, it would all go quiet. Then they would stare at each other in relief, wipe the smoke from their faces, rest their weary limbs and wait for the next time.

But Eleanor was wrong; it did not play out as she expected. The arrows did not fall harmlessly. One tore through Fulk's neck and the impact threw his body against her. They hit the ground hard together and Eleanor rolled into a crouch beside him. Fulk was trembling with fear and pain but she could find no soothing words to calm him. The wound hardly bled at all but the arrow was lodged in his throat and she dared not pull it out. It took a long time for the lad to die and whilst he lay dying she stayed with him, her hand on his shoulder and her eyes locked on his.

Afterwards, she did not want to move and instead sat on the cobbles watching the servants and men at arms hurl water against the gate - until it became clear that this time their efforts would be in vain. The fire at the gate caught hold and their few leather buckets and leaky wooden pails proved insufficient to put it out. It seemed that tonight their attackers were trying harder for the gate was now a mass of flame.

Ragwulf was gathering a line of men at arms across the gateway. She sighed, laid Fulk's head gently down upon the stones and got to her feet. She moved awkwardly, her legs stiff with cramp, and went to stand beside Ragwulf. He gave her a cursory glance and said nothing, but then she was used to that. There was noise enough with the howling voices outside the walls and the crackle of burning timber within. Something crashed against the gate, now wreathed in smoke. It shuddered and sparks exploded into their faces. Eleanor took a pace back, the air ripped from her lungs. She sucked in a deep breath only to choke on cinders. She tried not to swallow, spitting out the ash, her throat as dry as old leather. The men were no better off than she and staggered back from the flames, coughing and spluttering.

More water was tossed against the gate, but the fire on the outer timbers was too strong. Another great blow battered the gate and a blast of heat struck her in the face, forcing her back a further step.

"Stand ready!" roared Ragwulf. "Don't crowd - give yourselves a yard!"

A moment later the flaming timbers split apart and bright shards of red hot wood spiralled out at them. Eleanor drew her sword, Will's sword, from its worn leather scabbard and cast the scabbard aside. She took up guard beside Ragwulf with her blade raised high above her head.

"We can manage well enough without your help, my lady," he said without a glance at her.

Her bitter smile gleamed in the firelight. "Aye, well you'll have to cut me down to move me!"

The centre of the gate disappeared in a confusion of smoke and flame and through it hurtled several screaming figures. At first Eleanor thought the men themselves were on fire but their spears thrust hard and their axes hacked away the charred timbers. The point of a spear darted at her through the smoke. She chopped her blade down on it, leaving only a broken shaft. The wild man holding it fell upon her with a snarl and slashed down at her with his long knife. She could not raise her sword fast enough and screamed in frustration. Suddenly she was shoved aside and the knife carved only through smoke-filled air. A great axe thudded into her attacker's body and his savage cry died with him as he fell.

"Take more care!" Ragwulf raged at her, "I can't be looking out for you! And watch that blade - you nearly took my arm off!"

"Then keep out of my way!" she barked at him, furious, and knowing he was right on both counts. As the remains of the gate blazed in front of them, they fought in a confused melee and soon it was hard to tell friend from foe. How many men came through the gate she had no idea, but few went out again. She was on the edge of it, skirting the great tangle of men and steel, and choosing her targets with care. She stabbed at a leg or sliced an unprotected arm to the bone until the slaughter ceased and all that remained was the smouldering wood, dying flames and mortal cries.

She looked about her: there were bodies aplenty by the blackened gateway and in the yard, including some of their own. At first she could not see Ragwulf and her anxious eyes scoured the courtyard until she found him. She discovered him leaning against the well. He was breathing heavily, coughing from the smoke he had taken into his lungs during the fight, but he looked unharmed. He glowered at her, but she patted his arm and smiled before leaving him.

She joined Maighread, Becky and several others in the Hall where some of the long tables already held blood-soaked bodies. Her aunt nodded to her but Eleanor decided there were enough helpers and turned away. She wandered back out into the dark to recover her discarded scabbard.

§§§§§

At dawn Eleanor and Becky went up to the highest rampart the castle offered at the very summit of Crag Tower. They stared out across the valley to the north where several spirals of smoke twisted up until the brisk wind seized upon them and scattered them eastwards. So, there had been other attacks in the night.

"I will go mad here," said Eleanor.

Becky grimaced. "You won't be alone…"

The breeze was cool but they did not mind for it discouraged others. Eleanor would have stood out in the pouring rain if it meant she could find some privacy, and a little peace.

"Here we all are crammed into this overstuffed kitchen garden, slowly rotting away. How kind of the good Lord to ease the crowding by killing some of our young men at arms. My brother released the men from their oaths three years ago - pity for them they didn't leave then."

"But not for us - we still need them," said Becky, "and three years ago they had nowhere to go."

"Aye, but we can't afford to pay them or feed them," said Eleanor, holding out her tattered clothes in disgust. "We're beggars in our own castle. This is a God-forsaken place…"

"Aye, lady."

"We can't go on like this. Everyone knows it; but no-one says it. Every week brings another attack. Have these border folk nothing better to do? It's not as if we even want to be here!"

The door up to the rampart swung slowly open and Lady Maighread Elder stood in the doorway. She smiled, or at least the left side of her face did whilst the other half, ravaged years ago by fire, merely creased awkwardly. The breeze caught her copper hair and threw it across her scarred cheek.

"Oh, shit," said Eleanor.

"God give you good morning, Eleanor," said Maighread.

"I pray He'll give me more than just one good morning, aunt."

"I do wish you wouldn't call me that," said Maighread, "I'm hardly older than you - we could be sisters."

"No, we couldn't," replied Eleanor, turning away. Looking at that tarnished beauty was more than she could bear. Instead she returned to looking out over the North Tyne, watching it flow in its great curve to the northwest.

"I'm sorry," said Maighread, "I was just seeking a little peace."

"So are we all." Eleanor knew her voice was cold and

regretted it at once.

"I'll leave you then," said Maighread quietly.

"No," said Eleanor. "This is more your home than mine. Even after four years here, Crag has never felt like home."

"I never wanted it to be so."

Her aunt was always so generous to her but fair words often grated in her ears. Maighread did not deserve her hostility but she received it nonetheless. It was not Eleanor's fault that they were all thrown together in this way, yet she knew it was not Maighread's either.

For a time the three of them stood together looking out over the battlements, silent as the stone. Then the door slammed open and the garrison commander, Sir Stephen, tramped up to them.

"Oh, Good Christ!" exclaimed Eleanor and pushed past him to descend the steps to the chambers below. Becky smiled an apology and ran after her.

§§§§

Maighread sighed in disappointment. Despite all her efforts to get to know her niece, they remained strangers. Sir Stephen gave her a sympathetic nod.

"I'm afraid the Lady Eleanor can be a fickle friend," he said.

Maighread frowned. "Perhaps you know her better than I," she replied, "but we can hardly lay the blame with her. We're all victims here."

"In another year, Lord Elder will return and all this will be forgotten."

Maighread winced. Another year? Could this man not see what was happening around him?

"We'll not survive another year like the last," she said in a low voice.

"Perhaps these border men will just give up and leave us

alone - they've taken heavy losses."

"I know these folk, Sir Stephen. What they see is a stronghold without its lord - that makes it very weak in their eyes. Aye, and getting weaker with every attack they make!"

"Ned Elder will come."

Maighread gave him a rueful smile. "Your lord is not a saint, Sir Stephen, who can work miracles in our lives."

"I know that, my lady - and, more important, so does he."

"He may come back to England but he'll not come here to Crag Tower. Why should he? There's nothing for him here. There's nothing for any of you here. You know that."

"Oh, he'll come here, my lady. I've no doubt of that." Stephen gave her an awkward smile.

There was a sudden outburst of shouting from the courtyard below.

"Oh, God rest us - what now?" muttered Sir Stephen. He excused himself and hurried down the steps.

Maighread tried to see over the parapet but whatever the commotion was it was out of her line of sight. She did not follow Sir Stephen but sat down on the stonework by the rampart wall. She closed her eyes and put her hands over her ears but still the shouts echoed up towards her. She knew what was happening - it was not the first argument amongst the men and there would be many more if nothing changed. In a moment it would stop and either Sir Stephen or the dependable Ragwulf would harangue the younger men involved before devising some utterly pointless and menial punishment. Well, this time they could at least be put to work on repairing the gate. Then peace would reign...until the next time.

She took her hands off her ears but still the shouting continued. She began to pay more attention to the voices for this argument sounded somehow different. The voices were not just loud they were hurling harsh, unforgiving words. A chill went through her as she recognised them:

Ragwulf and his son, Wulf - and she knew at once what the argument was about: Bess. It was certain to be about Bess. Scarred Maighread might be, but she could still use her eyes and ears. She had been expecting this, whilst hoping and praying it would not happen. They had enough problems without falling out with each other.

She got up and with a weary step made her way down the spiral stair to the floor where her chamber lay. It had never really been her chamber, but one she had shared for several years with Eleanor and before that, her cousin, Joan. At the sudden memory of Joan, her hand moved unbidden to stroke the rough skin on her right cheek. She hesitated on the threshold and thought of going on down to the courtyard but instead went into the chamber, which was mercifully empty. When the dispute showed no sign of abating, she shut the door - a waste of effort since she could still hear every word through the narrow arrow loop.

Wulf sounded furious. "I ask you again!" he bellowed, "before witnesses here."

Maighread knew there would be a crowd of men around the pair by now. They would have stopped work on the gate to listen.

"What business is it of yours if I've lain with Bess? We're going to marry!" declared Wulf.

"She's not for you!" retorted Ragwulf. He did not sound angry, but wounded, almost desperate. His self-control was legendary amongst his men; Ragwulf always remained calm. Always - but not now.

He raised his voice again. "Young John still needs Bess - she's been the only mother he knows."

Wulf's reply was blunt: "He's your bastard, not hers. She owes nothing to you - or to him."

"This is not the place-," said Ragwulf.

"Aye, it is the place! Bess and me are going to be married. Speak up, Bess!"

The girl spoke for the first time and her voice rang clear

and true. "Aye," she said, "married. I've done all that you asked of me and more."

For a moment there was a silence then much muttering and restless shuffling of boots on the cobbled yard until another voice was raised. Eleanor: as loud and uncompromising as ever.

"Ragwulf is right. Listen to your father, Wulf. Bess will stay here and continue her duties to John. She will not marry you, Wulf. You must be patient, the two of you. Perhaps, when Lord Elder returns…"

"And what if Lord Elder never returns?" roared Wulf. "We've waited long enough as it is. If we can't marry here, then I'll take Bess somewhere else."

"No!" said Eleanor. "She will not leave here. If you want to go, then go - you know Lord Elder has released you from all oaths. But you'll not take Bess with you."

"I've no wish to go, my lady," Wulf pleaded. "I only want what is right. Give me a reason why I can't marry Bess."

"You've been told," shouted Ragwulf. He was hoarse; he had shouted enough last night, Maighread thought.

"You shouldn't need telling again," he continued. "Lady Eleanor doesn't need to explain herself to the likes of you!"

Maighread heard the iron in his words. How hard it must be for him to speak so to his own son. Wulf must have heard that iron too for he did not reply. There was a further awkward silence and then she heard the footfalls as the knot of men and servants began to disperse about their business.

She found a tear on her cheek and wiped it away. The tension was beyond bearing: too many young men, their appetites whet by the blood of war, and now they grew resentful. Some had found brief solace with local girls but there were few enough of those. Her own bitter memories seemed nothing now, lost in the general misery of a beleaguered garrison waiting in vain for its lord to return.

No-one knew where he was and his exile had more than a year still to run but Maighread knew that the inhabitants of Crag Tower could not wait another year.

§§§§

Below in the Great Hall, Eleanor stood silently beside Ragwulf. She had come to know him so well and yet he was as distant towards her as he had ever been. It seemed that some wounds just would not heal. She could read his face better than she could read a book - though that was no great claim in her case. His eyes were fixed upon the wall; his anger had gone and his face now bore only the dark lines of regret.

She touched his shoulder but he shrugged her arm away. She opened her mouth to speak but he held up a hand.

"Don't, my lady," he said. "Don't say a word. It'll help nothing." Then he turned away.

He was probably right; when had she ever said a word that made things better between them? 'Between them'? Even her thoughts threw them together, though there was a chasm there long before this morning.

"I only wanted to thank you," she said, "for not telling them."

He faced her again. "Thank me? High born ladies don't thank men for keeping oaths freely given."

"But it was hard for you, I know. Wulf's your son, after all…"

"I knew what had to be said and I said it, my lady. The last thing I want is your thanks for it!"

His bitter words cut her but he would have known that. He meant her to feel some pain too. She could not stop looking at him, waiting for him to meet her eyes but he didn't. Instead he turned on his heel and left. She stared after him listening to the familiar footsteps echoing in his wake.

§§§§

Hal was left by the well, alone. Everyone else had disappeared, most to continue repairing the gate, but he had seen his friend Wulf go to the stables, his face set in anger. He went after him and found him there brushing down one of the few remaining horses.

"That's your father's horse," he said softly.

Wulf did not look around but carried on brushing with long angry strokes. "I know."

"You can't leave," Hal said simply.

"We're not young boys any more, Hal. And our lord has freed us from his service. We can go - and we can make our own way."

"We need you here - and they won't let you take Bess..."

"Oh. I'll take her. You know that. It's not as if she doesn't want to go! We could have just wed - and stayed. But it seems not…"

"I don't know what all the fuss is about," said Hal, "but I could talk to Lady Eleanor-"

Wulf looked round sharply. "Don't bother. Bess has already asked her a hundred times. It'll do no good."

"Don't do anything sudden."

"Sudden? I've thought of little else for a year or more. There's too many of us here anyway. I'm going and I'm taking some of the lads with me. This place will fall sooner or later and I don't want Bess to be here when it does. Are you coming?"

Hal winced. Sooner or later he had known the question would be asked.

"Wulf, you're my oldest friend; we've fought side by side and faced death together more than once…"

"But?" said Wulf with a rueful smile.

"My service to Ned Elder is … it's beyond oaths. When I was alone he gave me a life."

"And you've repaid him time and again, my friend. How

many more times do you have to repay him? Or do you have to die in his service? You don't even know where he is - he might be dead by now."

Hal smiled. "Wherever he is, he's not dead; I'd know it. He always comes back - always."

Wulf shook his head. "Well, come Lammastide, I'll be back - for Bess. Perhaps you'll have changed your mind by then."

"If you take your father's horse he'll kill you," said Hal.

"Only if he catches me," grinned Wulf. "Best say 'God be with you' today for, by the morrow, we'll be gone."

§§§§

The following morning Hal stood in the Hall. On the small dais before him was the Elder family's pale blue banner and beside it was Ned Elder's great battle sword. Hal had brought it with him to Crag Tower and Lady Maighread had put it in a place of honour. Now Hal stared at it wistfully, wondering whether he had done the right thing. Wulf had gone at first light. He had taken eight men and all the remaining horses. Lady Eleanor had raged about the small castle all morning. Ragwulf had taken it in silence but his face was grey and drawn. No-one dared speak to either of them.

His friend had gone but, if he was true to his word, he would be back at Lammas. Then there would be words, harsh words, and more besides. It was all so... unnecessary.

Bess walked into the Hall with John toddling in her wake. She smiled at Hal and he put an arm around her. Her dark eyes were red-rimmed and her cheeks puffed.

"I'm glad you're still here," she said. "I'm not very popular with anyone just now."

John hugged her leg and she bent down to him.

"I can't find Wulf," said John.

Bess smiled at the lad. "He's gone for a while - but he'll

be coming back. You'll see."

The boy took the news well, Hal thought. "Come on," he told him, "I'm going out to the butts with Will to practise. You can come and watch if you like."

John grinned. Hal knew Ragwulf did not like the lad to go outside the castle walls but the butts had been set up out there to keep the young men out of the way and out of mischief. If John was with him it could do no harm. He turned to Bess. "Will you tell Ragwulf where I've taken him?"

Bess shook her head. "No, I won't! Not unless he asks me. He'll be livid."

"John's safe enough with me."

"Aye, I know, but Ragwulf and Lady Eleanor won't see it that way, I promise you."

Hal shrugged. "Just at the moment I don't much care what they think," he said.

He took the boy's hand and led him out into the courtyard. Will, Lady Eleanor's seven year old son, was waiting with his bow and arrow bag. He handed the bag to John to carry as they went out to the butts and the small boy skipped along beside them. Hal shook his head - oh, to be just four years old again. It occurred to him then that when he was that age, he still had a father and a mother. He remembered being happy. Perhaps his parents were too, though he knew now how hard life was for those who toiled on the land. At least John still had his father - if Ragwulf was indeed his father. It did not always seem so for he scarcely ever looked at the lad and there was certainly no resemblance. Whereas when you saw young Will and Lady Eleanor together, the likeness took your breath away. Will was tall, as his father had been, but he had his mother's blood red hair.

Hal was one of the few who actually enjoyed the butts for he lived and breathed archery. He could never practise enough but after several hours of watching, fetching and carrying, the novelty wore off for both John and Will. Hal decided they had been gone long enough in any case and that was confirmed when he saw Ragwulf striding through the long grass towards them.

Hal bent down to John and whispered. "I hope you enjoyed your morning, John; 'cos now we're for it."

John grinned and Hal sighed in resignation.

Yet when Ragwulf came up he was strangely quiet. He had taken Wulf's leaving badly. He did not chastise Hal for taking John out; in fact he seemed almost grateful and clapped him on the back.

"I'm thankful you stayed," he said gruffly. "It must've been hard for you."

Hal looked at him. "Harder for you to bear than me, I think," he replied.

"Best take the lad back though," said Ragwulf and he turned and went back to Crag Tower.

Hal waited for a while, watching him trudge up towards the gate. He should look like a warrior in his prime but he walked liked an old man, his shoulders hunched and his head bowed. What weight did he bear on those broad shoulders?

2

25th June 1468, on the waterfront of Sluys in Flanders

Strange, Ned thought, where you could end up. He stared out across the ageing quays and warehouses of Sluys - not a very inspiring sight. Four years ago he had never heard of Sluys - in fact he had never heard of Flanders - and now Sluys was home. Ned was hardly an authority on ports but it seemed to him that Sluys was a tired port. Well, he was a tired knight so perhaps they were made for each other.

This evening the weary old girl was putting on a brave face: paths were being brushed and steps washed down. Piles of rubbish, which he knew for a fact had littered the quays for months, were now being removed in carts. All of this was because, in an hour or two, a little piece of English royalty would arrive in Sluys and the small town wanted to welcome Princess Margaret of York, the sister of King Edward IV, in style. The problem was that Sluys no longer had much style left to offer.

So, on this particular evening the port was busier than usual. Ned ignored all the fuss and, as was his habit, strolled along the bustling waterfront to the Golden Ship Inn. The Golden Ship, like the rest of Sluys, had seen better days. Merchants used to conduct much business there he had been told but now what few transactions occurred were of a more doubtful nature. He gave the proprietor, Pieter, a lazy wave and sat down at his customary table beside Spearbold where he was pleased to see that a pot of ale already awaited him.

"Thomas Gate!" hissed Spearbold in greeting.

Ned sighed and shook his head. "Let me sit down at least."

"It's Sir Thomas Gate, I tell you!"

Ned paused in the act of raising a pot to his mouth and stared over its pewter lid to the figure across the other side of the room. The man sat in the corner shadow where the glow of the rush lights did not venture. Ned regarded him thoughtfully for a moment. Spearbold was observant, it was true, and no-one knew the Earl of Warwick's agents better, but Ned had his doubts.

"Thomas … Gate," he weighed the two words carefully.

"Not so loud," whispered Spearbold.

Ned lowered his voice. "My dear Spearbold, are you sure? Might it not be … Robert Thwaite, or perhaps Benjamin Warner?"

"I may have been wrong about Thwaite," muttered Spearbold, "though in God's name there was an uncanny likeness. And Warner - well it was dark and I scarce glimpsed him - but, I assure you, this man is Sir Thomas Gate."

"Sir Thomas Gate," repeated Ned, almost to himself. "And who, or what, is Sir Thomas Gate - always assuming that it is Thomas Gate?"

"Sir Thomas Gate is Warwick's man - a trusted man; close."

"Trusted and close - like you were once," replied Ned with a wry smile. He was weary of Spearbold's sightings and, after four years, he was weary of exile.

"My lord-"

"I'm no longer a lord, Spearbold. I'm 'Master Young'. And don't tell me you've forgotten. It was you gave me the wretched name in the first place!"

"Aye, aye, of course, Master Young. Of course you are - you see how distracted I am," said Spearbold as he continued to observe the stranger through his fingers.

Ned said nothing more but, as he savoured a mouthful of ale, he kept one eye on the far corner of the room.

"What will you do?" prompted Spearbold.

Ned ignored him and took another long draught of ale. He owed much to Spearbold. It was he who had found them lodgings when they had disembarked from The Catherine at Sluys and too he had found employment for Ned. Without Spearbold's help Ned doubted he would have survived four weeks of his exile, let alone four years. Now he had come to believe he would survive the one year that remained - but then what? He was not sure what would await him if he returned home. Perhaps it would be safer to stay in Sluys; not just for him, but for Spearbold and Agnes too. For once, death had not followed in his footsteps and in Sluys he had found a sort of peace.

He glanced across at Agnes, now serving a knot of seamen with some bowls of hot potage. He remembered her when they first arrived in the port: thin and skittish, yet ready for whatever further sorrows the Lord might choose to hurl at her. She had filled out well - a comely figure of a girl - and she had lost none of her fire. As she passed by each rush light her golden hair glowed but the dim light hardly did her beauty justice. She would be coming up to seventeen now, as far as anyone - including Agnes - could work out. Spearbold had taught her to read and to write a little. For a girl who grew up in a forest with more animals than people, she was an able pupil.

Agnes placed the steaming bowls on the long table in the middle of the room and Ned studied the group of men who sat along it. He knew nearly all of them and that was good enough. Agnes would not be at risk from them - she had grown up with some of them and they had come to see her as they would some sort of lucky charm. A superstitious lot, were sailors. Her smile warmed them when they came back from the sea and perhaps it helped that she was mute and so had never pestered them with idle chatter.

Ned realised that he was grinning like some proud father but it was pleasing to see her so safe and well. He wished that Agnes' father had lived to see how she blossomed - it was about the only good thing to come of their exile.

Agnes finished serving the food and then took several pots of ale to one of the smaller side tables where the man who might be Thomas Gate sat with several others. Gate leaned towards her into a pool of light and Ned was able to see him clearly for the first time. He was thin-faced with unfashionably long hair that straggled down to his shoulders. He exuded an air of easy self-confidence, bolstered no doubt by the sword at his side.

Spearbold tapped his hand. "He's speaking to Agnes," he breathed.

"Aye, I can see - and why wouldn't he?" retorted Ned. "She serves here, doesn't she? And she's very pretty."

"But who knows what he's asking her?"

Ned frowned. "Well we know she's not going to tell him much, don't we? Now stop fretting! How could he find me anyway? Felix of Bordeaux is the only man in Christendom who knows where I am - and he's not even telling my sisters! Whether this fellow is Gate or not, he's doing no harm and that's what Pieter pays me to keep an eye on. Now, sit at peace, drink your cheap wine and let me worry about him."

Ned looked across at Gate who was now in earnest conversation with his companions. Then, at that very moment, Thomas Gate looked up and stared straight at Ned and in that instant everything changed. Gate clearly knew who he was and, if Spearbold was right, they were in trouble. Yet it was not a look of satisfaction that crossed Gate's face. If anything he looked shocked and confused, perhaps even worried. Gate recognised him but seemed anything but pleased to have found him and that puzzled Ned. Surely, if he was Warwick's man, he would know that his lord would be only too glad to find Ned Elder. It was Warwick's enmity that had forced him into exile, after all. Gate looked away and withdrew back into the shadows.

Pieter, not only the owner but also Ned's employer, was pouring more jugs of ale. Ned watched as he called Agnes over to serve them out. She had a grace of movement that set her apart from the other serving wenches. He wasn't surprised that men could not take their eyes off her. She returned to Gate's table with more ale. Gate took her by the arm and Ned stiffened for a moment. But he should not have worried for Agnes slipped effortlessly from Gate's grasp and moved away to serve more jugs of ale.

"You see," whispered Spearbold. "He's up to something…"

"I'd say he wants Agnes," said Ned, "but he's hardly the first, is he? And she knows how to handle herself."

"But it's Thomas Gate, I tell you." Spearbold was almost pleading now.

"Aye - and I believe you."

"You do?" said Spearbold, taken aback. "Why?"

"Because he knows who I am."

Spearbold looked crestfallen. "Then … our time has run out…"

"Perhaps not - he doesn't seem too interested in me - and that's a mystery in itself."

"Don't be fooled. He's a good dissembler is Gate. He doesn't want you to run, so he appears indifferent."

"Well, he's convinced me. Who's with him, do you think?"

"Frenchmen, by the sound of them. The port is crawling with all sorts today, with the princess coming."

"Aye, it's got a deal too busy around here in the past week."

"It'll all die down again soon enough," Spearbold reassured him. "Once the princess and the young Duke of Burgundy are married I doubt they'll come to Sluys much.

They'll be in Bruges or somewhere else more fashionable."

"If Gate wasn't expecting to see me, then why is he in Sluys at all? Only traders and seamen come here - and not so many of them now."

"He's an Englishman," mused Spearbold. "Perhaps he's come to see Princess Margaret wed, like many others…"

"I know nothing of these matters, Spearbold, but I seem to recall you telling me that the Earl of Warwick desires a French alliance."

"Indeed," said Spearbold.

"Yet the princess is marrying Duke Charles of Burgundy. The earl can't be too pleased about an alliance with Burgundy can he? So why would he send his man Gate to celebrate the bride's arrival?"

Spearbold's face clouded with worry. "Whatever Gate is up to, we must keep our heads down and let it pass us by."

"Aye, perhaps Gate is here to observe how the princess is received and report back to his master," said Ned.

Spearbold looked up sharply. "Thomas Gate does not observe; he acts. And whatever he's doing here it will be at Warwick's command."

"What then?" asked Ned.

"It's not our concern," said Spearbold. "Perhaps you're right and he's not interested in you."

"At present he seems engaged in some other business but I wouldn't be surprised if he didn't come for me afterwards… now that he's seen me."

Spearbold fell silent.

Ned stared at him. "You can guess as well as I can why he's here," he said. "Frenchmen, you say, are with him?"

"Perhaps."

"And this Burgundian marriage is a problem for the King of France, is it not?"

Spearbold nodded. "I imagine that King Louis has done all he can to stop it."

"And Warwick is in touch with the King of France?"

persisted Ned.

"Yes, so I believe, but-"

"The princess is about to arrive here …and Warwick's trusted agent sits in the port sharing a quiet drink with some Frenchmen."

Spearbold said nothing.

"I want you on the next ship to Bristol," said Ned. "You must hasten to Ludlow and find Felix."

Spearbold looked appalled. "There may not be a ship bound for Bristol for weeks! And in any case, I couldn't leave you now."

Ned put a hand on the older man's shoulder. "What will you do for me, Spearbold? Will you fight Thomas Gate? You are twice my age and no swordsman. If Warwick finds out I'm here then we'll need some help. You'll do me more service by letting Felix know. Get him to send over Bear and Hal - and perhaps a few of my other men at arms."

Spearbold stared at him blankly. "Have you forgotten? You released them all from your service three years ago. They'll have scattered to the four winds by now."

"Some perhaps, but not all. At the very least, Felix will know where to find Hal and Bear."

"But all that will take weeks! Gate's here now."

"I'll keep an eye on Gate," said Ned. "But if he sends to Warwick he'll get a response no quicker than you can from Felix."

"Gate is well known for his prowess with the sword," said Spearbold.

Ned stared at him. "So am I, as you know!"

"You've not fought in earnest since we arrived here, lord, only banged together a few drunken heads. And …"

"And what? Say what you think, man."

"There's your head wound - who knows how it will stand up to another blow?"

"There only one way I know to learn that, Spearbold. Listen, my head is fine - battered, but fine. Agnes tended me well."

"And what of Agnes?" said Spearbold. "If I go to England what will become of Agnes?"

"Agnes isn't made of glass, Spearbold. I'll be here so she'll be quite safe."

"Are you sure, my lord?"

"Just go, Spearbold! Start asking in here now for a ship. Now. There are some ship's masters in tonight. If not Bristol, then London, but get to Felix as fast as you can."

"And what are you going to do?" whispered Spearbold.

"I'm going to find out what our friend Gate is up to."

Spearbold looked at him aghast, but he left his master and went to speak to Pieter. Ned nodded in approval. Spearbold might be appalled at what was unfolding but, as always, he thought clearly. Pieter was an excellent man to start with for he knew more about the comings and goings of vessels in the port than most folk.

Ned turned his attention back to Thomas Gate. Perhaps he was wrong and Gate's presence in Sluys had nothing to do with the imminent arrival of Princess Margaret. Ned had served King Edward loyally and, though the king had exiled him, he bore him no ill will. The exile had been an act of clemency and Ned knew it. If there was any risk to the king's sister then Ned would do all he could to stop it. If doing so included eliminating one of Warwick's agents, then so much the better for the earl was no friend of his. So, how to proceed? It was quite straightforward, he decided: he would simply watch and follow Gate. Either he was up to no good or he wasn't. Either way, Ned would find out.

It became a long evening. Gate and his comrades seemed in no hurry to leave and Gate never even glanced again in Ned's direction. Spearbold passed from one seaman to another, engaging in earnest conversation. Gate must surely have noticed but, if he did, he showed no sign of it. After a time, Spearbold returned and stood opposite Ned with his back to Gate.

He spoke in a low voice. "Pieter's heard that the ship carrying the princess should dock shortly. And I've found a ship. The best I could do was London but she sails on tomorrow's tide!"

"Good," said Ned. "Now go and get yourself ready."

"Are you sure about this?"

Ned gave him a grim nod. "We'll talk again before you go," he said.

Spearbold walked to the door and gave him a sly wink.

Subtle as a pollaxe, thought Ned. He felt a gentle hand on his arm. He smiled up at Agnes and she perched on the bench opposite. He had got to know every nuance of her facial expressions: she was silently asking him why he was worried. She knew him too well, it seemed. He shook his head and she smiled at him - a wary, knowing smile. She got up to return to her work but gave him a peck on the cheek before leaving him.

He felt suddenly weary and stifled a yawn. He leant back against the battered wood panelling - a relic from a time when the Golden Ship had attracted a rather better class of clientele. Then he slumped forward and rested his forehead on the table to observe Gate through half-closed eyes.

He started awake... he must have dropped off for a moment. He looked up and glanced around the inn. Pieter was pouring and Agnes was serving; all was as it had been - except Thomas Gate and his friends were gone. God's blood, so much for watching Gate! He waved Agnes over and she came to him, an enquiring look on her face.

"The fellow who was in the corner, Agnes - has he just left?"

She nodded slowly. Then she frowned and regarded him doubtfully.

"It's nothing," he said with a smile. "Go back to your work. I'm going to take a breath of sea air. I'll be back later."

He got up and shook the stiffness from his legs. He did

not hurry to the door but signalled Pieter to let him know he was stepping out for a while. Outside, the evening air was warm though there was hardly a trace of salt in it for the sea was some distance away up the channel from the port.

"God's blood!" he muttered as he cast about him in the sunset glow. The light was beginning to fade now though he could still see the dockside with its warehouses and sheds clearly enough. Along the quay he heard the gentle, reassuring slap of the water against the hulls of a score of ships. Ships' masts pierced the skyline - though not as many as a few years before. Sluys had been a bustling place then. It still was, sometimes, such as tonight. Some would have come to welcome the princess - and a few to jeer probably. The English marriage was unpopular with some of the merchant houses who operated from the port. If Gate had some action in mind to threaten the princess and prevent the marriage then he might find a few willing helpers amongst the Flemish. However, there was no sign of Thomas Gate. Ned cursed his carelessness. Gate could have gone anywhere.

He walked along the quay past the first ship, picking his way around the forest of tuns that lay beside it - wine from Gascony no doubt waiting for flat-bottomed boats to take it on the last leg of its journey up the river Zwin to Bruges. He peered around large bales of raw wool but there was no sign of Gate, just a crowd of seafarers sitting on the dockside. Most were drinking and he had no doubt that in several hours' time there would be a few cracked heads. Others had sought out the whores who plied their trade along the Sluys port. Some of the women he knew well from their frequent visits to the Golden Ship; others looked as if they had just arrived from one of the nearby villages - bright ruddy-faced newcomers, looking to make a living. Well, they were making a living, but they could not hide the disappointment in their eyes. Sluys was a place where hope flourished for some and perished for others. He himself had arrived with no hope only to discover that dear Agnes had hope enough for two.

As he stood pondering what to do next, he noticed there were more people milling about at the far end of the quay. He continued slowly along the dockside, eyes eager for a glimpse of Warwick's man. He glanced up towards the town, unusually well-lit where the bell tower dominated the square. The lanes which led down to the wharves were already choked with people and wagons. Beyond the crush he spotted one or two fine coaches and a host of horsemen, struggling to get nearer to the port. On the quay there was already a hum of excitement and he assumed that Princess Margaret's ship had been sighted further along the channel.

He scanned the shore for Gate but still could not see him - not surprising: he was hardly going to stand on the dock in the open. Yet, perhaps he was wrong and Gate intended the princess no harm. Perhaps he had already left the docks and was in his lodgings with his boots off and his feet up. Even if Gate was still there, Ned could see there was little hope of finding him. The crowd was growing as more people squeezed through the narrow approaches onto the wharves.

Among the throng there were some mounted men at arms and there would be knights and archers aboard her ship. The princess would be closely protected - and probably by better men than he - so what was he doing? She did not need his help and he had been a fool even to think she might. Once he was a trusted lord at the heart of King Edward's affairs, but those days were long gone. He was yesterday's man now.

He ambled away, back towards the Golden Ship. That was where he belonged now, settling sailors' brawls and tossing out overripe whores. After a few steps, he halted again. He might not be needed, but it would do no harm to see King Edward's sister come ashore, if only for the comradeship they had shared in the days before Edward had become king. He turned back towards the quay and looked out over the water. There were several ships in the channel, making for the shore. One was larger than the rest and, as it came closer, he could make out the red cross of St George on the white ensign fluttering atop the main mast. A host of smaller vessels scuttled around it, shepherding the ship towards the dockside and there was a flurry of movement from the men on the dock preparing to receive her.

He was peering into the sun, its power almost spent now and leaving only red trails amongst the long strands of cloud in the western sky. He would get a better view from the first floor of one of the warehouses and, since all the merchants and their clerks knew him, he was able to slip inside with no trouble. In fact there were few bothered enough to notice and they merely nodded knowingly to him as he clambered past a mountain of grain sacks: here was the renegade Englishman coming to see his king's sister.

He hurried up a flight of steps to get to the upper floor where a goods hoist protruded through a large opening. It would be an excellent vantage point and he began to feel quite pleased that he had come back to watch. Then at the top of the steps he came face to face with Thomas Gate.

Beyond Gate he glimpsed several others crammed onto the loading platform, two with crossbows ready to loose. That was all he saw before Gate drew his sword and stepped forward. Ned tried to do the same but lost his balance and lurched back down the stairs. He rolled down trying to protect his head with one hand whilst gripping his sword hilt with the other.

He hit the floor heavily, which winded him, but still he clung onto the sword. He staggered to his feet. Gate came down after him, taking the steps two at a time, but in his haste he too stumbled on the narrow treads. Ned slashed at him as he clattered past and thudded into a pile of furs. The sword made little contact but when Gate got up Ned saw there was blood on his cheek. Gate wiped a hand across the cut and examined the blood on his glove. He looked at Ned and shook his head. Then he swayed forward and Ned clubbed him down with the hilt of his sword. Gate dropped once more and lay still. So much for Gate's prowess with the sword, thought Ned.

He puffed out his cheeks and took a deep breath. His back hurt and his head was sore but he climbed the steps once more. Another swordsman met him at the top and thrust down at him. Ned parried easily and seized his opponent's arm to pull him forward down the stairs. He tumbled down to the bottom and lay still. Ned stepped up towards the loading platform. The two crossbowmen were crouched with their backs to him, showing rather misplaced faith in Gate and his comrade. He stood still and peered over them down to the wharf below: Princess Margaret's ship had docked and he could make out several men at arms on the deck.

The bowmen were muttering to each other but did not even glance behind them, as they aimed their weapons down, intent on finding their target. Ned hesitated. Then he saw the princess emerge onto to the deck, uncloaked, for the evening was still mild. She was tall - like her brother then, he thought - and flanked by several other women. The crossbowmen leant further forward and at once Ned fell upon them. More blood upon my hands, he thought, stabbing at the nearer one. The hapless bowman groaned and loosed his quarrel wildly at the ship. There were cries of alarm and men looked up to the warehouse. A tall knight threw himself in front of the princess, bellowing commands to his men.

The second bowman half-turned towards Ned who dropped his sword and seized the loaded crossbow for he could not risk another quarrel being loosed at the deck. He wrestled for control of the bow but the stranger was strong

- stronger than he. Ned got a hand to the trigger and as soon as the bow pointed upwards he pulled it. The bowman cursed as the bolt thudded harmlessly into the roof timber. He broke free from Ned and angrily swung the heavy bow at him. It caught him on the temple and he went down at the top of the steps. His vision was blurred but he could make out the bowman beginning to reload, snatching another quarrel from his bag and putting his foot on the bow's stirrup to draw it tight.

Ned struggled to get up. The bowman stood up and the ratchet of the crossbow whirred. Ned grabbed his leg but he kicked off Ned's feeble hand and placed the bolt. Suddenly, man and crossbow flew back from the opening and landed on top of Ned. The man's face came to rest alongside his. He was stone dead, his eyes wide open in shock, and two feathered shafts sticking out from his chest. It seemed that several on board the ship had done their duty well.

There was a clamour on the quay now and Ned finally managed to get to his feet. His head cleared and he could see a little better. Perhaps he should have paid more attention to Spearbold: his old wound was still not right. He retrieved his sword and gingerly headed down the steps but when he reached the foot he noticed that only one man was still lying on the floor. He lurched around but too late as Gate struck him on the side of the head with something hard and heavy.

3

Late evening on 25th June 1468, in the port of Sluys

It was dark by the time Spearbold made his way back to the Golden Ship. There had been much excitement in the port at the arrival of the princess and he felt a little cheated that he had witnessed none of it himself. Pieter and Anna were just trying to prise loose their last clients when he arrived. He gave them a cheerful wave and Anna smiled. Pieter nodded slightly and gave an incomprehensible grunt which for him amounted to a high-spirited welcome.

Spearbold hurried upstairs to the room that he shared with Ned and Agnes. One look around the room, however, told him that his master had not yet returned. He carefully drew aside the curtain which separated off the area where Agnes slept. There she was: safe and lying peacefully in her narrow cot, reading in the flickering light of a tallow candle - Ned spared Agnes nothing. Still, Spearbold too felt a little pride at how far his pupil had come with her reading.

Agnes looked up and he perched at the foot of the bed.

"Have you seen Ned, my dear?" he asked.

She shook her head and gave him that penetrating stare she could produce at will. It said: you know I can't speak so tell me all I need to know - now. So he did, but it did not help either of them much for Agnes had not seen Ned since he left the inn.

Spearbold was not worried, though it was his master's habit to be at the inn when Pieter was closing up and his absence was therefore a little surprising. Then of course there was Thomas Gate - he did not tell Agnes about him.

"I shall await him below, my dear," he said and left her to her reading.

He descended the stairs in thoughtful mood but he did not wait below. Instead he told Pieter he was going out and would not be long.

"I lock up soon!" Pieter called after him but Spearbold's mind was elsewhere, trying to think where Ned might be. He set out to scour the dockside but it could be a dangerous place at such an hour. He patted the long knife at his side - it was the only weapon he carried for the local men knew whom he served and left him well alone. But there would be others abroad tonight, who were not local and who did not know - and some too who would not care.

§§§§

His search proved fruitless and, after what he judged to be several hours, he reluctantly headed back to the Golden Ship. Still, he had not seen or heard anything to give him cause to fret. Ned knew Sluys very well and was more than capable of coping with any danger it might pose. When he considered it carefully, he realised his behaviour was just a little ludicrous. After all, even if Ned was in trouble, of what possible use could Spearbold be? He chuckled to himself - better he got a good night's sleep, for his ship to London sailed on the morning tide.

He hoped that Pieter had not locked him out. It was late - unusually late for him to retire but Pieter knew he was out. He would be cross if the landlord had barred the door but he was encouraged to see a glimmer of light from downstairs - if the rush lights were still burning then Pieter must still be up. He arrived at the door way and raised a hand to tap lightly on the door. His hand stopped in mid-air and he grinned as he looked at the door. It was ajar - Pieter must have left it open for him. He listened carefully but could hear no sound from within: he hoped Pieter was not already asleep.

He gave the heavy door a tentative shove. It swung half-open and he stepped inside. The large room was empty. There was a dim glow from a rush light on the table nearest the door and several other rushes guttered by the stairs. Pieter and Anna must have retired. Yet on the far side of the room a candle stood, still alight. Spearbold suddenly felt a prick of alarm, for Pieter hated waste and whilst he might, just might, have left the door open and a few rush lights burning out, he would never have left the candle thus.

"Pieter!" he whispered.

He thought he heard something then, but not a reply, more of a whimper. He wiped a bead of sweat from his forehead and gulped down a deep breath. He stood still and used all his senses. The room seemed to have a different smell to it from before - an entirely unwelcome smell. He could not stand there forever. So he took several hesitant paces forward - and fell over Pieter. The inn keeper lay between the two larger tables and Spearbold ended up on his knees beside him.

His fingers slid across something sticky congealing on the floor - of course: it was blood he had smelt! He knew at once the man was dead and scrabbled over the floor in a panic. Then, leaning on one of the tables, he struggled to compose himself. After all, Pieter's was not the first dead body he had seen. Serving Ned Elder, he had seen death a good deal more frequently than he would have liked. Now think, he told himself.

Ahead of him in the back room he heard the sound again - only now he knew very well what it was. He passed through into the small chamber at the rear of the inn where Pieter and his wife lived and slept. Anna was sitting on the floor with a great cleaver resting across her lap. Her shoulders heaved up and down as she sobbed. When she saw Spearbold she cast the weapon aside and leapt into his arms.

"Oh, Master Spearbold!" she wailed. "Murder, murder!" she cried and then continued in such rapid Flemish that he struggled to follow.

"Slowly, my dear," he soothed, "slowly. Where is Ned…Master Young?"

But his question only increased the torrent of words she produced so he led her to one of the benches and sat her down. She caught a glimpse of her husband's corpse and began sobbing uncontrollably.

"Wait here," ordered Spearbold. He tried to calm himself. Panicking would not help, he told himself. He must find Ned Elder.

He was about to pick up the candle but did not have the heart to leave the woman in the dark so he took up one of the rush lights and made his way up the stairs. On the first floor was a landing with two large rooms off it. Here were the chambers where anyone staying at the inn would be sleeping - there would always be a few and tonight, with Princess Margaret's arrival, the inn was full. He opened the first door and peered in. The two large beds were occupied and he heard snoring. Was it conceivable that these folk had just slept through their host's murder? He went out and closed the door. When he entered the other chamber he found a similar scene except his entry disturbed one of the guests.

"Who are you?" he croaked grumpily at Spearbold. "We've had enough noise tonight to wake the dead!"

Spearbold shook his head. "I fear not," he replied. "But please, do go back to sleep. I wouldn't want you inconvenienced by the occasional murder."

"Murder!" cried the guest. "What murder?" But Spearbold had already shut the door and was heading up the second, narrower flight of steps to the garret room that he, Ned and Agnes occupied. Seeing the lodgers all safe and sound had brought him some relief; all the same, he knew that Ned Elder would not have lain in bed whilst the landlord - his employer - was being butchered below. So it was with some trepidation that he opened the door. He might find Ned wounded, having beaten off an attack - or Agnes might rush to him in grief if Ned had been killed.

In fact neither scenario occurred when he stepped into the chamber. There was no sign of Ned. Worse still, the curtain across the room was now drawn aside and there was no trace of Agnes either. The attic room was empty. There was no sign of a struggle. All was neat and tidy - as was usual where Agnes was concerned. But where was she? Where had the silly girl gone? She must have gone looking for Ned too. Spearbold sat down. His ordered world was unravelling further as each hour passed - and it had all begun with the arrival of Thomas Gate.

§§§§§

By morning Spearbold had discovered nothing more either about the disappearance of his companions or the murder of Pieter. He had covered Pieter's corpse with linen cloths and calmed his widow, though that was achieved more by strong spirits than by Spearbold's counsel. The guests at the inn had been awoken by the man Spearbold had spoken to and at first light they all disappeared. He paid them little attention and let them go; he was more concerned about Ned and Agnes. As soon as he could he alerted the port authorities and then spent the morning scouring the docks, questioning closely anyone who knew Ned - which amounted to most of the population of the port. Some had seen Ned the previous evening and, from what folk told him, Spearbold was able to track Ned's movements up to the moment the princess arrived. Then nothing, though an old woman he knew well told him that he was not the only one who had been asking questions about Master Young.

As for Agnes, she had not yet returned and it seemed there was even less to tell, though she was well known and well-liked in the port. The same old woman told him in halting English that she had seen a girl of Agnes's colouring in a small boat heading out to one of the ships in the channel. But he doubted it was Agnes - for Agnes would not have gone anywhere without Ned.

So he returned worried and disappointed to the Golden Ship. There he found a man waiting for him - a confident fellow who sat with his feet up on a table unconcerned by Pieter's stiffening body on the next table where Spearbold had laid it out earlier. Spearbold regarded the stranger suspiciously and his hostility must have been obvious for the newcomer put his feet down and stood up.

"William Crabber," he said.

Spearbold did not reply.

"I would ask that God give you a good day," continued Crabber, "but I can already see for myself that would be a forlorn hope."

Spearbold gave him a nod and waved him back to his seat.

"I don't know you," he said. "Are you employed by the port?"

Crabber grinned and shook his head. "I'm looking for a certain Master Young," he said.

Spearbold frowned. Still, he was not averse to a direct approach - it often proved helpful.

"You've told me who you are," he said, "now tell me what you are: who does William Crabber serve?"

Crabber smiled. "Perhaps I serve only myself."

"Then you should be able to explain your business very quickly," retorted Spearbold.

Crabber nodded. "I should have told you at once but..." He glanced at Pieter's shrouded body. "I thought to be cautious."

"Aye, caution," said Spearbold, "caution is prudent."

"And you are?"

"George Spearbold."

"Very well, Master Spearbold. I serve Lord Scales."

"And I serve Master Young. What does Lord Scales want with my master?"

"Do you know who Lord Scales is?"

"Aye, of course. He's Anthony Woodville. So, what does the queen's brother want with Master Young?"

"You're a suspicious fellow," commented Crabber.

"Aye, well, finding a corpse is like to make a man suspicious."

Crabber grinned, revealing several blackened teeth; yet there was a certain warmth about the man, Spearbold thought.

"Lord Scales merely wishes me to convey his thanks - and those of the Princess Margaret - for Master Young's intervention last evening."

"Intervention?"

"Are you sure you're Master Young's servant?" asked Crabber.

"Aye!" snapped Spearbold. "What intervention?"

Crabber proceeded to explain how Ned had been seen grappling with the assassins at the dock side. Spearbold was only mildly surprised. Ned Elder could sniff out a brawl in a nunnery. Yet what Crabber told him seemed of little help in finding Ned.

"Lord Scales is in Bruges at present but he would like to see Master Young before he leaves - to thank him personally."

"I'd like to see him myself," confided Spearbold and he explained his predicament to Crabber. "And, after what you've told me, I'm not sure I will."

"You fear then that the French have killed him?" said Crabber.

"It may be they've tried, though in truth he's a hard man to kill."

"That much I can vouch for myself for I saw him from the ship's deck. I'll make enquiries. And the girl is still missing, you say?"

Spearbold's eyes clouded with tears. "Aye, Agnes - a beautiful young maid, though she has no speech. She's like a daughter to Ned."

"Ned?"

"Ah, Master Young," he corrected himself belatedly.

Crabber stood up and clapped Spearbold on the shoulder. "Don't worry. I'm sure Lord Scales will want to help such a man. We'll see if we can find them."

He moved towards the door but turned on the threshold. "Strange the maid should be gone too," he murmured. "And this dead fellow here? What connects them all, I wonder?"

Spearbold stood motionless as a sudden shiver passed through him. He knew what connected them all. He was much distracted by what Crabber had told him for he had no doubt now that Thomas Gate was involved and he was already beginning to fear the worst about Agnes. He had warned Ned about Thomas Gate. Should he have told Crabber about Gate? He had decided not to. He didn't know Crabber well enough yet to pass on that name. Even so, Lord Scales and the rest of the Woodville tribe had no love for Gate's master, the Earl of Warwick. Perhaps the Woodvilles, with their close connection to the king, might be powerful allies for Ned if his feud with Warwick continued - if Ned was still alive.

In the meantime, what was he to do? His ship had already have sailed without him. Ned had told him to go but surely he could not leave now with both Ned and Agnes missing?

§§§§

Spearbold did not seek another passage to London. Instead he busied himself with his enquiries about Ned and

Agnes. He questioned everyone he could find but he got nowhere. No-one had seen Ned since the attack on the princess. After several days, Crabber returned to see him but he too had nothing to offer. Any trail there might have been had gone cold; Ned and Agnes had just disappeared.

After a week Spearbold decided, though he did not like to admit it even to himself, that he could do nothing more on his own. His continued presence in Sluys would not help. So he made fresh enquiries for a ship and found one leaving for Southampton and Bristol in three days which would suit him well enough. If any hope remained of finding Ned, then he was going to need help to do it. He must carry out Ned's last order and go to Felix of Bordeaux.

4

16th July 1468, at Middleham Castle in Yorkshire

Thomas Gate was relieved to see the great square towers of Middleham in the distance - relieved and yet a little apprehensive. His journey from Flanders had taken longer than he had hoped. Despite his haste to leave, he found there was no ship to Newcastle for several weeks so he had taken one bound for London. His ship was then delayed by a summer storm in the Channel and was blown badly off course. The ship's master was a cautious man and they sheltered for several days before resuming their voyage and then there was a dearth of breeze to take them.

Both Gate and his companion, Walter Grave, were poor sea travellers and loathed every minute aboard ship. Gate supposed that the Lord had his reasons for delaying him and prayed daily for their safe deliverance. After a further week of delay, God saw fit to release Gate's poor body from its torment and allow the ship to reach its destination.

Through it all and much to his astonishment - the girl, Agnes, met all setbacks with surprising fortitude. She had even mopped his brow when the wretched sickness seized him. It endeared her to him in a way he would not have believed very likely when he had taken her from Sluys. Admittedly she still believed that he was taking her to Ned Elder and when she discovered he wasn't, he suspected she would be a good deal less cooperative.

From London his journey became easier for mention of the earl's name bought him three fast horses and provisions for his ride north. So, here they were: Middleham - the place he had called home for the past five years. He had done well under Warwick, who was generous to clients who served him well - and Gate had served him very well. Not openly, but most certainly covertly. He was relieved to be back but his apprehension stemmed from the failure in Sluys. Warwick was astute: he recognised the difficulties of the task he had set Gate but he still expected success. His previous successes had earned him a small suite of rooms on the top floor of Middleham's west range and Gate was anxious to keep it - or perhaps even merit a move to chambers in the coveted, and more modern, north range.

It had been a dusty ride for the north road was baked hard from the summer sun. Gate nudged his weary horse up the rough track through the village towards the north gate. Grave and the girl followed him. She looked pale now and worried, he thought. Well, she had every right to be.

The new north gate might have been built for his own convenience since it gave swift and easy access to his chambers. It was late afternoon and the gate lay open still. He nodded to the men who stood beside it and rode on through. They took little notice of him or Grave but took more than a passing interest in the beautiful Agnes. Once inside, Grave took their mounts over to the stables and Gate led Agnes through the courtyard between the keep and the north range. He glanced up at the wooden walkway ahead of him which linked the first floor of the north range to the keep and his spirits sank at once. On the walkway stood the tall figure of Richard Neville, Earl of Warwick. Gate stopped and closed his eyes for a moment.

"Gate!" His eyes flicked open as Warwick's voice echoed around the walls. His master was clearly expecting him. "Inner chamber!" Warwick called down and disappeared into the keep.

Thomas thought swiftly. He had hoped to keep Agnes a secret and had not expected Warwick to be out to greet him.

"Wait here," he told Agnes. "You don't want to get lost. I'll be back as swiftly as I can."

Agnes frowned and not for the first time he was glad that she could not speak. He turned and retraced his steps to mount the long flight of steps which gave access to the keep and made his way to Warwick's inner chamber which lay off the Great Chamber. The stone passages were crowded with men and servants going about their business and he was obliged to push his way through at times. He was tired and not exactly at his best to talk to his lord. He was most surprised to find the earl waiting outside the chamber to usher him in. It did not bode at all well for the earl to be in such a hurry.

Warwick sat down in his customary chair, high-backed and French. Gate remained standing and, of course, now that Warwick had him standing there he was going to make him wait.

"My lord?" Thomas tried to get it over with.

"I thought you were never coming out of hiding," said Warwick, his voice even - however angry Warwick might be with Gate he would not show it. Thomas felt no less nervous all the same.

"Hardly in hiding, my lord. I was delayed," he said.

"Aye, delayed by fear and guilt. I dare say. I take it - from the gaudy spectacle which took place in Damme - that your visit to Flanders was not exactly a success."

"No, my lord. The French proved unreliable and..." Thomas hesitated.

"And the wedding went ahead?"

"Our design was forestalled by ... rogue interference."

"Rogue?" queried Warwick. "Explain."

"Ned Elder."

The earl stared at him for a very long time - or so it seemed to Thomas.

"Ned Elder." Warwick sighed. "Will I never be rid of

him? He hangs about me like a leper's curse. So, he's been in Flanders all this time. I thought he would have run further away."

"Aye, my lord. But I have him now - securely locked up and awaiting your pleasure." Thomas was relieved to get to his better news, but Warwick greeted it with a steely glare. Beads of sweat formed on Thomas's brow; it was an unusual experience for him - not much worried him - but this man's power to destroy was immense.

"Thomas, are you suggesting to me that the capture of Ned Elder is in any way recompense for your failure to prevent the marriage of the king's sister to the Duke of Burgundy? Do you seriously believe that my irritation with that warlike knight, a man of no consequence, is of the same order as preventing the Burgundy alliance that the wretched queen's relatives have been pushing for?"

Thomas shuddered. "No, my lord, but the attack had already stalled and I knew that you would want me to take the chance to capture Lord Elder…that it was important - important to you. He is in your hands now…my lord."

The earl was already shaking his head. "Well, the attack in Sluys was very much a last ditch effort - and you're hardly to blame for the marriage. As for your prisoner, he is no longer 'Lord' Elder - or lord of anything. Ned Elder is rotten meat. He's of no threat to me now: his power is dust, his lands and titles lost. You should know that better than anyone since you'll soon have some of them. The Elders are subdued and we have more important matters to work on here in the north."

"And Ned Elder, my lord?"

Warwick gave a sigh. "Go back to Flanders and make sure Ned Elder is gone for good this time. I don't want to hear his name again – and don't make it too easy for him after all the trouble he's made."

"It will be done, my lord," said Thomas, and he had every reason to make sure it was.

"When that's done, return here with all speed. You want the marriage of Joan Elder?"

"Aye, my lord." Thomas was wary now. He had been angling for the Elder marriage for two years. Joan Elder's marriage belonged to Warwick but why was the earl raising it now, he wondered? Did he know why Thomas was so keen? You never knew with Warwick.

"Well, do you want the marriage or not?" snapped Warwick.

"Aye, my lord, aye – if you are willing to agree to it."

"It'll come at a price," answered the earl, "but you knew that. I'll require some robust service from you in the coming months and you'll need some clout here if you are to do me that service. The Elder lands and estates that come to you through Joan Elder will give you some substance among other men in the shire."

Ah, thought Thomas, here comes the rub. "I have ever served you well, my lord."

"These are unruly times, Thomas."

The earl, often a plain speaker, could be irritatingly obscure at times, Thomas reflected.

"You want me to help restore order in these parts, my lord?"

Warwick smiled. "This goes far beyond restoring order, Thomas and is a most…privy matter – privy enough to cost you your head if it goes wrong."

"My lord?" Thomas specialised in 'privy matters' as the earl well knew.

"Restoring order, Thomas, is not what I have in mind. More likely, I'll want you to create more disorder. I may need you to light me a fire, Thomas – a fire in the north, hot enough to burn the fingers of a king. In the coming months you will need to prepare. There will be much to do."

Thomas considered for a moment. "Does the Elder marriage bring me all Ned Elder's lands and titles?"

A trace of a smile crossed Warwick's face. "No, not yet. The king – out of some remaining affection, I assume - allows Ned's sister to keep several manors and lands. Of course, your own actions could change that."

"I understand, my lord," said Thomas.

"I knew you would. Thus, when you come back from Flanders you'll be married to Joan Elder. You'll take up residence at Yoredale Castle and start recruiting men. Speak to the Conyers brothers - they know what's in my mind on this matter and what may need to be done. But this is not a matter for other ears, Thomas."

"Aye, my lord. I shall go to Sir John Conyers upon my return."

Thomas was annoyed that he must go to Flanders again so soon but elated by Warwick's confirmation of his marriage. It would give him everything he needed to establish himself as a leading figure in the north. He knew that Warwick wanted to remove the influence of the queen's family at court. When that was done, there would be opportunities for other, ambitious men and then he would then be able to claim his own birthright. He took a pace towards the door.

"Thomas," said Warwick softly, "who is the girl?"

Thomas had forgotten Agnes and the question took him unawares.

"Oh, she's of no consequence, my lord. A mute girl I took a liking to along the way. I'll put her to work here somewhere - the kitchens perhaps."

"Hmm, very well. When you return, I'll likely be in the south, or at Calais. Sir John will tell you what to do - but first make sure of Ned Elder."

"Aye, my lord, you may rely upon that."

5

20th July 1468, at Crag Tower in Northumberland

Maighread was in the Great Hall when John ran in, chasing the wooden ball as it rolled crazily across the stone flags. The boy wielded a short cudgel of wood and skilfully controlled it as it ricocheted off the legs of benches and tables. Intent upon his game, he did not see her until the ball came to rest at her feet. Then he stopped dead and looked up at her; he looked worried. He was a sweet young boy, she thought, how hideous she must seem to him.

She turned her disfigured cheek away from him. "You fear my scars still," she said softly.

He studied her face for a moment - all of it. "No, my lady," he replied, "I just don't want you to take my ball away."

She grinned at him, her best twisted grin, and bent down to pick up the ball. John waited whilst she examined it. She could see that it was well crafted.

"Who made this for you?" she asked him.

"Bear, my lady."

She smiled again. She should not be surprised for Bear seemed capable of almost anything.

"Are you going to take it, my lady?" he asked.

He spoke well, she thought, for a boy of four. A clear, strong voice.

"I think you should give it back, my lady," John suggested, holding out his hand. He was confident, this little soul. She went to drop it into his waiting palm but the ball slipped from her grasp. John dropped his wooden stick, dived to the floor and deftly caught the ball in his other hand. Maighread was astonished to see such speed of movement from one so young. He quickly jumped to his feet, clutching the ball and gave her a wry grin. "Can I go now, my lady?" he asked.

Maighread was lost for words and just nodded. She watched him skip out of the Hall and staggered back until she felt the wall, cold against her back. She was in shock, not because he was a clever, agile little boy, but because she had seen that boyish grin before, several times and she remembered it well. How had she not seen it before? She had spent four years with that boy and only now did she realise that he was Ned Elder's son. By God, how had Eleanor kept such a secret? And who else knew?

Suddenly, all became clear: Eleanor and Ragwulf had brought the boy to Crag Tower four years before. Now their refusal to let Wulf take Bessie and the boy with him made some sense. Poor Ragwulf, the boy was not his and yet he was trapped by a pact he must have made with Eleanor four years ago. Maighread sat down on one of the long benches. She felt like weeping but a shout from the courtyard distracted her and she got up to discover the cause of all the noise.

§§§§

Felix of Bordeaux dismounted slowly in the small cobbled courtyard. It was not just that he was stiff and saddle-sore from his journey, but also that he wanted to delay the moment for as long as possible. Now that he had actually reached Crag Tower, he was dreading what would come next. He glanced at Spearbold briefly but long enough to know that his companion shared his fears. His unease was increased by what he had seen on his way in: the blackened walls beside the newly repaired gate.

His feet had hardly touched the ground before Lady

Eleanor rushed out to greet him. She crushed him in a fond embrace that quite overwhelmed him.

"Felix! You don't know how glorious it is to see a friendly face!" she said.

"But, my lady, you are surely surrounded by friends here," he said, gently disentangling himself from her grasp.

Eleanor stood back from him and smiled. Her smile lit up the deep shadows of the courtyard. Felix forced a smile of his own but she knew at once that something was amiss.

"You bring news of Ned," she said, her voice betraying her uncertainty.

"Lady -"

"Wait!" she said. "Come into the Hall. Whatever you have to tell, there are others who need to hear it too."

She took his arm and walked him up the few steps to the Hall. Spearbold followed them and others had already begun to gather, probably from the moment they identified him from the rampart.

Sir Stephen almost ran to him. "At last! You have news, Felix…" he declared.

"I do," Felix said but he could not keep the misery from his voice.

Eleanor slumped down onto one of the long benches. "He's dead, isn't he?" she said in a whisper.

"I'll not believe it!" cried Hal.

Felix looked at the young man, not so young these days really. He put a hand on his shoulder. "Let me tell it how it must be told, Hal."

Hal nodded and the others settled themselves around the Hall. Felix looked about him; they were all there: the ladies, Eleanor and Maighread; Sir Stephen, Ragwulf, Hal, Bear and Rob, Maighread's brother. And yet some of the younger men, such as Ragwulf's son, were not there. Ned had freed them from their oaths long ago so it was hardly surprising they had gone.

"Your lord may not be dead," Felix announced, "but he

is missing."

"You have all waited a very long time," he began, "It is four years since Ned left these shores in exile. As you know, he escaped in a ship called The Catherine. Until now I have kept all of you ignorant of his destination but now there is no longer anything to be gained by doing so."

"So, what has happened?" asked Eleanor.

"Gently, my lady gently," soothed Felix. "Let me tell this tale - with Master Spearbold's help - for this man has been a loyal servant to Ned Elder throughout his exile."

"Well for the love of God, Felix, make haste and spit it out!" growled Eleanor.

So Felix explained what had happened, with occasional helpful interjections by Spearbold.

When he stopped speaking there was no reaction, just stunned silence. Then Eleanor, eyes afire, began to ask questions.

"You've heard nothing at all of him, Master Spearbold?"

"Nothing, my lady. And I assure you I've done my best."

"The girl, Agnes, could she have been involved in some plot to take him?" asked Eleanor.

"Never!" cried Hal, surprising Felix with his vehemence. "Agnes is the most loyal soul…"

"What about this Thomas Gate?" said Eleanor. "Where is he?"

"I've made some enquiries," said Felix. "It seems that Spearbold was right: he is Warwick's man and he is almost certainly back in England by now."

"Then there is our link," said Eleanor. "If Gate is behind it, then we must find him."

"My lady," said Spearbold, "Gate is a shadowy, privy fellow. You'll not find him easily - unless he is at Middleham and you'll not get close to him there."

Eleanor sighed and turned away. Lady Maighread, Felix noticed, walked briskly away up the stairs - though whether from excess of grief or lack of it, he could not tell. Others drifted away, servants to their daily tasks, the boys in ignorance of what had passed and some men perhaps to shed a few tears into their ale. Sir Stephen stepped forward and took Spearbold's hand.

"We are grateful to you both for your loyalty," he said. "You must be weary. Come up to the solar and take some rest and refreshment."

Eleanor did not leave. Instead she followed Sir Stephen and took Felix's arm once more to lead him into the solar. Hal, Bear and Ragwulf went too and Becky was despatched to bring up some refreshment.

In the solar, seats were found for Felix and Spearbold.

"Tell me, Felix," said Eleanor, "do you believe Ned is dead?"

"Indeed, my lady, it is the most likely outcome," he replied.

"Then there's nothing more to be said."

Felix took her hand gently in his own black hands. "My lady, I have not made this long journey simply to grieve with you. Never underestimate your brother's ability to escape death - I've witnessed it often enough! If your lord and brother is still alive, then you will have to go looking for him - and that I will help you to do. Spearbold has passage on a ship back to Sluys in a weeks' time. Several of you must go with him and take one last chance to track Ned down."

"But how?" asked Sir Stephen. "Where would we start? If Spearbold couldn't find him before, what makes you believe we could do any better?"

Felix gave him an indulgent smile. "Well, Sir Stephen, because we have one here who knows Flanders far better than Master Spearbold..."

There was a brief silence and then, as one, they all turned to look at Bear. He had been a mercenary, a fugitive from Flanders, when he happened upon Ned Elder. He was a giant of a man who could have earned much in the service of any great lord. Yet he had chosen to fight beside Ned all those years ago. Now he stepped forward to face Felix and slowly nodded his head. In his deep guttural tones, he announced: "Bear will go."

For several moments the others were silent again; then everyone spoke at once and it seemed all wanted to go. Felix shook his head.

"Peace, peace!" he said, raising his voice, and when his words had no effect he crashed the iron-shod butt of his staff down upon the floor. The timbers shuddered and an uneasy quiet descended.

"Peace," he repeated quietly. "I ask myself sometimes, why I go so far out of my way so frequently to help you folk at all."

He thought that without Ned they would fritter away their strengths like unruly children. Ned Elder was the one that bound them together.

"Well, I shall go, of course," said Lady Eleanor at once. Felix was about to reply when Ragwulf spoke up.

"No, my lady, of us all, you may not go." He stared at her, fixing her eyes with his. Who would dare to hold that fiery glare, thought Felix? But Ragwulf did and Felix watched in fascination as Eleanor capitulated. He never thought to see it; nor did others fail to notice.

"My lady?" asked Felix.

She looked forlorn, her sad eyes downcast. "No," she said at last. "I will not go...but who then will go with Bear?"

"I will go," said Ragwulf. "I'll go with Bear." All the while his eyes rested on Eleanor's ashen face. Felix observed the look that passed between them, a look of understanding, of acceptance of their diverging fates.

"I regret I must remain here," said Sir Stephen. "Nothing would please me more than to help deliver my lord, but he charged me to remain here, to hold Crag Tower and protect Lady Maighread and all who live here. Given the troubles we have had, I must stay."

"I'll go," said Hal but Felix shook his head. "No Hal; better that you are on hand if there is word of Agnes - no-one else here would know her. And, aside from Spearbold, she knows you better than anyone. She would trust you."

"But she could still be in Flanders," said Hal.

"In which case, Spearbold will be there to reassure her. No, it's better you stay here. In any case, three is enough. Any more will attract too much attention in Sluys."

So it was agreed and all that remained was to fit out the small expedition. Felix was appalled to discover that there were no horses left at Crag Tower, and he had only to cast his eyes around him to see the poverty of his hosts: their clothing was ragged, all looked thin and haggard. He would have to reach into his own purse once more if Ragwulf and Bear were to accompany Spearbold.

6

30th July 1468, somewhere in Flanders

Dripping walls, dripping roof, every stone, every scrap of rusted iron or rotten wood was wet. God's blood! If there was a wetter place in all Christendom, Ned had never been there.

He lay on a thin slick of water, not the sweet clear water of a Yorkshire beck but a slimy, stinking sludge. It stank like death - and so did he, but he wasn't dead. He should be, but he wasn't. Why he was still alive, he knew from the first was an important question but as time slowly passed, he cared about the answer less and less.

For a while he counted the days, scratching a mark on a stone; but then it seemed pointless so he did not bother. He tried to pray but he knew the Lord would not be listening and he didn't blame Him. Ned had too much blood on his hands. All he could hope was that the good Lord had not given up on Agnes and Spearbold. Always it seemed he was destined to wreak havoc upon his friends. It may be that he had saved the life of a princess - but was her life worth more than the life of Agnes? Not to him it wasn't.

He cursed his wretched fate. He had got so close: his exile had only one more year to run. Exile was bad enough but Spearbold and Agnes had seen him through it. Then he had to ruin it. In spite of Spearbold's warnings, he had followed Thomas Gate and, God curse him, he had found him. Blood of Christ! What had he done?

His head still hurt, which was a pity after the trouble Agnes had taken to repair it. Agnes - what would become of her? Spearbold would do his best but Spearbold was a clerk, a man of letters not a swordsman.

Why had they not simply killed him? Gate could have cut his throat with ease. How he must have wanted to after Ned had stopped the attack on the princess. But Thomas Gate was cautious, clever and he hadn't just lashed out in anger - even though he must have been in great peril, fleeing from the docks at Sluys. Gate decided to keep him alive, locked up somewhere and surely by now Warwick must know where he was. So far they had left him alive but he could not help thinking that would soon change: Warwick would want him dead.

He did not have any idea where he was being held, or by whom. He could remember little of his journey there, except coming to in a covered wagon only a few hours after his capture, unless perhaps that was a dream. No, the smell stayed with him: the scent of fleeces. He could still smell it on his clothes. Someone regularly moved wool bales in that wagon. He thought he had been on route for several days but he could have been mistaken.

When Ned considered it, he could not recall ever being imprisoned before. He hated it, being caged and manacled on the end of chain like some miserable bear. Day by day he could feel his strength ebbing away - aye, and his will too. He heard the echo of boots outside the cell, he could hear them coming from some distance - this was a large place then. Then came the familiar grating noise as the door opened.

They brought his food late in the evening, if they brought it at all. It seemed almost an afterthought, which did not augur well. He barely glimpsed his gaolers - he knew there were at least two, though neither was Thomas Gate himself. He had not seen him at all. Thomas Gate was no turnkey - he would be elsewhere by now, back with Warwick no doubt, engaging in matters of more importance.

By now Ned knew very well what to expect: they would

open the cell door and one of them would throw a chunk of bread in his general direction. The other would wait for Ned to throw him an empty leather flask and then sent an identical flask spinning through the air towards him. He sometimes asked them where he was but his Flemish was rudimentary and whether they understood him or not he could not tell. They never said a word, just stared at him with unseeing eyes. He might still be alive but he was clearly as good as dead as far as they were concerned.

Once or twice the bread fell out of his reach - as happened now - and he would spend half the night listening to the rats gnaw their way through the stale, coarse-grained loaf. By morning there would not be a crumb left. This evening the stopper was jolted from the flask as it struck the stone floor and some water spilled out. He quickly rescued the remainder and swilled a little around his mouth as the door clanged shut. It was not the sweetest water he had ever drunk. In fact it tasted like bog water; he would have preferred ale.

He waited for sleep to claim him but it didn't. Instead he was forced to listen to the rats worrying away at the bread. In the darkness other, older memories came crowding in upon him once more, first of the dead and then worse, much worse, of the living. One thought led to another and soon he had called them all to mind: Eleanor, Emma, Amelie... He had tried to forget in Sluys, and the ale had helped at times, but the guilt always came back. It would never leave him. He forced the memories out, one by one, slamming the doors in his head and chaining them shut once more.

One image lingered after all the others, one he could never quite dislodge: Maighread Elder's face: one half a work of exquisite beauty, the other ravaged by fire. Tears rolled down his cheeks, unbidden and unwanted. They dribbled down his face and dripped onto the damp floor where he lay. Somewhere water was still dripping. Drip,

drip, drip.

In the morning his hunger was worse - that must be normal, he told himself and it would pass; it didn't. A bold rat scuttled across the floor a few feet away from him. The rat looked fat enough and he had considered trying to catch one but they were too quick for him - too quick and too clever.

At first he had tried to move about - at least as far as the short chain would allow. But now he did not bother. His legs ached. His arms ached. His head ached. Not for the first time he cast his eyes around the cell and, not for the first time, the little that he saw did nothing to cheer him. The stone walls were black with damp. Did stone rot? He thought not, but the stones looked worn by the water. If he could reach the walls he thought he might burrow through them but he was chained to a ring in the centre of the floor and the stone that held the ring was not loose. The only wall he could reach was the internal wall. Besides, even in the unlikely event that he might remove a stone, he was still chained up.

He must wait. He must be patient. They were keeping him alive for a purpose and eventually it would be revealed and they would take him out. Then he would have a chance. Aye, then they would have to be careful with him for he would take his chance and they would be dead men. After a while he realised that he was saying his thoughts aloud. He laughed. "Dead men!" he shouted. At least he tried to shout but only a dry croak came out and then he coughed until his chest felt like it would explode. The coughing was another problem - the constant damp, he supposed, but it wasn't doing him any good.

He forced himself up on his knees. He should keep moving, keep alert. Be ready for when they came for him. Then he would rip their heads off.

§§§§

They came as usual in the evening, but they did not come to feed him, nor to take him away. They came to talk - and that did surprise him. They strolled in and pushed the door closed behind them.

"Time to go," said one.

"You're English!" said Ned, unable to hide his surprise. He had just assumed they were local men.

"We are," said the other.

"Why did you not speak then?"

"Nothing to gain by talking to a dead man."

"Aye, but I'm not dead am I and now you've come for me," said Ned, he could not keep the grin from his face.

"No," replied one of his gaolers, "We've not come for you." The cold hostility began to worry him and his grin slowly faded. He crouched, tensing himself for them to come at him. They didn't and instead he heard more footsteps approaching.

The pair sniggered. "You won't be getting a quick death, "Lord" Elder. You'll be all on your own - apart from the rats." He looked at his companion. "Pity," he said, "it'd be good to know which gets you first: hunger or the rats."

The cell door opened and Thomas Gate stood on the threshold.

"Sir Thomas?" Ned's voice was a whisper.

"The earl sends his compliments," said Gate.

"I very much doubt that," muttered Ned.

"He wanted you to know that you're of no further interest to him. He was most anxious that I tell you that…before I send you on your way."

Ned sat on the floor, trying to make sense of what was happening.

"So I'm to be…released?"

"Nothing quite so generous as that," replied Gate. "The earl felt you would need some time to reflect upon the misery you have caused him - and others. I decided that staying here in this place would give you plenty of time."

So he was to be abandoned there, to a slow death. How many times had he fought his way out of trouble, sword in hand, loyal comrades at his side? But these men had no intention of fighting him. Why bother when they could just leave him to rot in his cell.

For himself, he knew he could make no complaint: he was lucky to have survived so long. But there were others…

"I would ask something of you, Sir Thomas," he said, "if you will do it."

"If I can do it, I will," replied Sir Thomas.

"This is not an easy thing for me to ask. There is a young girl - I have acted as her guardian these past four years - will you give me your word that you'll see she is safe?"

Gate smiled at him. "Well, that's easily done. You needn't worry upon her account. She's quite safe. There's nowhere more secure than Middleham Castle and that's where she is now."

Ned sighed and turned away. "Middleham? Why Middleham?"

"Because I'm at Middleham - for now," replied Gate, "and she is … with me."

Ned looked up at him, meeting his eyes. "If you hurt her, I'll kill you."

Gate gave a chuckle. "No, you won't - but she'll not be hurt, I promise you that much."

Ned gave him a stiff nod of the head. It hurt him to do so… it hurt him a great deal. Then he turned away from them all so that they would not see his face. He heard Gate walk out and listened to his footsteps as they receded. Soon only an echo remained and then nothing. Yet he realised that his gaolers were still staring at him and he could feel their animosity. He turned back to face them.

"Have I wronged you in the past?" he asked.

"You killed some of the earl's men - men we knew… men we fought alongside."

"The earl wronged me many times," said Ned. "If I killed, it was to defend myself or my own men! Blame your lord, not me!"

One of his captors took a swift step forward and kicked him in the leg. He crumpled to the floor and the other struck his chest, knocking him onto his back. He hadn't expected that and was badly winded.

"You're not worth a tenth of our master. He's a brave knight and a great lord. He looks after his own. You're not fit to shovel his shit! Think about that while you lie there getting weaker. You'll have lots of time."

He placed a flask beside Ned and whispered: "See how long you can make that last."

They went out, slamming the door so hard that the iron rang around the cell. Ned did not cry out after them. He lay on the floor, stunned - but not by the boot that had no doubt bruised a few ribs. It was their praise of Warwick that shocked him. They clearly worshipped the earl and they certainly had no love at all for Ned Elder. For the very first time it struck him that he was not every man's valiant warrior. To them, he was the villain and he was going to die for it, slowly.

7

Lammas Day, 1st August 1468, at Crag Tower

Hal watched them from the rampart as they came up along the track from the south. There were about a dozen of them which surprised him - Wulf had clearly gathered a few recruits. The men on the gate were Wulf's friends and they opened it without hesitation. Hal walked down to the Hall to greet his comrade. It was a blessing, he thought, that Ragwulf had gone for at least they would be spared a fight between father and son. Even so, by the time he got to the Hall he could see that the time for negotiation was long past.

Sir Stephen, Lady Maighread and her brother, Rob, stood on the dais. All had their eyes fixed upon Lady Eleanor who had planted herself in the centre of the Hall with a naked sword in her hand. She kept Bess and John behind her. Wulf was in the doorway, framed by several of his young men at arms. Lady Eleanor's face was flushed with anger. Those present were certain of only one thing: they had no idea what the ebullient lady intended to do next.

"Lady Eleanor," said Sir Stephen, "please put up your sword. We are all friends and allies here."

"Be quiet!" Lady Eleanor snapped. He took it like a slap on the face and Hal could see he was fuming, but he made no reply. Lady Maighread beside him said nothing either.

"I did not come here to shed blood, my lady," said Wulf, "I just want Bess."

Hal was proud of his comrade: he spoke with calm but also with strength. His case was clear: he wanted to marry Bess; she wanted to marry him. What could be simpler? Hal watched Lady Eleanor carefully. She said nothing, as if weighing up the extent of Wulf's resolve.

"Come, Bess," said Wulf, holding his hand out to her. The girl hesitated as if she dared not take a step towards him without her lady's permission. John was clutching her hand tightly. It seemed to Hal that the boy was almost holding her back. Yet surely John was far too young to understand. The thought crossed Hal's mind that he did not fully understand himself. But surely Lady Eleanor must let them go - why was she making such a stand?

He saw her glance around the Hall, perhaps estimating who would stand with her against Wulf if the need arose. When her eyes came to rest upon Hal, he shook his head slightly. She ought to know that he would not fight Wulf, least of all to keep Bess from him.

"Very well," agreed Lady Eleanor, resting the point of her blade on the dead rushes that covered the floor. "Bess, you may go with him."

Hal could feel the relief spread around the room but something in her tone told him it was not over yet. Bess took a step towards Wulf and took John with her.

"No," said Lady Eleanor flatly. "You can go - but not the boy. John stays."

Bess stopped and went down on one knee. "Please, my lady. I can't leave him. He's more my son than anyone's. You can't want the lad to grow up without a mother."

"I did," growled Lady Eleanor. "But you're not his mother! Go with your young man and leave John with me."

Bess looked across to Wulf and shook her head. He sighed in resignation.

"We'll take the boy with us," he said.

Lady Eleanor raised her sword again. "No. I will kill anyone who tries to take him. Anyone." She seized John's other hand and wrenched him free of Bess. Bess ran over to Wulf and he pushed her behind him to the door. Others now drew their swords.

"Hold! This has gone far enough!" shouted Sir Stephen. "As Lord Elder's steward, I command you all to put up your arms at once. You disgrace your lord! Lady Eleanor, put up your sword and let the boy go."

She gave him such a venomous look that he took a step back in shock.

"You do not command here." She ground the words out at him. "And if you say another word, you must call me enemy."

John looked utterly bemused by all the fuss but to Hal's surprise he did not shrink from Eleanor or try to pull away. Remarkably, he seemed more inclined to stand still and watch what happened.

"Wulf, take Bess and go - while you may," said Lady Eleanor.

Wulf stood his ground. "My lady, we won't go without him and you are alone in this."

"No," said Lady Maighread suddenly. "I believe the boy should stay here too. I'm sure Lady Eleanor and I can see that he is well cared for."

Even Lady Eleanor looked surprised at that and stared at her aunt in some confusion then acknowledged her support with a curt nod.

Wulf turned to Bess and for the first time he looked unsure, but she was not.

"I've nursed that boy from his birth and he needs me still. Will you have the boy watch us fight over him, my lady?"

Her voice was no longer deferential or subdued and her words rang with determination. Lady Eleanor dropped John's hand.

"John, come over to me, please," instructed Bess.

So at last, Hal thought, it was over. But it wasn't because

John stayed exactly where he was - which surprised everyone. He looked behind Lady Eleanor to the wall where her son Will, his friend, crouched in the corner. Hal thought there were no more surprises left but he was wrong again, for Lady Eleanor laid her sword on the floor and knelt down by John. She gave him a hug and he buried his head in her shoulder. Somehow - and Hal could not see how - there was a close bond between these two. A bond that John understood in a way that no-one else seemed to.

So there was an impasse: Bess would not leave without the boy and now the boy himself seemed unwilling to go.

If anyone had asked him, Hal could not have explained at that moment why he stepped forward and said: "Let young John decide."

It sent a ripple of consternation around the Hall. Several voices muttered at once that it was a ridiculous idea. Hal shared their doubts for he did not think a four year old was capable of deciding either. But it was the only idea that came into his head and instead of standing by as a silent observer, he decided he must intervene.

He took John away from the others and spoke quietly to him.

"You understand, don't you," he said. "You can go with Bess and Wulf or you can stay here with Lady Eleanor."

John nodded unhappily.

Hal tried his best to be even handed. "There will be dangers outside these walls. This place is all you've known. I know it is hard for you to decide…"

"No," replied John, "it's not. I'd like to see what's outside."

He walked briskly across to Bess and took her hand.

"We're going home," said Wulf. "Back to Yoredale. That's where the boy will be…if you want to see him."

"No," breathed Lady Eleanor, "not there – anywhere but there…" Her lips trembled and her face was ashen.

Hal was suddenly puzzled. "Is that a good idea?" he

asked.

"Aye, it is. At least we know folk in Yoredale," said Wulf. "We've a chance there."

"Yoredale has changed, Wulf. I've told you what was done there - Lady Joan Elder is to be feared."

"That's in the past, Hal. We need to make our way and we should have no fear of going back home to do it."

Hal saw Lady Eleanor bend down and at once he put his foot upon her blade where it lay on the rushes. She shook her head. "You don't know what you've done," she said, weeping now, "and when you do, you'll want to cut out your tongue in penance."

Wulf, Bess and the others hurried out of the Hall.

Lady Eleanor put her hands around Hal's neck and pressed her fingers into his throat.

"Go with them," she said. "And if any ill befalls that boy, you'll answer to me with your life."

Hal was nonplussed. He had not intended to go with Wulf. "I thought it would be better if I stayed to help defend the castle..."

"Yes," said Sir Stephen, "we've few enough men as it is!"

"Leave us!" ordered Lady Eleanor and waited whilst Sir Stephen and the others left. She did not relax her grip on Hal's neck.

"Listen to me!" she told him in a harsh whisper. "You'll go with John and you'll leave word for me so that I know where you are."

"But how, my lady?"

"Do you remember Canon Reedman?" she said.

"The monk at Coverham Abbey?"

"Aye, the white canon. You must tell him where you are – trust no-one else. I will follow after you soon and when I get to Yoredale I'll go to him."

"Yes, my lady."

She released her hold but put her face an inch away

from his, her green eyes glaring into his.

"There's more. I'll be close but you'll be closer. You'll stay with John day and night. You'll protect him with your life - with… your… life," she repeated, "as if you were protecting your very own lord, Ned Elder, his own …body." Her eyes bored into him. "Do you understand me?"

Hal met her stare and nodded because for the first time he believed he really did understand and the knowledge of what he had just done filled his heart with fear. He wondered too how he had not seen it long ago.

"With my life, my lady," he replied softly.

§§§§

Eleanor was still seething with a cold rage days after Wulf had left and she vented her anger on every soul left at Crag Tower - though there were few enough of those. She would have followed Hal at once but that night there was another raid. This time there was no Ragwulf, no Bear and no Hal. Eleanor knew Sir Stephen was an able knight but he struggled to inspire the remaining men at arms and archers. Their spirits were already low and the renewed attack by the border folk had all but broken their morale. Nevertheless, the repaired gate stood up well to the assault and they now drenched it with water late every night to help slow any fireballs thrown against it. Thus their assailants did not get in this time and the tiny victory put a little hope back into them all. Yet her own courage was wavering and she saw it too in all their faces - except Maighread - and Eleanor suspected that was because, for her aunt, things could get no worse.

All their efforts over the past years had been towards one end - Ned's return after his five year exile. But Spearbold's news had snatched away that hope and replaced it with a dull aching dread: Ned Elder was not coming back.

So, Eleanor began to consider what she should do if her brother was indeed lost. However long she thought about it, the answer was always the same: John. She should never have let him go; she should have killed if need be to keep him safe. He was Ned's sole heir and she must watch over him. She had lingered at Crag Tower too long already.

That evening, as they sat in the Hall consuming a thin tasteless potage, she told them all.

"I'm going after Wulf."

Her announcement did not seem to surprise anyone. They all nodded silently and continued eating. She wasn't sure what she had expected: objections, expressions of regret - or support, or offers to accompany her but none of these were put forward. After they had eaten, each one took their leave and she did too, leaving the Hall to the few soldiers and servants who remained. Only rush lights now burned in the castle for they had no candles left. Eleanor crept up to her chamber hoping to find it in darkness but she was disappointed. Maighread had hung a rush light from the wall and it gave a dull glow.

Eleanor ignored Maighread and began to disrobe. Then she remembered that Becky had laced her into the bodice in the morning and Becky now slept with Will… now that John had gone. She wrestled with the bodice. She felt like ripping it apart but she had little else to wear.

She flinched as she felt Maighread's hands on her shoulders.

"Be calm," said Maighread. "Let me do it."

Eleanor had barely spoken to Maighread for days, even before Wulf's return. The friction between them sometimes seemed to make the air itself crackle. She allowed Maighread to help her but only because it was better than the embarrassment of struggling in vain. Her aunt had a soft touch and nimble fingers and swiftly helped remove the offending garment.

"Thank you," Eleanor said stiffly.

By the time she had stripped naked, as was her habit, especially when the nights grew warmer, Maighread had returned to her own bed.

Eleanor climbed under her covers and looked across at her aunt. She felt that somehow the wall that divided them had been breached and she might pose a question that had been troubling her.

"Why did you - of all people - support me when I tried to keep John here?"

Maighread smiled. "Because I knew why you wanted him here."

"You couldn't have known that," scoffed Eleanor.

"He's Ned son, isn't he?" said Maighread.

"How could you know that?" breathed Eleanor. "Only Ragwulf knew - and he wouldn't have told anyone!"

"I didn't notice when he was younger-"

"He's only four now!"

"But old enough to show his manner, his natural skills, his strengths. He's quick, with hand and eye and-"

"Many lads are - so is my Will. That tells you nothing!"

"- and ... he has his father's smile," said Maighread.

Eleanor suddenly saw her aunt in a different light then. Clearly Maighread was very observant but, more than that, she seemed to remember Ned remarkably well from what must have been a very brief encounter. In a few moments Eleanor learned more about Maighread than she had in four years - and now suddenly she wanted to know more.

"How long have you lived here?" she asked.

If Maighread was surprised by the question she didn't show it.

"I really struggle to remember," she replied. "That must seem foolish, I know, but I've lived here a long time. I came here as a bride when I was about ten years old. Your grandfather and my father made a truce and my marriage was part of it."

"Who was your father?"

"My father was - and for all I know still is - the head of a large border family, the Halls. He was a much feared man in these parts and a constant trouble to your grandfather, Sir Thomas Elder."

"Who did you marry?"

"I married one of your uncles, Richard, his name was. I think his first wife died of a fever. He must have been about thirty…"

"And you were ten?"

"Aye."

"That must have been … hard."

Maighread smiled her lopsided smile. "It could have been but your grandfather had agreed that the marriage wouldn't be fulfilled until I was fourteen."

"You were fortunate then."

"Aye, perhaps I was then, for your uncle went off to the French wars with his brothers and never came back. I was a widow before my eleventh birthday - a virgin widow - but I was well looked after by your grandmother, Lady Margaret. I had a good life but there was no more talk of marriage. So I kept my maidenhood until… your half-brother, Henry, came along and then…."

"I knew he killed her and burned you. He raped you too?"

Maighread pulled a face. "Before you arrived here, I was seen as something of a plain speaker. Perhaps that's why we've not found it so easy to talk."

Eleanor grinned. "When I open my mouth, everyone holds their breath. My words leave no-one content."

"Well, you describe my fate well enough: I was burned. I was supposed to die - and most days I wish I had. When I was burned I wasn't a virgin anymore either. I took it as the Lord's displeasure…"

"I'd have thrown myself from the highest rampart if…"

"…If you looked as I do? Well, that would have been a mortal sin and... I think now that God saved me for a purpose."

Eleanor could not help smiling.

"You mock me," said Maighread.

"No, it's just that I'm told it was Ned who saved you and I'm sure the good Lord gave up on him a long time ago. The thought of Ned in some way serving God's purpose is quite difficult to believe."

Maighread looked across at her. "God does not give up on a man so easily."

Eleanor thought she could discern the glint of a tear glistening on Maighread's cheek.

"So," said Maighread, "you are going after them. What will you do when you find them? Have you thought about that?"

"Aye, I'm not going to argue with them. I just need to be close by - to go where they go, just to keep an eye on John. I swore an oath over his dead mother to look after him until his father came back. I can't keep that oath sitting in Crag Tower."

"Will you go alone?"

"Aye, I can't see anyone rushing to go with me!"

Eleanor struggled to interpret the look Maighread gave her. "I think you might get some company on the road," her aunt said. "How soon will you go?"

"Now my mind's made up I'll leave at first light. They've a long start on me."

"You'll leave your own son, despite the dangers here?"

"As I said, I swore an oath. Besides, he'll be safer here with all of you than outside these walls with just me to protect him. And Becky will look after him."

"Your servant loves you well."

"I've known her since I was a small girl - we grew together. She's more than a servant, though she plays that role when it suits her. She's suffered more than any of us and she'll be livid with me when I leave her but she'll stay for Will's sake."

They said nothing then for a long time as the rush light slowly burned itself out and Eleanor thought Maighread was asleep.

Then a quiet voice from the darkness said: "You don't expect Ned to return, do you?"

"No, I don't," said Eleanor softly. "Not this time."

"Well … I do," replied Maighread.

PART TWO: HOUSE OF DEVILS

DEREK BIRKS

8

5th August 1468 dawn, at Crag Tower

Eleanor leant on the table and surveyed the limited resources laid out before her. She had one of Will's swords - what would she have given to have her lover himself with her? Lover, swordsman and father of her son, but that Will was long dead. She had Amelie's small knife - and if she met Joan Elder then the blade that had killed sweet Amelie would be the blade that avenged her. She had waited four years already, but she would meet Joan again - of that she was certain. Her hand caressed the knife's jewelled hilt as it caught the early morning sun.

She sheathed the sword and the knife, which left only a freshly baked loaf wrapped up in a short length of linen cloth and a leather flask of ale. That was all - that and the clothes she stood in and of those, the breeches and cap were borrowed.

She had cut her hair short. Becky wept to see it for it had taken years to grow again after her time at the nunnery. Her son Will stared at her in shock as the vivid crimson locks fell to the floor. It felt as if she was naked in front of him. She sighed. It did not do to reflect too much, she decided. If she thought about it any longer, she would not go at all.

Rob Hall sauntered in. "Ready then?" he said with a cheerful grin.

Eleanor looked him up and down. Not for the first time she questioned why she had agreed to take Maighread's brother with her. Sir Stephen had insisted that she could not go alone, even though she had shorn her hair and dressed as a man. She argued that he could spare no-one since the garrison was already far too small. It was Maighread who suggested Rob and he had readily agreed. They all knew that Rob was the least effective man at arms at Crag Tower - indeed he never claimed to be anything else. He had only ever been a skirmisher, darting in and out on the fringes of a fight. She knew that he still limped from his fall from the castle wall and it was likely he always would.

"I am ready," she replied, "though I'm not sure you are. Will that leg of yours carry you as fast as I can walk?"

"That depends on how fast you walk," said Rob. "Have you ever walked any distance before?"

"What do you mean by that?" she snapped.

"Well, I mean travelling a distance…without a horse under you."

If he was trying to annoy her he was making an excellent start but she resolved not to show it and instead forced a smile. "Don't come, then."

"Are you sure you know what you're doing?" He gave her an odd look, condescending, almost as if he was dealing with a child.

"I didn't ask you to come." Her patience was fraying fast.

He grinned and shook his head of shaggy black hair. "You won't be rid of me that easily. I think you'll need a guide," he said, "let's be honest you get lost going down to the village."

She fixed him with a piercing stare and was gratified when he turned pale.

"When I need help from you, I'll tell you."

She pulled on her worn leather jacket - it had fitted her perfectly four years earlier but now it stretched tightly across her breasts, too tightly. She had certainly not grown fat these past years but somehow her shoulders were broader. It was not encouraging: the whole point was to disguise her womanhood not exaggerate it. She tore off the jacket and tossed it onto the table. She picked up her woollen cloak: grey and plain. It would have to do. It would be warm for the summer but she would need all its warmth later in the year. She could feel Rob's eyes upon her.

"Bring the bread and ale," she ordered, and walked out into the yard.

It was even harder than she expected, embracing her son and Becky to say farewell. Even Maighread had a tear in her eye and Sir Stephen gave her a bleak, despairing look as he stood at the gate. She leant against it and the smell of the new wood reminded her of the threat the defenders still faced.

"I pray God that Ragwulf and Bear will return soon," she told him. "And that they have my brother with them."

"May God be your guide, my lady," said Sir Stephen.

Eleanor took a pace through the gateway. It felt like a step into another world. Never before had she feared the unknown, but fears crowded in upon her as she took that first step. Rob seemed to sense her uncertainty and put a hand on her shoulder. She glared at him, shrugged off his hand and set off from the wall onto the track which led down to the river.

"Let's be clear," she said as she walked along the grassy path at a brisk pace. "I am taking you with me only because Sir Stephen insisted. Be assured that I don't need your help or your witless advice."

"Of course, my lady," agreed Rob.

"We'll head south along the river."

"I know," he said, with that irritating grin.

"I'll decide where we go and when we stop."

"Aye, my lady."

"And if your leg isn't up to it then I'll leave you behind."

"Fair enough."

"Good Christ, stop agreeing with me! You're already a burden and we haven't gone twenty yards!"

She walked on in silence for a while and he fell in beside her.

"And don't keep addressing me as 'my lady'," she said. "I'm supposed to be a man."

"What then?" he asked. "It won't do a lot for your manly image if I call you Eleanor."

Her frosty glance warned him to be careful.

"Very well," she conceded, "you may call me Jack."

"What about 'Red'?"

She scowled at him. "Jack."

"Red would suit you better."

She stopped and faced him. "Go on then," she said, "call me 'Red' and see if it suits me."

"It's a fine day for a walk, Red," he said, with a grin.

Her sharp slap to his face swiftly removed the grin.

"No," she said, smiling, "As I thought: it didn't suit me at all!"

They walked on and this time the silence lasted a very long time. She smiled to herself; it had not been so difficult to stop the fool's prattling. Now he was sulking - no surprise there. Men hated to be put down by women.

They were still not speaking when they stopped around noon to share some of the bread. By then she decided he was overdoing his dumb show. His idle chatter was like the buzzing of a troublesome fly, but she had to concede that his silence was worse. How was it that men were so difficult to be with? If you weren't in love with them, they could be intolerable company.

By nightfall she had hoped to reach the place where the North Tyne joined its great namesake and began to flow eastwards but she was disappointed to find that she could not sustain her early pace. She had forgotten how slow it was on foot and it was nearly dark when she was forced to concede defeat.

"We'll have to stop soon," she said, "your leg won't take much more."

He smirked at that. "We could stop for the night at the ancients' wall," he suggested.

"I'll decide," she replied curtly and walked faster for another score of paces. "Do you know the wall?" she asked.

"I've been by it a few times."

"Is it safe at night?" she asked, slowing up.

He stopped. "Be clear: nowhere is safe. Others travel along this river."

She hated being in his hands but she decided she must learn to bend a little if they were to survive: they could not be fighting each other all the time.

"Is it far?"

"No."

The wall was not quite what she expected and the part of the wall they discovered was a disappointment to her since much of it had fallen away, leaving only one tall stack of stone standing to about twice her height. Still, she could see that it was a useful place to sleep and with no coin they had little option but to sleep in the open.

"I'll sleep here," she said, sitting in the lee of the wall. "You can sleep on the other side."

"It's colder on my side. And there's a moon, I'll be lit up if anyone comes along here. We'll be better together on your side."

"Do as you're told," she said and rolled her cloak into a ball. She placed it with care among the fallen stones and then kneaded it until it provided a soft hollow for her head and shoulders. Then she lay down to rest with her sword by her side. Rob shrugged and retired, muttering, to the other side of the wall. She heard him settling himself down and almost laughed out loud when the phrase "selfish bitch" reached her ears. After a while though, he peered around the edge of the stonework and said: "Sleep well, Red."

"Pisspot!" she retorted, but she fell asleep with a smile upon her lips.

§§§§

She woke up to the sound of voices - one of them quite loud: Rob Hall. Weary from the day's walk, she wanted only to sleep. Rob was determined to annoy her even when she was at rest. Who was he talking to, anyway? She was about to tell him to be quiet when she began to take in the conversation.

"I'm on my own!" he shouted. "I've already told you that once!"

"Well you can keep quiet now," said another voice.

"Why should I?" cried Rob.

She winced at the sound of a blow.

"Because you'll get that again if you say another word," growled a deeper voice.

"Now, what have you got that's worth having?" asked the first man. "And if you've got nowt, I'll slit your throat for wasting my time."

Eleanor sat up, alert now. She slowly reached for her sword, careful not to scrape it on the stones around her. Then she got to her feet, keeping close to the wall. It was a clear night and, as Rob had warned her, the wall was bathed in moonlight. As soon as she stepped out from behind the wall, she would be able to see Rob's assailants but equally they would have a clear view of her. She drew out her knife and crept along the wall. As long as she stayed in the wall's shadow, she was safe. Shit! That's why he had spoken so loudly, to warn her. She inched her way to the edge of the high wall and then picked up a small piece of stone and threw it behind her so that it skipped off one or two other stones before rolling still.

The voices on the other side of the wall fell silent. She could hear nothing but a moonlit shadow loomed beside her: someone was coming to investigate. She held her breath and watched the shadow slide towards her as she leant against the cold stone. Sword or knife, she asked herself? A figure leapt around the wall and she struck him with both - sword low and knife blade high. If she had practised all night she could not have done it better. Her knife plunged into his throat and she felt the weight of him as her sword sliced through his stomach. He said not a word but his body slipped from her grasp and flopped onto the ground beside her with a soft thud.

"Walter?" said the deep voice. "What have you found there?"

Now there was only one, she felt much emboldened and stepped out from around the wall.

"He found me," she said.

"Oh, shit," said Rob, lying prone on the ground. "You foolish lass."

She swallowed hard: there was not one man left; there were three. One held Rob's sword and the others had knives in their hands. They looked at her in surprise.

"Lass, is it?" laughed one of them. "We're in for a treat then, lads."

Eleanor glared at Rob. She wanted to hit him very hard for revealing her sex.

"We have nothing for you," said Rob.

"Oh, I wouldn't say that. She's a scrawny lass, to be sure, but a woman is a woman, after all."

"There's blood on my sword," said Eleanor, "and there'll be much more on it, if you don't leave us be."

"Brave words, little girl. You may have caught our Walter by surprise but if you don't drop those blades, I'll cut your man open from chin to cock."

Eleanor stared at him. "Go ahead then. He's an idle little shit and he's not 'my man'. But if you want anything from me you'll pay for it with your own blood."

She knew that Rob's wide eyes were fixed upon her but she did not dare glance in his direction. Her eyes were on the man with the sword, following every move he made. He looked just crazy enough to carry out his threat but then what he didn't realise was: so was she.

He smiled across at her and dropped the point of the

sword onto Rob's groin.

"Wait!" she cried.

"Hah! There you go, lads." He turned to his fellows with a satisfied grin. "Never fails!"

"No, just wait," said Eleanor, feigning annoyance. "He has something of mine and I want it back." She sheathed her knife and lowered her sword, putting the men more at ease.

"It'll be round his neck," she went on and, as she spoke, she moved. "I don't want you getting blood all over it!" She took three strides towards Rob and pushed the other man aside. He was wrong footed and she needed to keep him that way.

She focussed on Rob. "You lying, thieving excuse of a man," she shouted and kicked him in the ribs. He cried out and rolled onto his side. The men behind her were laughing now as she beat Rob's shoulder with the flat of her sword.

"This should be worth seeing," said the one holding the sword and he stepped back so that he and his companions stood in a small arc around the fighting pair.

Rob got to his feet and she slapped him on the face. It had to hurt, she decided - this was no time for half measures. He seized her roughly and tried to wrestle the sword from her. She leant forward and bit his ear.

"You bitch!" he yelled. She thought his pain and alarm sounded genuine enough.

"Thieving little shit! Where is it?" She wrapped her arms around him, her back towards the ring of men, and pressed her lips to his bleeding ear. "Take my knife?" she hissed. "Take it and then push me towards them."

She half pulled away and his eyes met hers for a fleeting instant. Then he dragged her to him and put one hand on the knife hilt.

"I'll tear the rest of your hair out, you foul- mouthed slut!" he roared and swung her around so that she spun away from him. The man holding the sword was still laughing as she slashed with all her strength down across his neck and shoulder. The blade did not cut deep but deep enough. He let his weapon fall and clutched at his throat. In the sheen of moonlight, dark blood trickled between his desperate fingers.

She moved on as the nearest man brandished his knife at her and without a moment's hesitation she lunged with her sword at his groin. Ned had always told her: go for the throat or the 'jewels'. The sword missed its target but sliced into his thigh. He screamed and fell back with her sword still skewered through his leg. When she tore it out, he roared with pain and hurled his dagger at her. She batted it aside with her sword but stumbled back off balance over one of the stones. She landed heavily and her sword flew from her grasp.

He limped towards her and she could see the blood glistening down his leg. She struggled to get to her feet but was too slow and he threw himself on top of her.

"I'll pop your eyes out!" he growled, seizing her around the throat. His thumbs pressed into her neck, squeezing the life from her. She couldn't breathe. She felt lightheaded. She panicked, and flapped her hands aimlessly until one hand lighted upon a stone. She wrapped her fingers around it and cracked it against the side of his head. He was stunned for a moment, allowing her to roll aside and rise to her knees. She darted a glance at Rob but he was grappling with the third man.

She faced her opponent. They were both on their knees, two yards apart. He shook his head, wiped the blood from it and stared across at her. Between them on the ground the moonlight glinted on her fallen sword blade. He grinned and leant forward to pick it up, but she was quick - much quicker than he expected. She grasped the hilt first and drove the steel up through him with all the force she could muster. He shivered with the pain of it, his body arching in mortal agony. Then he simply sighed, went still and fell backwards.

"Cold steel, my friend," she murmured, "is the answer to all ills…"

A hand gripped her shoulder and she turned swiftly.

"Hold!" said Rob. "Enough. They're dead."

He held out his hand to her and, for a moment, she gripped it tightly, feeling the slick of blood upon it. He pulled her to her feet and she let him hold her for a while. She was trembling and they were both breathing heavily.

"We were fortunate tonight," he said quietly. "A few lucky blows and much blood spilled. Another time it might not be so easy."

She gave him a kiss on the cheek. "Thank you for giving me a warning," she said and let him go.

He gave her a rueful look. "You didn't have to bite my ear."

"Well, I'm sorry for that but I wanted to make it seem real…"

"Believe me, it was real!"

"I got a little excited... is all. Does it hurt?"

"Of course it hurts!" he retorted.

"It can't be that bad - let me look at it."

"You can admire your handiwork another time," he grumbled and went to search the men for anything of value. They recovered all their belongings and took those of the others. Then they piled up the bodies on the far side of the wall. When they had finished, Eleanor stood bathed in the silver light and examined the many stains upon her clothes. It felt as if there was blood on everything.

"I'm going down to the river to wash off some of this blood," she said. "Bring all our goods."

Eleanor set off at a slow walk down alongside the wall towards the river. After ten paces or so she stopped and turned around. He was still standing there.

"Oh, one other thing," she said, as she waited for him to join her.

"What?" he asked wearily.

She slapped him full on the face.

"What it Christ's name was that for?" he demanded, rubbing his cheek.

"That was for telling them I was a woman!"

§§§§

They awoke late the following morning, finished off the remains of their loaf and ale and then shook the stiffness from their legs. They said little as they prepared themselves for their journey. Eleanor had much to reflect upon as they walked and was content to let Rob take the lead. After only one day and night they had almost perished. She shuddered to think what the pair of them must look like to other travellers, yet as they headed south to cross the Tyne she was struck by the appearance of others they encountered: they looked haggard, weary and above all, poor.

They passed through Corbridge and crossed the Tyne at a ford to the east of the village. The water was low and there were many using the ford.

"Every man we see looks as if he carries his troubles upon his back," she murmured to Rob.

"The north bled during the wars and in the revolts after," said Rob, "and it bleeds still."

She pulled a face and he continued. "Have you never wondered what drives those who attack Crag Tower so frequently?"

"They're used to a life of thieving?"

"No! They had little to start with and they have less now. The law won't help them so they live outside the law. King Edward promised good government but we're not seeing much of it up here. The Nevilles and their clients rule here and they do as they please. And in the shadows the Percies lie in wait for the moment when their great rivals look the other way. Men of the north know all this;

they know another struggle is coming."

"I have not the least notion what you're talking about," said Eleanor, as they reached the far bank of the Tyne.

Rob stopped on the gritty sand bar that reached out into the river.

"That's because you're not poor," he said simply.

"Not poor? Look at the state of me! Don't tell me I'm not poor."

He shook his head. "Your son Will, is his skin stretched tight across his cheeks? Is his stomach forever empty? Does he live in a filthy hovel or sleep under a cold sky?"

"So be it," said Eleanor, "perhaps I was born into a landed, titled family, but I've had all that ripped away. The law has hardly protected my family either. What can I do for others if I can't get back what I've lost?"

Rob nodded. "It'll get a deal worse yet."

"Why do you say that? The king will bring justice to the land soon. It takes time… I think, doesn't it?"

"I'm not sure how much longer he's got," said Rob.

Eleanor sat down on the riverbank and he perched beside her.

"Never mind him," she said, "it's going to take us longer than I thought, isn't it?"

He nodded.

By the crossing a column of men approached them heading north. They were armed mostly with primitive weapons, axes and homemade spears, though a few wore swords. The first man in the column stopped.

"God give you good day, masters," he said. Eleanor smiled at him, feeling ridiculously pleased to be addressed as 'master'.

"And a good day to you, sir," she said in the deepest voice she could manage.

"Sir?" the stranger laughed, "I don't think we've been called 'sirs' before!"

"We seek some friends," said Rob, "a small party of

mounted men - they have a young boy and a lass with them and they'd be wearing this livery." He pointed to the faded blue Elder badge he wore on his breast.

"Hmm, I don't remember them and I doubt you'll find them," he replied. "There's a lot of folk on the road this summer - the north's in a bad way."

"Aye. That it is," said Rob.

"Where are you bound for?" asked Eleanor.

"We're looking for men - if you want to join us."

"Men? For what?" she asked.

"Men who don't like things as they are," the stranger replied. "Men who might be willing to do something about it."

"We've our own matters to deal with," said Rob.

"Well, when we've been to Hexham we'll be going back to Yorkshire. Perhaps our paths will cross again there."

He gave them a wave and moved on. Eleanor watched the men trudge past them: there was much misery in their faces but also, she thought, a trace of hope.

"So many men," murmured Eleanor, "wandering the land… It truly is a bad time, isn't it?"

"Aye," said Rob. "And we wander as they do, my lady, more in hope than belief."

They spent the night huddled together in a stand of trees not far south of the Tyne. It was a damp night but the trees afforded them enough cover to keep them dry. The days after that passed slowly as they walked on for mile upon mile. Eleanor hated it and though she tried to keep her spirits up, she found herself growing more impatient as each day went by. She was increasingly worried by the route Rob was following. They walked across fields, sometimes on local tracks and by ways but never on anything that looked at all like a road. When she had come north to Crag Tower four years earlier with Hal and Ragwulf, she seemed to recall that they had taken the great north road for a large part of their journey.

On the evening of the seventh day, she decided it was time to raise her concerns. She flopped down onto a grassy bank to rest.

"Do you have the least idea where we are, Rob?" she asked.

"Aye, I do," he said.

She was surprised. "You know where we are?"

"Aye, we're further south than I've ever been, 'Red'."

"Stop calling me that! You've never been this far before then?"

Rob grinned. "No, I've never been south of Durham!"

Eleanor sighed. "Well how can you find your way? Why did I ever let you take the lead? We're lost then."

"No," he replied indignantly. "I'm a fair hand at finding my way about - ask your brother!"

"Difficult…just now," she said. "Well, where are we then?"

He grinned at her again - that inane and exasperating grin. She wanted to slap his face across the field - but she didn't. Instead she stared at him to indicate that she was still waiting for an answer.

"Well, we're south of Bishop Auckland and Durham and north of Richmond."

"How can you possibly know that?" she persisted. "And don't answer me with a grin."

He smirked. Eleanor frowned but held her tongue.

"Because I know the signs: the call of the land, the flight of the birds, the direction of the furrows, the angle of the sun - it's my world."

"And you're telling me that you found your way almost to Richmond by those…signs?"

"Aye," said Rob, "those signs, and of course…we've been walking about a hundred yards west of the north road - we've been following its line for days."

He grinned then hastily ducked under her hand as she aimed an angry blow at his face.

"Then yesterday I thought it was time to turn south west," he continued.

She screeched at him and hit him with her clenched fist.

"Hey, lady, that hurt," he complained, backing away from her.

"It'll get worse!" she snapped and began to chase him around the bank at the field's edge. "Why must you always grin and tease me? Why can't you just tell me something straight?"

He slowed and she caught up with him, seized him around the waist and pulled him down on to the grass. They rolled down it into the cultivated land and crushed half a bushel of wheat under their bodies. Somehow Eleanor found herself in his arms as they lay still. They simply stared at each other for a moment and then he kissed her - and for a moment she let him. And then she clubbed her fist against the side of his head and knocked him off her.

She sat at the bottom of the bank, stiff with anger, her hands still balled into fists.

He stood on the other side of the bank rubbing his head.

After a while she got up and went to stand beside him. "What did you think you were you doing?" she asked in a quiet voice.

"I thought you could tell what I was doing."

"Do you have to make mirth out of everything?" she said.

"I'm very… fond of you, 'Red'," he said. "I didn't mean to…"

"Rob, I am not someone called 'Red'. I am Lady Eleanor Elder and we are not going to be lovers. What were you thinking?"

"I was thinking no more or less than you. Don't tell me it didn't feel good to you too."

"No man has kissed me for years," she said. "Of course I liked it, but … I am not for you - and you'd be a fool to want me."

"But, perhaps…"

Eleanor put her arm around him. "When we left Crag Tower I thought you a fool; and I've found that you're not. I could love you, Rob, but as a brother - be glad of that."

9

13th August 1468, at Yoredale Castle in Yorkshire

Joan Elder stood on the battlements above the gatehouse, staring at the trail of dust to the east which marked the approach of a column of horsemen. Had they come from Middleham, from the Earl of Warwick? She had been disappointed in the past few years; she had expected more from him. He promised her Ned Elder's lands but she was merely the steward at Yoredale Castle. She remained there at Warwick's pleasure and the fruits of the estate mostly found their way to Middleham. What's more, Warwick still held Emma Elder's son, Richard, at Middleham. She had known from the start that the boy could be the key, for he could claim to be heir both to the Radcliffes and the Elders. She should have slit his throat when she had the chance - she doubted she would get another.

The riders were closer now, but the dust obscured her view. She could not help feeling apprehensive: one or two riders might convey a message, but a score or so threatened much more serious business. Well, whatever the column meant, she had no option but to accept it. She had only a few men at arms of her own: and most of them wore the bear and ragged staff of Warwick. If it came to it, only Weaver and one or two others owed their allegiance to her.

The column slowed as it joined the track to the castle and the dust settled a little. She recognised first the red pennant carried by one of the riders and then their livery. It was not the earl himself but then that was no surprise. He would have more important matters to deal with than her. She recognised Warwick's man and nodded thoughtfully then she turned away to descend to the courtyard below.

"Let them in," she ordered the men at the portcullis. "I'll be in the privy chamber."

By the time she had crossed the yard the first riders had bent low to pass under the rising portcullis and their horses clattered over the cobbled stones as they came to a halt.

Joan climbed the steps to the privy chamber and sat down. She did not have long to wait before Sir Thomas Gate strode in.

"God give you good day, Lady Joan," he said and kissed the hand she offered.

"And to you, Sir Thomas. You come here in some haste, I think. I'm intrigued to know what the urgency is."

"Urgency, my lady? I would not say urgency exactly."

She gave a wry smile for he looked suitably discomfited. "Well then?"

"The earl has made a decision about your marriage, my lady," said Sir Thomas, "and he has sent me to acquaint you with that decision."

So that was it. The question of her marriage had been left in the air for too long but why was Gate coming to speak to her about it? She was irritated that the earl himself had not come.

"May I ask how my marriage concerns you, sir?" He sounded nervous she thought and now he hesitated before answering her.

"It concerns me, my lady, because the earl has decided that you will marry me."

It was a flat announcement that left no doubt or question - a statement of fact that came as a body blow to her. She had aimed higher, much higher and hoped for better: an earl perhaps. Gate was good-looking, to be sure, but good looks brought her nothing.

"I see that the earl's decision leaves you a little shocked, my lady," ventured Gate.

He handed her Warwick's letter. She broke the seal and she made a show of reading it but she did not need to. She knew that Gate was one of Warwick's favoured men and she knew the match made sense for both Warwick and Gate. It was only her influence that would diminish, her claims which would be subordinated and her ambitions that would be unfulfilled. Still, she remained in the game and it was in her nature to make the best of a poor situation. She smiled at her prospective husband and graciously accepted what was unpalatable, but inevitable. And too, she reminded herself, she had already disposed of one husband.

"We shall wed at the earliest opportunity," said Sir Thomas, "as soon as the formalities of church and law can be completed. Tomorrow we shall give thanks in the chapel."

Joan raised an eyebrow at that and could not resist replying. "I'm breathless with anticipation, Sir Thomas. I had no idea you held me in such high regard."

"Truly, my lady, I have long been an ardent admirer and was most pleased to receive the earl's blessing."

"It's quite overwhelmed me as well," she replied, all too aware that his ardour had little to do with her undoubted charms and much more to do with her claim to the Elder lands.

"I shall take up residence here at once," he told her. "Please arrange a suitable chamber for me and ensure that my men are adequately housed. I've brought several servants with me and my baggage should arrive this evening. In the meantime I'll use this room as my base. I have much to do and Yoredale Castle will now be at the heart of it all. There will be frequent messengers to and fro. Life will be busy and I'll need you to manage provisions and billeting carefully."

She stood in silence. She must be wearing a look of

horror. She was not used to being ordered about in her own castle, nor treated as if she was a glorified housekeeper.

"Perhaps you would like me to serve in the kitchens too, Sir Thomas?"

He smiled at her - a wickedly handsome smile. "No, my lady, don't trouble yourself. I have a girl who can do that for you. She's a mute, so she'll do it very quietly."

Joan grimaced. "I can't wait till our wedding day!" she said and stalked out of the room seething with anger.

§§§§

Agnes sat upon a great oak chest in the midst of the mound of baggage which belonged to Thomas Gate. She sat unmoving and watched unblinking as servants came and went, adding more to the pile: pieces of leg armour, a box of documents, hunting clothes, a very large sword, woollen cloaks and fur-lined cloaks. Steadily the possessions multiplied before her eyes and there she sat, little Agnes, just another of Gate's many trinkets.

"Wait here," Walter Grave had told her. So she had.

It had taken her a long time to realise that the dashing young Thomas Gate was not her saviour and that he was not going to take her to Ned. She had been foolish, it was true and she winced to remember just how gullible she had been that night in Sluys. Yet, at the time it all seemed to make sense: Spearbold himself had told her that her guardian was missing and then along came this captivating man who had complimented her in the Golden Ship earlier that evening. He told her Ned was in trouble and swept her away with him. She took no other clothes, just what she was wearing then and a cloak. She remembered Gate's tenderness as he wrapped the cloak around her before they left.

Even on the ship to England she had believed him still. He told her that Ned had been taken and that he was in pursuit, that he would find Ned no matter how long it took. She believed it all, every word and even sought to repay him by nursing him through his sickness aboard ship and washing his clothes.

Even when they arrived at Middleham, she suspected nothing. He had given her a small chamber of her own and even a candle to read by - she had been so grateful to him, so ridiculously grateful. Then one night he had come to her, sat on her little mattress of straw and hugged her to him. And she let him because he was kind to her and because he was looking for her friend, Ned Elder.

But Agnes was not a fool and she had learned enough from watching the girls at the Golden Ship to know that Gate's embrace was that of a lover. Yet she was grateful to him for all she believed he had done so when he kissed her on the lips she had let him. When he caressed her breasts, she had let him and then she had let him do whatever else he pleased, because she needed his help to find Ned. She was not like the girls at the inn who opened their legs on an easy promise of a better life. She did it because she believed he was a good man and because she was a serving girl and he was a handsome knight. He was gentle and kind when he stole her maidenhood, but she took no pleasure in it and cried for the rest of the night.

He did not come to her again, but continued to treat her well, and so she explained it to herself that she had given him the only gift she had to give for the trouble he was taking to find Ned. Even when he told her that Ned was dead she did not doubt him. Even then, when he lamented with her that he had done all he could to save Ned and had promised Ned that he would look after her, she wept with him and was glad of his comforting arm.

Then within a day or so, all became clear. He told her that he was to marry Lady Joan Elder and that Agnes would go with him to Yoredale Castle - or rather she would go with his companion William Grave. She would work in the castle kitchens and answer only to Grave. On no account should she attempt to speak to Thomas Gate again. Thus she became a part of Gate's baggage, to be transported by covered wagon to Yoredale Castle - a place she remembered only too vividly. There Ned was grievously wounded, there she prepared salves and liquids to help him and there she embraced Hal so fondly before they parted. But she did not have Hal, she had Grave. Up to now Grave had been courteous and aloof towards her but now that she was his to command that had changed. He gave her curt instructions, clearly assuming that her lack of speech was matched only by a lack of wits. So, Grave said wait and that's what she was doing.

When he returned it was to supervise the loading of his master's goods and that included her. The journey to Yoredale by wagon was not one she would care to repeat and at times she was so uncomfortable she got off the vehicle to walk alongside. Then she found that the dust got into her face, mouth and eyes and she climbed back up onto the wagon. The driver gave her a swig of ale and she drank it down gratefully. It took all day to cover the few miles to Yoredale Castle and by the time she arrived, Agnes was exhausted.

The wagon rumbled through the gate and into the yard. At once the driver and Agnes were joined by other household servants running to help empty the wagon. She was about to start unloading when Grave seized her arm.

"Not you," he said in a sharp tone, "I have my own chamber upstairs - next to the chapel! You can take my baggage up there." He laughed. "It's not as if you've any of your own!"

When she stared at him, he slapped her around the head. "Go on, get doing - and don't look me in the eye again!"

There was already baggage scattered all over the cobbles so she had to hunt to find out what was Grave's. Then she set off to find her way up to the chapel.

"Wait!" called Grave. "Do you know where you're going?"

She turned to him and nodded briefly before carrying on her way, feeling his eyes upon her as she crossed the yard. She went in through the bake-house on the ground floor and stood for a short while on the threshold, remembering the last time she stood there.

"Get a move on then, lass!" shouted Grave from the yard. So she did.

§§§§

Later she was pressed into service at the meal time. The great Hall was crowded. She had only ever seen it empty. Now, as well as Sir Thomas and his bride to be, Lady Joan, there was a clutch of knights in his service and other men at arms, as well as all the servants. She was well used to serving food and drink so the bustle and lively atmosphere did not concern her in the least. But she was very wary of Lady Joan. She had heard enough about Joan from Ned, Hal and the others to fill her full of dread. She had only glimpsed her once before but, if Joan recognised her, her life would be worth nothing.

She was thus determined not to draw attention to herself, but the mere sight of Joan, sitting where her lord should be, unsettled her. When Agnes brought a jug of wine to the table, Joan called out for some. Agnes hesitated, stared at her for a moment and then proceeded to bring the wine. She cursed silently. She had looked into Joan's eyes and the insult had not gone unnoticed but Agnes did not care. She was trembling as she put down the jug of wine and managed to bang the pitcher of wine so hard onto the table that wine slopped over the rim and splashed the lady's hand. Joan looked furious.

"Well, serve it, girl!" she snapped and turned to Thomas Gate. "Is this your mute?" she asked.

Agnes picked up the jug again. Gate nodded and Agnes paused with the jug half-raised. A sudden devilment overwhelmed her as she started to pour the wine into the goblet in Joan's hand. Anyone who knew Agnes well would have noted her stern countenance and taken cover. She kept pouring the wine until the goblet overflowed and then carried on pouring the remaining contents onto Joan's hand and arm.

Joan snatched her hand away and cried out in anger. Agnes slammed the jug down onto the table and it shattered into several pieces. Then she simply stood there, brazen and defiant. This woman had hurt her lord and was therefore her enemy. And if Ned Elder was no more, then she would rather die where she stood than serve wine to this unworthy woman.

There were stunned faces along the high table, not least Thomas Gate. Joan was screaming at her but she paid no attention. Instead she smiled and turned to walk away.

"Take that bitch!" cried Joan and several men at arms seized Agnes and dragged her back to Lady Joan.

"Kneel!" Joan told her.

Agnes tried to stand as tall as she could but her captors forced her down upon her knees anyway.

Joan stood up, a little unsteadily, for she had consumed much wine already and walked around the table to Agnes. Agnes darted a look at Gate but he turned away. Joan saw the glance and lashed out at Agnes, slapping her across the face. Agnes flinched but did not cower from the blow; instead she lifted her chin and stared at Joan, inviting another. Joan's face turned purple with rage and she reached for another flagon.

"No!" said Thomas, but before he could stop her, she picked up the wine pot and smashed it down on to Agnes' head. The shattering blow stunned her briefly and blood-red wine smothered her head, hair and smock. Guests nearby took evasive action as great gouts of wine splashed everywhere. The men holding her let go and stepped back allowing her to fall down onto the flagstones. She watched as the Hall swirled around her until it was in darkness.

10

14th August 1468, in Flanders

It took Spearbold and his companions several weeks to get back to Sluys but Crabber had not been idle in his absence. He had harnessed some local knowledge to conduct a thorough search of the lands around the port of Sluys. The search, however, had so far yielded nothing and Crabber would soon be obliged to follow his master, Lord Scales, back to England. Spearbold was forced to accept that their enterprise now had even less hope of success.

They sat in the Ship discussing what few options remained to them.

"The problem is that they must have taken him further from Sluys than we first thought," observed Crabber.

Spearbold shook his head. He had only just told Crabber about Thomas Gate and now regretted he had not trusted him sooner. It might have made a difference.

"He could be anywhere by now!" Spearbold said miserably. "It's almost two months - he could have been shipped to the Holy Land by now!"

"Exactly," agreed Crabber. "Where would we even start to look?"

"I did not come here to give up or drink myself stupid," said Ragwulf. "It's time we thought about this more carefully."

"But what in God's name do you think I've been doing for the past weeks?" declared Spearbold. He had had enough of Ragwulf. The soldier was a dour companion at the best of times, always looking as if he bore the weight of all Christendom on his shoulders.

"I don't doubt your effort, Master Spearbold, but we should be looking at this from Thomas Gate's standpoint," said Ragwulf.

"I have!" insisted Spearbold.

"Go on," Crabber urged Ragwulf.

"Well, as far as we know, Gate took Lord Elder during the evening. He then came back for Agnes later that same evening."

"You state what is already well known," muttered Spearbold.

"Aye, but when Gate was taking Agnes, where was Lord Elder?" asked Ragwulf.

"Well, clearly Gate had help," agreed Crabber, "that much is obvious. But for all we know, your lord is drowned in the River Zwin somewhere. Gate had no reason to keep Lord Elder alive."

Spearbold suddenly slammed his jug of ale down on the table, splashing out the contents.

"But he did!" he exclaimed. "Ragwulf is right: Gate had every reason to keep Ned alive if he could because Warwick didn't even know he had him! He needed to find out from Warwick what was to be done - he couldn't just kill him out of hand."

"If that's true," mused Crabber, "then he needed some secure place to hide Lord Elder and men to watch him."

"His helpers were French, you think?" he asked Spearbold.

Spearbold nodded. "But he might have had his own men too - unlikely to cross the Channel alone, I should say."

"He'd need somewhere out of Sluys," continued Crabber, "not to the north but closer to France perhaps…further south."

"Closer to Bruges though, so not so safe?" said Spearbold.

"But no-one was looking for him nearer to Bruges…"

"So," said Ragwulf, "what sort of place does Gate need?"

"He'd need somewhere well hidden..." said Crabber.

"A place where others would not usually go, remote perhaps," suggested Ragwulf.

"And secure," added Spearbold. "He would have to wait for Warwick's response, unless he went back to England himself..."

"All this would have taken time, which means that Lord Elder could yet be alive," said Ragwulf.

"But even so, where do we start?" asked Spearbold.

"The forests," said Bear, speaking for the first time. "Much forest near Bruges."

"Aye, perhaps," acknowledged Spearbold, "but he'd need a place to hold Ned."

"Castles, ruin," said Bear, "many ruin."

"Are there such places?" asked Ragwulf.

Bear delivered a withering glare. "This is my land, I know."

Spearbold called over Anna whose English was marginally better than Bear's.

"Explain to her," he told Bear. The big man nodded and immediately launched into a long discourse in Flemish. When he had finished Spearbold turned to Anna. "Well?" he asked.

Anna sat down on the bench with them. Spearbold cursed himself for not paying more attention to the poor woman for her grief was greater than theirs. For them at least there was a chance: Ned might yet be alive. Her man was not and when she spoke it was with tears in her eyes.

"Bear tells of the time he was young... he lived in the land east of Bruges...when Ghent rebelled against the duke - the Duke of Burgundy. He says there was much fighting ... many were killed, including his own father and ... many forts were taken... burned... abandoned."

"Do you know of such places?" Spearbold asked Bear.

"I know, but there are many…to look at all…"

"How long would it take to search them all?"

"All?" Bear looked incredulous. "That will take all our days."

"Even if we found the right place, we couldn't just ride in," said Ragwulf. "If they're holding him still, they're not going to just hand him over, are they?"

"True enough," said Crabber, "They might kill him just at the sight of us."

They fell silent for a moment and Anna took the opportunity to slip away. Spearbold stared after her for a moment. It occurred to him that Gate had left Anna alone and yet had taken Agnes. Why, he wondered? Anna was a fine looking woman, if it was a woman Gate wanted. But then of course it was not any woman he wanted but someone that Ned Elder cared for.

Ragwulf interrupted his thoughts. "There may be many, and we may need to be cautious, my friends, but is this not the reason we came here, to find him?"

"Aye, well said, Ragwulf," said Spearbold.

"I regret that I must follow Lord Scales tomorrow," said Crabber. "But the new Duchess has sent a sum of money to aid you in your search - it'll pay for your horses and more."

"She takes a keen interest in this, then?" said Spearbold.

"Indeed, Master Spearbold, she is most interested in the man who saved her life - and would be glad of any news from you. Before I leave I'll furnish you with a name in her household that you might call upon - if you need to."

Spearbold looked at his fellows. "So, masters, on the morrow we shall spread our net wider, south towards Bruges, and see what we can catch."

11

15th August 1468, at a castle east of Bruges

When his gaolers left him in darkness, Ned felt sorry for himself and he continued to feel sorry for himself well into the small hours. His anger and frustration kept him wide awake for hours but just before dawn he was shocked out of his torpor. All night he heard the rats scuttling across the floor around him. Occasionally one would brush against him and he would thrust out a hand to discourage it. But then one took a bite out of his calf and he screamed in outrage, seized the cocky little animal and hurled it squealing into the darkness. He heard it thud against the wall and drop to the floor.

The cell went quiet then, aside from the constant dripping of the water. Then once more the crafty, snuffling bastards were on the move again. If he stayed where he was, he might be gnawed to death by rats long before he starved. He lay awake fending off the rodents till dawn and by the time the light drifted into his cell he knew what he must do. He explored his prison cell again as if for the first time but now he was not looking for a way out for he knew there was none. He was looking for the means of staying alive and, in particular, he was looking for a weapon.

He examined every inch of the floor and walls as far as the restraining chain allowed him. Every crack, every dip in the floor, every defect in the stonework was probed. It took him hours and his fingers grew chapped and sore. When he had finished his search, he considered what he had found.

He had discovered a place at the base of the wall where the constant beat of water drops had worn away the mortar and scooped out a hollow in the stone. The leather flask they had left him was now half empty but he worked out that if he wedged the flask in the crevice at exactly the right angle, the water would drip into it. He would not die of thirst at least.

In places he saw the stone floor had been repaired in the past, filled in with pieces of brick, tile and old mortar and then pressed down hard. From such patches he recovered several rocks which might serve as primitive weapons, but his prize find was amongst a scattering of human bones. They were almost out of reach and he had done his best to ignore them up to now; it had felt somehow wrong to disturb the remains but now he was desperate. He muttered a brief prayer over the bones and sorted methodically through them.

It was a grisly task but after a while he found one that he thought he could use: it was two bones still loosely joined together - he suspected part of an arm or leg. He pulled the two slender bones apart and discarded the thinner of the two. The other he turned over in his hands, feeling its shape and weight. How strong would it be, he wondered? Well there was only one way to find out. He placed it carefully down on the floor. Then, using one of his newly discovered rocks, he smashed it down onto the narrower end of the bone. It took several sharp blows to fracture the bone and then he carefully prised the splinters of bone away. In the end he had exactly what he hoped for: a tapering bone with a jagged end. A few hours of honing it on the stone would give him a dirk as sharp as steel - though of course it might snap in two when he tried to use it. He had also unearthed a short length of frayed rope fibre which he wound around the blunt end of the bone and tied to give his new knife a hand grip.

Food was more of a problem - he didn't expect to find

any of that. He was already quite weak for he had only eaten dry bread at best since he arrived. He would have to survive on water alone - and dirty water at that. How long could a man last without food? He did not know. He would need his guards to return soon to check on his progress towards death - everything depended on that. If these men were not the curious sort then he was finished. What if they had already gone and left him for dead? But there was no future in believing that; he must assume they were coming back. He must conserve what little strength he had left and wait - waiting would be hard enough. He decided to make scratch marks on the stone again so as not to lose track of the passing time. It was important now to know how long he had gone without food.

§§§§§

Every morning, another mark and there were seven marks now. Seven days gone and they were not easy days - indeed each one seemed to last forever. His gaolers did not return. He had established a sort of routine. The rats tended not to bother him by day so he slept for much of it so that he could remain alert to fend off their increasingly vicious attention during the long nights. The water collected in the flask more slowly than he had hoped and most times he had barely a trickle to drink. He tried to conserve his strength by lying still but then terrible cramps wracked his legs and sometimes he doubted he would ever stand again let alone fight his guards at the end of it all.

By the time he marked off the fifteenth day, stomach cramps too had become a regular part of his existence. He spent less and less time awake and every night the rats came for him, every night bolder and every night he fought them off. That night, that fifteenth night, they tore at him and he twisted and turned, wriggled and rolled to discourage them - but with little success. They kept biting and scratching at him, their damp fur rubbing against his face as their legs sought purchase in his matted hair. They were survivors and it did not take them long to work out that his right ankle was his weakest point for he could not move it much with the weight of the manacle and the chain pulling on it. Several gnawed away there and in desperation he struck at them with the rocks he had put aside.

In the morning his ankle was raw and bleeding and he found that he had thrown away all the rocks. Only one remained within reach. He did not bother going to fetch it, nor did he make a mark to count the new day. He knew he would not last the next night. He would have to fight off the rats with his makeshift knife and when that failed, as it undoubtedly would, he would be slowly torn apart. Still breathing, perhaps crying out, but growing weaker until one of them bit into something vital. It would be a bitter end and hardly the sort of heroic death he had once envisaged.

He accepted that his guards were not coming back. He had been a fool to think they would. Why would they? He was going nowhere so it was certain he would die and his gaolers did not need to come back to confirm it. They would be long gone. How they would have roared with laughter had they realised that he was still lying in wait for them. Ned gave a bitter laugh himself. He had been a dead man all along.

12

30th August 1468, near Bruges

It was early morning and a thin haze smothered the low scrub and scattered trees. In a few hours the damp air would be warmer and a steamy mist would drift upwards, revealing shallow pools and boggy ground. Ragwulf stepped forward, keeping one eye on Spearbold on his left. He had the feeling that Spearbold would rather be somewhere else, perhaps anywhere else. Well, he should be: this was not the place for him. Ragwulf carried on, taking a lead from Bear who was picking his way across the soft ground with apparent ease over on their right flank.

Crabber, with Bear's help, had located several ruined buildings that seemed likely places to begin their search. They had begun with optimism but after several days searching they had found nothing except bleak, abandoned ruins. There was no certainty that Ned Elder was a prisoner anywhere; he could be lying in a ditch somewhere with his throat cut for all they knew. Still, they had to do something or they might as well have stayed at Crag Tower.

So here they were at the next place and it was by far the worst to approach. Tree cover was sparse and they must cross large stretches of open water to reach the building. Ragwulf was soon wading up to his knees in sludge. The rain of the past week had been torrential, leaving the area they searched half flooded and treacherous. Spearbold, he noticed, was lagging behind and he did not blame him. With every step, Ragwulf thought he might sink into the marsh and be sucked under. Then a dark outline arose out of the mist ahead - at first just an impression, then a solid shape.

Soon Ragwulf could make out the detail of it. It was clearly falling apart and its breached walls and misshapen towers gave it an ugly countenance.

He walked on, disturbing the still morning with his noisy splashing. But stealth would make no difference here for if there was anyone watching from the ruins the three of them would soon be in full view. As the sun rose higher, its rays played upon the castle walls. The stone looked lighter, almost white, but as he closed in, he could see the walls were crisscrossed by irregular strands of foliage. He was barely thirty yards away and wading thigh deep now. There was no movement anywhere on the broken ramparts, nothing. Bear glanced across, giving him a signal to go around the left side of the building. He veered that way and carefully drew out his sword - if he dropped it here he might never recover it. Bear headed in the other direction, climbing up a great pile of stones at the foot of a battered tower. That was one way in - a frontal assault through the breach in the wall - and Bear was just the man for it.

Ragwulf hurried to explore around the left flank but paused to wave Spearbold to a halt. The fellow would be more of a danger to himself than anyone else and it was better he remained outside. Ragwulf went on, clambering forward over the moss-covered rubble. Bear had already crossed the shattered wall and gone inside. Ragwulf circled around a corner tower of the castle. It had been badly damaged by attempts to undermine it, yet it still endured. Beyond it though, the curtain wall was devastated, with hardly a stone left standing. Ragwulf paused on the low course of stones that remained and scanned the interior of the castle: it was only a shell now for the chambers which must once have filled the void of the walls had been utterly demolished. There was little left and no sign of recent occupation. If Ned Elder was being held there then he must be below ground.

Bear appeared in a crumbling doorway across the yard

and waved him in. He crossed the courtyard and followed Bear inside. It would have been dark but for the gaping holes where sections of the wall had given way. There was a spiral stair leading down into what could only be cellars. The walls were green with damp and water dripped from the ceiling. Bear put his fingers to his lips and drew out his axe. Ragwulf nodded and Bear began to descend the steps.

§§§§

Ned heard a muffled sound. At first he ignored it: it would be the rats. But something about the noise nagged away at his dull brain. The noise was surely too regular for a rat. Mind you, those little beggars were clever: you could never trust them. He must remember that: don't trust rats.

The noise persisted, a kind of knocking or tapping noise. It echoed strangely and he thought it was getting louder. The idea burst into his head like a lightning bolt: footsteps! He told his arm to move swiftly and pick up the bone knife. His arm did not respond at first and when it did begin to slide across the stone, it occurred to Ned that he could not remember where the bone knife was. The footsteps were getting louder; he must move. He looked around him. There it was, right beside him. He knew he had planned carefully what he would do if his gaolers returned but he was struggling to recall exactly what that plan was.

The footsteps were ringing in his ears now and slowing down. They were almost at the cell door. He got to his knees and gripped the bone firmly in his hand. He crawled towards the door until the chain stopped him. Then he hid the bone under his body and waited. He felt elated, he felt crafty: his plan had worked; his gaolers had returned. He did not know why that made him start to weep when they opened the cell door.

He did not look up but he could hear them and knew their voices.

"I told you!" one said with a hint of triumph. "I told you he'd still be alive."

He laughed with satisfaction.

"You've cost me a month's pay, you bastard!" complained his comrade.

A boot struck Ned in the ribs and he rolled over. He could see where both men stood now. The fellow who had lost some money was right in front of him. This was it: this was his chance. He must get up off his arse and stab the little shit where it hurt most. He was going to enjoy it. He staggered to his feet and was greeted by more laughter from both men. Well, he would soon stop their mirth. He brought his makeshift dirk up from behind him and aimed a stab at the gaoler's eye. His intended victim continued to laugh as the weapon arced towards him, then he snatched it from Ned's hand as if he was taking it from a child. With a casual brush of his hand he sent Ned crashing back to the floor and examined the piece of bone.

He shook his head. "You tried," he said, "I'll give you that."

He knelt down beside Ned. "But you're too weak now - might have worked a few weeks ago, but not now. You're too near the end."

Ned tried to reach out, to strike him, to land a blow. His hand barely even twitched. The gaoler's expression softened. There was no hate in those eyes now, only pity and that did not make Ned feel any better.

"Here," said the gaoler and laid the bone knife onto the floor by Ned's hand. "When it gets too hard, give yourself a swift end, my 'lord.'"

The gaoler got up and moved away. Ned's stomach chose that moment to go into a spasm again and he curled up in agony. He could hear the two men talking but their words were lost in his pain. He hoped they would just kill him. And they were so noisy. Their words echoed around the stone cavern but had no meaning for him, just noise hurting his head.

§§§§§

Ragwulf followed Bear down the steps and into the chamber below. It was dark and they had to wait for their eyes to adjust. Even then they could see very little because there was nothing there. No stores, no wine or ale, and most definitely, no trace of Ned Elder.

They went back to where Spearbold was waiting. Ragwulf felt as if he'd been kicked in the stomach and Bear's face was set like stone. Spearbold would know from their faces that their search had ended fruitlessly.

"Never mind lads," he greeted them, "it's not the only place."

"Aye, but Master Crabber thought it was one of the most likely," said Ragwulf, "and we've lost some more time…"

"It's Sunday morning," observed Spearbold. "Perhaps we'd do more good on our knees praying."

No-one spoke again as they splashed their way back through the swampy ground and into the trees. By the time they returned to where they left their mounts, the sun was at its zenith.

"So," said Spearbold, "where next?"

"Male," replied Bear.

"Male?" said Spearbold.

"Male," agreed Ragwulf.

"What is Male?"

"Male is a village on the outskirts of Bruges," said Ragwulf, "perhaps a score of miles away."

"Are we wasting our time?" asked Spearbold. "We know almost nothing about these places; we might as well forage for him in the swamps!"

"Well," replied Ragwulf, "I'd rather find him alive in a cellar somewhere than dead in a bog."

"Of course, of course," muttered Spearbold.

"Good," said Bear giving them a brief nod. He mounted his horse and set off at a canter.

Spearbold looked at Ragwulf.

"Come on then," said Ragwulf.

The castle near Male was not as ruined as the other but it was even more difficult to reach. There was a lake surrounding it on all sides and the area around was heavily forested. Once there would have been a wooden bridge across the narrow stretch of water before the gatehouse but it had long ago rotted away. Only a few timber stumps protruded from the water to show where it stood.

"No-one's been here for ten years or more, I'd wager," said Spearbold. "There's no way in."

Ragwulf considered the gatehouse: there was no gate and the stonework was falling apart. "We can get in - if we can cross the water. It's only a little water, master Spearbold. That's all."

"What is the point?" argued Spearbold. "If no-one has been here, then Ned's not here, is he?"

Ragwulf shrugged. "Let's find out how deep it is anyway."

He leapt into the water and was pleased to discover that it only came up to his knees. He waded towards the far bank.

"You see, Spearbold, someone could easily have-" The fall was so sudden it took his breath away as he plunged into deeper water. Since he had been speaking his open mouth took in a great gulp of filthy water. He could see nothing and it took a moment for his feet to touch the bottom. He was confused and choking. He waved his arms about to try to lift himself up but couldn't. His weapons and breastplate weighed him down. He gagged on the water he had swallowed and promptly took in some more. Then he clamped his lips shut.

He was falling to his knees still thrashing his arms around when something hard struck him on the shoulder.

The water was so cloudy he could not see what it was. God's breath! Let it not be lampreys! He had heard bad tales about lampreys. He was struck again, this time on the head, and then prodded in the chest. He saw it was a branch - but why by God's sweet breath was a branch attacking him? He pulled at it and it pulled back, lifting him a foot off the bottom, but he lost his grip. It came back towards him and he lunged for it, holding on as tightly as he could, while the branch raised him.

He reached the surface and a strong hand lifted him bodily out of the water. Bear, his sluggish mind realised. He coughed up some water and a few other very unpleasant items. He looked on in horror as one tiny object crawled back into the water. He felt very sick.

"You gave us a mighty scare!" said Spearbold.

He tried to speak but choked and simply nodded. Bear clapped him on the back and he started coughing and spat out a little more water and grit. It took him a while to recover and by the time he did the afternoon was almost over.

"I'm sorry, my friends," he said. "We've little time and my foolishness has wasted much of it. And my thanks to you, Bear. That's another life I owe you!"

"The time has not been entirely wasted," replied Spearbold. "Bear has discovered something. Come."

Ragwulf got up. They had stripped most of his clothing and weapons off him and the sun had dried him a little but his boots were still damp. He dressed and followed the others around the lake. On the other side of the ruin, Bear pointed and Ragwulf saw a small boat on the far bank near a breach in the outer walls.

"So, someone is here then!" he said.

Spearbold nodded. "Aye, but we can't get to them without the boat."

"If we stand here in the open for much longer, they'll see us," said Ragwulf.

"Whilst you were flirting with death, Bear has been busy," said Spearbold, beaming.

Bear smiled. "Come," he said.

Bear led them back to the main entrance and proudly indicated a small stack of tree branches.

"He collected them and the idea is-"

"I can see what the idea is," Ragwulf interrupted for Bear was already throwing the branches into the water where he had sunk earlier. "But won't these logs just sink as I did?"

Bear shook his head.

"They are not just logs but small trees which he's ripped out in the forest," explained Spearbold. "See how he's placing them in different directions and they bind together a little. He thinks we can just run across if we have enough of them."

Ragwulf looked on in disbelief. "Well, I'll not be the first across," he said. "I've played that game already!"

Bear worked swiftly until he had created a narrow raft of trees. It seemed to Ragwulf that it was too narrow and moved too much to be at all safe.

"You go first then, Bear. If it holds you, it'll hold all Christendom!"

Without a moment's hesitation Bear sprinted across and his floating bridge barely swayed.

Spearbold followed and reached the gatehouse, breathless but dry. Ragwulf eyed the flimsy tangle of branches warily. He put one foot on it and it sank under his weight. He drew back in haste.

"Go fast!" barked Bear, in a rare moment of impatience.

"Oh, shit," muttered Ragwulf. He took several steps back and then ran on to the floating bridge. It dipped a little but held and he was surprised how easily he reached the other bank. Bear, as always, had delivered.

Ragwulf joined the others in the gateway. They had crouched down to keep out of sight and he saw why.

Across the far side of a large central courtyard a man leant against the remnant of a low wall. Ragwulf studied the figure carefully. He was armed, a scabbard was at his belt - worse still, Ragwulf thought he could make out a crossbow hanging on his back. He wore no mail, just a leather jerkin and breeches. There was not much else to tell from so far away.

"It's a wonder he didn't hear us," he breathed. "Do you think he's awake?"

"Perhaps not," whispered Spearbold, "but perhaps there's more of them."

"If Ned's being held here, we must hurry," said Ragwulf.

"Best be cautious though," said Spearbold. "He's waited this long; if he's still alive there's no reason he's going to die in the next few moments."

"Perhaps you're right. Bear, circle around to the right and see if you can find enough cover to get to that fellow. Spearbold, move left outside the curtain wall until you can see where they landed the boat. Keep a close eye and shout out if anyone goes to the boat. I'll go in the front door."

Each began to move as silently as they could. It was not easy across the stone littered ground. Ragwulf soon lost sight of the others but fixed his attention on the man on the other side of the courtyard. He could see he would have to take some risks, dodge from one ruined wall to another and hope the man did not casually glance behind him at any point. He moved to the first wall and ducked under its shadow. Then he peered over the wall and made for a stone buttress against the wall which still supported the rotten remains of a storehouse. He sighed with relief when he got there for it hid him completely.

He suddenly caught a glimpse of Bear as he approached through a breach in the wall to his right. Then Bear disappeared behind a large chunk of fallen masonry.

"Now where?" he muttered to himself, tapping his fingers against the timber frame beside him. Without warning it slid away from the wall and the remains of the storehouse collapsed around him, raising a cloud of dust and splinters. He dived to the ground and jarred his knee on a lump of stone. He could not breathe for the dust. He looked to the spot where the man had been. Of course, he was not there. Where then? He scanned the courtyard: nothing. Had he bolted somewhere? Perhaps Bear had caught him.

"Sod it," he said and got swiftly to his feet. He ran across the yard and found that Bear was hurrying in from the flank. They converged on the spot where the guard had been. They searched frantically from place to place, in doorways and behind stubs of wall but could not find him.

"Perhaps it was only him and he's gone to the boat," said Ragwulf, but they heard no warning cry from Spearbold.

Bear said nothing, but his expression was not very encouraging. They explored a nearby archway which once would have given access to a tower. Rubble blocked the entrance. Another doorway led upwards and Ragwulf hurried up only to come to a sudden stop. Below him was only a sheer drop where the core of the building had fallen in upon itself.

"Down," said Bear. "We must go down."

"Aye down, but where?" said Ragwulf. "Where? It can't be far."

Bear was staring at a ruined archway to their left and he began walking slowly towards it. Ragwulf joined him and they passed through it. Bear stopped and reached for his axe. Ragwulf drew his sword. They moved with care now: they had at least one man on the loose, there might be others.

"The fellow we saw?" whispered Ragwulf.

"What of him?"

"He might just be a guard - employed to protect his lord's land."

Bear stopped. "So? What do you say?"

"I say: we should not harm him unless we know this is the place," hissed Ragwulf.

Bear nodded grimly. Ragwulf took the lead and they set off again.

The passage was illuminated by the late afternoon sun streaming through windows that faced onto the courtyard but at the end there was a wooden door. It lay wide open and beyond it there was only darkness. They passed through the door and after a few yards the passage turned at right angles and it was impossible to see ahead. They could hear voices though, loud and animated.

"Come on," said Ragwulf and started to feel his way along the stone wall. Bear was close behind him. "Good Christ! Take care with that axe!" warned Ragwulf, but he kept going.

The passage took another turn, then another. Both times he banged his head on the wall and cursed silently. They were now walking down a slope, quite steeply. The air smelt damp and he realised they were walking through a few inches of water. The voices sounded closer now. Ahead there was a faint glimmer of light. They turned yet another corner and met the full glare of torchlight.

A shout of alarm greeted them and a crossbow bolt struck the wall by Bear's head. It ricocheted on down the passage. In the wavering light Ragwulf saw two men with swords drawn by an open cell door. Inside the cell was a third man, standing over some poor wretch on the floor. The two armed men came at them with a fury and Ragwulf instinctively parried the first blow but his attention was on the prisoner.

"It's him!" he called out. "God's breath, Bear, it's him!"

"Well, you're wasting your stinking lives on him because he's dead now!" said one of the men who came at them. "You're too late!"

§§§§§

Ned's stomach cramps slowly subsided, for which he was grateful, but the noise continued. There seemed to be more of them, arguing among themselves outside his open cell door. He could escape... if he wasn't chained to the floor... if he could run... if he could walk even. Perhaps they were arguing over who was going to finish him off. Yet they had given him back his blade to kill himself so why had they not left him? Did they want to watch him cut his own throat or stab himself in the thigh, watch Ned Elder's blood flow away to mingle with the water that lay there?

He picked up his bone and tried to listen.

"Go up and take another look!" shouted one of them - the one who had returned his knife. That was a kind gesture from one who clearly hated him - aye, a kind gesture. He decided he liked that fellow. There was more shouting. Swords were drawn. Oh, shit, they were going to finish him after all. He wished they would make up their sodding minds.

Then from out of sight down the passage came a booming voice that he knew so well.

"I come, lord," it roared, "I come!"

A fire flared suddenly in the depths of his soul.

"I must stay alive," he breathed.

Then he was hauled abruptly to his knees. It was the one he liked; that was a pity. He must stay alive. The man took out a long knife and bent down to strike. Ned used both hands and all his remaining strength to plunge the length of bone up through his captor's neck as it descended towards him. The bone knife snapped, as he knew it would, but not before it left six inches of its length in his opponent's throat.

The man stared at Ned, choked briefly and dropped his knife. He still clutched Ned's neck and when he fell he took Ned with him. On the floor, Ned could not move. He had nothing left. The dying gaoler kept one hand on his throat, squeezing on his windpipe until an axe blow severed the hand from his arm. He stopped squeezing then and Bear wrenched his lifeless hand away.

"You're too late," murmured Ned.

Bear ignored him, hacked the chain from his bloody ankle and lifted him up.

§§§§§

Ned came suddenly awake and found himself being jostled from side to side. He was lying on his back. He looked up and saw grey sky. He tried to work out where he was. He was in a cart - he could tell that much from the movement. As he considered why he was in the cart it must have hit a rut or a stone. His head was dashed against the wooden side board and he lost consciousness again.

Loud, urgent voices woke him.

"Hurry!" barked Bear. "Brugge is close now!"

The cart moved faster and the jostling got worse.

"Have a care!" warned Ragwulf.

Ned grinned. Ragwulf and Bear were his men...his men.

The voices carried on but he heard little and understood less. He tried to reach out a hand to steady himself but his arm barely moved so he succumbed once more to the rolling motion of the cart. He wanted to tell them to slow down but his lips wouldn't move either.

They were arguing he thought. Bear was arguing in Flemish - they might all have been arguing in Flemish, he thought as he passed out.

There was a dull ringing: insistent, annoying, getting louder. Ned wished it would stop. It didn't. He tried to lift his head but the muscles in his neck would not respond. He stared up: the sky was darker. The bell was now so close he thought it might have crept inside his head. Then the cart came to a stop. He became aware of other men close by and a certain smell he recognised from a dim memory: the stink of a town. Large stink, large town. He felt cold. The cart lurched forward a few paces and halted once more.

"Where am I?" asked Ned, or rather that's what he intended to say but since his lips didn't move the words remained unsaid.

Those around the cart began to argue again; some voices he recognised, some he did not. Strident, harsh voices all speaking at once. A giant hand flashed before his eyes and a thick finger stabbed down at him - Bear had the biggest hands in Christendom.

Bear spoke, but not to him. His guttural tone grew threatening and the other voices faltered. There was a pause and then the cart moved forward again, slowly. Its wheels crossed a rutted surface and Ned was thrown about like a sack of wool. Spearbold's worried face loomed over him.

"Slower," he said. "I fear he's bleeding again."

Ned did not want to be bleeding at all, let alone again. The cart stopped again and torches flared above him. He screwed his eyes shut against the glare. When he opened them a moment later he found an ugly face peering at him which then disappeared from view. The cart rumbled forward and he passed beneath the dark teeth of a great portcullis. More torches flickered by under a vaulted archway. He closed his eyes again.

He spluttered awake. Water was splashing onto his face. It was almost dark and the motion of the cart was somehow different, not jolting, more bobbing up and down. His cart was afloat!

"Are you trying to drown him?" asked Spearbold.

"Hold your tongue!" hissed Ragwulf. "If we're caught out in Bruges after curfew they'll likely drown us all!"

"Stay still," growled Bear. "You sink boat."

Ah, a boat, thought Ned, not the cart then. The boat lurched and Ned rolled onto his side. Ragwulf's face appeared close to his.

"Sorry, lord," he breathed and turned Ned onto his back again.

"Can he hear me do you think?" Ragwulf asked the

others.

Spearbold looked down at him. "It doesn't seem so," he said.

Look closer, light a torch, Ned urged them silently.

"What is this place?" asked Ragwulf.

"Waterhalle," replied Bear.

Water hall? Ned didn't know what a water hall was but he could make out huge roof timbers above him and the tops of the columns that supported them. The boat moved slowly. There were low voices in the water hall. Then, close by, a wicked, giggling laugh shattered the silence. The boat stopped and no-one spoke. All was silent save for a regular grunting sound, punctuated by the occasional squeal or moan. Ned wanted to laugh…or cry - he was inclined to do both. Footsteps thudded on the wooden boards of the landing and then clipped away along a stone quay perhaps, fading swiftly.

"There's something that never changes," observed Ragwulf.

"I should think this 'Waterhalle' is a popular haunt for such women," said Spearbold.

As if Spearbold would know, Ned thought, as he felt the boat move off again.

"Are you sure you know where you're going?" asked Spearbold. "We should have gone straight to the fellow Crabber told us about."

"We will," said Ragwulf, "but not with Lord Elder."

"But we must get him some help," Spearbold pleaded.

Aye, Ned agreed. Help was what he needed, right enough.

"That's why we'll leave Crabber's man till tomorrow," insisted Ragwulf. "First we must find somewhere to leave Lord Elder."

Leave me? No, don't leave me, pleaded Ned.

"Only one place to go," answered Bear, "St John's Hospital - if they don't take him, no-one will."

Ned began to feel sick and tried to retch. He had nothing to bring up save the lining of his belly but he tried nonetheless. There was panic in the boat.

"Dear God!" exclaimed Spearbold. "He's choking on something!"

"Peace!" said Ragwulf.

Ned found himself abruptly turned over onto his front. That hurt, but not as much as the sudden blow to his back that followed. After everything, Bear had now broken his back. Nevertheless, the gagging ceased and the wave of nausea passed. Ned's face flopped down onto the flat bottom of the boat and landed in a shallow trough of water. The water was cold. It lapped against his lips; it tasted like liquid shit and he spat it out. He felt wide awake now, all his senses alerted. He could feel pain, every bruise and cut, the soreness on his ankle, the ache in his head. Pain assaulted him, ravaged him. The boat grazed against stone and he passed out.

When he woke next, it was not so dark. There were torches or oil lamps - he did not care to know which. He looked up to see that he was in a cavernous hall yet it seemed cramped, overcrowded. There were many others there. He could see their shadowy forms beside him on narrow beds. All about him he heard their cries, their moans, their prayers or just their rasping breath. Hooded figures circled around him in the gloom. Where were his friends? He cried out their names ... inside his head. Then the pain returned and he knew that the rescue was only a cruel delusion. He was dead all along, had died in his cell and now his soul languished in purgatory. Here he would wait whilst his sins were weighed up and Ned knew what the outcome of that would be, for was he not a man mired in the blood of others?

13

25th August 1468, on the road north of Yoredale

Damp branches crackled and spat upon the fire where only Hal and Wulf remained. Horses shuffled restlessly, disturbed by their voices. The others had drifted away to sleep in the darkness leaving the two of them alone - and the boy, John, already fast asleep. Hal had not let him out of his sight - nor would he. Every waking moment he remembered Lady Eleanor's whispered words and they never ceased to chill him.

"Where did you go this morning?" asked Wulf. "You were gone a long time."

Hal sighed. Sooner or later they would have to talk about it and tomorrow would be too late.

"I went to see Canon Reedman at Coverham Abbey - to leave word where I am and where I'm going. I told Lady Eleanor I would."

"Why take John with you?"

"The lad likes an adventure," replied Hal, improvising.

"And where will this …adventure take you then?" asked Wulf, lowering his voice.

"We must take different paths, my friend," said Hal. "I'm not going back to Yoredale Castle and nor is John. Too much happened there…"

"Aye, but that's what I don't see, Hal. I can see you might not want to go back…with all that went on. But John, what harm can he come to? He'd be safe with Bess - and she's the only mother he knows."

"That may be, but she's not his mother, is she? I'm still not happy any of you are going there. Men were slaughtered there - our men! And worse too! I know Joan Elder for a murdering bitch."

"But this morning we talked to folk around here. It seems Joan Elder holds little power now -she's married to some local knight. I don't know who - and I don't care. All I've heard is that he's after men at arms. If you know someone else that's recruiting, then tell me!"

"Why's he looking for men then, when no-one else is?"

"We have to have work, Hal and we can't afford to be too particular. When winter comes, we need a place, some food on the table. We can't ride around the north forever, hunting wild and proclaiming our lord's good name and honour. Whether he's dead or alive, Ned Elder can't feed us now. You said it yourself: few are taking on men at arms just now - and there are plenty of men wandering the byways looking for work, or turning to thieving. Would you rather we do that? Because that's all that's left, and even living outside the law doesn't pay well - the north is too poor, too weary."

Hal nodded and patted his friend's shoulder. He had no reasonable argument to counter what Wulf said, none except his fear of Joan Elder. She had killed those who were most dear to him, sweet Jane and old Gruffydd. But most of all, he owed her for Lady Amelie. The only reason he would return to Yoredale Castle was to kill Joan Elder and he could not risk John's life to do that. So Joan Elder would have to wait.

He wanted to explain all to his friend, but it was not his secret to share. Hal did not dare trust even his friend with the knowledge that Lady Eleanor had made plain to him. Wulf was sure to tell Bess and before he knew it the word would be out and Joan Elder would hear of it. He could barely imagine what she might do if he found out Ned had a son and heir.

"Different paths then, Wulf," he said, "but I'll come back here after winter - to see how you've fared."

His comrade grinned. "It's harder than I thought," he murmured, "making the decisions. If we've nothing to eat, they look to me; if we meet someone on the road, they look to me. By Christ, Hal - if a dog shits on their foot, they look to me. I never knew…"

"You'll do them proud," said Hal, with the smile of an old comrade.

"When will you go?"

"I'll ride with you to Yoredale. When you ride into Yoredale Castle, I'll leave you - and I'll take John."

"Bess won't like it, Hal."

"Then you'd better speak to her. Be ready to take my part in this, Wulf, because I'll not be leaving without him."

§§§§§

In the morning they took the once familiar track that followed the river Yore. It was narrow in places where the water had washed away the bank or in others where low scrub grew down into the river itself and the traveller was obliged to change course to continue his journey. They rode in a long, straggling column with Bess and John in their midst. Hal decided to let John share Bess's mount whilst he could.

Long before they reached Yoredale Castle they were met on the road by a group of armed riders.

"God give you good morning, all," announced the leading rider as he drew up to them.

"And to you," replied Wulf with equal courtesy.

Once pleasantries are exchanged there is often a pause whilst those who meet on the road make a swift assessment of each other. Hal looked first at their livery and saw at once that they did not wear the pale blue Elder colours. He did not recognise their badges at all but he was glad to see that they did not wear the bear and ragged staff of Warwick at least.

"I am Sir Walter Grave," the horseman informed them.

"And I'm Wulf Ragwulfson," said Wulf.

Grave turned to his fellows and laughed. "We've an old Norseman here, lads!"

Wulf frowned. "I'll take your words kindly, sir," he said. "Do you come from Yoredale Castle?"

Grave eyed him with suspicion. "Why do want to know?" he asked.

"We've been told that the lord of Yoredale is looking for men at arms and archers," said Wulf, "and we'd like to offer ourselves for service or hire."

"For hire, eh?" echoed Grave. "You must think highly of yourselves then. I wonder if you're as sharp as you think…"

"If you're not from the castle then I'll bid you good day and move on," said Wulf, nudging his mount forward.

"Hold hard, youth," said Grave. "We are from the castle, sure enough. You can come back with us. Whether you can do useful service of any kind, our lord will decide."

"Very well," replied Wulf.

"I'll leave you here then," said Hal and he turned his horse to go back to collect John.

"Wait!" said Grave. "All will come to the castle. We like to keep an eye on strangers."

Hal turned once more and rode back to Grave, only pulling up when he was alongside him.

"I am not offering myself for service here, Sir Walter," he said.

"You're merely passing through my lord's estates then?"

"Yes, indeed - just travelling through." Hal smiled.

Grave did not. "Across my lord's land?"

"Yes, but-"

"All will come to the castle. Matters will be dealt with there. Some may be taken on for service and others perhaps not."

Hal glanced to the rear of their group where several more mounted men had appeared. He was in no position to argue and gave a nod of acceptance.

"Who is your lord?" he asked.

"Sir Thomas Gate - a warrior of great renown."

Hal tried to appear calm but the name Gate struck him like a blow to the chest.

"I've heard of him," he stuttered.

"He's made a name for himself, to be sure," agreed Grave and rode on.

Wulf trotted past him and shrugged. "I'm sorry Hal, but I'm sure you'll be on your way soon enough."

Hal had so many conflicting thoughts in his head he could barely concentrate on riding. Thomas Gate was the name Spearbold had given them, the knight who had acted against Lord Elder and probably taken Agnes too. But what could Hal do about it?

"Are you alright. Hal?" asked Wulf, reaching across to touch his arm.

Hal looked up. "Yes, why?"

"Because you're dripping sweat and you've turned a colour to match the autumn leaves, my friend, that's why!"

Hal shuddered. He dared not say too much for Grave's men rode amongst them.

"We must be very, very watchful," he breathed. "Thomas Gate is not to be trusted, Wulf. Take that as the iron truth. As soon as I can, I'll leave but I must take John with me. Must! Make sure Bess is clear about that."

"Aye, of course, Hal - that's what we agreed."

"Yes, but it may get awkward, Wulf. Just trust me."

"Always, Hal." Wulf slapped him on the back and rode on ahead whilst Hal allowed his mount to drop back nearer to Bess and John. He said nothing to them but spent the remainder of the ride observing their escort carefully.

His mind raced ahead trying to foresee what might

happen when they reached Yoredale Castle. The more he thought about it, the darker the outlook seemed. Going into Yoredale Castle was madness. He should be riding like the winds of Hell in the opposite direction for he was putting Ned's son at great risk. If Thomas Gate and Joan Elder ruled at Yoredale Castle then Hal was taking John to the most dangerous place in Christendom.

14

26th August 1468, at Yoredale Castle.

Hal, Wulf and the other young men stood in the yard, a yard that some remembered very well. They were waiting for a moment of Sir Thomas Gate's valuable time and they would have to stand there until it pleased him to see them. Bess and John waited nearby with the horses but the rest of them talked quietly, nervously, amongst themselves for they knew the importance of this meeting. If they failed to make a good impression they might be turned out of the castle with less than they came in with. As winter approached they would be condemned to wander the dales in search of work. Their very lives depended on persuading the new lord of Yoredale that they were exactly the sort of men he was looking for.

Hal moved closer to Bess. "Whatever happens," he said, "do not give up the boy."

Bess looked puzzled. "Why would I need to?" she asked. "No-one else is going to want to look after him, are they?"

"As soon as I can, I'm going to leave with John," he said, "take him somewhere…safer."

"Where could be safer than here?" she argued. "He can stay with me and Wulf. You'd be no use looking after him."

Hal assumed that Wulf had already had his conversation with Bess. It seemed not and now he had raised it in a clumsy manner but he must assert his hold on the boy. He gripped Bess by the shoulders. "Listen Bess, John will stay with me now and I won't be crossed in this - even by you."

Too late he realised that his stern tone had only frightened her, making her still more determined to keep

John with her. At that moment, a ripple of expectation spread through the group as the new lord of Yoredale strolled lazily across the cobbles towards them. Beside him was Sir Walter Grave but there was no sign of Joan Elder, for which Hal was grateful.

"I am Sir Thomas Gate," the man announced cheerfully, "and I own all of the lands you have just passed through."

So it was true enough, thought Hal. This was Thomas Gate, Warwick's man. Hal stared at him long and hard. If this man had harmed either Lord Elder or Agnes, then he would answer for it. Yet he looked more than capable of coping with a single opponent. Hal only half-listened to what Gate was saying about recruiting his comrades. He knew what would be said, and afterwards Gate would either recruit them or he would not.

After what seemed a lot longer than just a few moments, Hal found that everyone was looking at him and began to pay closer attention.

"I'm told that you do not wish to serve me as your friends do?" said Thomas Gate.

"No, Sir Thomas."

"What are you?" Gate asked him.

"A simple archer, Sir Thomas."

"And why would a simple archer refuse to serve me?"

"I don't refuse, Sir Thomas. I rode this far with my friends but I have business to finish elsewhere and I must take this boy along with me."

"Your son?" asked Gate.

"No, but his nearest relative here," lied Hal. John's nearest relative there was in fact Lady Joan Elder but Hal thanked God that no-one knew it.

Gate nodded and Hal was relieved that the knight did not seem unduly interested.

"Well, as it happens, I have archers enough for now," said Gate, "so you and the boy can be on your way."

"Thank you, Sir Thomas," said Hal, hoping his relief

was not too obvious.

He held out his hand to John and the boy took it willingly.

"Wait," said Bess suddenly. "The boy should stay with me!"

"Keep out of this," Wulf growled at her quietly but Bess was not to be denied and seized John's other hand.

Gate looked annoyed. "Is the boy yours…mistress?"

"No, my lord, but I've nursed him since he was a few days old. I'm the nearest thing to a mother the boy's ever had."

"Is this true?" he asked Hal.

"Yes," said Hal, "but-"

"Then should he not stay with her?" demanded Gate.

"No, he belongs with me," said Hal, knowing how lame his words sounded.

Gate frowned. "Well, I don't care either way but for the boy's sake, I'll ask my lady to judge the matter. You can remain here until then."

Hal could think of no response that would change Gate's mind, so he watched him leave and then went straight to Wulf.

"You were supposed to tell her!" he said.

"I couldn't…find the right moment," said Wulf.

"You know my mind on this," Hal retorted, "make Bess understand: John must come with me. She's already put him in grave danger because his fate is now in the hands of Gate's lady, Joan Elder. If she recognises me then I'm a dead man, Wulf. I don't even want her to look upon the boy. Bess must say she was wrong to object."

Wulf sighed and gave him a doubtful look. "Bess can be a bit stubborn on things, Hal. Leave her to settle for a while and I'll talk to her."

"Let's be clear with one another, Wulf, just between us two old friends: I would kill every man here to keep that boy safe."

Wulf looked shocked by Hal's vehemence and did not answer.

"If you love me at all," persisted Hal, "then persuade her to give way on this."

§§§§

By the evening, Wulf had indeed persuaded Bess to let John leave with Hal, though with little grace and only thinly veiled resentment. But it was too late to avoid a meeting with Joan Elder for Gate had already told his wife and she seemed keen to assert her control over household matters in the castle. Thus, in the morning, after Sir Thomas had ridden out early with some of the garrison, Hal, Wulf and Bess were summoned to the Great Chamber to see her.

They stood before her, caps off and heads bowed. Hal was almost shaking to see her so close. Here was the murderer of his dear Amelie who had lifted him from the gutter and given him a reason to live. He would gladly have given his life to protect her. Even now he ached to strike the woman down but there was John to consider and he must come first.

Lady Joan stepped off the dais and took several paces towards them, examining their faces carefully. Hal knew he was sweating and when she stopped in front of him for a moment, he ensured his eyes remained cast down to avoid meeting hers.

"What is this all about?" Lady Joan asked Bess.

"It's all a mistake, my lady," said Bess. "I nursed the boy when he was a bairn but I know that Hal will look after him; I never thought otherwise. I just wanted him with me a little longer, that's all. But it's best he go with Hal now."

Well said, Bess, thought Hal.

"Well, let's find out," said Joan. "Where is this boy? I'd like to see him. You," she told Bess, "go and bring him here to me."

When Bess left, Lady Joan turned her attention back to

Hal.

"Have you served here before?" she asked.

It was a question Hal had been dreading. "No, my lady," he lied, offering up a silent prayer.

"But my lord, Sir Thomas, told me that all of you had served here before - when my cousin, Edward, held the lordship."

Wulf spoke up. "The rest of us, my lady, but not Hal," he said.

"Have I seen you before," she asked Hal. She seemed somehow wary of him.

"I don't believe so, my lady."

He was saved from further scrutiny by the return of Bess with John. Joan studied the boy for a moment.

"He is very young to leave this girl who has been his mother for so long," she observed. As she spoke her eyes remained upon John.

"Why do you want to take him with you...Hal, is it?"

Hal had given some thought overnight to the tale he would tell. "I'm an archer, my lady. The boy's keen to learn and I want to train him early so that he can become a great archer in time."

"By God, man, you'll have him in the field before he's five years old! Besides, we have practice butts - you could teach him well enough here."

She went to John and he gave her that look which he reserved for all strangers, the unblinking stare that announced: I'm John Elder and I bow to no man - or woman for that matter. Lady Joan could not fail to notice it and her displeasure was soon evident enough in her expression.

"Well, John," she said, "what say you? Do you want to go with this man?"

"Aye, my lady," he answered. Even if he was terrified out of his wits, Hal knew the boy would never show it.

Lady Joan returned to the dais and sat down. She

seemed to be studying them all thoughtfully.

"No," she said finally, "the boy will stay here - and you, Hal, will also stay to teach the boy and at the same time to serve my husband."

Hal wanted to scream. If only Bess had kept her mouth shut, he and John would be long gone by now. He quivered with anger but said nothing for there was no point in arguing. Like the others, he bowed slightly to her ladyship and prepared to withdraw but John had other ideas.

"No, my lady," he piped up, "I don't want to stay here."

Joan had already turned to leave but her head whipped back at the boy's sudden announcement.

"You'll do as you're told, boy!" she snarled, "And I'll have you whipped for that!" She glanced at Bess, "the ungrateful little bastard - for that's what he is, I'm sure."

Bess scooped up John and Wulf put his arms around them both.

"Please, my lady," they cried.

She turned to Hal. "The boy needs to learn his place before he learns the bow!"

Hal went on his knees before her. "Please, my lady, let me take his punishment. He's but a small boy. If he is ill-mannered, the fault lies with me."

"Very well," she said with a bemused smile, "you will be whipped since you wish it…but so will he. If he's old enough to insult me, then he's old enough to be punished."

She swept out of the Hall and left them. Hal turned to John, who had never been whipped before. For once, the boy remained silent.

§§§§§

At midday, Hal and John stood together in a corner of the castle yard. Both were stripped to the waist and the boy was bent forward over a small barrel. Hal was tied between two old wooden posts set in the cobbles. Most likely they were the remains of an animal pen judging by the pungent smell of dung that lingered there.

The pair of them faced out across the yard where many had come to watch. Others stood on the ramparts above. Hal had insisted on taking his twenty lashes first, hoping to encourage the lad that the punishment could be endured. Even so, he grunted with pain when the lash began to fall. He had not been beaten since he was a lad at Corve Manor. The watching crowd cheered each stroke of the lash with growing enthusiasm and he knew that even his friends would be cheering to give him encouragement. He picked out familiar faces nearby: Wulf, Bess in floods of tears and a few others he knew well. Beyond them were many more: men of the garrison, servants, kitchen wenches, they were all there.

When it was over, it was John's turn. Hal reckoned that a child might well have been whipped here before but this was public and that was enough to make this a novelty for the castle inhabitants.

"Be strong, John," he whispered. "It'll hurt, but if I can bear it - so can you. You're a brave lad. Now shut it out of your head and think of something else."

John nodded but said nothing. He looked strangely calm but Hal knew it could only be because he had no understanding of how much what followed would hurt. The fellow with the whip was called Weaver, one of Joan's men, not Gate's.

"Go easy on the lad, Weaver," said Hal.

Weaver gave a shrug. "You keep your mouth shut - or you'll get another hiding."

"Get on with it!" ordered Joan looking down from the rampart.

Hal felt that the mood in the yard had changed. Many who had been more than happy to cheer each stroke of his beating seemed less certain how to receive the young boy's punishment. There had been a murmur of chatter from the onlookers but now an awkward silence fell.

When the wiry strands of the whip first struck John's back, he flinched but uttered not a word. As blow after blow landed, he gritted his teeth and made no sound at all as the watching crowd held their breath. He was to have ten strokes but when he bore the ten with so little reaction, Lady Joan bellowed down. "Give him another ten, Weaver - and don't go so easy on him this time!"

The slap of the whip on the boy's bare skin echoed around the walls and a collective gasp came from those in the yard. With each stroke, John kept his gaze fixed firmly upon Lady Joan on the far rampart. At the end though the tears poured down his face and his whole body shook, still he did not cry out. Hal was almost in tears himself and, if he had ever had any doubt whose son John was, all his doubts fled that day.

When it was over Lady Joan stalked from the battlements into the nearest tower. Most of the crowd drifted back to their duties but a few willing hands remained to treat their bloodied backs. Only then did John slide from the barrel onto the damp cobbles and sob. Hal's hands were swiftly untied and he bent down to lift the boy up. Bess was beside herself. She went to touch John and recoiled at the sight of his wounds.

"It looks worse than it is," Wulf tried to reassure her as she buried her face against his chest.

"Not if you're a four year old," murmured Hal. He was vaguely aware of a few of the castle household helping them into a storeroom by the castle well - a priest was there muttering the soothing words of God though Hal found little consolation in them. He was concerned for the boy - only the lad's fierce pride had held him together and now the pain of the raw wounds would really hit him hard. He laid him gently down on his chest upon a trestle table, stroking his head and talking to distract him from the pain.

"Well done, lad. Brave lad. Well done," he said. Looking at the bloody weals made him simmer with anger.

"I'll not forgive Weaver for this," muttered Wulf.

His friends and the priest tried to take Hal to another table and bade him lie down there.

"The boy, first," he insisted, shrugging off their helping hands.

Then one of the kitchen girls planted her hand on his chest, leaving it lingering for a moment above his heart. For the first time he looked at her anxious face and his mouth opened wide to speak, but he could not find the words. She smiled and then pushed him firmly away as she turned to apply her salves to the boy's raw wounds. But then, after she had seen to John, she came to him and rubbed a salve on his back. At first it burned like a torch held against his skin, but gently her skilled fingers worked it into the ragged cuts. His back felt slightly numb and the pain began to fade.

When she stopped, Hal sat up and looked at her. They were alone in the store. When Agnes had laid her hand upon his breast he thought he must have conjured her up in his anguish. She was beautiful now, but looked older and somehow, more careworn. She seemed calm, though not at ease, and when he wrapped his arms around her, she sobbed silently.

All he could say was "Agnes." He repeated it softly over and over. And then she left the warmth of his embrace, brushed her fingers against his lips and was gone.

15

27th August 1468, at Yoredale Castle

Hal was left to sleep in the storeroom for most of the afternoon and when he awoke he found that Bess was there, watching over John. Hal was relieved to see the boy sleeping at peace.

Bess put a tentative hand on Hal's shoulder. "I wanted to be here when you came to… I wanted to say…"

"It's done, Bess," said Hal. "John's alright. There's no more to be said."

"But it was my fault!"

"Your fault we're still here maybe, but don't take the blame for his whipping. That belongs elsewhere and it won't be forgotten either. John best stay with you as long as he's in here but keep him with you all the time."

"Aye, I will," she said.

"All the time, Bess," he insisted. "He must never be from your sight. Do you understand me?"

"Aye, Hal, aye, but … I've never understood why you think anyone would harm John?"

"Do you not see something in him?" he said, staring at the boy.

"He's just a little lad."

Hal nodded. "As you say, Bess… he's just a little lad."

Bess gave him a sombre nod. "He may not be mine but he's precious to me too, you know. It's like he is mine and for Ragwulf's sake, I'd never want him harmed…"

"Take him with you then. He can sleep with you and Wulf."

Hal watched her go. Poor Bess, she must be so confused, he thought. Well, she wasn't the only one. Seeing

Agnes had changed everything for him: his first thought had been to get John away but now he knew that, having found her again, he could never leave Agnes behind.

Gingerly, he raised himself up. His back was still sore but he'd known worse pain - much worse - nevertheless, he decided to remain down in the storeroom for the night.

In the morning he found his way to the great kitchen. When he asked the servants about Agnes, they looked away and would say nothing. They would not even tell him if she worked there. When he paused to think about it, he was not surprised. They had probably all witnessed his punishment. He was not exactly in favour and they knew not to make an enemy of their lord and lady - especially their lady. He decided he must be more careful about asking questions. Agnes must be in the castle somewhere and he knew it well enough to know where to look. It should not be so difficult to find her.

Below the kitchen were the dry stores and he worked his way through there and then through the wine store and past the postern gate into the stables. From there he crossed the yard and searched all the other ground floor store rooms, then the bake house and brew house. The alewife sent him packing with a playful punch to the shoulder, but he believed her when she told him that Agnes did not work there.

He stood in the middle of the yard, aware that if he stood there for too long then someone would decide he was fit enough to work. If he searched above the ground floor, he would be taking a risk and if he was caught wandering near the privy chamber or the solar he would be in deep trouble. He had no business poking around up there and anyone would know it. But, the garrison mess and its kitchen were on the first floor too - he would perhaps be more welcome there.

So he mounted the spiral stair in the south east tower which housed the castle garrison. When he reached the first floor landing he heard footsteps coming down and waited. Then - as if the Lord had willed it - Agnes appeared above him on the steps. But she looked horrified to see him and turned to run back up the stair.

"Agnes!" he called but she moved fast and when he followed there was no sign of her on the landing above. He tried to remember the rooms that lay nearby. By the landing were the garrison sleeping quarters and he found those empty. Above lay only the ramparts, so where else could she have gone up here? His two old comrades, Bagot and Gruffydd, had once shared the next chamber along and beyond that was only the chapel. He went to the chamber door first and listened: nothing. He knocked lightly on the door. No response.

Why had she run from him? Surely he must be her only ally?

He opened the chamber door and stepped inside. The room was a good deal less cluttered than when the two old soldiers had occupied it. There was just a bed and a chest now - and, standing by the window, there was Agnes. She looked ashen.

"Agnes, why did you run?"

She ran across to him and hugged him. Then she pushed him firmly towards the door.

"No wait, Agnes," he said, "we need to talk."

She gave him a withering look

"Alright - I need to talk to you at least."

She shook her head and pushed him back out of the door into the passage outside. She glanced along it, worry etched on her face.

"It's alright, Agnes, be calm. I'm here now." But his words only made her look more terrified. She steered him away from the chamber and back towards the steps. They were nearly there when they both heard someone coming up. Agnes looked at him in panic and ran back to the chamber. She shut the door leaving him alone at the top of the steps.

It was Sir Walter Grave ascending the stair and he did not look pleased to see Hal.

"What do you want up here?" he demanded.

Hal nodded towards the sleeping quarters. "I'm just going to lie down, Sir Walter," he replied, "to give the wounds some time to heal."

Grave shrugged. "Make sure you don't get yourself into any more trouble," he warned. "I know everything that goes on in here - every last thing."

"Of course, Sir Walter," said Hal.

Grave continued along the passage and Hal's heart sank. He doubted that Grave was going to the chapel to pray. The chamber Agnes was in must now belong to Grave.

§§§§

When the chamber door opened again, Agnes thought it must be Hal returning and moved towards it. When she saw Grave she paused mid-stride. He looked anything but pleased.

"The youth outside," he said, "the one who was whipped - did you see him?"

She shrugged and then shook her head.

"Well, avoid him. He's trouble - and you've already had enough of that. You're not to work in the great kitchen any more. I've arranged it. You'll spend your time in the garrison kitchen up here and if you're not there then I want you in this chamber. I want to know where you are. Is that clear?"

Agnes nodded. She tried to comply with Grave's wishes for he was not a cruel or unreasonable man - unless she crossed him. Then she would feel the back of his hand across her face. Survival for all these months had meant keeping Walter Grave on her side. That had been her plan - such as it was. But now Hal was there and at first she thought her troubles were at an end. Then she realised that Hal's presence changed nothing for he was as much a prisoner as she was.

"You'll sleep in my chamber every night now," Grave continued. "You can sleep on the floor by the window - unless I want you to warm my bed. If you continue to please me Agnes, I'll keep you safe from her ladyship. You know that, don't you?"

Agnes nodded.

"Good. Now go and fetch what few belongings you have and bring them here."

Agnes smiled at him and left the chamber at a walk, knowing that Grave disliked haste and fuss. She closed the door behind her and leant for a moment against the plastered stone wall. She forced back a few tears and then made her way, tight-lipped, to the stairs. Hal came out of the men at arms' sleeping chamber and blocked her path. She shook her head in disbelief. Was he trying to get them killed?

"Is Grave using you, Agnes?" he asked, seizing her arm.

The question stung her and he knew she could not answer, so why did he even ask?

He looked fierce with anger; she had never seen him like that. He brushed past her and headed for Grave's chamber. She tugged at his arm but he shrugged her off and strode to the chamber door. She ran after him and pushed him past it, pushed him hard along the passage and held him against the chapel door. She shook her head at him vigorously.

"Agnes…"

Behind them Grave's chamber door opened. Swiftly Agnes lifted the chapel door latch and shoved Hal through it. Then she turned and closed the chapel door to force a smile at Grave who was standing in the passage staring at her. She put her hands together in front of her to mime the act of prayer. Grave nodded thoughtfully. "A brief prayer, my girl? Perhaps you should spend longer in there."

But he seemed satisfied and went back into his chamber. Agnes fled back along the passage and down the stairs.

§§§§

When Hal was thrust into the chapel, he gave the priest something of a shock and they simply stood facing each other for a moment. The priest looked strangely familiar to Hal but he could not think where he had met him before. His mind was still consumed by thoughts of Agnes and Walter Grave.

"I'm Father Baston," the priest told him. It was a northern voice and Hal remembered the name too.

"I'm Hal," he said absently. "Do I know you?"

"Do you?"

Hal considered. There were many times when a priest had ministered to them before a battle. "Did you pray with us the night before Towton?" he asked.

"I wasn't at Towton field, I'm glad to say," replied the priest, "but I think we've met before."

"Where then?"

Again the two men stood in silence.

"It was not on a battlefield," said Father Baston, "though there was slaughter enough." His eyes glistened with the memory and Hal examined the rugged face more closely.

"Ah…Crag Tower," said Hal softly. "Sweet Lord. You were the priest… you were the priest when we buried the bodies, those charred bodies."

Like the priest, he found the bitter memory hard to contemplate - even for a moment.

"Aye. I was a fresh-faced, young priest, trained in Newcastle and sent out to call the border folk to worship. I was born in the village below Crag, you know. I'd been a wild youth and I was pleased to return a better man. The first person I met on my way into the village was Sir

Stephen. He seized my arm and dragged me along to Crag Tower. He wouldn't - perhaps couldn't - explain but he looked so frantic I thought I'd better go with him. I thought I'd find someone close to death and needing the last rites. When I stood over the pit that carried those tortured, twisted remains of people, I could understand why he was lost for words. I had never seen the like and I thank God I've seen nothing like it since. It was my first act as a parish priest... and I never recovered from it."

"But how are you come here - of all places?" asked Hal. "You must know…"

"That, my friend, is too long a tale for today. But we'll speak of it another time. Did I see young Agnes with you?"

"Yes, I knew her years ago - with Lord Elder."

"Not a name I'd use too much around here," said Father Baston, "Not unless you want me to be saying a few words over you."

"I'm worried about her."

"Well, you're right to be - but she's a strong girl. I've seen it in her - Godless, but strong."

"Hardly Godless." protested Hal, "She's one of the kindest people I've ever met, Father."

"Aye, kind she is, Hal, but she knows nothing of the saints, nor even the Blessed Virgin. She was born and raised without God."

"She was raised in a forest by her father - that's where her faith lies."

Father Baston nodded. "I've some duties today," he said, "but I'll speak with you again. There's much here that you don't know. I've made it my business to know and you're the first person to come here that I believe I might be able to trust. Come to me tomorrow. Take care though."

"I'll come up by the main stair next time," said Hal.

"No, don't. The small door you came through is my private entrance and, as you've found, you must pass Sir Walter Grave's chamber to get here. But the main stair carries more danger still for it leads past Lady Joan's bedchamber. We certainly don't want to raise any suspicions in that cunning little head. Go out the way you came in - but take care, Hal, for this is a house of devils."

PART THREE: BROTHERS AND SISTERS

DEREK BIRKS

16

5th September 1468, in Yoredale

Eleanor and Rob stood, still and silent, the dawn air fresh upon their faces.

"The forest of Yoredale," breathed Eleanor. "After the last time, I never thought I'd miss it." But now she was there, under its cavernous oak canopies of green, it somehow drew her in, like meeting an old friend of years gone by. It was hard to believe that in her youth she had been a child of that forest. Wild, angry and rebellious - well beyond her father's belated attempts at discipline. A trace of regret caught her then. If only her mother had not died so young, perhaps all their lives would have taken a different course.

"Red?" Rob looked at her uncertainly.

"Don't call me that - I hate it!" she snapped and strode off once more along the woodland track. After a few steps she risked a glance back and was reassured to see him only a few yards behind her. She continued along the forest track until she glimpsed the castle towers in the distance. For a moment she stopped, her confidence stripped away by the dark memories that flooded into her head: stark, vivid scenes of blood and death.

"What is it?" asked Rob, following her gaze.

"The past," she muttered.

He put an arm around her. She batted it away and prowled forward through the trees, her eyes never leaving the towers of Yoredale. She was grateful that Rob fell silent now for the care he paid her only irritated her more. Then she heard horses, coming their way through the trees. She seized his hand and dragged him into a thicket of hazel and birch, burrowing under the bracken.

"Together at last," he breathed as they lay close.

"Peace, you fool!" she whispered.

A column of horsemen threaded its way past them and the pair lay still until the riders were well out of sight. Eleanor found herself in his arms and she was surprised how good it felt. Perhaps he was good for her, this Rob Hall. He amused her and stopped her black moods from taking hold - and he cared about her. He kissed her softly on the cheek and she grinned as she felt him tense, no doubt unsure of her reaction.

"I am deep in love with you, Lady Eleanor Elder," he said.

"I know," she murmured, enjoying the way he held her.

"I was hoping that by now you might feel the same."

"I don't, Rob," she said. "I've told you already: I don't love you - but I do like you, and there aren't too many men I can say that about."

The moment was sweet but it passed as every moment did, good or ill. Slowly she extricated herself from his embrace and stood up.

"We'd better keep our distance from the castle until we know who holds power there now," she said. "It was my cousin, Joan Elder, but after four years, who knows?"

"How will we know…who does hold it now?" he asked.

Eleanor turned to face him and favoured him with one of her sweetest smiles. "Because you're going to find out for us."

Rob heaved a sigh of resignation. "You know if I was your lover, I'd walk into fire for that smile but… as only your friend, I'm not so sure."

Eleanor contemplated slapping him. She admired directness but not so much when it strayed near the truth.

"I suppose you want me to go into the nearest alehouse and ask someone," he said.

"You suppose right - better you than me. I'm sure I make a convincing man but that might be one risk too many."

"My lady, nothing would please me more than to drink myself to hell and back in your service but sadly your idea lacks a little something…"

"What?" Sometimes she wearied of his endless banter.

"Coin!" he replied simply. "We have none - unless you've been keeping it from me."

"Ah," said Eleanor, "coin…no…" She sighed. "I don't know why I call you fool," she muttered. "Put a weapon in my hand, Rob, and I'll fight to my last breath, but I can't even think of something as simple as coin."

Rob gave her a mischievous grin. "Perhaps because you're not used to needing it?"

She pounded her head with her fist. "What then?"

"Listen, my lady, you stay here," he said, "and I'll go down into one of the villages and strike up a casual conversation… then, by and by, I'll get to asking about the lordship of the estate. It'll be easy."

She noticed he always called her 'lady' when he wanted to get his way.

"But can you do it?" she asked. "Can you be that cunning?"

"Me? I'm the most cunning fellow I know," he declared. "My charms can't be resisted by mortal man or woman and my good humour is a legend in the borders…"

Eleanor covered her ears with her hands. He was good enough at prattling in this empty-headed sort of way but could he do it without arousing any suspicion?

"Enough! They'll know you're an alien as soon as you open your mouth," she said.

"So? I reckon there are plenty of strangers about just now. I can say I'm looking for work."

"Now that, if they knew you, would truly surprise them," she retorted.

She appraised him thoughtfully. He looked the part: scruffy, but with his sword at his belt he might pass for a soldier - a poor man's mercenary perhaps.

"Very well," she conceded, "but you must make no mention of me, or Ned…or Ragwulf… or Bess - she might be known here too. In fact don't mention anyone!"

"I'll give no names - not even my own," he reassured her. "I'm not that great a fool, my lady! You know that."

Eleanor gave him a fond, indulgent smile. "Aye, but I know shit about men. Sometimes I think you're all fools… and then other times I think you're all heroes."

"So, the only question is: where shall I go?"

"We'll go further south towards Coverham Abbey - further from the castle. I ought to find Canon Reedman in any case - always assuming he remembers who I am. Aysgarth village would do - it's on our way and you'll find some folk about."

"One thing…" said Rob.

"What?" said Eleanor.

"It might be a good idea to leave your sword somewhere - and that knife with the fancy hilt. You'll attract attention. I mean, normally, with your long, red… and those eyes… I mean normally a sword's the last thing any man would notice…but just now…"

Eleanor grinned at him. "You mean dressed like this, with my ragged stubble of hair, you don't find me so … desirable?"

She was pleased to see his cheeks redden. "I've spent a month in ditches and hedgerows with you and I still find you desirable…"

She smiled. "But you're right. There are falls near Aysgarth. I'll wait for you there and hide the weapons nearby."

They found their way down into the valley and walked along the river towards Aysgarth.

"I'll feel naked without Will's sword and Amelie's

knife," she said.

"You won't look naked," he said. "You can borrow my long knife if you get the urge to kill someone," he offered.

"I've got the urge to kill someone right now."

But she relented, moved closer to him and patted his arm.

"It'll take us the best part of the day to walk to Aysgarth," she said, "and my boots are worn through already. I've never walked so far in all my life."

"This, my precious lady, is how most folk travel all the time."

"Aye, I know, but they don't do it because they like it!"

§§§§§

The river water gushed noisily past her, scouring the rocks on the river bed as it raged eastwards over the falls. A fine spray of water caught the breeze and tiny droplets washed over her face. He had been gone for some time, the light was fading... and he was not back. The evenings were getting shorter now in any case. Soon it would be dark.

She stood up and shivered, her limbs stiff with cold. She tugged at her cloak, wrapping it closer around her and paced along the broad stone ledge. She had stowed away her weapons in the undergrowth amongst the trees near the river. She wondered whether she would need them again sooner than she thought.

Several hours had passed since he went into the village but her doubts had begun soon after he left. The longer he was away, the more certain she became that something had gone amiss. Rob Hall was clearly a fool - even more of a fool than she. All he had to do was talk to folk - and that was one thing they agreed he did passing well. He had probably just left her there. Men always abandoned her in the end.

It was a fault, she knew - this mistrust of those who

tried to help her. She was not good at accepting help, nor was she good at waiting, not very good at all. But then a thought sprang to mind and she wrestled with her doubts, remembering her rage at Ragwulf - loyal, brave Ragwulf. She had misjudged him badly once and treated him appallingly - another wrong that she could never erase.

She must learn to trust her friends better. What would Ragwulf advise? He would say: be calm, lady, be calm. Trust Rob Hall. She wiped a tear from her eye, smiled to herself and took a deep breath. She sat down again and watched the turbulent course of the river as the breeze strengthened and whipped up more spray onto her.

"Very well, Ragwulf," she whispered, "I'm calm. I'm very calm, but…what should I do if he doesn't come back?"

§§§§§

A hand shook her roughly from her sleep. She opened her eyes. It was dark.

"My lady!" An urgent whisper of warning and then the hand was clamped over her mouth.

She bit one of the fingers hard and the palm was torn away. "Oh, Jesus!" cried Rob.

"Rob?" she said.

"What did you do that for?" he replied crossly.

"I don't like to be attacked in my sleep!"

"Why would I attack you?" he hissed. "And keep your voice down!"

"Why? What's happened?"

"I'm being followed."

"Why?"

"I might have… stolen something…"

"What? You're an even greater fool than I imagined! Shit! What did you steal?"

But he was not listening to her and then she too heard above the noise of the rushing force. Horses.

"What did you steal that men would track you through the forest at night?" she demanded.

He held out a fat purse. "We had no coin, my lady…"

"You'll suffer for this folly!" she growled.

"Time for that later, my lady," he breathed and dragged her to her feet. "We must run!"

She was livid and would have hit him hard but if they must run, then she would run. For an instant she thought of retrieving her sword until she glimpsed a flicker of torchlight through the trees higher up the bank. She moved swiftly then, down along the river to the lower force. It was too dark and the water level was too high but crossing at the lower force was still the best option.

She stopped at the river's edge and tore off her cloak, bundling it up in her hands. Rob looked aghast at the river.

"We're not crossing that, are we?" he said.

"Aye, just follow me - swift but sure. It's the shortest - and nearest - crossing. I did it a hundred times in my youth. Come!"

"No!" he protested. "It's madness - you can't even see where to tread."

"I don't need to see," she said. "I could do it blind."

"We are doing it blind!" he cried.

She reached out to him. "Here, hold on to me - just cross quickly. Do you trust me?"

"Aye, of course!"

"Well don't! Because if you stumble and fall, I'll let you go!"

"I'll drown…"

"Then you'll sodding drown! Are you coming or not?"

She stepped out into the stream. His timidity fuelled her anger and made her reckless. His cold hand clamped onto hers as she strode out. A shout came from the trees near the bank behind them and instinctively they both turned towards it. Rob lost his balance and as she tried to pull him upright, his feet shot from under him.

She gasped as he fell and his weight dragged her down. He clung on to her hand.

"Shit!" she cried. She could have let him go, should have let him go, but she didn't and they sped towards the edge of the force together. They slid for ten yards and she tried to cling to the slippery rocks but Rob's flailing arms were little help.

The first fall knocked the air from their lungs. The second filled them with river water and then they crashed into the rocks below.

17

5th September 1468, at Bruges in Flanders

Ned woke up. It was very light, so bright he didn't want to open his eyes. He tried to recall where he might be. He wasn't in the damp cell any more. The last memory he had was a large, dark hall and this was not it. He was in purgatory…but, he couldn't be…because he wasn't dead. He blinked his eyes open and looked into the face of a complete stranger.

The man stared back at him. He looked surprised. Ned opened his mouth to speak. The stranger put a finger to his lips and Ned closed his mouth again. He tried to swallow but his throat felt as dry as sand. He tried to sit up but the stranger - who was beginning to annoy him - pressed a gentle hand down on his shoulder.

At last the man spoke, but his words brought Ned little relief for he spoke in Flemish. Ned's fogged mind could not recall a single word of Flemish despite having spoken it in a haphazard fashion for several years. It mattered little. When Ned ignored the stranger and tried to rise he found that his body made little response. So, whether he wanted to get up or not, he couldn't.

The stranger spoke briefly again and then walked away. Ned listened to his footsteps until he heard a door close. Then it was quiet, in fact silent - not even the sound of dripping water. That was good, at least.

Memories slipped unbidden into his head and every one brought questions. He had no answers. He felt like a small child who knew nothing, so he waited for others to come. He did not have to wait long. The chamber door banged open and he heard several men approach. A familiar face came into sight: Bear; then another, Ragwulf and finally, Spearbold.

Before he knew it, Ned was weeping. He thought they had abandoned him. He tried to speak but only a rattling croak escaped his lips. He tried again to get up and this time his friends helped him and sat him up against the bolster. For the first time he could see where he was: in a large and comfortable bed, in a plush chamber, with richly coloured tapestries on the wall in gold and green. The window to his left was tall and lavished light upon him. He was in a palace, it seemed.

He had a hundred questions and struggled to blurt out a single one. Fortunately, the faithful Spearbold anticipated his needs.

"My lord, you are safe and recovering - albeit slowly. You've been here for five days."

Ned looked about him.

"Where is here?" said Spearbold. "This place of opulence is a house in Bruges at the disposal of the new Duchess, Margaret of Burgundy, who has taken much interest in your recovery. As you see, Ragwulf and Bear have brought about your escape and the good physician who was here when you awoke was provided by the Duchess herself. All is well and you are in good hands, but you are very weak and it will take time for you to get your strength back. The doctor thinks it will be months… but then he does not know you very well."

"Thank you all," Ned attempted to say. He thought the words did not come out quite right but they all nodded so perhaps they understood.

"Now you must rest, my lord," said Spearbold.

Rest, thought Ned, he did not need much more rest…

§§§§

It must have been hours later when he opened his eyes again. It must have been, but it wasn't. Spearbold told him he'd been dozing for two days. Spearbold became very angry with him the first time he tried to get up and fell to the floor at once. It was then that Ned truly acknowledged that he had never felt so weak, that he needed to rest.

"My lord," Spearbold said sternly, "you went without food for weeks. You're lucky to have survived at all. The best way to kill yourself is to keep pushing and pushing when you've not an ounce of strength left in you!"

Weeks passed before Ned recovered sufficiently even to walk unaided around his chamber. And all that time his thoughts raced ahead. He was impatient to move, to get on, to find Thomas Gate - and, by the blood of Christ, to find Agnes.

"But there is so much to do, Spearbold," Ned cried.

"Well, you won't live to do it if you don't take it more slowly!" shouted Spearbold and went out, slamming the door behind him.

The day that Spearbold shouted at him, Ned reflected, was the day to take notice. So, he took it more slowly. He should have known better; it was not as if he hadn't been wounded badly before, but patience was not a quality he possessed in excess.

A week later, he had a visitor. She came alone and unannounced and stood next to his bed He worked out who she was almost at once. She was tall, he thought almost as tall as her brother. Her hair was fair, though a little golden perhaps. It was difficult to tell with the sun on it. It reminded him of someone else's hair. She was impressive rather than attractive but she had a pleasing smile and countenance.

"I am Margaret," she said, "Margaret of York." Her voice was light and soft. She smiled with embarrassment. "No, Margaret of Burgundy now," she said and sat down on the richly upholstered chair beside the bed.

"You honour me, your Grace, by coming here - and by all you've done for me."

"Lord Scales assured me that you did more than enough to save my life in Sluys. It seemed only right to do as much for you... if I could. You are a little better, I am told."

"I hope so, your Grace." He wondered how much she knew about him but it soon became clear.

"Lord Elder, I have written to my brother and told him of your deeds. I have asked him to end your exile - at once, if he is able."

"You are very kind, your Grace, but I fear the king may find it difficult to do so. I have enemies at court..."

"Not so many, my lord."

"Well, at least one - and one who matters a great deal to your brother."

The Duchess smiled. "We may share a common enemy then, my lord..."

"I should be pleased if you would call me Ned, your Grace. I'm Ned to your brother so I may as well be to you."

"Are you comfortable, Ned?" asked the Duchess. "Do you have everything you need?"

"Aye, your Grace, I'm well cared for - and by your own physician, I believe."

"Between us, I find him a very irritating man but the duke tells me he is most capable."

"This is a fine chamber, your Grace, a beautiful chamber. I suppose you must have many such houses now..."

"Alas, I have very few houses, Ned. This is the house of Louis van Gruuthuuse, a loyal courtier of the duke, and it is he who has made these rooms available to you."

She stood up abruptly. "But I can see that you are tired and still far from well. You don't need to entertain me with wit and conversation, Ned - I have plenty at the duke's court who can do that."

"Your grace, I will not stay more than another day or

two. You and your servants have been generous enough already."

She smiled. "Nonsense, Ned. You'll go when my physician allows it and not before. Let's see what the king, my brother, says. But first, my lord, you must get well."

"Thank you, your Grace," said Ned.

When she had gone Spearbold came in to see him.

"Where are you lodged?" Ned asked him.

Spearbold beamed. "Why, here in the house," he replied. "We've all three been well treated - Ragwulf and Bear are billeted in an excellent room near the stables."

"The Duchess is keen for us to stay," said Ned. "I'm not; we should be on our way - I've not forgotten Agnes. God knows what she's been through with Gate."

"Aye," acknowledged Spearbold, "and I think that Ragwulf's worried about Crag Tower."

"Oh? Why?"

"Well, we've not had time to discuss it, my lord, but Crag's been under attack for months."

"Attack? What, by Warwick?"

"No. It seems that the peace that once existed in your grandfather's time is no longer respected. Clans from across the border must see Crag Tower as weak and vulnerable or they would not take the risk. Ragwulf says that defending it has got harder and harder - especially with Wulf and some of the others gone."

"And I don't expect my sister was of much help either," said Ned. He had not forgotten how she had abandoned Amelie at Yoredale - there would have to be a reckoning between them for that.

Spearbold shrugged. "If Ragwulf is to be believed, Lady Eleanor has been a staunch defender."

"Hmm. I doubt it," grumbled Ned.

He tried to remember what it was like before when he had been badly wounded. But then he had Amelie, sweet Amelie to nurse him, body and spirit. Amelie, who had been left alone with her unborn child to meet her bloody end. Left there by his sister... his dear, flawed Ellie.

He slowly shook his head. It had started to ache the moment Spearbold began to relate their troubles. Ned did not want to face such problems. He was weary... the Duchess was right: he was not fit yet to go anywhere.

"Perhaps I'll need to rest a few more days," he said, "but you can start looking for passage to England."

Spearbold nodded. "Very well, my lord, it will be done."

"Wait... Spearbold..."

"My lord?"

"If I go back soon - and I'm going to - I shall break the terms of my exile. As soon as Warwick learns of my arrival in England, it'll get dangerous. I need to be careful for another six to eight months, or until the king is willing to receive me. I'll need to keep my head down but if Crag Tower needs me, we'll go there first. But..."

"My lord?" prompted Spearbold.

"Once I take ship, it will be hard to stop word getting out."

"I'll be most discreet, my lord," said Spearbold.

"I know, but I thought... see if you can find out where Finch is these days."

"My lord, I can try, but Master Finch could be anywhere from Genoa to Sweden!"

"The thing is, Spearbold, we can trust Finch, which is more than you can say for some ship's masters. Send word to Felix. He's certain to know where Finch is. That'll give me time to get stronger."

"Aye, my lord, indeed, Finch is a good fellow, a sound fellow. I'll write to Felix of Bordeaux at once."

18

6th September 1468 at dawn, in Middleham Castle

Her wrists were sore and she had hardly slept at all. If she could get to Rob, Eleanor would surely kill him, but he was at least a yard out of her reach. He hung from his chains, oblivious to all that had happened, most of the time unconscious or at best incoherent. Yet, Eleanor resolved to kill him if she got free, well... perhaps not kill.

Until they were taken to the guardroom, her captors did not see that she was a woman and Rob did not witness how they treated her when they found out. She almost got away with it but as they put the manacles upon her and held her up to chain her to the rusted iron rings on the wall, it all went badly wrong.

Her linen shirt, already torn in the descent from the falls, ripped open and there, in the gloom, a pink, scarred breast poked out. The men's surprise did not last long and they then wasted no time in exploring what they had uncovered. Several tried to kiss her, their hairy lips crushing her exposed teat and then moving on to her mouth. She bit one and kneed another. That extinguished their ardour a little but it also persuaded them to strip off her shirt and slap her about.

They would have done worse but for a man at arms who came in and sent them away. He looked at her and she smiled at him through her bleeding lips. She thought he would apologise, release her from her chains and take her out. He didn't do any of those things. All he said was:

"whore!" and went out, bolting the door shut after him.

Rob moaned.

"Be quiet," she said, "you useless, shit-headed…thief!"

If he heard her, he made no response; but then if he heard, he might think that no reply was the safest course. In that, if nothing else, he would be right.

After a long time in her own desperate company, however, Eleanor began to wish that she could talk to him. Aye, he was to blame - squarely to blame - for their troubles yet she did not really want him hurt. If she had, she could have let him go at the falls. Instead she had clung on to him and they rolled over the force together, swept along the river course and battered by boulders in the lower levels. They staggered to the bank and fell down, utterly spent. There was no fight left in them and their pursuers simply rode along and picked them up.

Now, they were at Middleham - and in Warwick's hands, she assumed.

Rob moaned again - if the bastard could manage more than a moan, it might help.

"Rob?" Her throat was dry and her voice cracked a little as she spoke.

He moaned once more, louder this time.

"Rob!" she shouted. "Wake up, you idle, thieving little shit!"

His head came slowly up and his eyelids fluttered, then a pair of glazed eyes opened. As he looked at her his eyes widened. He mumbled a few incomprehensible words.

"What?" she asked.

"You look great," he muttered with a sheepish grin.

She looked down at her naked breasts and groaned. At first she wanted to scream, or cry but in the end she just grinned back at him. Rob did that to her, he made her see humour even in the most trying of circumstances.

"Well, here I am, lover," she said, in a deep lust-filled voice. "Come and get me… oh, I forgot - you're all chained up."

"I'm sorry," he said and he looked it, she thought.

"If I ever get free you'll be even sorrier," she said, but said it without malice, said it because she knew it's what he expected her to say; said it, because it meant defiance rather than despair.

"Where are we?" he asked.

"In a makeshift gaol in a guard room at Middleham Castle."

"Is that bad?" he asked.

"Bad enough. Who were you stealing from - the Earl of Warwick himself?"

"No…it was an accident…almost. The purse…"

"…just dropped into your hand, did it?"

"Well, almost. It was just hanging there from his belt, a ripe apple begging to be plucked from the branch. And we had no coin…"

She sighed, beyond anger now. "And you were the man to take it. I suppose it didn't cross that feeble little mind of yours, as you reached out to pick the fruit that I sent you on a rather different task."

"Sometimes, I can't help it," he replied.

"Well you should learn to control your urges!" she snapped at him.

Where he had been contrite, now he smirked and then burst out laughing.

Eleanor could feel her blood rising, her face flushed. "And now, you laugh at me?" she growled.

"Aye, I do," he replied, still chuckling to himself, "for you, my dear lady, are not the one to tell me to control my urges."

She closed her eyes, deflated by that. How right he was: a subject best left well alone…

"What do you think they'll do to us?" he asked.

"You know that: they'll hang us both for thieves," said Eleanor.

"That's always the way it is, I suppose," he said, "but it's rough on you."

Eleanor said nothing.

"Now, hear me out on this before you jump at me," he said. "Your best chance is to let them have you and hope they'll let you go when they've finished with you."

"Have you lost the rest of your wits now?" she said crossly.

"No. Listen. Do you want to die? Make it easy on yourself. If you please them, you could escape quite lightly."

"Quite…lightly," she said. "I'm not sure whether to be pleased that you value the attractions of my body so highly or disappointed that you value my honour so little. If they made you such an offer, would you take it?" she asked.

"Well, no, but that would be different…"

She shook her head, cross that she could feel hot tears on her cheeks. "So, it's fine for me to be fucked by them, but not you. Because that's all women are good for isn't it!"

"I didn't say that!"

"It's more or less what you said though…"

She was angry but her anger subsided quickly. He was not her enemy, merely telling her accurately enough what her gaolers would do. She was a woman, even if she was not looking her best. She was a woman, she was chained up and half-naked. It did not require a wise man to tell her what to expect. Rob just wanted her to use it to her advantage.

"Lady," he said gently, "I don't want them to hurt you…"

"I know," she said, "I know."

Perhaps there was another way. They were at the Earl of Warwick's castle so she could ask to see him. But would he see some whore just because she asked? No. She would have to say who she really was and then he might see just her out of curiosity. But would he even know Eleanor Elder if he saw her? She could not recall ever seeing him - unless perhaps when she was a child. And if he looked upon her now, with her hair shorn and clothing in tatters, he would not see Lady Eleanor Elder; he would see a whore.

So, better not to risk announcing who she was. After all, Warwick had given Yoredale Castle and its lands to her cousin and Joan would certainly not be pleased to see Eleanor return - in fact no-one would be pleased. Perhaps Rob was right: there was only one way out.

"How long do you think we've got?" he asked.

"Not long, I'd guess. They'll want us hanged and buried early in the day."

"Will they not hear us, first?" he said.

"There's nothing to hear - they saw you steal and I ran with you. It's enough to pass swift judgement. Besides, we're in their way - they can hold us here for a few hours but this room's not used for locking folk up for long."

"We shan't draw a crowd then."

"No crowd, Rob. Be glad of that. We'll be hanged as common thieves and forgotten, that's all."

Soon they heard footsteps approaching the gatehouse, pounding a brisk passage towards their prison.

"Sounds as if they're in a hurry," observed Rob miserably.

"Listen," she said suddenly, "I'm going to take the other way…to live - if they'll let me."

"It's worth a try," he said, his voice quiet, defeated.

The door opened and three men came into the room. Between them they removed the manacles and unfastened the chains.

"Are you releasing us?" she asked.

"Hah! Hold your tongue girl or we'll cut it off!" said one. She saw the red welt on his mouth where she had bitten him the previous night.

"I want to make amends," she said in what she hoped was her sweetest voice. She seized his hand and put it on her breast. "Like this."

He looked at her suspiciously, but did not remove his hand and she felt his fingers exploring her. His two comrades stared at her.

"I could please all of you," she added hastily, "whenever you like - if you keep me and protect me from others."

"We're not taking a whore's word for that," said one of the others, a fat, round-faced fellow. "Do each of us now and then we'll see."

"We'll see?" she sneered. "I want more than 'we'll see.'"

"Take it or hang," said the first man, removing his hand from her breast.

Now she hesitated. She could not trust them but it was the only offer she had.

"Alright," she said, "let's do it."

The gaolers looked at each other and grinned.

"I don't want him watching!" she said, looking at Rob.

"Easily done, lass," said the fat one and brought his cudgel down onto Rob's head. He dropped like a woolsack and lay still.

"You've killed him!" she said.

"He'll be fit enough to hang later," he reassured her, "now forget about him and pay some mind to us."

He turned to the third, younger looking man. "Jack, keep an eye outside the door."

"Why me?" whined the lad.

"You'll get your turn - never worry. Just keep a good look out, that's all."

Eleanor forced a smile to her lips. "Who's first then?" she said and, even as she said the words, a crazy notion came into her head. She dismissed it at once and put her hand on the fat man's shoulder.

"Aye, alright then, "he said with enthusiasm, "I'm for first dig!"

"Hold hard," said the other, "she asked me first. I was the one made the deal."

"Do as you're told," replied the fat man, "you'll enjoy

watching me first."

"Come on, plenty for all," soothed Eleanor. She just wanted to get it over with before she lost her nerve completely.

"Shut your cow's face!" said the fat man and pushed her back against the wall. He held her there with one hand whilst he argued with his comrade. The insane idea crept once more into her mind and began to take root. She slipped from his grasp and threw herself at the first man. "You want me first, don't you?" she said. She wrapped her arms around him and kissed his neck.

"Wait there," he told her and pushed her away. He turned to the fat man. "There's no need for a scrap over her," he said, "you can go first. The tricky bitch is just trying to play us, is all."

Eleanor noticed that Rob was already stirring.

"I don't care which of you I have first," she said, "but it's cold and I wish you'd just get on with it!"

"Spoken like a true whore!" laughed the fat man.

It might have been his words or the way he said them or it might just have been her natural instinct but suddenly her wild idea took hold. She smiled at him and slid easily into his arms. She rubbed her bare breasts against his chest as he fumbled to undo his breeches. Her hand glided down as if to help him but her fingers found the hilt of his knife. As she put her other arm around his neck, she drew out the blade and stabbed him twice, hard, in the belly. His moans caused his comrade to guffaw loudly.

"Doesn't take much to please you," he said, laughing. "I'll want a bit more than that from you," he told Eleanor.

The fat man was whimpering and she could barely support him as his legs began to crumple. Breathless, she replied. "I'm going to give you everything I've got!"

He licked his lips but his amusement turned to horror as he watched the fat man fall and she came at him. He barely glimpsed Eleanor's blood-covered hand arcing towards him. He reached down for his weapon but her blade plunged once into his throat and he choked on blood. His final act was to fling an arm at her sending her slamming into the door.

Jack's voice outside called: "Is aught amiss?"

Eleanor with her back against the door gave a great moan and cried: "More, more, give it more!"

Her victim was still standing but blood poured from the wound and he could not speak. He looked at her with pure hate and staggered towards her, his hands outstretched to seize her neck. She dropped to her knees on the stone floor and thrust her knife up hard into his groin. He groaned and fell down upon her. She slipped aside and crawled across to Rob who had found his way onto his knees and was slowly taking in what she had done. There was blood everywhere.

"By Christ, my lady, I take it you changed your mind!" He got to his feet and lurched against her.

The gaoler, Jack, called out again: "it must be my turn by now!"

Eleanor pulled open the door. "It is. Come in," she said and, when he did, Rob cracked him on the skull with the gaoler's cudgel. Eleanor pushed the door to and leant against it.

Rob puffed out his cheeks. "I'll say this, my lady, travelling with you is never dull."

She wiped some of the blood from her upper body and wrapped her torn shirt loosely across her chest. Rob took a knife from Jack and kept a hold on the cudgel.

"We'd best move fast," he said. "Someone will come in here very soon and when they find this lot, they'll hunt us down like rats. We're not thieves anymore; we're murderers."

Eleanor took some deep breaths as she looked about her and took in what she had done.

Rob opened the door a crack and they peered out. "I don't suppose you know this place at all, do you?" he asked.

"No, only that it's vast."

"Excellent," he replied. "Well, there are men on the gate and we're not going to get past them looking like this. I say we go up and try to find an empty chamber - somewhere to hide till nightfall."

"Then what?" said Eleanor.

"How do I know? Perhaps by then it won't matter because they'll have found us already!"

She shrugged and they left the cell, closing and bolting the door. Then they hurried away from the gatehouse through an archway into a short passage. Beyond it lay an open courtyard which they crossed with a few swift steps. Eleanor was sure they must be seen - at the very least by the servants bustling about as they hurried from one building to another. She realised they were simply walking around the great stone keep and if they carried on would soon arrive back where they started at the guardroom.

"Let's try one of the ranges," she said. "There must be fifty chambers in this place."

She paused by an entrance, drawn in by the smell of freshly baked bread. The bake house - perhaps they could hide in a store nearby. She pulled Rob inside after her and the warmth from the ovens hit her at once. Two men turned, startled by their arrival and transfixed by Eleanor's appearance.

"Come on!" she said and led Rob back out and up an adjacent spiral stair to the floor above.

They hurried up the flight of steps and found themselves in a small vestibule with three doors leading from it.

"Which one?" he hissed. She shook her head.

Before they could make a decision, one of the doors opened abruptly and a woman appeared on the threshold.

"Alice? Nurse, is that you?" she called. Then she saw the pair of them and her jaw dropped.

Eleanor stared at her and blinked.

19

6th September 1468, at Middleham Castle

Eleanor bit her lip and, since it was already swollen, it hurt.

"Sister, you look dreadful," said Emma. "Your hair, your clothes, the blood..."

"We can't stand talking out here!" snapped Eleanor.

Emma hesitated and then ushered them into her chamber and shut the door.

"Are we safe here?" demanded Eleanor. "Is anyone likely to walk in on us?"

"No... I don't believe so...no...but where have you come from? And who is he?"

Eleanor was still in shock at finding her sister in Middleham of all places. She supposed that her arrival was equally shocking to Emma. So the two sisters stood facing each other for a while, saying nothing, whilst Rob looked from one to the other in confusion.

"I'm Rob Hall," he announced.

"What is he to you?" Emma asked her.

"He's our aunt's brother but don't mind him," said Eleanor. "We're prisoners, or rather we've just escaped."

"In here?" breathed Emma. "How? How are you a prisoner?"

Eleanor shook her head. She most definitely did not feel up to explaining that, besides which she had other concerns. "Never mind what I'm doing here, what are you doing here - here in the midst of our enemies? You told me you were taking holy orders - and I, like a fool, believed you!"

"It was more complicated than you think, Ellie - it's always more complicated than you think." She stared at Rob again. "Who did you say he is?"

Eleanor turned to Rob, seeking an ally. "Meet Lady Emma Radcliffe, my elder sister…mother…confessor … and judge."

"I'm Rob Hall, Lady Emma."

"So you said, but what is Rob Hall?" asked Emma, not even looking at him.

Rob hesitated, unnerved, Eleanor supposed, by the chill of her sister's question.

"What she said," he replied, "your aunt's brother…"

"He's my friend too," conceded Eleanor, realising the truth of it for the first time.

"Your friend?" said Emma, unable to suppress a smirk.

"Not in that way!" said Eleanor.

Emma turned away. "Well, you can't stay here for long - a few hours perhaps…"

"A few hours - is that all I'm worth?" said Eleanor.

"We're alright then for a while," Rob said. "Perhaps you could help us to get out?"

Eleanor frowned at him. "Sit down and be quiet," she told him. "I need to speak with my sister." She turned to Emma. "Well, did you take holy orders or not?"

"What does it matter whether she did or didn't?" Rob said. "She's clearly not in holy orders now, is she?"

Eleanor glared at him. "I told you to keep quiet!"

"Just now, my lady, we need clear heads not sharp words. Now please, talk to each other - or if not to each other, then to me!"

Eleanor sat down on Emma's bed. He was right…again. How could a man so foolish sometimes see so clearly? She might have asked him who had got them arrested in the first place - but she refrained. She rubbed her hands over her face and dragged her fingers back through what remained of her hair. She could feel the smears of blood in it.

"Oh, for God's sake, cover yourself!" said Emma.

Eleanor looked down to see that her torn and bloodied shirt had come untied. She rearranged the linen rag to cover her modesty.

"So," said Emma, "some plain speaking then?"

"Aye," agreed Eleanor.

"How do you come to be in Middleham?"

"We were trying to find Hal and the other young folk who left Crag Tower," she said.

"Hal is here?"

"Aye," said Eleanor, "so we believe."

"And did you find him?" asked Emma.

"No."

"So how did you end up here?"

"Well, Rob's a thief," said Eleanor, "and it seems he's not very good at it." She softened her words with a smile to Rob. "It also seems that they arrest thieves who aren't good enough. Now: your turn."

Emma sighed and leant back against the wall hung tapestry. "I did intend to take my vows as a nun. But then, a few months after you left for Crag Tower... I found I was with child."

"Garth's child?" said Eleanor, remembering the youth who had died at Coverham Abbey.

"Of course Garth's - who else would it have been?"

Eleanor nodded. "Go on."

"I couldn't stay at Coverham but I had to go somewhere to have the child. Canon Reedman went to Middleham to plead on my behalf."

"He went to Warwick?"

"No, not the earl, his lady, the Countess Anne. She's a kind lady and is much interested in children - she has two daughters of her own - and Richard, my boy, was already here as her husband's ward."

"Aye, taken here by Joan Elder!"

"Aye, but here nonetheless. Reedman asked the Countess if she would take me in for the confinement - and she did. As you see, several years later, I'm still here."

"Does she know who you are?"

"Of course she does - and she told me that the earl had no quarrel with me - or you, for that matter."

"Aye," said Eleanor, "but he has a blood quarrel with our brother…"

"I thought only of my children: the new child and Richard."

"Where are the children now?" asked Eleanor.

"Richard will be at his duties. He's seven now and quite the little page. I've come to love him better now, to forget his father. Alice, my daughter, is three. She's a sweet girl - she's with the nurse this morning."

She jumped away from the wall at a sudden outbreak of shouting and banging of doors outside.

Eleanor got up and peered out of the window. "They know now. They'll be after us. We can't stay here."

"Do they know who you are?" asked Emma.

"No, I'm sure they don't," said Eleanor.

"Very well, you can stay here till they've searched all the storehouses and the other obvious hiding places, then I'll take you down to one that's little used at present."

"We must get out," said Rob, "or we'll be taken for certain."

"Stay here," said Emma, "I'll find you something to eat - and by the look of you there's a little binding up needed too."

§§§§

It was dark. Eleanor pushed Rob's snoring body away. Whenever she woke up, she seemed to find Rob lying half on top of her. She was beginning to think it could not always be by accident. They were sleeping behind a stack of logs in the cellar of a tower which housed several latrines. The stench of the privies was appalling but at least it discouraged others from spending too long in the area. The tower was not far from the nursery which gave Emma a convenient excuse for using the spiral stair there. Her sister had brought them half a loaf that afternoon - for the bake house ovens were also, as they knew, nearby. The bread tasted like heaven and lifted their spirits a little.

Rob had slept most of the afternoon - not something that she was well equipped to do. Instead she brooded upon their situation and, however she turned it over, she could see no way out. Yet get out, they must. They would have to wait and hope. She would need to trust in her sister - which she never found easy.

Late in the evening Eleanor heard footsteps on the stair. She roused Rob from another period of dozing and he went to stand by the pile of logs from which he could see the steps. They had no light and the darkness was impenetrable. Eleanor recognised the footfall of a woman and, sure enough, it was Emma who stumbled on the last few treads and fell into the woodpile. Rob seized her and she gave a startled yelp. He let her go at once.

"You two will be the death of me," Emma groaned. "I dared not show a light for fear that it was seen and questions asked. I had forgotten fear, sister, until you returned."

"We're most grateful for your aid, my lady," said Rob.

"So you should be, but it's not going to be easy to get you out," she said.

"The gate is well guarded," said Eleanor. "We saw that much when we were brought in."

"That would have been the new north gate," replied Emma. "It has every latest means of deterring anyone from going in or out. But there are two gates…"

"Aye, we were housed near the other - on the east wall,"

said Rob.

"That is truly the only way out," said Emma, "and even that is a risk no-one would take lightly."

"Unless of course, they were sitting in here having killed a few of the castle watch…" said Eleanor.

"Aye," said Emma, "I know you're impatient to move. I know that well enough but you must wait a day or so - perhaps more. Then I can try to get you out of the east gate."

"How will the east gate be any easier?" asked Rob.

"Because it's in use all day and much of the evening. The gate is opened early and shut very late because it allows many of our craftsman and labourers in from their lodgings in the outer yard. There is much to and fro."

"When then?" asked Eleanor. "Tomorrow?"

"Be patient, I said. Give me time. I can get some clothes for you and perhaps some tools or other means of disguise. I assume you don't object to dressing as a woman, sister?"

In the darkness, Eleanor glowered at Emma. "I'll manage."

"We can cover your hair easily enough, but the cuts and bruises…well, we'll just have to hope the guards aren't too curious."

"We can explain those away - Rob is a notorious wife-beater," laughed Eleanor.

"Are you?" Emma asked him.

"No, of course he's not!" said Eleanor.

"This is no matter for merrymaking!" her sister said angrily. "I'm taking all the risks here. I walk in the shadows to bring you succour. It is I shall be lying to and thieving from people who've taken me in and called me friend!"

"And we are grateful, sis. We are," said Eleanor and she meant it.

"I don't want your gratitude, I want you gone - and gone forever from my life and the lives of my children!"

Emma's tone was cold and her words struck Eleanor

hard. "I always thought that we were poor friends, but rather better sisters…" she said.

She felt Rob's arm slide around her waist and for once had no desire to shrug it off.

"I must go," said Emma. "Don't wander out of here. I'll return sometime tomorrow; I don't know when."

And she was gone; her light step padding up the stone treads of the stairwell until it faded away. For the rest of the night Eleanor was grateful for Rob's comfort. He asked nothing of her and she fell asleep feeling secure in his arms.

§§§§

They spent another two days in the tower cellar but it could have been much worse, Eleanor reflected. Emma brought them bread and some ale whenever she could and they even had the use of a privy at night if they risked climbing a few steps. Finally, Emma brought a clean linen shift, a kirtle and wimple for Eleanor to wear and a small bag of tools for Rob.

"I thought you might pass for a stone mason and his wife," she said, "if no-one looks too closely!"

"When do we go?" asked Eleanor.

"Now."

"Now?" said Rob.

"Aye, now! The gate will be open for a while longer and it's near dusk now. It's the best time. You'll say you've been doing some work in the north range, Rob - there's always something being added there, best say it's a fireplace. Tell them you are housed in the outer courtyard. After that, you're on your own. You'll have to take some horses from the stables - don't take ones that have clear markings. There'll be trouble over that but I suppose if you're tried as horse thieves it'll be no worse than murder. At the outer gate you'll have to use your wits, make something up but try to cause the least disturbance you can."

"You've done very well for us," said Rob.

"Aye," said Eleanor, "I won't forget."

"No, do forget. Forget me and never come back. Leave me to my quiet, safe life here."

The two sisters faced each other in silence for a time whilst Eleanor laced up her bodice and Rob fiddled with his clothing.

"One last thing," said Emma. "I went to see Canon Reedman today. He told me that Hal had left word for you: he has gone home to Corve Manor."

"Oh, thank God!" said Eleanor, feeling the relief almost overwhelm her. If Hal had taken John to the safety of Corve, then it was the best possible course he could have chosen.

"Then we shall follow him there," she said and embraced Emma one last time.

"I'll go back up now," said Emma. "Wait for me to leave and then go: left out of the tower, past the north range and round to the east gate. And…may God watch over you - both of you."

She was gone in a moment and after a short while they set off up the steps, with Rob leading and trying not to crash his tools against the wall. It would not do to be discovered before they got outside into the yard. Eleanor kept prodding him in the back to go faster. At the top of the steps he halted.

"Lady," he whispered, "stop pushing me. We must move slowly, naturally, lest our hurrying causes us to be noticed."

"There's no-one here to notice us yet!" she hissed.

As they passed the north range Rob said "Let's start talking about fireplaces."

"Not till we have to," grumbled Eleanor, "for it's going to be a very brief discussion."

To their surprise they passed through the east gate with no trouble at all. The outer yard was a noisy, busy place even at dusk and an assortment of unpleasant smells assaulted them at once.

"Slaughterhouse to our left, I'd say," said Rob, holding his nose. "By God - that's a place I'd not like to work all day."

"Pay attention!" snapped Eleanor. "Stables are in the far corner to the right. Look."

"Right, lady, Wait here. I'll find a couple of mounts."

"Let's hope you're better at stealing horses than most other things," retorted Eleanor, "but I can't just stand here like a whore touting for clients."

"We could do with some coin though," said Rob.

She slapped him fondly around the head. "Go on. I've an idea. I'm going to speak to the men on the outer gate."

"Oh, shit! Is that wise? What for? You'll get us caught before I've even got the horses."

"No," she said firmly. "Just get the horses and come straight to the gate - but not as if you're in a hurry."

"But I am in a hurry!"

"Go!" she said and watched him trot off towards the stables. Then she covered her face a little more with the wimple Emma had provided and headed straight to the gate. There were several men at arms on guard by the gatehouse and more above on the rampart. Even in the dying light she could make out bows and crossbows up there. Their departure must seem right or they would be cut down before they travelled more than a few yards.

She began weeping - or at least the appearance of it. She stopped twenty paces or so from the gate and stood as if waiting impatiently. She had a knife under her skirts but it occurred to her just then that getting it out swiftly would be almost impossible. She began to pace up and down before the gate, sighing loudly and occasionally weeping. She knew that sooner or later curiosity would encourage one of the guards to speak to her - and eventually one did.

"What's the trouble, mistress?" he enquired. He was

actually quite well-formed and rather good-looking, she thought.

She could already see Rob making his way slowly out of one of the stables with two horses but she turned her back to him. She would hear soon enough if someone yelled out "thief!" Instead she drew nearer to the man who had spoken to her.

"I've just had word that my mother's ill in Carperby," she said, with a voice full of woe. "My husband's not keen to take me this late?"

"I don't blame him!" grunted the guard. "You could lose your way in the dark. Best wait till morning."

Eleanor clutched his arm. "But she's near to die and I'm the only one of her children who still lives. My husband knows the tracks to Carperby well - he's just too idle, that's all."

The guard glanced behind her. "Well, he's bringing your horses now, mistress," he said.

She looked at Rob. "Aye, but see how slowly he's coming. Perhaps you could hurry him up for me - put the ire of God into him."

"Aye," nodded the guard with a grin, "why not?"

When Rob arrived with the horses, he smiled at Eleanor but the guard spoke harshly to him.

"Show a bit more haste, man," he urged, "or this poor woman's mother'll be in the grave before you get her to Carperby!"

Rob stopped and looked at him in astonishment.

"Don't just stand there like a pudding; help your wife to mount her horse! Come on move, you sluggard!"

Eleanor choked back her laughter but there were truly tears in her eyes now. She favoured the guard with a wan smile and pressed his arm in gratitude.

Rob was shaking his head as he lifted her into the saddle and held her hand long enough for her to adjust her legs and skirt to sit on the mount.

The guards hurried them through the gate and wished them: "God speed!"

They rode off, turning at once to ride around the castle walls and take the track that led out to the west.

When they were a mile or more from Middleham, Eleanor could contain her amusement no longer and spluttered into a fit of laughing.

Rob stared at her. "Sometimes…" he said.

"Your face," she giggled. "You looked terrified."

"How was I to know you'd made up some story? I didn't know what the bastard was talking about."

She reached across and took his hand. "It worked though, didn't it?"

"Aye, it worked, but we might have ridden out without all that fuss!"

"Well, I enjoyed it," she said.

"Where now?" he asked wearily. "Unless you're intending to ride on all night."

"No. There's a place I know, a ruined mill. We must collect my sword on the way but we can stay at the mill for the night and then ride on at dawn."

"Where is Corve anyway?"

"I don't know, well not exactly."

"Well, how will we find it then?"

"We'll go to Felix in Ludlow - he'll take us to Corve."

"And do you know how to find Felix - or Ludlow?"

"Too many questions, dear Rob - and too much noise. I need to pay attention to where I'm going now or I'll never find the mill in the dark, let alone Ludlow!"

20

10th September 1468, in the chapel at Middleham Castle

"The priest here thinks that you come to hear my confession," said Emma.

Canon Reedman smiled. "But, I do," he protested. "And to offer any spiritual guidance I may."

"Your advice goes far beyond the spiritual," she said, "and I would have been lost without your kindness over the years."

"We white canons have a rather broader brief than most monks," he said.

She shook her head. "Not as broad as you make it."

Only a day after Eleanor had left, she was relieved to find that her life returned very easily back to its comfortable routine. She did not want it to be disrupted again. Her children meant more to her now than ever before. To see her son, Richard, grow and flourish was something she had not been able even to imagine before. They sometimes called him Dickon as a jest after the young Duke of Gloucester who had spent a year or so at Middleham. He had been good with the younger pages, encouraging them in their learning and in their practice of knightly skills. And Alice, so young and so pretty - in time she would make a good match with the help of the Countess. Emma had no quarrel with the Earl and the Countess of Warwick - and she didn't want one.

"I assume that I am not just here to receive your praise," said Canon Reedman.

"No. I needed to speak to you about … my brother Ned."

"You've heard from Lord Elder?"

"No, but Eleanor told me that he has been found. Well, it seems he's been in Flanders these past four years and has now just recently disappeared."

Reedman listened impassively, as he always did.

"It's possible that he might come back," she continued. "I've heard the gossip around here of late. There's talk that he may be back already. I'd paid no mind to it but, after what Eleanor said, he could be here now!"

"And… you aren't too pleased about that," said Reedman.

"I do not wish harm upon my brother, Canon. I would never want that. It's just that wherever he goes, wielding his great sword, it seems that sorrow is not far away. I just want to live in peace and see my children grow up and prosper. Is that too much to hope for?"

"You've had much sorrow in your young life, my lady, and I see no reason why you should endure any more of it."

"But that's the problem. Ned will come to you - as Hal did, and Eleanor would have. And he will ask about Hal, Eleanor and the others."

"And I will tell him what I know, as I did Hal."

"But you did not tell Hal about me," she said.

"Hal did not ask about you - besides it was not his business to ask."

"Aye, but it will be Ned's business and he will ask about me."

Reedman fell silent for a while. "You don't want me to tell him you are here?"

"If he knew I was here, he would try to 'rescue' me and I don't need rescuing."

"But I could tell him that," said Reedman.

"And he would ignore you and come for me - I know my brother. You would need to lie to him, Canon. Lie to his face, deny you know what became of me."

Reedman gave an involuntary shiver.

"You must tell him that the rest have gone to Corve and that you know nothing of me at all," she said.

"I have always been prepared to bend some rules to help you, my dear," said Reedman, "but to tell a deliberate falsehood - that is rather different."

"A deliberate falsehood aye, but one that will protect me and my children."

"I shall have to consider this. I shall have to discover whether God thinks it is the right thing to do or not."

"In your heart," Emma said, "you'll know it is the best course."

Reedman shook his head. "A lie might make matters worse - who can know except God?"

21

10th September 1468, at the old mill near Carperby in Yoredale

Eleanor woke up and shuddered. A chill breeze rattled the old mill's fragile walls where shafts of watery sunshine broke through. The abandoned structure had deteriorated a great deal since she was there with Ragwulf. The blackened shell of the building had not weathered very well since she had last seen it. More roof timbers had rotted away and fallen. It would not survive another winter, she thought. She felt somehow disappointed.

She shook Rob awake and he crawled stiffly up onto his knees.

"By Christ! Why would you want to come here?" said Rob.

She could see his point. It seemed a sad and lonely place now and even she found it hard to conjure up the fond memories she held, memories she had lived on for four years, memories of Ragwulf …and John.

"Something to eat?" he mumbled.

She pulled a face. "There's water still in the mill race…" she said, "better take the horses along there at least."

He shrugged and stood up. They took the horses to drink and then Rob saddled them.

"We'll need to beg or steal a loaf somewhere," said Rob.

"You are not to steal anything else! Do you understand?" she asked as they set off southwards. "You can eat when we reach Corve."

"And how long's that going to take?"

She laughed. "A day or two!" She was guessing for she had no idea.

"Back to stealing then…"

"No! You'll only get us into more trouble."

"You're riding a stolen horse now…"

"That's different," she said.

"So stealing's alright if you don't want to walk but not if you're starving?"

"Be quiet!" she snapped.

"Ah, you see. You don't like hearing the truth -"

She pulled up and seized his arm. "No, I mean just stop making a noise!" she said but it was too late. She had heard the hoof beats and now they could both see the riders heading along the track towards them. Instinctively they turned and fled.

"Halt!" someone shouted. Never a good sign, thought Eleanor.

"Come on," she said, "we'll cut through the trees."

"Are you sure?" asked Rob, eyeing the forest warily. "It looks damned thick in there!"

"Don't argue!"

Eleanor launched her horse off the narrow track and into the forest. There was always a way through if you knew the forest well enough - and she did. Here, higher up the valley slopes, the trees were thinner, hazel and birch mostly. She was heading south down into the valley where there was a spread of oak and ash, with hazel filling the spaces between the larger trees. If they could get there, then they could lose any pursuer.

She did not look back despite the shouts and was reassured to hear Rob's mount just behind keeping up well with hers. An arrow suddenly thudded into a great oak branch by her head. She ducked belatedly and gave a nervous laugh. A quick glance behind told her Rob was still there hunched low over his mount as wiry hazel branches scratched at his face. They rode on for another mile or so then she came slowly to a halt in a stand of large oaks. There she sat and listened but all she could hear was Rob gulping in lungfuls of air.

"Hush! I'm trying to listen," she whispered.

Rob was about to speak but she silenced him with a gesture and then carried on listening until she was satisfied.

"That arrow was close," she grinned, "almost made me jump out of my saddle!"

He grimaced. "I wasn't… quite so lucky."

She looked at him properly then and saw his face was grey. "Oh no, dear God, you were hit."

"Nothing mortal," he said. "Nothing that won't heal. It's just a bit sore, that's all."

She helped him dismount and saw the patch of blood at once. She examined the shaft protruding through his worn leather jerkin and swiftly snapped it off. He gave a yelp.

"Don't be such a child," she scolded him and took off his jerkin. Then she helped him sit down against one of the tree trunks. The wound was in his side and did not look too bad.

"Does it hurt much?" she asked.

"Of course it fucking hurts!"

"Oh, I'm sorry," she said.

He gave her a weak grin. "I was just fishing for some sympathy," he said. "It's not so bad. I don't think I've lost much blood."

Eleanor gave him a playful punch on the shoulder but she was still concerned. Rob would not be able to ride far without making the wound worse. He certainly would not get to Corve or even Ludlow where Felix was.

"If we can get the head out, it'll be fine," she said.

"Have you ever taken out an arrow head?" he asked.

"No."

"Thought not…"

"Have you?" she asked.

"Oh, aye," he said, "but not out of my own flesh. I

could tell you how to do it though."

"I'm sure I could do it."

"The blood wouldn't put you off and you're good with a blade. Depends how far it's in…"

Eleanor tore his shirt away from the wound and examined it more closely.

"It's gone in a long way, I think," she said. She spoke quietly for she knew already that she could not do it.

"Listen," Rob said, "if you can stick a man with your knife to kill him, then you can do the same to save him, can't you?"

"But I don't care what happens to someone I'm trying to kill."

"Well, I'm pleased that you care - but what difference does caring make?"

Caring, she thought, made all the difference in the world. She forced herself to think: they could not stay where they were. The old mill was still close, but exposed. If they were trapped there they would not get away a second time but there was nowhere else. She needed help - someone like Canon Reedman - but he was all the way over at Coverham. The chances of getting there without being discovered were remote. Emma was at Middleham - but that was just as far and twice as dangerous.

"We're going back to the mill," she told him.

He grinned at her - that silly, familiar grin. "I put myself in your capable hands, Red."

"Aye, but you're a fool…"

§§§§

They were obliged to take their time getting back to the mill and it was almost midday when they reached it. Eleanor settled Rob down in the driest, warmest part of the ruin which still possessed the remains of a roof. She gathered what dry kindling she could find and built a small fire. In the bag of tools Emma had given them was a flint, but she was unused to handling it and lighting the fire took her a long time. She looked again at Rob's wound. Watery blood leaked from the ragged hole where the arrow had gone in.

"You can do this," he urged. She shook her head.

"You must do this," he said softly. "There's no-one else…"

She took out her knife.

"It needs a keen edge on it," he said.

She nodded and spent a little time sharpening it against one of the mill's old grindstones and then held it in the fire for a time.

"Try not to burn me to death," he quipped but she was in no mood now for laughter. Her stomach churned just thinking about what she was going to do. He seemed to understand for he put his hand gently over hers.

"It'll be fine," he said. "Just do exactly what I tell you."

She nodded.

"Now, the first thing you need to know is that a knife is not the best tool to use for this."

"What!"

"Now don't panic," he said swiftly, "but usually it works best with a couple of rounder objects - spoons or something like. It stops the head ripping the flesh on the way out."

"Shit! Why are you only telling me that now?"

"So that you know to watch for that and that you'll have to make a bigger hole to get it out. You need to understand that. There'll be blood but don't rush it or you'll tear the head out. That's not going to be a good idea."

She nodded, incapable of speech. She was trembling with fear - it was ridiculous, a woman that could face down several armed men and yet could not face a task where there was no danger for her at all.

He cut a piece of leather from his jacket and folded it into a thick pad. "Something for me to bite on if the pain gets too bad," he said.

She took a deep breath. "Are you ready then?" she asked.

"No, but let's do it anyway."

She nodded again and put the point of the knife to the wound.

"You'll tell me what to do?"

"Aye, go to it lass. Slide the point of the blade into the wound alongside the arrow shaft."

She did as he instructed and inserted the blade. He grunted, taking short breaths.

"Can you…feel… the shaft?" he asked.

"Aye." Her hand was shaking as she gently eased the knife in.

He was sweating and breathing hard but she understood what he meant. She could feel the wood of the shaft, hard against the steel but the blade was already half its length into his flesh.

They were both trembling when the point of the knife reached the arrowhead.

"Now…pay…close attention," he said, grinding the words out slowly, "this is the hard part." Then he passed out.

"Rob?" gasped Eleanor, thinking for an instant he was dead. She hesitated, biting her lip till it bled. She was frozen there with her knife in the wound but frightened to do any more with it. Her ignorance could easily kill him. Gently she withdrew the blade and threw it aside. At once she regretted it. She should have persevered and cut out the head. She stared at the offending knife lying by the fire.

When he came to later, she could see he was disappointed that she had not removed the arrow.

"I didn't know how to do it," she said. It sounded lame and weak. She despised weakness - even more in herself than others.

Rob took her hand and squeezed it gently. It was a gesture of love and she knew it. She kissed him on the forehead and then, because she knew he needed it, she kissed him on the lips.

"I would have got wounded sooner," he muttered, "if I'd known what you'd do for a wounded man."

"Peace," she said pressing her fingers lightly against his lips. "I'll have to take you to Reedman - I can't take the arrow out."

"Let's just leave it there," he said, "as something for folk to wonder at."

"Fool."

"You know I can't ride to Coverham Abbey," he said. "You'll have to go and bring the Canon here."

"But what if someone comes while I'm gone, or you feel worse?"

He shrugged. "And what would you be able to do if either of those things happened while you were still here?"

Nothing, she realised, but leaving him would be hard.

"I'll go just before dawn," she said. She built the fire up a little then lay down beside him and held him close.

He winced. "Gently, Red, gently..."

22

11th September 1468, at Coverham Abbey

It took Eleanor several hours to get to Coverham but, once there, it proved easier than she expected to find Canon Reedman. There was a new gatekeeper since her last visit and she was heartily glad of that. She had reluctantly left her weapons at the mill - aside from Amelie's knife. Dressed as she was, and with her hair covered, the white canons of Coverham paid little attention to her. It amused her as she passed each one and they did not recognise her as the demonic woman who had railed at them - and in particular, their abbot - when she was last there.

Even Reedman did not recognise her at first.

"How can I be of help to you, goodwife?" he greeted her.

She resisted the temptation to laugh and instead revealed her true identity.

"Of course!" he said, unable to hide his consternation. "Lady Emma has spoken of you."

"Oh, I'm sure she has," said Eleanor darkly.

"Your sister has given you help at great risk to herself," Reedman chided.

"Aye, she has," admitted Eleanor. "And it was nearly enough…but my friend has been wounded." She explained what had happened and asked him to return to the mill with her.

At first she thought he was going to refuse.

"If you have been hunted," he said, "then you may be

hunted again. The mill is hardly a safe refuge."

"Would you rather have us here, Canon?"

He gave brisk shake of the head. "No - and you must be gone before the abbot returns. I fear he'll see through your disguise quicker than I did - but then he has more reason to remember you than most."

She recalled her threats against the treacherous abbot - and knew that she would deliver the same vile insults at him again if the chance arose. Reedman was right: best to avoid that. She had a talent for making a terrible predicament even worse.

"I'll come with you," he said, "but we must be careful."

He gathered all he thought he might need and fetched some bread, cheese and ale for them from the abbey kitchen. It was after midday by the time they actually left Coverham but the weather was dry, if a little cool, and they made good time alongside the river Yore. As they forded the river and ascended into the forest, Eleanor was alert for any sound of men or horses. This was when they were closest to Yoredale Castle and thus at most risk. Soon Eleanor pulled up.

"You go on along the track," she said. "No-one will worry about you - but they might recognise me from the chase. Just make sure you're not followed and I'll take a longer route and meet you at the mill."

Reedman nodded and rode on. She watched him go and headed back to the south, skirting along the forest's edge to loop around to the west before turning back north to Carperby. When she finally arrived at the mill she was pleased to see that Reedman had already tended to Rob's wound.

"You've taken it out?"

"Aye," said Reedman, but his tone told her that all was not well.

"And?" she prompted.

"It is a deep wound. I've done the best I could but…"

"But?" she asked. The need to coax him to explain was beginning to anger her.

"It's in God's hands now," was all he would say. "I can do no more. I've washed the wound with wine and applied a poultice of crushed yarrow and honey. Either the wound will heal or it will not."

"But, do you think it will heal?" she asked.

"I don't know. It's in …"

"…God's hands. Aye, you said."

"My lady, this is not the best place for him…"

"You hardly need to tell me that, Canon! As soon as he's fit enough to ride, we'll go on to Corve."

Reedman looked at Rob and then back at her. "And if his wound does not heal, what then, my lady?"

"I'll stay with him until it does."

"I'll return in three or four days. If you're gone, all's well; if you're still here, you'll need my help - one way or another."

"Thank you, Canon. And I am most grateful for your help."

"Do you want me to tell your sister?" he said.

"Wait until you return here. If we are gone then there's nothing to tell her."

Reedman nodded and left them. Eleanor tended the fire and pondered what she would do if Rob's wound did not heal.

§§§§

It took two days for Eleanor to be sure that Rob was getting worse. He became feverish on the second night and she decided to examine the wound, carefully peeling off Reedman's linen dressing. Under it the small mound of poultice had cracked and a small amount of foul smelling liquid was oozing from the wound. She had suffered some terrible wounds in the past but had never had to treat them herself. She did not recall the smell though; it was surely not a good sign.

Church bells tolled in the distance. It must be Sunday and the bells were summoning folk to worship. She had lost track of the days. Reedman would not be able to get away today. She must manage until the morrow. She replaced the strip of linen and used part of her shift to wipe the sweat from his face. His skin was hot to the touch and as day turned to evening he became restless. It was not an easy night and by morning his face looked ashen and the putrid smell of the wound was stronger. His eyes were open but nothing he said made sense. His breath was short and wheezing; he sweated constantly but seemed to shiver as if cold. He could not eat and when she poured some ale into his mouth he could not swallow it and it just dribbled down his chin.

She knew she could wait no longer. She needed Reedman now, or it would be too late. She hated to leave Rob and kissed his cheek.

"I'll come back with Reedman," she told him softly. He showed no sign that he had heard but before she left he gripped her hand so tightly that she was forced to prise off his fingers to leave.

She brushed away her tears and rode fast through the forest, abandoning all prudence in her quest to bring Reedman back. She had good fortune and encountered none of the patrols she had feared. She arrived at Coverham exhausted but relieved only to discover that Reedman was not there. Some of the canons thought he might be at Aysgarth but others suggested that he might have gone to the parish church in Coverham. She felt like screaming for in truth none of them knew for certain. All she could do was search for him so she left at once.

The mare she rode was already tired and she could not persuade it to go faster than a walk. It took her the rest of the day to get back to Aysgarth where she enquired of Reedman only to be told he was not there either. It occurred to her then that perhaps the canon had returned to see Rob again - sooner than he had promised. Whether he had or not, there was nothing to be gained from wandering Yoredale looking for him. Better that she got back to Rob to give him some comfort at least.

She was about half a mile short of the old mill when her luck ran out. She heard them coming along the track behind her. Her horse was spent and she was walking alongside the mare. She was too tired to run and quickly decided that perhaps it was for the best. At least Rob could be taken to Yoredale Castle and given some care there. She stopped and waited for them.

"God give you good even, mistress," said one as they rode up. "It's late for you to be riding on your own in the forest."

She was ready to play again the role of the stone mason's wife.

"My husband is wounded," she said, reckoning that she sounded pitiful enough without any further dissembling on her part. "We were travelling from Middleham, where he works as a mason, to see my sick mother in Carperby. Then we were set upon by thieves and my husband was injured."

She thought her tale was going rather well until one of the others said: "Arrow wound was it?"

She stared at him and he grinned back at her. "You're the pair who didn't stop the other day when we told you to. That's my arrow your husband's been wearing."

"We thought you were thieves!" she cried.

"Well, we're not," said the one who had spoken first.

"Well who are you then?" she demanded.

"My name is Weaver and I serve Lady Joan Elder. You can come with us to Yoredale Castle. She - or her husband - can decide what to do with you."

"Very well," she said, beyond caring. "But will you see to my husband first? He's at the old mill."

Weaver nodded to two of his men. "Take her up to the

castle and wait for me there."

Eleanor looked at Weaver. "You will take care of him, won't you," she pleaded.

"Never fear, goodwife," said Weaver, "you don't need to worry about that man of yours."

Eleanor mounted the mare and followed his men up to the castle. So, in the space of a few days she had escaped a cell at Middleham only to ride into a prison of a different kind at Yoredale. The sight of its towers chilled her for she knew what it meant: Joan Elder. She might pass as a mason's wife to some but not to Joan Elder. Joan had seen her close, very close and she would not forget Eleanor's face. All she could do was hope that at least Rob might be saved. Then it struck her with the force of a war hammer: Joan would know Rob Hall as well as anyone for he was Maighread's brother and Joan had lived with Maighread most of her life at Crag Tower. She would know Rob Hall very well and she would loathe him, just as she loathed his sister.

Eleanor's misery was almost complete but she consoled herself that at least John was safe in Corve with Hal, so she could rest easy on that count.

§§§§

Weaver rode up to the burned out mill and dismounted swiftly. He took cover beside part of the remaining stone work, keeping himself hidden from anyone inside. If Master Hall was in there, he was damned quiet - but then he was supposed to be wounded. Still, a wounded, cornered man might still give him some trouble, he thought, if he was not careful. Weaver prided himself on being careful. He drew out his sword and listened for a while longer then he snatched a look around the wall: the mill was empty. He cursed under his breath. Perhaps he had not been so careful after all - the mason must have heard his approach.

He found the man's bed soon enough but there was no-one in it. He felt the woollen blanket - still warm and damp with pus or blood or some other unpleasant shit upon it. He wiped his hand on it and stayed crouching on the floor. The wounded man must have just left but, by the look of what was leaking out of him, he wouldn't get very far.

Weaver stood up and sheathed his sword. Cautiously, he cast about outside the mill. Where would he go? Not the river path - too open. He stared into the trees all around him. It would be hard going for an injured man, but the forest offered the best chance of escape. He examined the tracks around the mill but the ground was dry and hard, making tracking near impossible. He'd need a score of men to track the fellow down and he doubted it was worth the effort. By the bitter stench of his bedding, Master Hall would not last long. Alone in the forest, he was as good as dead.

23

18th September 1468 in the evening, at Yoredale Castle

"I swear, Thomas, you're feeding every wretch in the shire! They flock to us, more and more each day and yet you welcome them with open arms."

Joan stood in the gallery above the Hall, looking down upon the torch-lit chamber with ill-disguised disgust. Thomas also surveyed the crowded Hall, though for different reasons.

"What are you doing?" she asked him. "You are clearly gathering men - but why?"

He looked across at her and smiled. Her blunt manner amused him. She could be a charming woman - if she wanted to - but it seemed that she wanted to less and less frequently. The flickering light gave her features a hard edge. There was a severity to her beauty which she accentuated with tall, ornate head dresses. She wore fine cauls with elaborate horns, thinking them the height of courtly fashion. In her own way, Joan was a work of art.

"When I need to tell you about it, dear wife, I shall do so," he replied amiably. "For now, it's not your concern."

"It is my concern if my Hall is being crammed with the dregs of the north!"

"Well, legally, it ceased to be your Hall a month or two ago," observed Thomas.

"You told me that Yoredale would always be mine," she said.

Her words were not said in anger, he noted, and smiled

at her. She played the game with a cool head. There was something very alluring about that. He took her hand, so cold and stiff.

"Are you so easily satisfied, with this one castle?" he asked. "I don't believe so."

"What then?" she said, more interested now.

"We are allies, my lady, allies following a common path."

He suddenly pulled her close so that their faces almost touched. She was momentarily taken by surprise but soon recovered her composure.

"And what path are we following, my lord?" she said, her eyes blazing into his. There was her anger, he thought, seeking out his soul.

"The path that leads ever upward," he replied softly. "The path you took to seize this little castle…the path you took into Warwick's favour. That is still the path we follow."

"That path was bloody, my lord," she whispered.

He put his hands upon her shoulders and then began to dismantle her headdress.

"And it will get bloodier yet, my lady," he said and drew her to him in a fierce embrace. At first she gave a show of resistance but he swept her up and carried her into the nearest bed chamber. It was darker there where only a single candle cast its shimmering glow. He kissed her again hard, but she broke the embrace and twisted away from him. He smiled, because she was not running. She waited with her back to the wall and where before she had been cool and aloof, now she was hot and breathless. He tore the mesh caul from her head, releasing her dark brown hair to fall wantonly about her neck.

"And what do you plot then, my lord?" she said, gasping as he started to explore her body with his hands. "Why do you need so many men?"

He pressed his lips against her throat, feeling the

trembling anticipation there. Wrapping his arms around her, he began to loosen the ties at the back of her gown.

"A great prize requires a great many men," he said, easing the cloth from her shoulders.

"Great prizes carry grave risks, my lord," she said. Her face glowed as she stroked his chest and began to untie his shirt.

He kissed her breasts as the linen shift fell away to the floor. "Very grave risks…" he echoed softly.

"And what, my lord," she paused to nuzzle against his bare chest, "is the great prize?"

He pulled her down upon the bed. "Why, power, my love."

She hauled off his tight breeches and lay on top of him, wrapping her legs around his.

"And what will power bring me, my lord?" she murmured.

He turned her on to her back and her hair fanned out on the stark white of the bedcover. He caressed her from chin to waist.

"That depends how far along the bloody path you are willing to go?" he said, gently massaging her thighs.

"Oh, I will not be content in this small backwater, my lord. Like you, I want the great prize," she said. "And the great prize will need to be … secured with an heir." She slowly parted her legs and pulled him down into her.

Thomas smiled. His wife was a whore at heart, he thought, but for now he would let the whore have her dreams.

§§§§§

Joan was taking a bath. She liked to bathe in the morning; it helped her wash away the sins of the day before - God knew she had plenty of sins. She knew it did not really wash them away but that pathetic priest, Baston, who lolled about the chapel all day, certainly did little to assuage her guilt.

She had enjoyed the previous evening. Thomas did have his uses. The church taught that she would bear a child only if Thomas moved her sufficiently. Well, the priests could take it from her that she had been thoroughly moved last night.

Thomas had his plans it seemed, but she had some of her own irons in the fire. One advantage of all the newcomers to the castle was that it gave her an opportunity to recruit her own men - and women. It took care, of course, very much care to build loyalty and trust. She rewarded them with small favours - some men were content if she merely smiled at them, others were hers if she laid a gentle hand upon their arm. Women were different and they wanted different rewards. Some wanted the seniority of a post in her household; others craved only a word of praise where none other gave it. She had learned in the years she had been mistress of Yoredale. She had made a few misjudgements but now she was confident that those at the core of her household could train others in her service. Thus within Thomas Gate's circle of power there lay a small inner ring of trusted servants who answered not to Thomas, but to her.

She stood up in the small bath and stepped out into the waiting cloth held out to her by her most loyal, most privy servant, Margaret. She had been a constant companion in the past few years. Joan knew that in her darkest hours she had let Margaret get too close. Margaret knew her thoughts and dreams - but she was the only one that did. She was more than the mere servant of the body who dried her wet skin now so gently and expertly. If Joan trusted anyone in Christendom, it was Margaret.

"My lady?" Half the time she thought Margaret could tell what she was thinking. A trace of a smile crossed her lips as she wondered if Margaret was a witch - she had heard folk say it. What if it were true? Margaret held out a robe for her and helped her to dress.

"What new arrivals do we have?" she asked as Margaret laced up her bodice.

"Is that too tight, my lady?"

"No…you know it isn't. Why do you not answer me?" She indulged Margaret more than any other and waited, intrigued, for her to finish fastening the ties.

"There were several this week, my lady."

"And?"

"One of interest," said Margaret.

"And?" prompted Joan.

"A woman… but a strange one. There's something about her…"

"Where has she come from?"

"She was brought in by Weaver. Her husband's a mason, she claims."

"And were they up to some mischief, this mason and his wife?"

"Her face has been cut and bruised - you can still see the marks. But she doesn't hold herself like a mason's wife - there's too much swagger to her. She tries to hide it but it's plain enough to me."

"Where is she?"

"We've put her to work in the kitchens. We need every hand there with the numbers we've to feed now. I don't know how we'll manage the winter, my lady."

"Let my good husband worry about that. Keep a close watch then on this woman - what happened to the mason?"

"Weaver told me he'd finished him at the old mill. Didn't brag too much about it though - and that's not like Weaver!"

"One less does us all some favour - I swear we have the dregs of the shire here," said Joan. "And where is that mute girl, Agnes? I've seen little of her - though even that is too much!"

"Sir Walter keeps Agnes close with him now," said

Margaret.

"The fool. She'll betray him sooner or later - the evil, little bitch. I want Weaver watching them - all of them. Speak to Weaver. I rely on the pair of you to make sure there are no problems. What about the young man who was whipped?"

"Hal?"

"Aye, Hal."

"I'll have no trouble keeping both eyes on him, my lady." Margaret grinned.

Joan shook her head but she could not be cross with Margaret; too much had passed between them, too much merriment … too much heartache.

"Be careful," warned Joan, "that's all - and don't trust him."

"I wasn't thinking of trusting him, my lady," Margaret replied with a wicked grin.

24

22nd September 1468, Yoredale Castle

Eleanor lay awake. All around her on the floor of the Hall lay many of the castle servants and they seemed to have no trouble sleeping despite the cacophony of snoring, grunting, sighing and worse. To her left, the pair who had been enthusiastically rutting for what seemed like hours had finally ceased their exertions. To her right, a large man was breaking wind in his sleep - he was really quite skilled, she thought, developing a rhythm that she had never envisaged was possible - nor ever wanted to.

She could not imagine sleeping peacefully ever again. It had been a mortal shock for her to find Hal and John still at Yoredale when she had believed them safely on their way to Corve Manor. She was powerless though - and she knew it. She dared not even acknowledge Hal or John. She must remain a simple mason's widow, must play the role with care. Thus, it was no surprise that she found sleep hard to come by any night and, if by some chance she succumbed, she would wake in a sweat, haunted by the grey, haggard face of Rob Hall.

Weaver lost no time in telling her he had despatched Rob. It might in the end have been the kindest end for she knew in her heart that Rob had little time left. She had seen death many times and been its agent too, but she took his death hard. On the road south, when her spirit had flagged it was his humour and heart that sustained her - aye, and his love, too. She would have liked to be with him at the end.

No, she did not expect to sleep well at Yoredale.

She felt a movement nearby and suddenly a hand tapped

upon hers. She swiftly clamped her other hand upon it and swivelled onto her side. She still kept Amelie's knife close at night. It was probably some hopeful seeking what lay under her smock. She eased herself towards him thinking through a means of cooling his ardour without waking half the occupants of the Hall. The sleeping bodies were so close together any movement might cause a stir.

"You are Mistress Hall, I believe," whispered a familiar voice. Her sigh of relief was loud enough to wake them all. She grinned to herself and released his hand.

"You've a firm grip," said Hal. "We must talk."

Eleanor peered around the room. There were too many sleeping bodies to clamber over.

"Not here," she said. She thought about what she would be doing on the morrow - much as she had done today and the day before. Variety, she had discovered, was not a feature of work in the castle kitchens.

She put her lips close to his ear. "I'll see you by the well at midday tomorrow," she breathed. Then she rolled away from him and was relieved when he said nothing more. Around her, the rest slumbered noisily on. Eleanor dozed for a time but when the first servants stirred, so did she. The bread ovens were already at work and their smell had become a familiar part of the dawn. There were fires to be lit now that the cooler weather was upon them and food to be prepared in the Great kitchen - that was her lot.

She slipped on her kirtle and swiftly laced it up. She looked down at it in disgust, for it was already and grease-stained and stank of offal. She was not at home in the steam and sweat of the kitchens where harsh words greeted her every failure.

At noon she volunteered to fetch water, not a task she usually undertook willingly. The cook looked at her in surprise as she made for the kitchen door.

"You might need this!" he bawled at her, tossing an empty wooden pail in her direction. She dropped it and the cook added with a filthy look: "you clumsy bitch!"

Eleanor shook her head and went to find Hal. Sometimes she surprised herself with her patience - she must be getting old. She was relieved to find him alone by the well, but it was a busy thoroughfare for the wine cellar and other stores were nearby. Their meeting must be brief.

"My lady-" began Hal.

"Hush you fool!" hissed Eleanor, lowering her pail down into the well.

"I'm sorry," said Hal at once, "of course, I know, you're Mistress Hall. Is it true what's being said about Rob?"

"Aye, Rob's wound was bad, but I... I really wanted him to... Poor Rob."

"Add another to Weaver's victims," said Hal, "but he'll answer for it."

Eleanor darted a glance at the doorway to the courtyard. "Can you get me and John out of here?"

Hal shook his head and then paused as two men came in, grunting as they rolled a hogshead of wine into the adjacent cellar.

"I've found Agnes," he said.

"Ned's mute girl?"

Hal nodded. "She must come out with us too," said Hal.

Even without the desperate look he gave her, Eleanor knew that Agnes could not be left behind. "Who can we trust?" she asked.

Hal shrugged. "Wulf, Bess and some of the others - the priest is a friend too."

"I don't trust priests," said Eleanor. She struggled with the effort of raising the full pail. "I'm taking too long."

"Let me," said Hal. He quickly pulled up the pail and set it down for her on the stone floor.

"I must go, or it'll be noticed," she said. "We can do nothing for now. Where would we go?"

"I thought Corve," said Hal.

"It'll be winter soon."

"Yes, I know and we could never make Corve without mounts and if we take those, they'll come after us for certain."

"Aye," agreed Eleanor, "just you, me, Agnes and John - we'd have no chance. Better to wait here till the spring. Lie low and give no cause for suspicion."

She lifted the heavy pail and turned to go, but then on impulse she patted his arm. "Just in case one of us needs help, sleep near me at night."

"What's this?" The deep throated growl startled them both. "Making plans together, are we? Sleeping together are we?"

"Piss off, Weaver," said Hal, "I don't answer to you."

Weaver winked at Eleanor. "Well, the grieving widow here does," he said. "I didn't know you were on heat already, mistress. But I'd steer your warm arse away from this one, if I were you. He's already a marked man."

He laid a hand on her buttocks and gave a squeeze. "A new lass like you will need some friends," he said. "I'll do a lot for my friends." His hand slid between her legs and she gave an involuntary gasp at his boldness. "You sound like my sort of woman," he said.

He was relaxed, matter of fact; he might have been discussing the harvest. The weight of the filled pail was making her arms tremble and he noticed.

"Do I frighten you, mistress?" he asked.

"No," she snapped and hurried back to the kitchens where she slammed the pail down on the floor, spilling some of the contents.

"You took your time," observed one of the cooks.

"Weaver was talking to me," she said.

That produced a raucous howl from half the girls there. "Weaver talks to anyone without a cock between their legs!" retorted the cook. "Now there's work to do, so wipe up what you've slopped on the floor and get back to it!"

And that became Eleanor's day, all day every day, as

autumn ground on into early winter.

As the nights grew colder, the great fire in the hearth was kept burning all night and she grew accustomed to the close atmosphere, the haze of smoke and the flicker of firelight. Still restful sleep remained elusive. She had told Hal to wait until the spring, but she could not see how anything would have changed by then.

PART FOUR: RETURN

DEREK BIRKS

25

27th October 1468, at the docks in Newcastle

Ned stared at the wharves, silhouetted against the dying sun's reddish glow. He felt a flutter of apprehension, remembering his last visit to Newcastle. Behind him the master of The Catherine, James Finch, bellowed a string of commands to his crew. A knot of seamen rose up from the deck as one and Ned admired their skill and balance as they scattered across the ship. Some nimbly scaled the rigging and trimmed the sails whilst others leaned out along the side with a coil of rope in their hand. The small, bulbous ship lurched and slowed. The wind blew hard, making the landing difficult, but Finch seemed unconcerned.

"A good crossing, Master Finch," said Ned amicably.

Finch grunted his agreement - not one of life's great talkers, Master Finch.

"Fine and calm," Ned persisted.

Finch gave a mirthless chuckle and pointed to Bear and Ragwulf who stumbled up onto the deck. They looked a sorry pair, having suffered from the ravages of the ship's motion. Spearbold followed them up and he at least seemed quite unaffected. Ned too, now a veteran of three sea crossings, was pleased to find that he had adjusted quite easily to the movement of the ship. He would never have believed it after his first sea voyage, but he found the journey quite relaxing. Their landfall, however, was giving him a great deal more concern, though he tried not to show it.

The Catherine slowed so that she was almost stationary and Ned could see the space along the dockside that Finch was aiming for. He was a canny fellow, Finch. They would be berthed as far from the castle as possible for he knew that would suit Ned best.

"Well done, Master Finch," said Spearbold.

"Damn sight easier than Hartlepool," grumbled Finch, referring to their hasty departure four years earlier.

"You've a sound memory, Finch," observed Spearbold with a rueful glance at Ned.

But Ned's attention had turned to the wharves nearby. It was near sunset and late in the autumn so the usually busy port was far from crowded. A few lamps were already lit and some folk were still abroad, but it was ideal for their purposes. Finch drew The Catherine expertly in towards the wooden dock.

"Don't worry, my lord," Spearbold assured him. "All is arranged. We are to lodge overnight at the Grey Horse Inn. Felix has sent your letter of pardon by a trusted man. If he's not already here, he should arrive tonight. There will be mounts waiting for us and tomorrow we may set off in earnest. Felix has accomplished it all - with the king's aid, I dare say."

"I swear, Spearbold, I already owe Felix more than I can ever repay."

"I think you owe the Duchess of Burgundy a good deal more than Felix this time. She has worked a miracle with her brother, King Edward. Things will get better now, my lord. I feel it."

Finch gave him a withering look.

"I prefer to travel in hope," Spearbold told Finch as several of the crew manhandled the gangplank out and it clattered down onto the dock.

"You're a whoreson fool then," replied the master.

"I can hardly believe I'm here," said Ned, placing his foot onto the wooden platform.

"The Duchess was as good as her word," murmured Spearbold, following Ned off the ship.

The crew passed them what little baggage they had and Bear and Ragwulf shared the load between them. Ned, though he felt rested, carried only his sword in accordance with the Flemish doctor's strict instructions. Ned knew that he would need more weeks of rest and gentle exercise before he would be fully fit and there were times when he doubted that he would ever fight again.

Finch came off the ship to join them.

"Thank you, once again, Finch," said Ned, "I dare say you'll be hoping not to see me again."

For the first time Finch gave what might generously be interpreted as a smile. "Not at all, my lord, for every time I carry you somewhere, Felix pays me very well indeed!"

"And I supposed it was blind loyalty that made you do it," said Ned with a grin.

Finch slung a leather bag over his shoulder and set off. "Come on then," he said, "I'll take you to the Grey Horse."

"We're obliged to you Finch," said Spearbold.

"You shouldn't be," replied Finch, "since I'm lodging there too."

"Is it safe?" Ned enquired as he attempted to keep up with him.

Finch shook his head. "We're in a busy port, by a busy river where there are more cutthroats than rats," he said. "Of course it's not safe but, unless you want to stay at the Castle Inn under the noses of the authorities, it's the best we can do."

Finch set a brisk pace and soon Ned dropped back to walk alongside Spearbold.

"The Duchess must have written to the king in haste for all to be done in such a short time," said Ned. "I only hope you're right and the letter is waiting for us at the inn."

"Lord Hastings had it written, the king signed it - privily- and Felix arranged for its delivery here," said

Spearbold. "Surely you trust those three men at least."

"Aye, I do," replied Ned, "but little happens privily at court - and you know very well that Warwick has clients everywhere."

"Indeed, my lord, but Felix says the king and the earl are reconciled."

"And how does Felix know that?" said Ned. "And in any case, the earl may be reconciled with the king but I assure you that we are far from reconciled since he's been trying to have me killed all summer!"

"A fair observation, my lord," agreed Spearbold, "but the letter will be carried by one of Felix's trusted men."

"Well, if Felix trusts him, then I suppose I must too," said Ned.

They arrived at the Grey Horse without incident and were glad to find bread, cheese, and ale awaiting them. It was humble fare but Felix had thought of everything and soon some warm potage was served. The landlord told them there were horses for them in the stables. They remained downstairs all evening, drinking the health of Felix of Bordeaux with the generous amounts of ale he had provided. The inn was crowded, as Ned expected, and was not unlike the Golden Ship at Sluys with its raucous mix of sailors, whores and traders. They expected to meet Felix's messenger during the evening but if he was there, he did not make himself known to them.

Ned, weary from the journey, dozed off several times and was nudged awake from time to time by Spearbold. Gradually the inn's patrons left and it became clear that their envoy was not coming that evening. The inn was almost silent as they made their way upstairs. They were to share one of the two communal bedrooms that the establishment boasted. Bear insisted on sleeping on the floor, Ned took the smaller of the two beds and the others squeezed into the larger one.

Ned sat on the bed.

"Where is the fellow with the pardon?" Ragwulf asked no-one in particular.

Spearbold spread his hands. "If he is not here on the morrow, then we shall just have to wait for him," said Spearbold.

"The longer we stay here, the more danger there is," said Ragwulf.

"But… without the letter with the king's seal upon it our lord is still an exile, a fugitive - and we are all outlaws once more."

Ned was well past talking about it. "Enough," he said. "We can do nothing more tonight. Let's see what the morning brings."

They extinguished the expensive tallow candle and settled down to sleep - all except Ned, who had slept most of the evening. He found himself lying wide awake with only his fears to keep him company. He thought of getting up but reasoned that if he did, and by some great fortune managed to avoid falling over their luggage in the dark, he would then need to get past Bear who was snoring loudly against the door. So he remained where he was, brooding - which was becoming a habit.

He must have drifted into a half-sleep but he was awoken by a great crash at their door. If the intruder's intention was to take them by surprise, he succeeded. However, he failed to gain entry for the same reason Ned could not get out: the formidable obstacle of Bear, whose large feet rested against the door. Hence the weapon of surprise was compromised.

Everyone moved at once. Finch and Ragwulf leapt up from the bed, blades in hand. Bear rose unsteadily from the floor and Spearbold dived down out of the bed to hide behind it.

Ned was very stiff and could only move painfully slowly. There was a further clattering at the door. Two men smashed it open and then stood aside. Two crossbows appeared and a bolt thudded into each mattress. Ned felt one graze his thigh as he slid off the bed. Several armed men pushed the bows aside and charged into the room. Bear stopped one in his tracks, but the other got past and lunged at Ragwulf. Finch buried a knife in his back.

"Down!" roared Bear. Then all was silent for a moment.

Ned's eyes were already well adjusted to the darkness and he could see where the others were: Bear beside the shattered door, Ragwulf and Finch on the floor and Spearbold crawling along under the window sill. He rolled off the bed and landed on the floor near Spearbold.

"Stay down," he breathed, but it was clear from Spearbold's demeanour that he had no intention of doing otherwise. Ned drew his knife for there was no room to use a sword. He watched the door closely, waiting for one of the crossbows to reappear. Two quarrels flew in through the window and buried themselves in the daubed wall.

"My mother's oath!" hissed Finch. "There must be others on the stable roof across the yard!"

"They'll be shooting their bolts blind," said Ragwulf. "They can't see us."

"They can't get in," said Ned, "but we can't get out either."

"We could wait till dawn," suggested Spearbold.

"And let them take our horses? We need those mounts!" said Ned.

"What then?" asked Spearbold.

"Lord?" Bear waved him over. Ned crawled across to him and together they peered around the door frame. The landing was empty but the stairs below were in darkness.

"What do you think?" Ned asked him.

Bear gave a solemn shake of the head. "Stay here," he said.

"They want to draw us out, don't they?"

Bear nodded.

"Well, let's do it then," said Ned.

"No lord!" said Spearbold. "We'll be killed."

Ned ignored him and pointed to the large piece of timber that had once been half a door. Bear stared at it for a moment and then grinned. He swept it up and held it in front of him as he stepped out onto the landing.

"Come on!" hissed Ned and the others joined him. They crowded onto the landing and the door to the other bedroom flew open. Bear deftly turned the board to face it and a quarrel struck it with great force. Ragwulf and Finch dived into the room and made short work of the lone attacker. Then they began to descend the stairs with Bear still shielding them. Ned drew his sword. The treads creaked as they made their way down.

Their attackers waited until they had reached the foot of the stairs and then came at them from all sides. Bear smashed the remains of the door into the first man and then whipped out his axe to cleave the man's head in two. Ragwulf and Finch again combined to cut down another assailant and a third ran off.

The five of them stood in a tight circle back to back, breathing heavily and awaiting the next attack, but the inn was still.

"We know there are others out there," said Ragwulf.

"Aye," said Ned, "If we go for the horses, they'll have us. They know that too."

"My lord?" It was Spearbold who drew their attention to the two bodies in the inn. Two men. One, the innkeeper, had his head stove in and was slumped upon one of the long trestle tables. Also at the table was a stranger who had bled to death from a knife wound in his neck. Before him on the wooden board was a small heap of burnt paper and ash.

Spearbold rubbed at an oily smear in its midst.

"What is it?" asked Ragwulf.

"It's the remains of a wax seal, isn't it Spearbold?" said Ned.

Spearbold nodded. "And this poor fellow, I'd guess, is Felix of Bordeaux's trusted man. He must have ridden all night to get here."

"Hah! Much good it did him," growled Finch.

"So, we're going to be outlaws again," murmured Spearbold.

"We've lost before we've even begun," said Ragwulf.

"Not if we can get to the horses," said Ned. "We can worry about whether we're outlaws or not later, but first we must get away!"

"But they're waiting for us," said Spearbold.

"Perhaps," said Ned. "Bear, go and fetch that crossbow and dig out a couple of bolts. Ragwulf, take look in the yard - carefully, mind you…"

Bear plodded back up the stairs whilst Ragwulf went to the door at the side of the building which led around to the stable yard.

"Surely other folk would be alarmed by now?" said Spearbold.

"Alarmed, aye," grinned Finch, "but not stupid enough to step outside. This is the docks - no-one goes looking for trouble."

"You'd best go now, Finch," said Ned.

"Aye, I don't want to be answering any questions about all this," he said, but he did not move. "Still, you may need my blade…"

"No, go now. If I need you it'll be at the helm of a ship, not in a place like this."

Finch nodded. "Aye to that," he muttered and clapped Ned on the back. He moved fast then, darting out of the inn and into a side alley, running a dogleg line into the night.

Bear returned with the crossbow. "One bolt," he said miserably as he loaded it.

Ragwulf came back from the door. "I can make out the shape of a head on the roofline. There could be another.

I'm not sure," he said.

"It'll soon be dawn," said Ned. "Spearbold, gather up what you can carry. Ragwulf and I will make a run for the stables and get the mounts. Bear - are you ready? Try to save the bolt for when we ride up with the horses - that's when we'll be in most danger."

Bear nodded. They looked at each other and Ned smiled.

Spearbold gave a grimace of disapproval. "You look as if you've missed this, my lord."

"Whether I have or not," replied Ned, "I'm certainly not up to it!"

"Then you must take care - the physician was most particular-"

"I don't see him here now though, Spearbold. Do you?"

"Well at least let Ragwulf go first."

Ragwulf frowned. "Thank you, Master Spearbold," he said drily.

Bear crouched in the small porch outside, almost filling the doorway. Ragwulf pushed past him. Ned glanced around the stable yard, but saw no-one. Then he caught a flicker of movement in one of the stalls as someone changed their position. Cramped, he thought; their assailants were getting uncomfortable waiting. He sensed that the darkness was waning, though there was no glimmer of dawn.

He whispered to Ragwulf. "There's someone at the third door along."

"Aye, I noticed. I'll take him; you go for the first door?"

Ned gave him a nod and they set off, moving low to the ground, staggering to right and left as they made for the stables. Ned found it hard going and Ragwulf got there well ahead of him, crashing into the stall whilst he was still in the open. An iron bolt ricocheted off the cobbles at his feet and sped away across the yard. He stumbled on, slowing with the effort. He should have stayed longer in Bruges, he reflected.

He reached the stable as Ragwulf emerged from the other door. There was a smear of blood on his chin. He held up two fingers - so there were two mounts there. They went into the stable together and waited just inside, leaning against the beams of the timber frame. Ned could hear only the horses, nervous and unsettled, rattling the stalls in the dark. His eyes began to adjust to the gloom and he crouched down. There was a long row of stalls and Ragwulf started to move along the front of them, examining each one. Ned moved on towards the far end of the row.

Before he reached the end, a sword speared out at him from one of the stalls. It narrowly missed him, sliding along his parrying blade. Ned seized the arm that held it before it could pull back. He intended to drag his opponent out and throw him to the floor but it didn't quite happen that way. His assailant resisted and in an instant Ned realised that he did not have the strength to prevail. It was a new experience for him and he backed away in shock. The other man followed him and struck hard. Ned blocked several blows and was relieved when Ragwulf cut the man down from behind.

They saddled two of the horses and in the time it took Ned to saddle a third, Ragwulf had prepared another mount in the adjacent stable. Finally they stood ready to lead the horses out. It was beginning to get light and they could see Bear in the doorway to the inn. If they could see him, Ned decided, then the crossbowmen on the roofs would see them clearly enough when they moved out with the horses.

"They have only one chance and two bolts at most," he said. "By the time they can reload, we'll be gone."

They each mounted a horse and led the others behind them.

"Ready, lord?" asked Ragwulf.

Ned reassured him with a glance and then bent low to pass out of the stable door with the spare mount behind him. As he emerged he saw Bear come out of the inn, crossbow aimed steadily at the roofline. A quarrel thudded into the stable door frame and another flew high over his shoulder. Bear let fly his own bolt and then threw the bow aside as Ned and Ragwulf urged the horses towards him. Spearbold hurried out with their baggage and Bear lifted him bodily into a saddle. Then the warrior swung his own weight up on to a protesting mare.

They cantered away before the crossbowmen could reload and headed west through the town. After a short distance they slowed to a gentle trot; it would not look good to approach the gate at speed. The low clouds behind them slowly revealed the dawn which was just as well for the gates would only open at first light.

"Spearbold - do you know where you're going?" enquired Ned.

"Indeed, my lord - don't you?"

"Last time I passed through this town I was in rather a hurry to leave, as I recall. We crossed the bridge."

"We're making for Close Gate this time," announced Spearbold, "small, but large enough for us to pass through without trouble, I pray..."

Ned was relieved when Spearbold's prayers were answered and they passed through the gate the moment it opened, leaving the town behind them. There was only one possible place to go so they headed west towards Corbridge, the north Tyne valley and then Crag Tower. Perhaps there they could remain safe for the winter and prepare for a new beginning in the spring. Yet without proof of his pardon from the king, Ned could be arrested and condemned at any time. Sooner rather than later he must get to the king and persuade him to issue another letter.

Ned wanted to do so much - not least find Agnes - and to do that he must track down Thomas Gate. After what had happened at the inn, Ned was under no illusions now about his own health. If he found Thomas Gate today, then Gate would kill him with ease and that would not help Agnes one jot. It was as well that he was unlikely to face Gate today.

26

29th October 1468, in the privy chamber at Middleham Castle

Sir Thomas Gate left Walter Grave to wait down in the courtyard whilst he ascended alone to Warwick's privy chamber. He considered once more, as he climbed the long stairway beside the keep, why Warwick had summoned him. It could only be bad news. He expected to meet the earl alone but, to his surprise, there was another waiting outside the chamber when he arrived.

Gate had not seen Benjamin Warner for years. Warner was not one of the earl's bullish northern clients - he was altogether different. He carried no sword for he needed none - he struck fear into men's hearts wielding a very different weapon. In theory he was one of the earl's legal clerks; in practice he was deadly trouble. He knew how to get things done - legally and, if required, not so legally. As such he was more valuable to Warwick than a thousand men at arms.

His presence worried Gate and his apprehension grew when Warner responded to his effusive greeting with lukewarm enthusiasm. They both stood then in silence whilst Warwick kept them waiting. When the door to the privy chamber opened, Warner was called in and Gate had to wait even longer. When he was finally admitted into the earl's presence he was shocked to see that Warner was seated whilst the earl stood.

"Ah, Thomas," said Warwick, "sorry to drag you away from your important work in the dales. I trust it all goes well."

"Aye, my lord," said Thomas warily. "We're recruiting more men every day."

"Excellent news," replied Warwick with a smile, then the smile faded. "Ned Elder has escaped from Flanders."

Warwick said the words in a quiet understated manner though he well knew the effect it would have on his servant. For a moment Gate was too stunned to comment. How could Ned Elder have escaped? It beggared belief.

"My lord, I don't understand how that could have happened. Why, the man was half dead when I last saw him!"

"Half-dead Thomas, but clearly not wholly dead. And since his ... near death, he's been rather busy."

"My lord?"

"Aye, Thomas, he's been in touch with the king, through the king's sister, Margaret - you remember Princess Margaret, Thomas?"

"Of course my lord!"

"Only too well, I should think, Thomas. She was the one you were supposed to stop from marrying the Duke of Burgundy, wasn't she?"

"Aye, my lord."

"The king has pardoned Ned Elder...he's no longer an outlaw and he's to receive his lands back - you'll remember the lands too, I suppose, Thomas - since you're sitting on them at Yoredale Castle!"

The earl turned to Warner. "Master Warner - if you please - acquaint our friend Thomas with what you have discovered."

Warner inclined his head. "Well, Sir Thomas, Ned Elder has returned to England. I learned that he was taking a ship for Newcastle - there to collect upon his arrival a letter of pardon despatched from the king. He landed there two days ago but the earl laid plans to stop him."

"And?" asked Gate.

"Ned Elder managed to get out of Newcastle but ...

without his letter of pardon," conceded Warner.

Gate felt like laughing out loud but he did not. Warwick's failure helped no-one and he knew now - if he had ever doubted it - that Ned Elder was not an easy man to put down. In the end, it changed nothing for him - unless of course Ned headed for Yoredale.

"If he has no letter of pardon, then he might be mistaken for an outlaw again," said Gate.

"Aye," agreed Warwick, "he must go to the king or risk all."

"He's no threat to you, my lord," said Gate. "He's got no men!"

"Aye, but it seems he does have some allies. Warner?"

"Indeed my lord. As you instructed, I've been investigating his friends. The only man he's close to at court is Lord Hastings who of course is a formidable influence. They are former comrades in arms but I've found nothing to say that Lord Hastings has ever aided his escape."

"Hmm, Hastings knows a great deal and a great many owe him a service," said Warwick. "But let that pass. Go on."

"I had little to go on except the ship that brought him to Newcastle, The Catherine. The ship's master is one James Finch sailing out of London."

"I hardly think a single ship's master has any significance," said Gate.

Warner gave him an indulgent smile and continued. "A man who is hunted needs money and the owner of The Catherine is a wealthy goldsmith by the name of John Goldwell - a city alderman no less. There is another man, a rather more exotic fellow, a vintner, who calls himself Felix of Bordeaux and runs his wine trade out of Bristol and London.

"And what have you found out about these ... merchants?" asked Gate. He didn't trust Warner but he didn't trust merchants much either.

"I have discovered a great deal, Sir Thomas, by simple, but effective methods," replied Warner smoothly. "I have men who are good at following and observing - they are like leeches, Sir Thomas, they cling to their victim until they have sucked all the information out of him."

"Very…dramatic, Master Warner, but where have your leeches got us?" persisted Gate.

Warner looked across to the earl, who nodded.

"Steps have been taken, Sir Thomas, to…destroy Ned Elder's allies. There is much talk of traitors in London …words have been dropped in a few receptive ears: mention of clandestine meetings, men smuggled abroad, and so on. It doesn't take much…"

"And what of Finch?"

"He's at sea - but he'll keep."

"So," said the earl, "Ned Elder is once more on the run and he's in the north but he's hardly any men so he can't go to Yoredale. He must find men either at Crag Tower or Corve Manor - they're all he has left. Should he seek help from his former allies, he'll find them with difficulties of their own."

"He'll go to the king though," said Gate.

"Aye, he'll try, but even if he sees the king, all he'll get is his pardon. King Edward's not going to give him any men at arms - nor is anyone else. He can't buy men because he has no coin and he can't get it from his rich friends. So, he should be powerless."

"He can still go to Corve Manor," Gate pointed out.

"Let him," said the earl. "He can stew at his little marcher manor until he rots for all I care, so long as he keeps out of our way."

"What if he comes here anyway?" asked Thomas.

"Well, I suppose on past behaviour we can't discount that," sighed Warwick. "Then you'd best make sure you know about it. My coin's been feeding your men for months now - it's about time they did something useful for it."

"Aye," said Gate, "I'll send men out just to be sure."

"Good - and handle it quietly! No disturbances - I don't want any distractions. There are more important matters to come."

§§§§

Gate heaved a sigh of relief when he finally escaped from Warwick's privy chamber. He hurried downstairs to join Walter Grave in the courtyard.

"Ned Elder is alive and in the north," he told him. "How many men do we have?"

"Three score men at arms," replied Walter, "if you'd call them that for they're ill trained for the most part."

"But can they fight, Walter?"

"Aye, they can fight, my lord, but I'm not sure they all will. Many come to us because they've nowhere else to go. We should have waited until spring - we've to feed all these men through winter."

"We'll recruit more in the spring but we couldn't leave it all till then. Now's the time to raise men - when they're frightened and hungry. Rumours fly across the land fed by arrests and executions. Our king fears Lancastrian plots everywhere and while he hunts down spies, the kingdom's at the mercy of the queen's grasping relatives. Their greed will deliver this land into the earl's hands. And part of what falls into Warwick's hands will fall into ours, Walter."

"Indeed, my lord. So… Ned Elder?"

"Aye, we'd best not take any risks. The earl believes he's not likely to pay us a visit, but we know better, Walter. He'll come to find me - because he'll want the girl. We have plenty of men - so let's give them something to do."

"We already send out regular patrols my lord," said Grave.

"Aye, well I want more men out there keeping a tight watch over the valley - day and night. If any strangers arrive in Yoredale, I must know of it. Would you know Ned Elder on sight?"

"No, my lord."

"Then take no chances. Anyone you are not sure of, bring them here. I, or Lady Joan, will soon tell you if you have Ned Elder."

"It shall be done, my lord."

"Good, see that it is."

"My lord," began Walter. "What about the girl, Agnes?"

"She's harmless enough but just keep her close, that's all."

"I can't keep her any closer than I already do," said Grave with a rare smile.

Thomas regarded him thoughtfully. "I don't want her harmed, Walter. She doesn't deserve that."

"Aye, my lord, I understand - unless of course she was to play us false..."

Gate nodded, though he could not quite imagine how poor, mute, little Agnes could 'play them false.'

27

30th October 1468, at Crag Tower

"More water!" bellowed Sir Stephen. "Bring more water! For the love of God, more water!"

He stood at the gate with half of the men at arms at his command whilst the rest manned the ramparts. Maighread, Becky and Will fetched water to douse the fire at the gate - there was no-one else left. Maighread hauled her leaking pail to the gate, waited whilst the contents were hurled at the flaming timbers and then hurried back with it to the well. The cold sweat soaked her ragged clothes and the ash and filth clung to her skin.

Now and then a stray arrow flew over the rampart and skidded across the yard or struck one of the walls. Maighread had no fear of the arrows but it took every ounce of nerve she had to approach the burning gate. The wimple that once covered her hair had fallen off somewhere - she knew not where - and the searing heat made her scarred face feel as if it was scorched anew. Away from the fire, the cobbled yard was slick with a thin layer of melting ice. She had fallen twice already but she bullied her bruised body back to the gate with another load of water. As far as she could judge, it was making little difference for the fire burned ever more brightly. But this was all she could do to help.

They had repulsed another night attack the previous week and the following night the last few servants had fled. Sir Stephen warned that there would be, must be, more attacks. More men were coming down from the high pasture, driving their few scrawny cattle with them. They needed shelter for the winter and any stores they could scavenge. Crag Tower had long been a target but now their enemies were more numerous, gathered from both sides of the border. They knew the tower was undermanned and they grew ever more desperate to take it.

Maighread's next bucket was snatched from her and emptied. Just then some kind of ram crashed into the gate and a shower of sparks covered her. She screamed with fright and the men at arms turned to stare at her briefly before looking away again.

"I'm sorry, I'm sorry," she wailed and staggered back to the well again. Her fellow defenders could do without her screeching to the heavens but she could not help it. All she could do was carry water. Eleanor's son, Will, struggled past her with his pail, half the contents slopping out as he went. The boy was putting on a brave face.

As she lowered her bucket at the well she lost her balance and fell, colliding with Becky who grabbed her around the waist and held her up.

"Thank you," she gasped and leant on the stonework. "Young Will is doing well."

Becky nodded. "We're all of us doing well, but I don't think it'll be enough, my lady."

"You don't?" said Maighread.

"No, I don't," Becky paused. "There are some knives on a table in the Hall. When the time comes, we should take Will up to your chamber and bar the door. We may hold out there for a while…"

"Aye," was all Maighread could reply for she wondered what they would be holding out for.

There was a cry from the rampart and a figure tumbled down onto the cobbles: their last archer. Becky reached him first and bent down to him. When Maighread joined her, she was already back to her feet. "He's gone," she said flatly.

They resumed their toil but when they reached the gate

with their pails, one glance was enough to tell them it was over. The timbers were breaking up in great clouds of smoke and flame. There were only three men left to defend it - and it could no longer be defended. A flurry of arrows flew through the shattered debris of the gateway. One struck Sir Stephen in his right eye and he roared with impotent rage. Another pierced his thigh and blood flowed as he fell heavily onto the cobbles.

"Take him into the Hall!" shouted Maighread and followed them in.

Maighread just stood and stared as one of the men carefully snapped off the arrow shafts but even so, she could not see how the heads could be removed without killing him. He must have been in agony but he braved it well, though blood poured from his leg. She pressed a blood-soaked rag against the wound to staunch the flow.

"Back to the gate!" he told his men. "I'll join you … soon."

But when the men had gone out, he pulled Maighread down close to him.

"We are done, my lady," he breathed.

"Becky says we should lock ourselves in my chamber."

"No!" he gripped her right arm so that her old scars burned and she pulled away. Oblivious to any pain he caused her, he seized her again.

"Not to your chamber! Hide in the stables … or a store." He gasped for breath. "They'll come to the tower first - then you run…if you can."

He was spent and dropped back on to the table top, breathing hard. A thin dribble of dark blood leaked from his eye and ran down his pale face. Maighread still had one hand pressed against the leg wound but to no avail.

"Who'd have thought - damned arrows, after all the times …battle after battle and not a scratch."

He put his hand on hers and moved it off his bleeding leg.

"Leave it. I'm sorry, my lady… I've failed you." He whispered the words and they sounded like an epitaph.

She wanted to salve his wound and reassure him that he had done all he could but then his head simply dropped down to one side and he lay still. Their captain, Ned's loyal aide, was dead.

She slumped her head down on the table beside him for a moment. They were lost. The clamour outside was louder. She lifted her breast from the table, took a deep breath and cast her eyes for one final time upon Sir Stephen. He had nothing to be sorry for. Now she must be strong and she must be swift.

She looked at the knives laid out as Becky said. She picked up three of them and hurried outside. The ramparts were empty and only three men stood at the gate - not enough. Even as she watched, another man fell to an arrow.

"Fall back!" she ordered. They looked at her and hesitated. "Come!" she screamed at them. "Sir Stephen is dead!"

They sprinted to her then. She gathered them all to her, like a mother hen with her nervous chicks. She had only a moment to decide.

"The grain store!" she said. "There's nothing in it. We'll wait for them to storm the tower and then we'll make a run for it."

It was a futile idea and they all knew it, but no-one had a better one because there wasn't one. Maighread hoped Sir Stephen was right that the attackers would go to the tower first.

Perhaps their attackers had known her father - they might leave her be. But who would know her now? Not even her father himself would see his little daughter in her scorched face. She would be their plaything for a time until they tired of her ugly countenance.

The grain store was a wooden structure that leant on the curtain wall for support. They had barely squeezed in out of sight before the gateway was finally smashed in and a horde of men poured through, hurling aside the smoking timbers. She peered through a gap between two planks in the store wall and watched the figures, frantic shadows against the fire's flickering light. They scattered across the yard at the run and many went straight for the Hall - many, but not all. Others went to the stable but several headed for the storehouses. She grimaced. If they expected to find much of use, they would be mistaken - except, of course, they would find Maighread and Becky. It would go badly for them if they were caught and she decided that she would rather use the knife on herself than submit.

She saw two men coming and jumped as they banged at the door. She gripped Becky's hand tightly in hers. The men who had hidden with her launched themselves out with courage. It was their last hope but they were both old men. One fell almost at once and the other was dragged out and swiftly butchered. Maighread looked at Becky and locked eyes with her. Becky nodded. This was how it must end.

Several men came into the dark store one after the other. Maighread released Becky's hand and they flew at them, stabbing wildly with their knives. Will joined them and crawled between shuffling legs, slicing at tendons and muscle. The two women screamed, abandoning all pretence of hiding. Their victims screamed too and fell. Maighread kept stabbing her knife into them until Becky stayed her frenzied arm. Maighread grappled with her.

"Enough!" hissed Becky. "Come!"

They stepped over the bodies to the door but other men had heard the noise and were drawn to the store. Only one man could enter the low-roofed store at a time and when one tried he was met by a whirlwind of angry blades.

After a short while, a gruff voice sounded above the rest. "Leave them! It's just a few women."

The voice made her cower back into the store. Where had she heard that voice before?

"Throw some fire on it," ordered the voice. "They can choose to come out or burn. Do it now! Then we need to get this fire out and block up the gate or we'll lose our prize tomorrow."

Maighread stared at the open doorway. Fire. She would not be burned again, but what about Will? They could not let him burn, nor could they let him go out on his own. But if they went out, it would be to their ruin and the boy might still be killed out of spite. The border families had won but their victory must have come at a high cost and they would want blood.

A burning brand was held against the timbers and swiftly the flames ran up the side of the store. They saw the roof thatch catch light and the smoke began to billow in.

"I must take Will out," said Becky, tossing her knife onto the ground. "At least we'll have some chance. Will you come with us, my lady?"

Maighread nodded, hugged them both and watched them step out into the yard where a wild cheer greeted them. Inside the storehouse, the smoke and falling ash stung her eyes and stole away her breath. But she was not going out nor would she let herself burn to death. She still held the knife in her scarred right hand and now turned its point to her breast. She was poised to make the thrust but then she hesitated. It was harder than she expected to take a life - even her own. It was a mortal sin, she knew, but God would surely forgive her. She could not face death by flame a second time.

She knelt down on the floor where the smoke was not so thick. She tried to shut out the roaring of the fire and the shouts from the yard and set the point of the knife at her throat. She began to mutter a prayer: "Help me, Mary. You know I have lived my life with faith and courage, give me the strength to end it in the same way."

Maighread held the blade at her throat. She could not do it… yet she must. She had lived this moment before. She knew the horror that was about to envelop her. She had seen it, felt it. Her skin would dry, sizzle, burn and her hair would crackle.

Then she heard Becky's screams; she was screaming her name. What cruel abominations was the poor girl suffering? It made up her mind for her and gave her the strength she needed. She felt the knife point against her neck - it was cold and she almost laughed to feel it. It was sharp enough though and it broke the skin when she pushed gently. The smoke was choking her now. She must hurry.

"God forgive me," she said and pressed the knife hard at her throat.

28

30th October 1468 evening, in the North Tyne Valley

"Surely it cannot be much further now, lord," said Spearbold.

Ned peered through the gloom ahead where an icy mist had settled over the river valley. He looked for some confirmation from Ragwulf or Bear but both shook their heads.

"If they aren't sure," replied Ned, "then I'm damned certain I'm not!"

After another dozen yards or so, Spearbold said: "Perhaps we should make camp then?"

"You're probably right," said Ned, slowing his mount.

"No," said Bear abruptly and urged his horse from a walk into a trot.

Ned sniffed the cool air and glanced at Ragwulf.

"Very well," muttered Spearbold behind him, "let's not camp then..."

"We're close," said Ragwulf, "and something's wrong..."

He sped up to follow Bear and Ned did the same. Bear led them up onto the plateau above the river where the mist was thinner and the air colder.

When Ned saw the glow on the skyline he felt sick.

"Not again!" he cried.

He surged forward and took his horse to a gallop, overtaking the others. In the mist it was madness and he knew it but he did not care. He was dimly aware of Bear and Ragwulf just behind him, matching his speed.

"Take care, lord!" wailed Spearbold from some distance back but his words went unheeded. Ned thundered on towards Crag Tower - Crag Tower, where his sister waited for him and where his loyal friends were holding out. But he did not see Stephen or Eleanor, all he saw was Maighread, lying in a charred cellar, half-burned to death. Bear drew up alongside him and they exchanged a brief look. Bear had been there with him - he knew Ned's thoughts exactly. Ned glanced behind to Ragwulf and was surprised to see a man who looked as desperate to reach Crag Tower as he was. The three raced on and ahead of them a spray of smoke and flames erupted into the sky.

"The gate has gone!" yelled Ragwulf. He already had his sword in his hand and Ned drew out his. He could only hope that his weak limbs were up to a fight. They urged on their exhausted mounts as a torment of cries reached them from inside Crag Tower. Bear gave a great roar and drove through the burning gateway first, battle axe in hand. Ned and Ragwulf followed him through the smoke. Ned took in the scene at a glance: to his right a store house was on fire, illuminating the yard; a crowd of armed men stood in the yard, their savage voices tearing the night apart. Between them and the burning store lay a woman and a boy. The woman looked up at Ned and screamed at him but there was so much noise he could not hear what she said.

They struck hard and fast, scattering the group of clansmen celebrating victory in the middle of the yard. Bear plunged into them, hacking down, first one side then the other, and men fell, choking on blood. The startled warriors tried to back away from him but he ran them down. Ragwulf leapt from his horse and made straight for the Hall, carving aside any man who crossed his path.

Ned swept around in an arc towards the well, slashing wildly at the knot of figures there. He was badly out of practice and his sword struck mostly air. He lost his balance and slid sideways in the saddle. The sudden lurch saved his life as a spear lunged up him. He knocked the point aside and stabbed down at its owner. His sword passed through the man's hide coat and stuck fast in him. Ned let it go, reined back and steered his mount aside as two other men converged upon him. Bear's horse suddenly shouldered his own aside and the Flemish mercenary wrought misery upon the pair on foot.

Somewhere the woman - Becky, he decided - was still screaming. He suddenly realised that she was shouting the same word over and over again: "Maighread! Maighread! Maighread!"

He felt weak and slid awkwardly from his horse. Becky sank to her knees and cried: "She's in there! She's in there!"

He stared at the store, flames dancing along its roof. Becky pulled at him, punched him and screeched at him. "It's too late! Too late! You're too late!

He pushed her aside, angry and confused.

§§§§

Maighread stabbed but the blade barely moved. She gasped, feeling another hand on hers, staying the thrust.

"No!" she roared. "You'll not take me!" But the hand would not let go and she could not break its grip on her. She moaned in despair as she was dragged out of the store. She bit at the hand that held hers but could not break free. They were saving her from the fire to make her their grisly trophy. She was hauled out with her eyes tight shut but she felt the blast of hot air and ash as the store collapsed in upon itself. Her captor wrenched away the blade and lifted her up into his arms. Her eyes flew open and when she saw Ned's face her eyes opened wider. She sobbed against him and he kissed her burned cheek. She was shocked how grey and haggard he looked. She felt him trembling as he held her and then he buckled at the knees, dropping them both on to the cobbled yard. She rolled aside, winded and bruised. He was struggling to get up so she crawled towards him.

All around them was the clamour of battle but out of the smoke a figure staggered towards them. As he came nearer she stared at his blood-stained face - a face she knew somehow from long ago. A face once fresh and young but now grizzled by age and long years of struggle. He was almost upon them and Ned was still on his knees. Where had her knife landed? She cast about on the stones around her. Becky scrambled to her feet and ran at him but the clansman brushed her aside.

He stared down at Maighread and she sought for the face in her memory, a face that matched the voice from deep in her past… until she knew for certain. Unspeaking, he put out his hand towards her, and then Bear cleaved her father's head in two.

She blinked and wiped the blood from her cheek. She was blood of his blood, but she felt nothing. Bear began to drag the dead warrior away by the legs. "No!" she shouted. Bear looked at her and paused. "No," she repeated. Bear nodded and disappeared once more into the haze of misty smoke.

Ned heaved himself over to her. He looked pale, half dead - only half as bad as her father, then, she thought.

"Are you hurt?" he asked. His breathing was uneven, his voice hoarse, she noticed. He was gasping as he spoke.

"Better than you, by the look of it," she said. That sounded harsh - too harsh. Her tongue was ever the enemy of concord. How hard had her poor lord driven himself to get here?

"There's blood all over you," he said.

"It'll wash off… my father's blood…"

"Your father?" Ned fell silent.

"He died for me a long time ago, Ned," she said. "Tis just the shock, after all these years."

He knelt in front of her, uncertain and hurting. She got to her feet and pulled him up, hugging him tightly to her. "Thank you, my lord," she breathed in his ear.

She didn't want to let him go but he was exhausted, hardly able to stand.

"That's two lives you've handed me now, my lord."

He said nothing but kissed her on the forehead. She sighed, knowing that once the excitement wore off he would look more carefully at her scarred face and would not be so ready to kiss it. Then he kissed her lips and took away what breath she had left.

The smoke was clearing in the yard, the fight was over and the fires were out. Bear came and took Ned from her embrace, supporting him under the shoulder as he led him inside. She knelt down to her father's body. It was an ugly sight and she closed her eyes. All this time it was her own father leading the attacks on Crag Tower. Yet she could not blame him for that. She remembered how hard it was to scratch out a life in the borderlands. His truce with the holders of Crag Tower had died with Sir Thomas Elder. He was doing what he thought was best for the Hall family just as he had when he gave her in marriage at the age of ten to Thomas Elder's widowed son.

She walked away and found Becky and Will sitting on the steps to the Hall. Ragwulf prowled into the yard from inside. He stood before them, shocked and hesitant.

"Sir Stephen's corpse lies on the table, my lady. Where are the others: Lady Eleanor, Hal?"

"Gone," said Becky. "Wulf took Bess and John. Hal went after Wulf. Lady Eleanor and Rob followed Hal."

He looked crushed. "But where? Where could they go?" he asked.

"Lady Eleanor thought Wulf would take them home to Yoredale."

"Foolish boy! He's brought all this upon us. If you'd had the young men at arms here, this would never have happened. I wish he was not my son. I crave your pardon, my lady, for what he has done."

He was addressing Maighread but she merely shrugged and did not answer. Then she saw that he had misunderstood her silence. She reached out and took his blood stained hand in hers.

"Wulf was a victim here too, Ragwulf. All he wanted was young Bess. He did not know what else was at stake. None of us can blame him. I pray that God will watch over them all,"

He bowed his head and tramped off across the yard. There was messy work to be done and only he and Bear to do it. Well, she thought, at least it will keep his mind from dwelling elsewhere - if only for a brief time. Bear lit some torches around the yard and she watched the two men lift the bodies of the fallen and stack them in the gateway. She felt a new strength and stood up. Becky too seemed to decide that it was time to get moving.

"Come, Will," said Becky, "let's get you to bed before you fall asleep here." She smiled at her charge and half-carried him into the Hall. Maighread followed her in. Spearbold was pacing around the great room, perhaps he was avoiding sitting at the table where Sir Stephen still lay in a pool of blood. She smiled at him.

"Lady Maighread," he said, "Lord Elder has been laid in Lady Eleanor's bed in your chamber."

"Well," she said, "I'll go and join him - though not in her bed, of course," she added with an embarrassed smile. Spearbold looked confused, well it had been a confusing night for them all, she reflected. Her new-found energy did not last long and deserted her as she mounted the steps to the first floor.

A single rush light struggled to illuminate the chamber where Ned Elder lay slumped across Eleanor's narrow bed. Maighread went over to him and tried to shift his weight more onto the bed. She soon gave up and sat down beside him, watching him. She rested her hand on his shoulder and then began to stroke his hair. Then she sighed and stood up and walked across to her own bed. She ran her hands over her dirty hair, matted with sweat and blood. Tiny flakes of ash dropped onto her shoulders and she brushed them off. She looked back at Ned and then extinguished the rush light before flopping down onto her own bed.

Sleep should have come for her at once, but it did not. Of all that had occurred that night only one moment stayed with her: she could not forget how he had held her. All these years she had been a widow - and a virgin until Henry had forced her. She had never felt a man's embrace before, not close like that - and no man had ever kissed her on the lips. Yet she was no fool and knew that Ned had just been caught up in the moment. There would be no more kisses for her and knowing it hurt her more than she had ever been hurt before.

29

31st October 1468 in the morning, at Crag Tower

The chill of the morning woke Ned and before he could move, his legs went rigid with cramp. His head ached too but that was hardly unusual - more a part of life as he now knew it. He stretched his legs to banish the cramps and then clambered awkwardly off the bed.

"It was a…hard night," said Maighread.

She startled him for he hadn't noticed she was awake. She was sitting so still on her bed, leaning against the wall, her legs drawn up under her. She looked beautiful, he thought, but as he watched her she turned her scarred cheek towards him. It was deliberate, he knew. She was testing him: could he see the worst she had to offer and not look away?

He went over and sat down on her bed. "How are you?" he asked.

She smiled - that sardonic, half-smile which always promised a hint of challenge.

"Still alive," she said. He liked her deep border accent, he decided.

He slid closer to her. "Marry me," he said. The words just came out and hung for a moment in the space between them. He must have been thinking it before but he could not recall when.

Her response began with a resounding peal of laughter and ended with: "No!"

Upon which she turned away, showing him her scarred

right side again. The burns had healed as much as they ever would, leaving a swathe of red across her cheek and down the side of her neck. He leant in to her and took her face in his hands, turning it so that he could see both sides. The ravaged skin gave nothing away but her eyes told him all he needed to know.

"Marry me," he said again softly.

She stared at him, only now taking his offer seriously. "I thought you spoke in jest."

She pulled away and leant back on the wall. "Why you would want to marry a disfigured bitch like me? Why, for that matter, would I want to marry you?"

"You love me," he said simply.

"And you would know that, would you?" she said, the half-smile shone again.

"I don't hear you denying it," he said.

She took his hands in hers. "There are other women you could have," she said.

"But I want you. I love you."

"When did love become a reason for folk to marry?"

It was a fair question but he suspected that in her case it was born out of bitterness.

"How can you love me?" she asked him. "You haven't seen me for four years! And before that we'd not spend more than a few days under the same roof."

"When I thought I would die in Flanders, you were in my mind a great deal," he said.

"And what was I doing there…in your mind?" she asked.

"You were… helping me."

"Bah! A doomed man's delusions," she scoffed. "You know nothing about me!"

"I know I love you. That I would walk through…"

"…fire?" The bitter smile returned. "Well, I can't argue with that, I suppose."

He had walked through fire twice already: last night and

the first day he met her when he carried her out of the blackened bowels of Crag Tower.

"I'm sorry," he said. "It was a thoughtless thing to say."

"Do you fall in love with all the women you rescue?" she asked.

"Only Amelie and you."

"And how many have you rescued?"

"Two."

She grinned, but then gave a heavy, leaden sigh. "It would be a mistake. I would be terrible to live with."

"So would I."

"Aye. You're a dangerous man, to be sure…"

But the smile was still there, he noticed. "I'll keep asking until you say 'aye'."

"Well, you'll oft be disappointed then, because I'll not say 'aye'."

"Then… at least don't refuse me now - take your time to consider."

She hesitated and for a moment he feared she might reject his suit again out of hand but she suddenly leant forward and kissed his cheek.

"Should that give me hope?" he asked.

"No, but we will see how matters fall out in the winter. You are my lord and I will be guided by you in all things - except this one. Don't press me, I beg you."

"You need beg me for nothing. I'll not ask you again but consider the proposal is always there for you to take up if you please. I'm not likely to be asking anyone else."

She nodded. "Very well, but I'm sure that's what suitors always say."

"Not this one."

"Enough, my lord." She pushed him gently off her bed and got up. "What is to be done here now… at Crag?"

Ned had been considering that and he could see only one viable course of action to take.

"If we were to leave here, would it be hard for you?" he

asked.

She shook her head. "I've lived here a long while. At times it was hard, at others it was a fine place to be. But for the past four years it's been like a prison and just now I'd be pleased if I never saw it again."

"Good," he said, "because we can't defend it. We'll leave today!"

"Well then, my lord, we had both better get moving!"

§§§§

When Ned stepped out into the courtyard, tendrils of smoke still drifted up from the stables but elsewhere the fires were cold. The gates were burned to ash and all that remained of the storehouses was a heap of charred timber. A tidy, if grotesque, stack of bodies was piled up near the entrance. The yard was littered with the grisly debris of battle and in places the cobbles reeked of blood.

Even his first casual glance around Crag Tower confirmed that they could not defend it, but it was more than that: he no longer wanted to defend it. Too many good men had died here already; their lives wasted defending this stone tomb. It did not feel like an ancestral home. He should not be here amongst the squabbling families of the northern marches. His real enemies lay further south: Thomas Gate, Joan Elder and the Earl of Warwick. Those were the folk who had spilled the blood of his kin and friends. And there was Agnes - Gate would lead him to Agnes. As for his sisters, Christ alone knew where they were and he wasn't even sure he wanted to know.

Ragwulf joined him. "What now, lord?" he asked.

"We go south," said Ned.

"We've only got four mounts - and there are seven of us."

"We'll walk and the women can ride - if need be, the women can walk too. Listen, we have little enough here but

I want every scrap that's of any use put on those horses."

Ragwulf nodded and hurried away to busy himself with the necessary preparations. Ned looked after him thoughtfully. Ragwulf looked pale, haggard; perhaps he was ill. He was always quiet but now he seemed more distant, brooding. Well, he had been to that place himself often enough and nothing cured him faster than hard work.

He was surprised how soon they were ready to leave and it brought home to him how miserable Crag Tower had been for them all whilst he was in Flanders. In the end they loaded up all four mounts with an assortment of weapons, food and clothing. Thus all of them were obliged to walk and he was concerned for Maighread, uncertain how well she would cope but he need not have worried. After the second time he enquired about her, she responded with a terse question: "Do I seem unsteady to you, my lord?"

"Not at all," he replied hastily.

"Then you may take it that I am quite well able to walk unless I tell you otherwise."

Ned found all women difficult to fathom but he was beginning to think that Maighread was more difficult than most. Perhaps she was right about his sudden proposal and perhaps she really did not care for him after all.

As if she could read his mind, Maighread took his arm and linked hers through it, clasping his hand in hers. He smiled and saw that the gesture did not go unnoticed by the others, except for Will. For the young lad, who had spent most of his life inside a fortified tower, everything he saw was a new experience and he stumbled alongside Becky with his eyes wide open in wonder.

When they rested for a while beside the North Tyne, Maighread sat next to him and laid her head upon his shoulder.

"You're almost as hard to read as my sister, Ellie," he said.

Maighread smiled. "I am but a simple woman."

"Hah! I have yet to meet a simple woman," he said with feeling. They sat for a while, still feeling awkward in each other's company. He almost regretted the proposal now for it had somehow changed their way with each other.

"You know, you do your sister much wrong," she said abruptly. Her bald assertion took him by surprise.

"I think I know my sister better than you," he replied curtly, confident that it was an area where he had much experience.

"I wouldn't be so sure about that - I've spent the past four years with her."

He had forgotten that. Had this unlikely pair become close? He thought not.

"I know what she's like," he said.

"You know what she was like."

"I thought she'd grown up after young Will was born, but…"

"But?"

"I don't want to talk about her, Maighread."

"But I do - and I have a reason for it. Hear me out… please."

Ned could feel the cool anger rising in him. He had put it aside for a long time, buried the cold stone of resentment deep. The last person on earth he wanted to discuss it with was Maighread.

"There's nothing to be said about it."

Maighread stroked his arm. She had a gentle touch.

"I would not marry a man who would not at least listen to his wife," she said.

He sighed. She wasn't going to leave it, he knew. "I don't want us to argue," he said.

"All the same," she answered swiftly, "a husband of mine would need to be honest with me - and I with him. We must talk about this or it will lie between us like a great hedge of thorns."

"Very well!" he conceded. "Eleanor left Amelie to die at

Yoredale Castle - she let her down... and me. Amelie was not just her sister in law - she was her friend! She left her to die - and I can never forgive her for that."

"Eleanor left her with Bagot," said Maighread.

"God's blood! Bagot was old and already wounded! She should have stayed!"

"There were others to get out of the castle," said Maighread.

"You know nothing about it, so leave it."

"I know far more than you do about it." He noticed that she had lowered her voice.

"You see: we are arguing now," he said miserably.

She stood up and offered him her hand. "Walk with me by the river," she said.

"We should be moving on," he replied.

She continued to hold out her hand, knowing he must take it or insult her. He took the hand and they set off along the bank, conscious of several pairs of eyes tracking their every move.

"You say you love me. If you have love for me," she said, "then you'll hear me out and not say a word until I've finished."

"Very well," he said, resigned to it but fearing where this was going to lead them.

"You should trust your sister's judgement more," she said.

"Hah! Judgement? She has no judgement."

"I'll tell you when I've finished," said Maighread firmly. He said nothing more. She clutched his hand more tightly but spoke with tenderness.

"You must not judge Eleanor until you have heard her. Let her explain how it was and why she did what she did."

"Has she explained it to you then?" he asked.

"Not all, but enough."

"Then tell me what you know that would make any difference to the way I feel about her."

"Eleanor must tell you herself. It's her story, not mine."

He thrust her arm aside. "Then why bother raising all this at all?"

She snatched up his hand again. "Because you are following her course and, sooner or later, you'll find her - and I might not be by your side when you do. All I beg of you is that you hear her out - before you make any rash judgements!"

He studied her face. "It matters to you?"

"A great deal."

He nodded. "If it's so important to you, then I will hear her out."

She smiled her crooked smile at him and kissed him on the cheek. He shook his head and led her back to the others.

"Perhaps we should take a morning stroll along the river too, Will," said the mischievous Becky when they returned.

"You can hold your tongue, if it's going to wag!" Ned snapped at her. "Let's walk on. We've wasted enough time here."

30

15th November 1468, at Alderman Goldwell's house in Cheap, London

Felix hurried along Bread Street, glancing left and right as he passed every lane and alley entrance. It was past curfew - in God's truth it was nearing the end of curfew. He wondered whether all his haste and secrecy were really necessary but he had chosen a course now and must let it run where it would. A few more anxious steps took him to Alderman Goldwell's house. It was large, one of the largest in Cheap, as befitted a wealthy goldsmith. Yet neither the alderman's house nor his gold would do him much good if he was taken.

Felix waited briefly in the shadow of the doorway which lay at the side of the house. Had he been followed? He listened but heard nothing. This was the moment: if he went away now, he had done no more than break curfew - not the most heinous of crimes; but if he warned his friend and helped him escape then he would step outside the law. Yet the alderman was a friend of many years and he was most certainly innocent.

He turned and rapped sharply on the door. God's faith! That sounded loud! He would rouse the whole street if he wasn't more careful. All the same, despite his loud knocking there seemed to be no immediate response from within. What now? If he banged on the door any harder he would split the timber.

Then he heard the heavy iron bolts being drawn back on the door - John Goldwell's house was built to see off even the most determined thief. The door openly slowly and Felix saw a dull wavering glow in the vestibule.

"Put out the light!" he hissed.

"Master Felix?" It was Sarah.

He pushed the door open enough to squeeze through, closed it smartly and blew out the candle she held.

"Felix!"

"Yes, my dear. Felix. Go, wake your father. I thought he might be a little more prepared."

"Prepared?"

"Just go and wake him, dear girl - and no more candles!"

He hoped his tone was not too brusque but this was no time for lengthy explanations. Sarah disappeared up the stairs and met her father on his way down. Felix waited at the foot of the stairs.

"Father, it's Felix…"

John Goldwell nodded and swept past her.

"Felix," he breathed, "so soon?"

"Matters have moved swiftly, John," said Felix. "Torture was used and you have been named, along with a servant of Lord Wenlock."

"But I've done nothing, Felix! Why would anyone name me? I'm loyal to the king. It's only a few months ago I gave gold to the Princess Margaret, here in Cheap, as she began her procession to take ship for Flanders! And I've never had any connection with Lord Wenlock."

"Perhaps it's your connection with Thomas Cook that helps condemn you. He's in trouble too."

"But he was the Mayor! I was a young alderman," insisted Goldwell, "I was bound to have business with him. I don't even like him!"

"Cook's probably innocent too but once he was accused, we knew that you would be at risk. There's panic at court - they see Lancastrian plotters everywhere. No-one's above suspicion - save the queen's family, of course. But, by whatever means it's happened, you are undone,

John."

"How long have we got?" asked John.

"I have a friend in the offices of Benjamin Warner and he suggests they'll move in at first light," said Felix.

The alderman sighed. "Sarah, wake up Jack, the apprentices and the maid - we must leave. Get anything you need to carry with you and come back down as quickly as you can."

"Leave? Why? What's happened?"

Alderman Goldwell's expression was grim. "We're ruined," he said. "Our lives are dust."

"We must hurry, John," urged Felix. "Finch waits only for the tide."

"The Catherine is in the port?"

"Yes - the Lord has smiled upon us there for The Catherine has only just returned from Newcastle - but Finch must take his cargo to Bristol on the morning tide and the tide flows early."

John looked at his daughter. "Hurry, child!"

Sarah nodded and mounted the stairs swiftly.

John turned to Felix. "I was grateful for your warning yesterday - and again now. But what will I do in Bristol - and what of my store of gold? I can hardly take that with me."

"That's in hand," replied Felix. "Gather what you need to take. I've some of Finch's men coming to carry it. But make haste, man!"

He took pity on his old friend then. The alderman was always so calm and assured but this sudden calamity had rocked him. "Come on, I'll help you."

John nodded and seemed to gather himself a little. He walked briskly through the dark Hall, only breaking his stride when he thumped into the corner of a large oak chest. There was a door at the rear of the Hall which led out to his small store in a walled yard at the back of the premises. There his strongboxes were kept securely.

At the door to the store he fumbled with his bunch of thick iron keys, seeking the one he required. It was too dark and he was working by touch alone. In his haste he dropped the keys and Felix bent down to retrieve them. He touched the alderman's shoulder lightly.

"Steady, John. It's a time for haste but also for nerve."

John nodded and finally found the right key.

"How much can Finch's men carry?" he asked.

Felix surveyed the contents of the room and even he was surprised at the stack of boxes.

"Not all that," he said.

"I'll be ruined!" breathed John.

"Choose the smallest box and fill it with what is of most value."

There was a sudden banging on the outside door, making them both jump.

"Good Christ!" said Felix, "I hope that's Finch's men. Hurry - do it now or you'll have to leave all. We've run out of time, John."

"Indeed," said the alderman.

They both knew what would happen. The first thing the crown would do was confiscate all his goods - that would make someone well off. By God's faith, the alderman had enough gold in here to buy half of Cheapside. No wonder there was a shortage in the Bristol markets.

Felix left him tossing heavy bags of gold nobles and angels into one of the chests and made for the door. If his men knocked any louder someone in Cheap would set up a cry for the watch. He let them in. They looked strong and he was glad of it for they would need all their strength to lift Alderman Goldwell's strongbox. He ushered them through the Hall and then found Sarah, the maid, Elizabeth, a sleepy young Jack and the two apprentices, George and Thomas.

"What's afoot, Master Felix?" asked George, the elder of the two apprentices.

"You're all leaving."

"Yes. but … where are we going?" The apprentice looked nonplussed.

"You'll know as soon as I do!" snapped the alderman, coming in from the back room. The two porters followed in his wake with the chest.

Felix would have preferred to leave the apprentices, but he dared not - for their sake as well as his. If torture had been used on Cornelius, the first fellow to be arrested, then he feared the same methods might be used on the servants of any others who were accused.

"Come," Alderman Goldwell told them, "we're making for the docks - a boat awaits us."

"Take heed," said Felix. "We must go silently and swiftly - we don't want the watch down upon us. George, you know the way to Trig Wharf. You take the lead with Finch's men, then Jack and his mother. Thomas can help me carry the luggage. Jack, I'm sure you're old enough to carry your own bag." The boy puffed out his chest and picked up his small cloth bag.

They went well-cloaked into the cool autumn night and John was the last out. He closed the door and stared for a moment at his fine house. Then he turned to Felix.

"The Lord is testing me this night, Felix. I shall try to bear it well. Thank the Lord my other daughters are all safely married! And, if I ever forget, remind me always of the good offices of my friends."

Felix gave him a sympathetic clap on the shoulder and they set off, moving swiftly down Bread Street, the pace set by those carrying the chest. He wrinkled his nose in distaste as they passed the end of Pissing Alley and sped on down the hill.

The alderman must feel most aggrieved, thought Felix, for he had been a staunch supporter of the House of York and now to be falsely accused of involvement in a plot to free the old Lancastrian king. It was monstrous, yet he was not alone - and how many would stand firm, he wondered, in the face of royal pressure?

"Turn left," ordered Felix, as the party halted ahead of him at the junction of Thames Street.

Finch's crew were flagging under the weight of the strongbox and the last half mile seemed to Felix to take hours, but at last they descended on to Trig Lane at the end of which was Trig Wharf. Felix was relieved to see the waiting boat for the sky was already lightening along the river channel beyond London Bridge to the east.

"Get a move on," he urged. Finch's men loaded the chest aboard the small boat and the others crowded in around it.

"I leave you then in the capable hands of Master Finch," said Felix, shaking John's hand. "I'll ride to Bristol and meet you at the docks. Then we'll try to get you to Ludlow. God be with you all."

Soon Felix was left alone on the wharf watching the craft begin to crawl across into the stream and attempt to pass between the pillars of the bridge. Felix held his breath for the boat was heavily laden and going under the bridge could be a dangerous manoeuvre at the best of times since the river's flow varied alarmingly. They seemed to make it through safely.

"God speed you," he breathed though they would not have heard him for they were soon out of his sight on the other side of the bridge heading to where they would find The Catherine moored and ready to leave. They would be safe enough with Finch but now came the harder part of his task: to prevent the alderman being condemned for treason in his absence.

As Felix made his way from Trig Wharf, he noticed there were more folk about as the end of curfew neared. Several men were loading a small hand cart, a few women of the night with painted faces scurried past him and a boatman waited idly on the quay. When Felix disappeared the boatman got up and ghosted up the street after him.

31

16th November 1468, in the hills above Yoredale

Ned stood out in the open with the rain dripping from the filthy hem of his cloak. The horses stamped their feet, restless in the damp.

"This cattle shed needs a roof," observed Spearbold. The crumbling walls offered them precious little protection and he was soaked through, as were the rest of them.

"It's a shieling," growled Ragwulf, shaking the rainwater from his matted hair, "and it would be sheep not cattle that would come up here."

"Don't mind me!" said Spearbold. "It's like standing by a wet dog!"

"Peace!" said Ned. His head was still sore and he was tired of their moaning. "Another lord would flay the hides off you for your endless griping."

"Then we would not be following that lord," said Maighread. "But we have followed you. So, my lord, what would you have us do now?"

Ned examined the rain-filled sky once more but he could see no break in the great blanket of steel grey cloud. He weighed up the options which were few enough. He had hoped to spend the night at the shieling high above the Yoredale valley but the weather made his plan untenable. There were fewer trees on the upland slopes and in any case autumn had taken its toll of leaf cover. He had barely set foot in the vale for four years; how did he know where they could wait in safety?

"Ragwulf - any ideas?" he asked.

"Lord," said Ragwulf, "it may be that my cottage in Carperby is still empty."

"After four years? And it's not your cottage, it's the estate's. Someone else will have it now."

Ragwulf nodded. Ned was worried about Ragwulf - or perhaps his memories of the rugged soldier were false. Four years was a long time he was discovering … in every respect.

"There's an old ruined mill…" Ragwulf said.

"I know it," said Ned at once. He knew it and he would not easily forget it. The miller had been burned to death in it - and his wife with him. Ned had found the miller's son, John Holton, in a bad state. With nowhere else to go and few friends, Holton had been apprenticed at Elder Hall. It seemed… it was … a very long time ago. In the years since, Holton had repaid the debt a thousand-fold - and suffered for it. It would be good to see Holton again, he thought, but Holton was at Corve now.

"My lord?" enquired Spearbold.

Ned turned to Ragwulf. "Will the mill be any better than this?" he asked.

"It was last time I was there, but that was a lifetime ago."

Ned thought his own outlook was a little bleak but Ragwulf would easily outdo him in that regard.

"It's south of-"

"I know where it is," Ned cut him off sharply. "It's more dangerous than here. So, we'll walk west and go down into the valley west of Carperby where there'll be fewer eyes to see us. It'll take the rest of the day. Let's hope this weather keeps men inside."

They all seemed glad to move - anything, he supposed, was preferable to standing or squatting in the rain.

He took Maighread's hand to lift her to her feet. Her woollen cloak was sodden and her face was pale and streaked with muddy water.

"It will be harder going now," he said, "the slopes will be treacherous with all this rain." He offered her his arm. She hesitated for only an instant before she threaded hers through it and gripped him tightly.

"Then... I put myself in your hands, my lord," she said.

As they crossed the barren hillside north of Yoredale, the rain came on more heavily and soon obliterated all around them from sight. When they finally turned south to descend into the vale, they found the rocky slopes almost impassable. Angry becks cut across their path, impossible to avoid and lethal to cross. Their heavily-laden horses slid and stumbled as they tried in vain to gain some purchase on the slippery stones and muddy banks.

The horses were not the only ones having difficulty. Becky held tight to Will's hand and the pair helped each other along. They all fell more than once, heads were cut and limbs bruised. Maighread screamed as she and Ned fell together and were swept down a short stretch of water to splash into a deep pool where the water cascaded down upon them. Ned's feet just touched the bottom but Maighread sank like one of the stones. He put his arms around her and lifted her up, holding her close to him. They stood as one with a great spout of water drenching them from above. He could feel Maighread shaking next to him.

"Don't be afraid!" he said, pressing his lips to her scarred ear. She pulled her face back a few inches and he saw that she was laughing.

"For all your faults, Ned Elder - and they are many - there's much to love about you!"

"Then we should marry!" he declared.

"Are you mad, my lord?" she cried as the beck continued to pour its torrent on them. "I'm freezing! We should get out!"

He kissed her and then she was laughing. He couldn't remember her laughing much before. "Marry me," he said "and I'll get you out!"

"No good can come of this!" she replied, but she was still laughing.

"Aye, but shall we do it anyway?"

She shook her head and stopped laughing. She leant her forehead against his and let the water consume them. "Aye, we shall," she said softly.

"Did you say 'aye'?" he shouted above the roar of the fall.

"Aye, I'm such a weak reed. A few kisses and I give myself to the first man who asks."

He grinned back at her, astonished. And then she kissed him long and hard on the lips.

There was an ironic cheer from close by and Ned turned to see all the others lining the pool, watching them.

"Well…help us out then!" he shouted.

"We didn't think you needed any help!" replied Becky.

"Is everyone still in one piece?" asked Ned, looking around him.

"Aye," said Ragwulf, "but one of the mounts is lame."

"I think one man seems to have fallen!" cried Becky.

"Bear! That girl needs to be soundly whipped!" Ned retorted. They all laughed and willing hands dragged them the sodden pair out of the pool.

Ned shook his head for each one of them was covered in dripping mud from head to foot, except for Maighread and himself.

"Well," said Maighread, "we certainly can't get any wetter!"

"Aye," he said and pointed to the pool. "You'd best clean yourselves up. Then we'll make our way through the forest to the mill.

At the end of the dull afternoon, darkness came early. The rain steadied to a light drizzle as they entered the thick forest of Yoredale. Ned knew it as well as any, from a childhood spent there.

"No sound now," he warned, "just in case…"

He took Maighread by the hand and the rest followed: Becky with Will; Spearbold and Bear leading most of the horses and then Ragwulf at the back with the lamed animal. Ned led them well wide of Carperby with its small garths, giving way to closer rows of cottages on the east side of the village. He did not like it, skulking in the trees like a criminal where once he had ridden like a lord. But he was afraid now to meet those who once doffed their caps to him and wished him good health as he passed them at work in the open fields.

He stopped when he emerged from the trees onto a clear track through the woodland. In the failing light he could make out little. They joined the path and made faster progress for a time but he knew they were all cold and weary: Maighread clung onto him for support, Spearbold was grey with the exertion and young Will stumbled frequently as he plodded on. The lame horse was also struggling but eventually Ned could hear the river running nearby. They must be close to the mill now and soon he was relieved to see its dark outline emerge from the tree line ahead of them.

"Wait here," he said softly.

"I'll go, lord," offered Ragwulf.

"No, you'll stay with Lady Maighread and the others."

Ragwulf nodded. Ned eased out his sword; the blade would be rusting he had no doubt.

"Don't come in until I call you," he ordered.

The grass around the decayed building was long but it had been trampled down in places and he was on his guard. The mill had seen other visitors but some time ago, he thought. Much of the blackened shell had fallen to the ground and rotted but enough remained, he decided, to give them shelter - unless, of course it was already occupied.

He trod carefully but still stumbled, tripped by beams of timber or pieces of stone, half-hidden under the grass.

There was no light showing, no fire, no smoke, no sound. He stood in what had once been the doorway to the chamber which housed the mill's grinding wheel. Little remained of it: no door and not much wall. Beyond it lay a store room which, from the look of the roof, seemed to provide the most shelter. Others had clearly thought so too for there were many signs of occupation - not least a large charred patch on the stone flags that had once been the floor. He bent down to touch the ashes: stone cold.

"Come in!" he called out and the others slowly filed in. He went at once to Maighread and took her arm, guiding her through the hazards into the store room.

She looked about her and shook her head, laughing her low, growling laugh. "I see you choose your refuges with care, my lord!"

He gave her an apologetic smile. What he would have preferred to do was sweep her up now into his arms and kiss her. He wondered what her response would be if he did so with all the others gathered around them. He thought either she would return his kiss or slap him; trouble was he could never tell which.

§§§§

Maighread spent a restless night at the mill. She lay awake for long periods, unsettled by the damp odour of the charred timbers around her. But it was not just the place. Ned lay beside her and she was still not sure how she felt about that. He had fallen asleep with his arm across her shoulder. Somehow it made her feel safe but an array of nagging doubts assailed her about their sudden intimacy. His arm was still there when dawn brought a grey and miserable morning. She gently left Ned asleep and stood up. Wrapping her still damp cloak around her, she went outside.

In what had once been the doorway, Ragwulf was on watch, leaning against one of the few upright timbers that remained. He nodded to her. "My lady?"

"I need to take a walk down to the river," she whispered.

"I'd better come with you," he said.

"You'd better not!" she retorted. "Unless you want to watch while I relieve myself?"

"Your pardon, lady, I just meant..."

"I know what you meant," she said, "and I thank you, but I'm only going a few yards."

He nodded. "Scream if you see anyone," he said.

She rolled her eyes. Who would she be likely to see here at this time of day? Still, she favoured him with a grateful smile, and set off through the trees towards the sound of the water. The ground felt spongy, peat soil rain-sodden and squelching beneath her feet. The river was, as she expected, very close by and there was something soothing about the way it followed its course past her. There was always a rhythm to a river, she thought, and each one seemed different.

"You don't care, Mistress River, do you?" she muttered to herself. She looked down at her filthy, ragged clothing. It need burning, not washing! She walked a little further along the bank and then slipped away from the track to find a place to squat well screened by the trees. It already smelt pretty ripe, she thought as she lifted her kirtle. Then she saw the face. She felt numb. She stared at it, fighting back tears. The face stared back, grey, almost black. The young man, buried shallow in the peat, was long dead. His skin was discoloured, his flesh swollen and animals had gnawed at his ears. Birds had pecked fissures in his cheeks and eyes, yet it was still her brother's face which stared back at her.

§§§§

Ned dashed past Ragwulf after the first scream, racing towards the river, sword already in hand. The others followed swiftly behind him, another scream driving them on. After the third scream there was silence and he feared the worst - yet there she was still standing and not a mark upon her. Then he saw what she was looking at and Maighread fell into his arms sobbing. Ragwulf threw his cloak over the head before Becky and Will arrived with Spearbold and Bear.

No-one spoke. Ned walked Maighread back to the mill with a glance back to Ragwulf. He spoke softly to her. She had thought her brother dead once before, but now... to see him there, half-buried in the forest.

"Eleanor," she whispered suddenly. "Rob left Crag with Eleanor."

"Ragwulf and Bear will search," he replied. "If she's out there too, then they'll find her."

He did not expect them to find her though; Eleanor was a survivor, like him. She would still be alive, though all around her perished. He sat Maighread down in the mill and draped his cloak around her. She shrugged it off immediately.

"It's still damp," she said. "Besides, I'm not ill, I'm just shocked."

"I know," he said, feeling utterly inadequate. He needed to do something so he got up and left Becky to sit with Maighread.

He joined Ragwulf and Bear who had finished examining Rob's body and were now beginning to search the woods nearby. They found nothing. No-one.

"Can you tell what happened to him?" he asked.

"Wound in the back, lord," said Ragwulf, "turned to shit."

"And that killed him?"

"He might have died of it," he said, "or he might have starved or it could have been the cold that finished him."

"God's blood! Well, someone's buried him - or tried to."

"We don't think so," said Ragwulf. "It looks more like

he's piled leaves and peat over himself, perhaps to hide? Who knows?"

"Well, someone does - my sister must have left him."

"My lord, there's no sign of Lady Eleanor," said Ragwulf.

What sign would his sister leave, he wondered? A trail of bleeding bodies, probably - well, they had one.

"They left Crag together," observed Ragwulf.

"So?" He hoped the man might take the hint and stop going on about her.

"Well, she'd have stayed with him, if she could…"

"And what would you know about it?" He regretted his angry tone but it was enough to ward off any further comments from Ragwulf, who gave him a curt nod and turned to go. "Wait!" said Ned. "Who would know? Who'd know what happened? Who would she go to here?"

"Canon Reedman," replied Ragwulf without hesitation, "he's just about the only one she could trust."

"Would Reedman trust you?" asked Ned.

"Aye, lord, I suppose… if he remembers me."

"Go and get him," ordered Ned.

"Go to Coverham Abbey, now?"

"Aye, bring him here."

"What if he won't come?"

Ned sighed. His head was beginning to ache again. "Then bring him anyway. Take a spare horse for him."

He returned to the mill and crouched down beside Maighread. She looked up at him and frowned.

"What is it?" he said.

"I know that grim face."

"There's no trace of Eleanor," he said.

"Rob followed her willingly," she murmured, "and if you'd asked him if he would have followed her even to his death, he would have said 'aye'."

Ned shook his head.

"You can be swift to judge, Ned Elder," she said. "We

don't know what happened."

"No, not yet. But I will know… and soon."

§§§§

Ragwulf was gone most of the day and the longer he was away, the more anxious Ned became. He had been foolish to send Ragwulf out on his own when he suspected there were Yoredale men about. His headache had turned into a nagging, drumming throb and he could feel the anger and frustration rising in him. He was little use to Maighread and left her to find comfort with the others. He was not surprised to find that the one she turned to was Bear. Their bond had been forged in the hours after Ned had first discovered her, half-burned and half-mad from her ordeal. It was Bear who knew how to treat her terrible burns but it was more than that: the big man possessed a sensitivity which always eluded Ned.

It was cool by the river. No sun and a trace of mist. He kept an impatient watch, pacing in a great circle along the riverbank and through the thick forest that clothed the mill. He saw others from time to time, especially near the river, but easily avoided being seen. He had spent half his life in these woods and he'd wager that no-one knew them better than he… except perhaps Eleanor. Now there was a puzzle, his younger sister. Why did he doubt her? He just could not see clearly how it had all ended at Yoredale four years ago. If only he had not been wounded, much might have been different.

Close behind him the bracken rustled and he turned abruptly, hand on his sword hilt. Maighread flinched and then grimaced.

"Sorry, you surprised me," he said. Dear Lord, he sounded gruff.

"I'm a surprising sort of woman," replied Maighread.

"Are you alright?" he asked.

"Aye." She smiled and put her arm through his. "I'll walk with you."

After they walked together for a while he found that the throbbing inside his head was easing. Even in her own grief, she was able to work some miracle for him.

By mid-afternoon, the sky was closing in and the mist turned into a dense November fog - another reminder of his childhood by this river. He put his arm around Maighread and they returned to the mill along the river track. They had only just reached it, when they heard the horses and turned to wait.

It was many years since Ned had last seen Canon Reedman but the monk was only a little greyer than he recalled. He had never known the man well, as Emma had, but he thought he might be trustworthy. But then, as Bagot always told him, 'Trust no-one' - not even a cleric.

The canon was grim-faced as he followed Ragwulf off the track and headed towards the mill. There he dismounted and darted anxious looks into the forest before entering the derelict building.

"God give you good day, Canon Reedman," said Ned.

Reedman took several paces towards him and peered at him in the gloom.

"Lord Elder?" the canon hesitated.

"Not lord of very much at the moment," said Ned. "Has Ragwulf told you what we found?"

Reedman gave a slight nod and Ned took him to where Rob's corpse had been laid outside the mill. Ned watched him trying to make sense of what he saw and it was clear enough that he recognised Rob. Nevertheless, he looked puzzled.

"I'm sorry to see the lad thus," he said, "but surely you did not find him here?"

"No," said Ned, "someone, perhaps even he, made a half-hearted effort at burial in the forest off the track."

The canon nodded and seemed reassured. Ned took him

into the mill and introduced Maighread.

"This lady is his sister, Lady Maighread Elder - my aunt."

Reedman gave a slight bow to Maighread and went over to her.

"Your brother was brave, very brave at the end but there was little hope. The wound was a grievous one."

"You saw him?" asked Ned.

"Aye, my lord. Your sister, Lady Eleanor, brought me to tend his wound but the arrow head was in too deep and I came too late. I did what I could but I feared it would not be enough and thereafter I relied upon prayer."

"He probably died from the wound, canon," said Ned.

He nodded his head. "I know nothing more, my lord. I told Lady Eleanor I'd return after a few days and see how he fared then."

"And did you?"

"Aye, I did - and they were both gone. There was no sign of them, so I assumed he had recovered enough for them to move on."

"Well he didn't get very far, did he?" said Ned. "How long ago was all this?"

"Well, certainly it was before Michaelmas, so it must be more than two months ago now."

"Aye, so it appeared from the state of the ..." He glanced at Maighread.

"Where is your sister, Lady Eleanor?" asked Reedman.

"Now that's a question I find myself asking more and more. Where indeed? You'd better tell me all you know."

"I've already done so, my lord, except that Lady Eleanor told me they had just escaped from Middleham."

"Middleham? God's blood! What were they doing in Middleham - of all places?" asked Ned. "I was told that Emma's boy was taken to Middleham - might that be why they were there?"

"That, I couldn't say, my lord," replied Reedman.

"Do you know anything about how the lad's doing?"

"I've heard that he's a young page, my lord, and that he is doing well."

"What about the others? Have you seen any of my men? My sister was following Hal and Wulf, I believe."

"Indeed I have. I told Lady Eleanor what Hal told me: that Wulf, Bess and the others were to enter service at Yoredale but that Hal and the boy, John, would go on to Corve Manor."

"Hal has gone to Corve?"

"Aye, he has. I suppose Lady Eleanor has followed them."

"Leaving Rob Hall lying in the woods…" said Ned coldly.

"She would not have done that!" said Maighread.

"No, you're right, the Eleanor I remember was wild but I'd like to think she would not have left a friend. But then she left Amelie…"

"You don't know that either, my lord!" snapped Maighread. Her vehemence took him by surprise for he could not see why she leapt so swiftly to her niece's defence.

A sudden thought occurred to him. "Canon Reedman, you knew my other sister well, as I recall."

"Indeed, my lord, we first met a very long time ago."

"I don't suppose you've heard any news of her?" asked Ned.

"News, my lord? I have received no news about the Lady Emma," he answered. He looked disappointed, Ned thought, but the canon had been fond of her as he remembered.

"There was talk of her taking holy orders," said Ned.

"She certainly intended to, my lord, but what happened I couldn't say…"

"Did you say that young John is with Hal?" Maighread asked the canon.

"That's what Hal told me."

"That's good," she said.

"Hardly," retorted Ned, "what does one boy matter when the rest of my young wolves have taken service with Joan Elder!"

"Not Joan Elder, my lord," said Reedman, "Sir Thomas Gate holds Yoredale now…he married Lady Joan…" He broke off when he saw the look on Ned's face.

"Thomas Gate is at Yoredale?" Ned breathed the words, scarcely able to believe it. Gate had mentioned Middleham, but Yoredale…

"Aye, he's recruiting men and many have joined him…"

"Thomas Gate is here…"

"My lord?"

Ned ignored the cleric. His head had started throbbing again with a sharp, insistent pain - the head wound Agnes had treated for so long. He could not think. He let out an explosive roar and stormed outside. He put his hands to his temples but the lance of pain did not subside.

Maighread followed him. "Ned, don't do anything rash!" she pleaded and took his arm.

He shook her off and strode off along the river path but she ran after him and pulled him back.

"Leave me, woman!" he barked at her and raised his arm to strike her. She dropped down on to her knees and cowered at his feet. Then he stopped, looked at her and lowered his arm to lift her to her feet. She hesitated and then took his hand.

He could not meet her eyes. "I ask your pardon, my lady." He had spoken too harshly, he knew, though he had not meant to do so. Maighread kept a firm grip on his hand and the stabbing inside his head eased a little.

"I've just lost one man I loved," she said, "I'd rather not lose the other."

"There's much you don't know," he said. "There's been no time to tell you what happened in Flanders."

"I know that Thomas Gate has done you great wrong and that is enough, but don't let him draw you in to destroy you. Wait. Wait, until you can win!"

"But Agnes…"

"Can you take Yoredale Castle?"

"No."

"Then you'll not help Agnes by joining my brother Rob."

He felt her squeeze his hand and drew her to him. They stood together for some time on the riverbank and when the pain in his head finally subsided he led her back to the mill. There he found the others waiting, anxiety and fear etched on their faces. All save Bear, who stood as tall and still as a great beam of oak - impassive as ever and ready to withstand whatever fate hurled at him next.

They were all waiting for Ned to decide what to do and when he did they would follow; they would obey him - even if what he proposed might be dangerous. For his part, as he walked arm in arm with Maighread, he reflected that he should not lightly put them into danger. That was what good lordship meant.

"There's nothing to be gained by staying here now," he told them. "We'll give our loyal friend, Rob Hall, a decent burial and then we'll follow the others to Corve. We'll winter there and I'll raise men on the estates. In the spring I'll come back here, find Agnes and settle matters with Thomas Gate."

He glanced at Maighread who leant against him and whispered: "Well spoken, my lord."

PART FIVE: SEASON OF GOOD WILL

DEREK BIRKS

32

12th December 1468, Yoredale Castle

"This is madness!" muttered Hal. "We risk too much, my lady!"

"We can't just sit all winter and wait," said Eleanor. "We need to … make plans."

"Plans? Well I've none - no plans save staying alive a little longer, and trying to keep others alive too."

They were waiting in the small chapel but Father Baston had not arrived.

"Are you sure we can trust him?" she asked.

"I wouldn't have brought you otherwise, my lady."

"You'd best stop calling me that or you'll do it when you shouldn't," said Eleanor. She glanced furtively around her as she paced up and down the short nave.

"Where is he, then?"

"Lady, he'll be here. Be patient."

Eleanor stopped in front of him and her eyes smoked through him. "I may look like a stonemason's widow and I may tell you not to address me as 'my lady'," she breathed, "but don't forget who I am!"

Hal dropped his eyes down to his boots. "I ask your pardon," he said. "I meant no offence."

Eleanor relented and lifted his chin with her forefinger. "We're all mummers here, Hal; all playing our parts but I'm not a player by nature."

The main door to the chapel opened, Father Baston hurried inside and closed it firmly behind him. He stared briefly at Eleanor.

"This is-"

"Don't say it," said Father Baston, cutting Hal off. "I think I know who she is. Come."

He led them to sit beneath the oak rood screen. He glanced up and indicated the gallery window at the far end of the chapel. "If we sit here, Lady Joan might not hear us, but she can see us and she would not be pleased to see us together. She is not in her chamber at present so we must be swift."

"Before we are swift, let us be sure," said Eleanor. "I know how Hal and I came to be here - but I'm less sure about you. Tell me, how is it that a priest from Crag Tower finds his way to the very same castle as the lady who used to reside in Crag Tower?"

Father Baston nodded gravely. "Aye - a fair question my lady," he said, "and of course it is no accident that I am here."

"Tell us," said Eleanor.

"Time is short - we may be discovered," said Father Baston.

"Hal has told me a little but I can place no trust in you, unless I know what you are here for."

"Very well," conceded Father Baston. "It's not a long explanation - simply one I've never told and don't relish telling."

Eleanor said nothing.

"I was born in the shadow of Crag Tower," began Father Baston. "My father was Sir Thomas Elder's steward and my mother was Lady Margaret's companion. Sir Thomas provided for me very well and I was sent to school. I studied hard and-"

"Good Christ, man - I don't want to know every time you broke wind!"

Father Baston looked shocked. "Very well, in short I trained as a priest. When I was sent back to my home I was joyous, overwhelmed - until I arrived back at Crag Tower to find that my parents and my benefactors were all dead. Then I walked into Sir Stephen who asked me to say some words over the grave Lord Elder made. I could hardly speak - and at that time I didn't know that my own mother was amongst the poor burned souls in that grave."

Eleanor regretted her impatient interruption.

"So you see, my lady, I'm not here for any Christian reason. I came here for one reason only: revenge. But I am twice shamed."

"How twice shamed?" asked Eleanor.

"Once, for seeking revenge in spite of Christ's teaching and my own vows, and twice for being too spineless to carry through my design. Then Hal came…and I saw the boy whipped…and it brought it all back."

"The most important thing is to get Lady Eleanor and the boy out," said Hal.

"It's not just getting out," said Eleanor, "it's getting away. I could probably walk out the main gate and no-one would stop me, but if I take John with me, there'll be questions and too much attention will be drawn."

"You're wrong, my lady," said Father Baston, "you wouldn't get as far as the main gate. You're being watched - you too, Hal. Weaver has folk watching you wherever you go."

"But why would Weaver suspect me?" asked Eleanor. "I know he wants to bed me, but it can't just be that!"

"Why does Weaver do anything?" asked the priest. "Because Lady Joan wills it."

"She suspects us then," said Hal.

"Aye, she suspects," said Father Baston, "but she knows nothing. If she did, you'd all be dead by now."

"So, we daren't wait any longer then," said Hal.

"But to act too soon may kill us all," said the priest.

"Well, Father, no-one can accuse you of that!" said Eleanor. "But I agree. There's already a covering of snow on the ground and there's still the question of where to go."

"I could only think of Corve Manor," said Hal, "and it's a long way in winter with no mounts."

"Unless we steal them," said Eleanor.

"We'll have but one chance, my lady," cautioned Hal. "If we fail, we'll never get another."

"We should wait until the spring then," said Father Baston.

"But you've just said how close we're being watched!" said Eleanor. "Sooner or later, we'll give ourselves away."

"Not if we don't meet - just keep to ourselves," said the priest.

"I suppose we might last till spring," conceded Eleanor, "but if Joan Elder gets one clear look at my face, she'll know me."

"I'm concerned for Agnes too," said Hal. "Sir Walter keeps her tight to him, the old goat. When I think…"

"Well, don't," said Eleanor. "Learn not to think about it. Christ knows we've all got our fears. Just remember that if you die, you will never free Agnes."

"So," said Father Baston, "it's agreed: we'll wait till the spring, keep our heads down and not draw attention."

"We should try to get word to my sister or my brother," said Eleanor. She looked at Father Baston. "You can come and go, can't you?"

"So far," he conceded.

"Could you tell Canon Reedman at Coverham that we're here?"

"Yes, by God," said Hal, "Reedman will still think I've gone to Corve."

Father Baston nodded. "Aye, I suppose I could. But you two must not speak to me again - or to each other. He put an arm on Hal's shoulder. "Be strong, young man. God will watch over your Agnes."

"I hope so, Father."

"You leave first, Hal," said Eleanor, "best we don't go together."

Eleanor looked at the priest when Hal had gone. "You're wrong about Agnes," she said.

"But she's safe at least."

"Safe, Father?" said Eleanor in a quiet voice. "Aye, she's as safe as any whore - just how safe do you think that is? And she's not a whore by choice…Walter Grave may be her protector for now, but you may be sure that if Hal does not kill him for what he has made her into, I shall."

"We all have reason to hate and I wish it were not so. All my prayers tell me it should not be so. But I must find the will, somehow… to have my revenge on Joan Elder."

Eleanor nodded and went out.

§§§§

Joan watched from the gallery, transfixed, as the chapel door below closed. She looked down upon Father Baston, already beginning to doubt what she had overheard. She had noticed the muffled voices when she entered her chamber. As she walked swiftly to the tiny window overlooking the chapel she caught a snatch of the priest's final words. By the time she looked down, the woman was almost through the door and she glimpsed only the top of a wimple.

If only she had chanced to come back a few moments earlier. It was a conspiracy of that there was no doubt - and she had the priest nailed for a certainty. He would have his revenge, would he? She didn't think so. But revenge for what? She had never doubted the priest for an instant. What did he want revenge for? And what did he want with the woman? Surely they weren't…in his chapel…

It irked her not to know what was going on in her own castle. She glanced across at Margaret, whose stare demanded an explanation. The timing was appalling: she must shortly leave Yoredale with Thomas to spend the Christmas season at some God-forsaken place further north. The Lord only knew how long it would take to get there. In her absence she would have to rely on her faithful dog, Weaver - and Margaret, of course. She would let them loose and see if between them they could prise an explanation out of Father Baston, and find the woman. Weaver liked women…

It was not ideal though. Sir Walter would hold sway whilst she and her husband were absent. He must receive all the rents on Christmas Day - he was a fool but he was good at that, at least. Grave disliked Weaver and Weaver disliked him - the pair of them would fight like dogs whilst she and Thomas were gone. She would need to give Weaver some leverage, some influence, or Grave might act against him.

Margaret was still waiting silently.

"Go and fetch Weaver," said Joan.

33

18th December 1468, at Corve Manor north of Ludlow

Ned could not decide what he felt when the high walls of Corve Manor came into view. It was very much how he recalled it - even the light covering of snow seemed familiar. None of his companions had ever been there except Bear so he sent the great warrior on ahead to warn of their coming. After seven years, his steward, John Holton, might be forgiven if he never expected to see Ned again.

"So this is your other great stronghold, my lord," said Maighread with a grin.

"I know it doesn't look like much," he said.

She smiled wearily. "I was teasing - it looks like a royal palace compared to Crag Tower!"

The short drawbridge was already lowered in anticipation of their arrival and they walked across and straight into the courtyard beyond.

"You're tired, I know," he said gently, "and you're putting on a brave face."

She frowned and it dawned on him yet again that he had spoken thoughtlessly.

"Aye, I'm lucky," she said, "I've two faces I can put on simply by a turn of my head - and if you tell me you're sorry again, Ned Elder, I'll strike you."

Facing them in the yard were John Holton and his wife, Margaret - though to Ned she would always be Mags. Holton towered over his wife for he was even taller and broader than Bear. Ned noticed that even Maighread was staring at Holton's face, yet despite his size it was his most distinctive feature. It was a miracle he survived the wound at all for it had torn a broad gully across his face from ear to chin. Ned quickly introduced everyone and Holton ushered them all into the Hall where several servants waited.

"Our great lord, Ned Elder, has returned to us!" Holton announced with genuine joy but Ned observed the bleak look that Mags gave her husband. It was clear she was not as pleased as he to see Ned Elder once again.

"It's been a long time, my friend," said Ned.

"My lord, I trust I have served you well in your absence."

"I don't doubt it!" retorted Ned. If there was a more loyal servant than Holton, he had never met him.

"Lady Maighread," said Holton, "I hope you'll forgive my grisly face. God knows I was an ugly youth but I fear my face is now a mask of horror for those who must look upon it."

Maighread gave him a wry smile. "As you can no doubt see for yourself, master steward, we share a common fault."

"How long will you stay, my lord?" asked Mags quickly.

Ned almost laughed aloud. Still the same old Mags, he thought, as blunt as an armourer's hammer. But he understood better now than he ever had before. To her, he was an angel of death and she feared that his presence alone would bring destruction upon them all.

"We will spend a frugal Christmas here and make our plans in the New Year, dear Mags - and you need not look so worried. I shall never take your man from you again. He has done more service for me already than almost any other."

She thanked him before excusing herself to ensure that their rooms were ready.

"But where are the others, Holton?" asked Ned. "Surely Hal and Lady Eleanor are here by now?"

"My lord?" said Holton. "We've seen none here but

Master Felix - and we've not seen him for months."

Ned looked around at Maighread, Ragwulf and Bear. Maighread looked distraught but it was Ragwulf who spoke: "But surely they're here, Master Holton," he pleaded, "Lady Eleanor… and the others."

Holton shook his head. "I'm afraid we've had no other visitors, my lord, but Corve is yours to command."

Ned tried to collect his thoughts. Canon Reedman had been quite clear about Hal, less so concerning Eleanor. He intended to discover from Hal what was going on at Yoredale but now…

"Very well then," he mumbled hastily, "a chamber for Lady Maighread and one for me - though I could share with Spearbold, if needs be."

He needed to think, but more than that he needed to rest. Whilst the others saw to the horses and the few belongings they had brought, he accompanied Maighread up to her chamber. Unusually quiet, she sat down on the bed.

"This changes everything," he said.

"Aye," she said, "and more than you can know."

He took her bitter reply as further evidence of her weariness and left her.

§§§§

The following morning Ned wasted no time in putting his retainers to work. He sent Spearbold straight off to see Felix, to inform him of their arrival at Corve.

"Find out if Felix knows where the king is to spend Christmas - or the New Year. I must get to him as soon as I can."

Spearbold nodded and mounted his horse. He looked tired still from their long ride.

"And Spearbold…"

"My lord?"

"Find out all you can from Felix, but if you learn

nothing of import, you should stay awhile in Ludlow. We can do little now until we know where the king is. In any case you could do with the rest; I need your mind sharp."

"Thank you, my lord."

With Spearbold on his way, Ned tasked Bear and Ragwulf with assessing the strength of the garrison and how many men they thought might be raised from the Corve estate. Holton and Mags prepared the castle for a winter with more mouths to feed.

To Ned's surprise, Spearbold returned later the same day.

"My lord, Felix is not in Ludlow. The ... er... lady of the house said he set off for London several months ago and has not returned since - but is expected... soon."

"Well...I suppose I should not be surprised: trade is his business, Spearbold, and I can't expect Felix to be sitting waiting for me to bring more trouble to his door. I don't suppose the streets of Ludlow were able to provide any news of the king."

"No, my lord," replied Spearbold, "I'm afraid not."

"Then I must wait - we're as safe here as anywhere, I suppose."

§§§§§

As he had promised Ned kept a frugal Christmas in the household at Corve. On Christmas Day he received the rents from his tenants, something he had not done for some time. Many were women or young men. It must be nearly ten years, he reckoned, since his brother Thomas had stripped Corve of most of its fighting men. None had returned, leaving widows and sons to work the land or become beggars. He noticed the shocked looks on their faces as they filed into the Hall. The men took off their caps and the women loosened their shawls. Most, if they had ever seen Ned, would hardly remember what he looked like. They would have paid their quarterly rents to his steward for years and he suspected that seeing their lord might be a rather dubious pleasure.

Holton was seated at a table to his right hand and he read out the names as each tenant came forward. Then he noted down in the roll the amount presented.

"Walter Hinshell!" Holton announced. The man Walter stepped forward a pace. He was older than most of the others, Ned thought.

"God give you good day, my lord," said Walter, placing a small pouch on the table. "Rent of eleven pence, my lord."

Holton emptied the bag and counted the coins.

"How much land do you hold of me, Walter?" Ned asked him.

"One acre, my lord, and half an acre of meadow," he replied.

"Very good," said Ned, "and how many sons do you have?"

Walter hesitated before replying: "I've three sons and four daughters, my lord."

Ned could see in his eyes that the man had an idea why he was asking. Ned's father had taught him to expect his tenants to answer a call to arms, but he had not taught him to see the service from the tenant's point of view. He had taken four score of men at arms and archers from his Yoredale estates and few had ever returned. Most had died fighting by his side and the rest had gradually been lost in holding Crag Tower. And what had he gained by their sacrifice? Nothing. They had given their lives and he, like their families, had still lost all he loved.

He nodded to Walter. "Thank you, Walter. There are gifts for you and your kinfolk: pies, ale, and extra firewood in the courtyard, if you need it."

"Thank you, my lord. They're all very welcome."

Walter paid his respect with a nod then put on his cap and went to collect his gifts.

So the morning was taken up with such duties and it gave Ned pause for much reflection.

That afternoon he sat with Maighread before the warm fire in the solar. They sat at ease, their heads together and their fingers entwined.

"I was Lord of Yoredale when I was but twenty," he said, "and I was a poor lord to those tenants."

"I doubt it," said Maighread, "it's not in you to be cruel or unjust - though that's not to say you couldn't do better."

"When I saw those tenants today…spoke to them. I could see the fear in their eyes when I asked how many sons they had."

"Well, why did you ask then? I'm sure Holton could have told you."

He shook his head. "Aye, but I'm not twenty anymore."

"But you're a lord and lords know little of the suffering of their tenants, of their sweat and toil," she said. "Lords live their lives in a world of power and blood."

"Aye, sure enough, that's the world my father dwelt in. He sacrificed the men of Corve and Elder Hall to his ambition. I realise now: he didn't need to get involved with the Duke of York and the Nevilles. By doing so he laid his family open to the greed of the Radcliffes and they all but destroyed us."

"There are better models of lordship," said Maighread.

He smiled at her. "My grandfather?"

"Aye, Sir Thomas was a fine lord."

"I wish I'd met him."

She nodded. "He knew of your exploits from afar. He was so proud of you, though he never spoke your name."

"How do you know he was proud then?"

She grinned. "When he listened to men's stories about you his face would light up; then he bade them repeat what they'd said claiming his hearing was bad - he was a poor liar, like you."

"I'm just a weary soldier," he said. "It's what I know…

what I do best."

"Hah! It's what your father trained you to do - and he trained you well, Ned. But you're not a youth anymore. You've fought your feuds and won your battles. You've fought for your king and won his battles - and you carry the wounds, but you're still alive - like me. God has watched over us both."

"I can't think for what purpose - I thought God had abandoned me long ago. God must have planned for us to marry!"

She squeezed his hand. "I doubt the Lord goes out of His way simply to give in to your whims."

"You haven't changed your mind?" he said, suddenly troubled at the thought.

"No, but…"

"But?" he repeated.

"Our marriage will not last long if you carry on fighting. Promise me that when this is all settled, you'll live with me in peace and quiet here at Corve."

"And what if the king calls upon me?"

She sighed and stroked the crown of his head. "You and I both know that you're no longer fit to fight, not really. You do it out of obligation to your men but you know that the wound you took to your head will never go away. You may hide it from some, but not those who know you well, and love you. Bear and the others, they see it - and I see it too."

"But I must go back to Yoredale for many who followed me are there."

"Aye, I know that. There are many reasons you must go but then I want us to live at peace here."

"Very well," he replied, "if the king calls for me, I shall be ill."

"There is one other condition," she replied.

"You fight a hard battle, my lady," he complained. "What else?"

"You must go to the king to receive your pardon before you go back to Yoredale."

He shrugged. "That is no great condition; I'd do that anyway."

"You would now perhaps, but not in a few moments time."

"What do you mean? What are saying?"

"Not when I've told you what I must tell you - so swear to me you'll go to the king first."

He gave a nervous laugh. "Very well, if it seems so important to you, I swear it. Now what is it you must tell me?" He looked at her more closely. "There's a tear in your eye, Maighread. What is it?"

He felt her take a deep breath beside him and he began to feel a little uneasy.

"Tell me."

"I've wanted to tell you this since you arrived back at Crag Tower but I hoped that Eleanor would be able to tell you herself - and, better still, show you."

"Tell me what? Show me what? You're beginning to worry me." He clasped her hand more tightly. "What has my sister done?"

"It's so hard to tell you this now…"

"In the name of God, Maighread - will you just tell me and have done with it! It can't be that bad surely."

"Very well then, my love. Here it is: you have a son."

"That's a poor jest," he said.

"It's no jest, Ned."

"That cannot be!" He pushed her away and got to his feet.

"There is only one woman I've ever lain with and she's dead! Dead before she could give me a son!"

"Listen!" cried Maighread. "Listen to me. You have a son. Amelie's son."

He looked at her in disbelief. His head began to throb slightly and he rubbed it.

"But how can that be?" he whispered.

"Eleanor saved the child, with Ragwulf's help. But they couldn't get to you before you were exiled so they brought him to Crag Tower. We called him John after your father and we all raised him there. Oh, Ned! He's like a little you, the way he talks and moves."

She was weeping now and he did not know what to say. Her words had turned his world upside down. He swallowed hard and fought back the tears that ran down his own cheeks. He sat down and put his head in his hands. Maighread sat beside him and put her arm around him.

He looked at her. "A son - you're sure?"

She nodded with a tearful grin.

"A son," he murmured. "Poor Amelie…"

"Aye, I know."

"But after all we've said to each other, how could you not tell me this before?"

His joy was tarnished by the realisation that John was now almost certainly in the hands of his enemies.

"I would have told you at Crag but John had already been taken south. I didn't want to raise your hopes in case anything happened to the lad."

"But something has happened to him - he's in Yoredale Castle! Why didn't you tell me at Yoredale - when I could have freed him?"

"We didn't know he was there, did we? Canon Reedman told us he was at Corve and Eleanor too. I thought she should tell you. I thought it would be a joyous moment for you to see him as soon as you knew. And even if you had known then? What could you have done?"

"I would have given my life to rescue him!"

"And how would giving your life have helped your son?" she asked softly.

He knew she was right but it did not make him feel any easier about it.

"And Ragwulf? My own sworn man knew and did not

tell me! I'll kill him!"

"Hush, my lord! He saved your son's life too! Your sister was worried that if anyone discovered who the boy was he would be in danger. She was right! She made Ragwulf swear not to tell anyone and he kept his oath to her even though it meant falling out with his own son! Your man has paid a high enough price already for that oath."

Ned stood up again. "I'll leave for Yoredale in the morning; I'll gather all the men I can muster at short notice."

"No!" she snapped at him. "You swore to me that you'd get the king's pardon first!"

"That was before! You were deceiving me!"

She gripped his arm tightly. "You swore to me and it's the only reason I agreed to tell you. I knew what your reaction would be!"

"You tell me I have a son - and he's in danger. Do you expect me to leave him there a moment longer than I must?"

"Listen to me!" she cried. "Your son's a four year old boy with more courage than many grown men. He's in no danger as long as no-one knows who he is - but think about your sister, Eleanor, because she's in more danger than he is. Joan doesn't know your son but she knows Eleanor. She's trying to protect your son - as she has for four long years and she needs you too."

"Then all the more reason for haste!" He did not understand why they were even arguing about it.

"No! All the more reason to think!" she pleaded. "If you go to Yoredale now, you'll go as an outlaw, an exile. Go first to the king and get him to restore your lands and titles. Then you can go to Yoredale with the law on your side and whatever you do to free your own will be seen as just."

"But the king has already pardoned me!" he protested.

"Where is the proof, my lord? Where is the sealed letter which tells everyman that you are a lord once more and not an outlaw?"

She engulfed him in a great hug. "In the press of battle, Ned Elder, you must be swift but you must keep a cool head too - as you know very well. Take some time to what you do next. That's why I've told you now, on Christmas Day. Use this season to consider. Decide nothing until twelfth night."

He gave a great sigh. "I'm only just beginning to believe I might have a son," he said.

"Believe me: you do have a son and a son to make you proud."

"Aye, and a sister that I've cursed wrongly for the past four years."

"Speak to the others. Only Ragwulf knows but they are all loyal to you and, if you ask them, all will speak their mind. They are your council of advisers - use them."

He nodded and took her arm in his. "You will be the most perfect wife a man could have."

She grinned and replied: "No. I'll be the peevish bitch I've always been but… through all that, never doubt my love for you."

34
26th December 1468, between Yoredale and Coverham

Father Baston was terrified he would somehow give himself away. He tried not to appear as if he was hurrying and he tried to tell himself that all he was doing was making a seasonal visit to the white canons of Coverham. There could surely be nothing suspicious about that, yet he shivered as he recalled passing under the portcullis with Weaver standing beside it, watching every step he took. He kept glancing behind, expecting at any moment to be overtaken but his fears proved groundless and he tramped on unmolested across the thin, gritty snow.

A few passed him on the way but not many. There would have been plenty abroad the previous day when the tenants made their unwelcome journey to the castle to pay the quarterly rents. For much of the distance to the abbey he saw no-one - and was glad of it. He was also thankful that Reedman was there when he arrived for it spared the need for any awkward conversations with the Abbot.

"Canon, I have a most privy matter to discuss with you," he said. Reedman took him to his cell, where Father Baston proceeded to tell Reedman of his meeting with Lady Eleanor and Hal.

"But I thought both had gone to Corve Manor!" he said aghast. "Both told me they would do so - and, what's more, I passed that knowledge - as I thought it - on to Lord Elder."

"Lord Elder is here?" Father Baston saw a glimmer of hope.

"Not now, he's not! He's gone with all speed to Corve. Gone mistakenly, it seems, since all those he was seeking are still here! Even on foot, he'll be at Corve by now."

Father Baston sighed. "From what I am told you know the trials of this family better than anyone, could you send to Corve? To Lord Elder?"

Reedman shook his head. "Who could I send? This is no longer Lord Elder's realm. Who could I trust? There is no-one and if it is dangerous for us, it would be equally dangerous for another."

"But we must do something!" urged Father Baston, rubbing his hands together.

"We are in the minority here, my friend, you and I," said Reedman. "We are on the wrong side. Lord Elder should not even have been here - his banishment was for five years. Sir Thomas Gate and Joan Elder - they're Warwick's clients and all who dwell in the shadow of Middleham understand that. If even the Abbot learned of our conversation, we'd both be finished."

Father Baston felt powerless. He had needed no-one before when all he intended was to rid Christendom of the abomination that was Joan Elder. He would have struck swiftly and sacrificed himself for that end. But he had delayed, prevaricated, racked by guilt and cowardice. Now others were embroiled in the trail of chaos and deceit.

"There must be someone else who could help," he said, "even if just as a messenger. Someone we could send to perhaps?"

Reedman seemed to hesitate for the first time. "There may be one such person," he said, "but I cannot name them. I will go to them and see what can be done."

"There is a hope then, at least of getting word to Lord Elder?"

Reedman hesitated once more as if wrestling with his conscience.

"Canon?" prompted Father Baston.

Reedman gave a sigh and shook his head. "I will try but I would not mislead you Father: this person alone cannot help you. You are all in God's hands at Yoredale. Do nothing to make matters worse. Perhaps this person can call upon Lord Elder and then, if God wills it, perhaps he will come to your aid - but do not rely upon it!"

Father Baston nodded. At least he knew: they were on their own.

"I should return," he said. "I'm being watched and the last thing I need to do is arouse any more suspicion."

§§§§

Reedman took Father Baston to the Abbey gate and watched him set off to walk back to Yoredale, his shoulders hunched low - as well they might be with the burden he carried. He must do what he could for them all. It was already early afternoon but if he wasted no time he might be able to get to Middleham and back before vespers.

The walk to the castle gave him time to consider what he should say to Lady Emma. He had not been to see her since her brother had summoned him to the mill. He should have but his guilt kept him away. He had lied to Lord Elder and no amount of prayer could change that. He had done so for her but he regretted it all the same.

Lady Emma, however, seemed very pleased to see him and took him at once to admire her daughter, Alice.

"She grows by the day, my lady," he said.

"Not that you'd know that, of course, since you've not seen her for weeks and weeks!" she chided him.

"Other matters have taken up my time, my lady." He paused. "I regret to say… some of these matters concern you."

Lady Emma stared at him hard and ordered the nurse to take Alice away.

"You'd better come to my chamber," she said. He knew

her so well: he could hear the anxiety in her voice and what he had to say would do nothing to relieve it.

"Tell me then," she said. She stood by the narrow window as he told her about her brother's arrival, about Rob's death and that her sister, Hal and the others were all now at Yoredale. When he finished she said nothing and remained looking out of the window.

"My lady?" he said.

After a while, she asked: "You didn't tell my brother I was here, did you?"

He frowned. "No, my lady, I told him nothing about you at all - God forgive me."

She nodded. "Good."

"What is to be done then, my lady?" he asked.

"Done?"

"Aye, what is to be done?"

Lady Emma smiled at him. "You have ever been a loyal friend to me, Canon. You may leave this to me and I will see what can be done."

"Will you send to Corve Manor?" he asked.

She seemed not to hear him. "Leave all in my hands, Canon," she replied.

"Your hands … and God's, my lady."

"Indeed. God's hands too," she said.

It was clear to him that their discussion was at an end and she sent him down on his own to the kitchens to find some refreshment. He did not go there for he was in no mood to eat and instead he made his way through the east gate and on along the track that led back to Coverham. He did not know whether he had done good or ill by going to Lady Emma but he prayed that God would guide her in whatever she tried to do.

35

28th December 1468, Yoredale Castle

It seemed to Eleanor that there were all kinds of snow. What landed at her feet as she stood in the doorway to the courtyard was gritty and wet. She looked up at the wall that faced her: the great south east tower which housed the guardroom. The white dust clung briefly to the stone wall and then dissolved, but a few larger flakes were beginning to drift down from the ash grey sky. It was not a heavy fall yet but they knew it was coming and it would keep them marooned in the castle for days at best, weeks at worst. Not that it made much difference to her for she was trapped there whether there was snow or not. She remembered with some fondness the heavy snowfalls of her youth but such memories were buried forever in the slumbering ruins of Elder Hall. There had been few good memories since.

Christmas Day had come and gone. She had seen the men of Yoredale trudging to the castle, heads bent as they fought the wind and sleet. They paid their rents to Sir Walter and then crawled home to their wattle and daub hovels. They were not fed - there were no seasonal humble pies for them. Eleanor knew that the kitchens were already overstretched trying to feed the recruited men but, all the same, it seemed a failure of lordship.

This morning the castle yard was deserted for no-one cared to venture out unless they must. Wulf was on watch at the gate this morning and he stood now beside the great portcullis, a picture of misery. Eleanor permitted herself a rueful smile as she witnessed his cloak turn from dirty brown to speckled white. She wondered why they did not just close up the gate and take refuge in the guardhouse. Then she glanced towards the door opposite on the other side of the yard and caught her breath: Weaver stood there watching her, staring at her, still and impassive.

Suddenly the chill of the morning struck her and she hurried inside, closing the heavy wooden door, shutting out the cold ... and the sight of Weaver. She walked up the steps to the first floor and into the kitchen where the bellowed commands of the cook echoed around the smoky chamber walls. She escaped through into the buttery and ran into Bess. Whenever they met Bess looked flustered - probably unsure how to address her in their changed circumstances.

"What's going on?" Eleanor asked her.

"Sir Walter's been down - a rare visit indeed! He's just told the cook that the new Lord of Misrule wants a feast tonight."

"How long have we had a Lord of Misrule?" asked Eleanor, intrigued. The Lord of Misrule was usually one of the servants, briefly ennobled for part of the Christmas season, turning the natural order upside down. "Shouldn't we have a say who it is?" asked Eleanor.

Bess shrugged. "Aye, well, it's Weaver - do you want to argue about it? I know I don't."

"I suppose Weaver appointed Weaver," said Eleanor, "yet...I don't see Weaver as one to dream up festivities to cheer us all."

"Well, someone has: we're having a mummers' play at the feast this evening," said Bess, "if the mummers get here."

That at least explained the open gate and Weaver's brooding presence, thought Eleanor, but if it took up Weaver's time then at least he would have less opportunity to trouble her.

§§§§

When evening came there was a mood of good-humoured anticipation as the feast began. Torches burned brightly around the Great Hall and the Lord of Misrule held court at the high table. All was cheerful and festive, yet Eleanor knew how much sweated effort had gone into the preparation of the feast. No-one - not even Weaver - normally went out of their way to annoy the cooks. But Weaver's call for a feast had thrown the kitchens into turmoil. Food was already scarce from the overcrowding and she imagined that the cooks had taken their lord and lady's absence to mean that no extravagant feasts would be required. But they had reckoned without Weaver, who was revelling in his new position of authority.

Sir Walter Grave, by contrast, looked abject. He brooded at the far end of the high table as far from Weaver as possible. It was no secret they detested each other and he looked on disapprovingly as the contents of Thomas Gate's wine cellar were served up. Elsewhere in the Hall the ale flowed in large quantities.

Eleanor sat far from the high table with some of the other members of the household. She drank little ale and took only a small share of the squat, oblong pies of shredded beef. Some of the others from Crag Tower, Wulf and his comrades, were indulging themselves fully. She did not begrudge them but she knew that if she drank too much ale, she would either become loud or morose - possibly even both - and she could see nothing here to celebrate. Rob was still much in her mind. She missed him more than she would ever have admitted - add another good man to the roll of the sorely missed.

She was tired even before the mummers' play began and their theme, the massacre of the innocents, did little to lighten her mood. It was appropriate for the day, she recognised, but the solemn play changed the atmosphere in the Hall. Typical of Weaver, she thought, to end a merry feast with a tale of murdered children. The only blessing was that the play was not very long and afterwards the players, sympathetic to their audience, did their best to lift the gloom with a few bawdy songs.

Then Weaver stood up and Eleanor assumed he was going to toast the mummers but he did not. Instead he announced that the Lord of Misrule was going to choose his "Lady." Around the Hall, silence fell and a few of the women noticeably cringed. Those were the ones who already bore an invisible badge marking them as "taken by Weaver." Some of the younger lasses, emboldened by the ale, eyed their new "Lord" eagerly. Rather you than me, thought Eleanor, as Weaver called for all the women and girls to stand up. She rose reluctantly to her feet with the others, hoping that she was sufficiently far away from him not to catch his eye. Then a sudden chill ran through her as she saw that his attention was already fixed elsewhere.

"You girl, mute!" Weaver shouted at Agnes.

"Oh, shit," muttered Eleanor.

"Get over here and show everyone what you've got!" said Weaver.

Agnes did not move.

"Come on, lass. Don't keep your lord waiting!" urged Weaver.

At first Eleanor thought Agnes was rooted to the spot by sheer terror, but she did not look frightened, just determined. Poor fool!

Weaver, of course, was affronted when she did not obey his call. "Bring the stupid wench here!" he roared. "She can kneel before her Lord and pay penance!"

Before anyone else reacted, Joan's woman, Margaret, seized Agnes by the arm and dragged her to the dais.

Walter Grave staggered to his feet. "Leave her! I've had enough of this, Weaver! Misrule's a good name for it."

"Aye, but it's my misrule, Sir Walter, not yours. So sit down or get out!"

Many gasped at Weaver's boldness, thinking him drunk,

but Eleanor suspected that Weaver was barely affected by the Gascon wine. He looked chillingly sober to her. Sir Walter was still on his feet. He could end the revels now but he would be taking a risk: Weaver had his own men there and even Sir Walter would know that Weaver was so close to Lady Joan he was untouchable.

"Have your way for now, Weaver," he conceded, "but not with this lass."

Eleanor watched Weaver closely. He took his time, calculating the consequences no doubt, then he nodded and Margaret released her grip on Agnes.

"Go," Sir Walter told her and she ran out at once. He stared at Weaver. "Take care what you do," he said in a voice all could hear, "for you'll not be a "lord" beyond twelfth night."

"Good Sir Walter," replied Weaver with a grin, "follow your whore out or we'll have a reckoning here and now."

Sir Walter was clearly seething and he took a step towards Weaver. Then he thought better of it and turned on his heel to stalk out of the Hall in Agnes' wake. For a few moments there was a hush in the Hall as all looked towards Weaver. Eleanor sighed; Sir Walter had abandoned them. Without thinking she sat down and that was all it took for Weaver to notice her.

"Think you're a lady do you," he called to her, "to sit in your lord's presence?"

She looked up to find all eyes upon her. "Good Christ, what have I done," she breathed.

She stood up swiftly. "I meant no offence, my lord," she said.

"Well, are you a lady?" he demanded.

Did he know? Surely he could not, she told herself.

"No, my lord," she replied, "a poor widow, a stonemason's widow."

"A mason's widow?" repeated Weaver. "Perhaps you have a heart of stone then? Come let's see whether you might have the …er, qualities I'm looking for in my lady."

Some in the Hall began to chant "Aye" and bang their fists and ale jugs on the tables.

Eleanor was not going to wait to be dragged to him by Margaret so she walked to the dais and stood before him. He studied her curiously.

"Well, she moves like a lady," said Weaver.

For a moment she wondered if he actually knew who she was for there was such confidence in his eyes. All she could do was play along and if she must be his "lady" then so be it. She was not going to give herself away.

"You look proud enough to be a lady," continued Weaver, "perhaps too proud."

She disliked his tone; this was not going to be straightforward. She waited just below the dais and he moved around the table to stand over her. Out of the corner of her eye she noted that Margaret had taken several steps towards her. To her surprise he offered her his hand and helped her up onto the dais.

"Are you too proud?" he asked her.

"No, my lord," she replied.

"Kneel before your lord then," instructed Weaver and she obediently dropped onto her knees. A shiver of apprehension ran through her as he placed one hand upon her wimple.

"What service can you offer your lord whilst you're down there?" he asked with a leering glance to those in the Hall. Raucous laughter greeted that. Her face was level with his groin and she knew as well as anyone else what he was suggesting. She stared at his crotch, not sure how to answer.

"I can beg forgiveness from my lord," she said and the crowd gave a disappointed groan.

"They don't think that's good enough service," said Weaver. "They think my "lady" should give me a more… personal service."

She couldn't see his face but she could tell from his tone

that he was enjoying himself immensely. Well, let him do his worst; she had been mistreated by far worse than him. If she must, she would demean herself - she was no saintly virgin and staying alive was more important to her.

She rested her hands on his hips and leaned towards him. The assembly roared its approval. Weaver pulled her head closer until her lips brushed the cloth covering his groin. The smell of stale urine almost overpowered her and she swayed back onto her haunches.

"Is that it?" demanded Weaver in disgust. Abruptly he tore away her wimple and the Hall fell silent. Even Weaver was taken aback for, whatever he expected to see, it clearly was not her short, ragged hair. She stood up and snatched the head dress back from him.

"Down! Down on your knees, bitch, where you belong for, whatever you are, we can see you're no lady!"

She slumped down once more on the dais at his feet. She must keep her wits, not give him cause to go any further. She was lucky that Joan was not there or she would have been recognised at once - even with so little of her hair.

"You're not fit to suck on me, you bitch, you're only fit to kiss my arse!"

His remark was not greeted with the amusement he probably expected: some in the Hall laughed, but many did not. Weaver seemed to sense the nervousness in his audience, who were puzzled by her appearance.

"I'm tired of you, wench," he said and pushed her off the platform with his foot. "Get thee gone! Margaret, fetch me a better one this time."

Eleanor rolled to her feet, bruised and humiliated. She fled from the Hall and down into one of the cellars where she could not stop herself sobbing with relief. After a while, and a few deep breaths, she restored her wimple and dusted herself down. It could have been worse, she told herself. Christ knew it could have been a lot worse. She could easily explain away her shorn hair - perhaps even blame her dead 'husband'.

Footsteps sounded nearby and she fumbled out her knife and hid with her back against the wall. A man entered the cellar cautiously; he carried no light.

"My lady?" he whispered and her shoulders relaxed.

"Hal," she breathed, "what are you doing? Why did you follow me?"

Hal peered at her in the darkness. "I just... wanted to know that you were alright…"

"Of course I'm alright; I'm not a child! Now get back upstairs and watch what's happening. And be careful!"

The youth left her. She could be a hard bitch at times. Poor Hal, he only ever acted for the best and now she had crushed him for it. She waited a while longer and then followed him back up in the direction of the Hall. She did not go in but lingered behind the screens in the adjacent buttery, listening. She received a few sullen looks from some of the serving girls as they passed but most others ignored her, which suited her fine.

Weaver, it appeared, had moved on, and Margaret now sat beside him as his "lady" and presumably that had always been the intention: humiliate a few women of his choice and then appoint Margaret. Well, she was welcome to Weaver.

He was still holding court and she tried to make sense of what was being said.

"Our friends, the mummers," said Weaver, "have given us our story for this eve - the deaths of those poor innocent children at the hands of the bloody tyrant King Herod. I was speaking to our own priest, Father Baston, about this only this afternoon."

Eleanor felt a prick of alarm at the mention of the priest yet she could not imagine Weaver discussing King Herod with Father Baston.

"It's long been a tradition to choose one child to

represent the suffering of all those poor children."

What was Weaver gibbering about? These drunken sots didn't want to hear about suffering, they were trying to escape from it.

"Margaret," Weaver continued, "go and fetch our boy."

Eleanor moved to the Hall door and looked in. Margaret had lifted John from a corner of the floor where he had been sleeping. He groaned and Bess screamed: "No, leave my lad!"

"Calm yourself, lass," said Weaver smiling, "it's only make believe - like the mummers. The boy will come to no harm."

Others chorused their approval and told Bess to sit down. Bess looked at Wulf and he nodded. John was wide awake now and went with Margaret to the dais. Eleanor scanned the Hall for Hal and found him leaning against the end wall not far from the high table. He looked on, smiling, but he was a poor actor and one look at his tense shoulders told her enough. His hand rested on his knife hilt.

She looked around the Hall more carefully: there were several armed men around the room and two more near her by the door. She closed her eyes, feeling Amelie's knife in the garter around her upper leg. It would not be easy to retrieve if she needed it in a hurry.

Weaver had his hand on John's shoulder. "What are you called, lad," he asked him.

John, undaunted by his rude awakening and the noisy crowd, answered with his customary confidence. "I'm called John."

"...my lord," Weaver added through gritted teeth.

"Do you call me lord?" asked John in confusion since he had so far slept through the whole of the Lord of Misrule's reign.

Weaver gave him a slap around the head and Eleanor saw Hal flinch and move half a pace forward.

"You address me as 'my lord'," explained Weaver.

"Do I?" asked John. "Why?"

Eleanor held her breath. She doubted Weaver had met many four year old boys but she knew for certain that he had never met one like John. If he was not careful John would have him running round in circles. But that would not be good either.

"Enough, boy. Hold your tongue!" snapped Weaver. A knife appeared in his hand and he brandished it theatrically for the audience. Eleanor suspected that even Weaver would not hurt a child so publically so she doubted John was in any danger and just wished Weaver would get the show over with. It all seemed so pointless and not at all what Weaver was about. And then suddenly it struck her and she knew that all this was not about a ceremony, or entertainment at all. Somehow Weaver must have found out who had met with Father Baston and now, one by one, he was seeking connections to flush them out.

Weaver raised his knife, playing to the crowd and John kicked him in the shin. Knowing John, he would have kicked as hard as he could and Weaver yelped. John slipped from his grasp and Weaver made a wild grab for him. Many of those watching laughed and Weaver was stung by the insult. He lunged again to catch the boy but John was too quick and made for Hal who was already heading towards him.

"Catch the little turd!" shouted Weaver. "I'll skin him!"

John hugged Hal around the knees as several men closed on them.

Hal held out his knife. "I have him, my lord," cried Hal, "but surely this has gone far enough. He's just a boy."

"Let me judge whether I've finished or not!" bellowed Weaver.

Eleanor watched as he made his way towards Hal, followed by others of his men. Chaos had erupted in the Hall. Women were screaming and men were shouting. Some called for calm, others for arms. She feared that unless she did something, it would end badly for them all.

"Oh, Good Christ, keep me safe," muttered Eleanor and stepped into the Hall. She elbowed her way to Hal and punched his arm to get his attention.

"Don't try to help me," she whispered as she drew level with him, "just take the boy out."

"What are you going to do," asked Hal.

"Go!" hissed Eleanor and passed on towards Weaver. A glance back told her that Hal had lifted up John and was pushing his way towards the door. She concentrated then on Weaver.

"You! Pisspot!" she screamed at him. "I've not finished with you!"

Silence fell on the Hall like a hammer blow. Weaver was clearly surprised to see her return.

"Pleased to see me?" she asked and mounted the step to the dais. Margaret moved to intercept her. Eleanor paused beside her and gave her a brief smile then slapped her as hard as she could across the cheek. Margaret staggered back a pace and wiped a smear of blood from her lip.

"You'll regret that, you bitch!" said Margaret.

Eleanor swept past her and made for Weaver.

"I want an apology from you," she declared.

Weaver responded with a chuckle. "You've got a man's hair, have you got any other parts of a man?"

Eleanor raised her hand to strike him but he was very swift - too swift for her. He seized her arm and forced her down on her knees. She glanced towards the door: Hal and John had disappeared.

"You had me here before," she shouted at him, "but you were a bit of a disappointment when I got close."

The audience in the Hall loved that and their laughter stung Weaver into a response. He removed her wimple again and grasped her around the neck to pull her face into his groin.

"Well, try again!" he roared.

It was the moment to concede, to do what he asked, to abase herself and survive. For an instant she considered that course, but only for an instant.

"If you like," she said, "I can try harder." Eleanor thrust her hand between his legs and grabbed at what she found there. Weaver screamed and cracked her head down against the dais. She was stunned and cursed herself for underestimating him. She shook her head and a drop of blood dripped onto the wooden boards. He'd cut her. She could not reach the knife - and besides she might need it later - best to leave it hidden for now. Weaver needed to know that she could give a good as she got. She lifted her head and smiled to see him bent almost double. Too late, she saw Margaret swing the jug of wine at her.

36

Twelfth Night 1469, at Middleham Castle

Joan looked around the Great Hall of Middleham; it was a place of the utmost opulence and grandeur - could even the king's court rival it, she wondered? The feast was sumptuous. Course after course was paraded into the Hall and served to the vast number of guests. No wonder Thomas was so keen to keep the confidence of Warwick for the man lived like a prince. Her husband had spoken vaguely of 'great things' that might be accomplished by supporting the Earl of Warwick and what she saw seemed to make his claims become real before her eyes.

Her husband's privilege was clear for they sat at Warwick's high table with his wife, daughters and other honoured guests. For the first time she actually believed that her marriage might raise her higher - higher at least than the provincial position she had held so far at Yoredale. Over the festive period she and Thomas had travelled more than she had expected - all, he assured her, to a grand purpose. Now she had some grasp of how grand that purpose might be. Thomas told her a little but she had listened to what others said and also considered what they did not say. From all that she gleaned, it was clear to her that Warwick must be aiming very high indeed.

Yet for all her excitement about what was going on, she had only to look to the other end of the long table to find displeasure. For there, almost opposite her, sat Lady Emma Elder with her son beside her. It was Joan who had snatched the boy from her and taken him to Middleham. She had certainly never expected to find Emma Elder there; the Countess had shown her too much of the milk of kindness.

She stared at Emma who had studiously avoided her eyes throughout the feast. She willed her to look up but Emma kept her eyes down at the table except for a few words of acknowledgement to Lady Anne who sat nearby. Time that girl was married off - she must be thirteen already. It was common talk in the northern households whose bed her elder sister, Isabel, would soon be warming: no less than the Duke of Clarence, brother to the king. Was there no end to Warwick's influence?

Thomas nudged her arm and she stopped looking across to Emma to turn to him. He had just sent away one of the servants and he did not look pleased.

"What is it?" she asked.

"It seems that your man, Weaver, has come to Middleham and would like a brief audience with you."

"Oh?"

"Aye, I've told him to wait a few hours - the cheek of the man!"

"No," said Joan, "I'd better go and see him - it can be swiftly dealt with, I'm sure…" she began to rise.

"I've dealt with it," snapped Thomas, resting his hand firmly upon hers.

She forced a smile and murmured sweetly: "Move your hand, my dear, or I'll put my knife through it. I am not your dog."

"Aye, my dogs are more obedient," he said and lifted his hand.

At once she excused herself to the Countess and withdrew. Weaver was waiting for her at the top of a stairwell. She was concerned their meeting might be overheard for there were many milling about. If they were all engaged on the earl's business then it seemed to her that the earl's business must be thriving. She led Weaver down the steps to the cellar below. He was wearing his customary grin.

"This had better be important, Weaver," she said.

"Aye, my lady, it is," replied Weaver.

"Well what is it then? Every moment down here is a further moment of annoyance to my husband!"

"I know the woman Father Baston was meeting with."

"Well?"

"You'll like this, my lady," said Weaver. "It's Lady Eleanor Elder - mind you she doesn't look much like a lady now."

She thought Weaver no longer had the ability to surprise her but she was wrong. How delicious! "You have her? I mean locked up?"

"Of course," replied Weaver smoothly, "we've had a little sport with her - but she's chained up in a cellar."

"That's not enough!" said Joan. "She'll get out…somehow." A thought struck her and she gave Weaver a little smile.

"My lady?"

"Throw her into the oubliette - she won't get out of there."

"Very well, my lady," said Weaver.

She allowed Weaver a brief share in her amusement before her smile froze. "There are others," she told him. "Find them!"

She rejoined the feasting guests with a curtsey to her hosts. She noted that another course had arrived at the table in her absence. Thomas greeted her with a frosty look but she smiled and put her hand upon his thigh under the table.

"And what was so important?" he asked, cool but also, she could tell, very curious.

"Guess who we hold at Yoredale?" she teased him in a whisper.

He did not reply, clearly not prepared to play her little

games. Instead he waited for her to tell him.

"Your friend, the seemingly impossible to kill Ned Elder, has two sisters: one is sitting over there and the other is sitting on a cellar floor at Yoredale Castle."

She was rewarded by Thomas giving her a look of utter astonishment but he said nothing at first. Instead he seemed intent on the brutal dismemberment of the fowl on the platter in front of him.

"Weaver," she said, picking up a piece of flesh that fell from his plate, "should not be underestimated. I knew he would not have come with a trifle to tell me."

"Eleanor Elder," breathed Thomas. "It seems we have within our grasp all the women Ned Elder loves best."

Joan wasn't sure whether others along the table heard the name Elder or not but, when she next looked around, she found Emma's gaze fixed upon her. It confused her a little - not that she feared Emma in the slightest. The younger one was to be watched carefully, to be sure, but not Emma. Yet there was something about the look she received that she did not much care for. There was almost … defiance in it, yet to what purpose? Even if Emma knew that Eleanor was her prisoner and even if she wanted to get her out, she had no means of doing so. Joan broke the eye contact and concentrated on the usual small talk that such occasions required of her. Perhaps she would have to reconsider her view of Emma Elder.

§§§§

Seeing Joan at the same meal table, made Emma feel physically sick. She would have run out screaming: "murderess!" but for her seven year old son, Richard, by her side. She picked at each course as it came and spent most of her time studying the table top. Occasionally dear Lady Anne would try to engage her in polite conversation but Emma could barely stumble out a few words. After a while even Anne gave up and talked to Richard instead.

Emma had many reasons to hate Joan but most of all because of Garth. Joan had robbed her of the one man she loved and the father of little Alice. For years she had buried that hate, was forced to bury it deep. Only on those terms would the earl allow Emma and her children to live at Middleham. The Countess had made that very clear: Emma was to forget what happened with Joan and start her life anew. It had been hard to do so, but she had done it.

Eleanor's abrupt re-entry into her life had stirred her feelings once more and Canon Reedman's recent visit had rekindled her hatred of Joan. Yet, despite all that, she had done nothing more to help her sister. She feared for her children if she acted against the mistress of Yoredale in any way. But now Joan was but a few yards away - the woman who had killed her loved ones and stolen the Elder inheritance was staring at her across the table. Though several years had passed, there had to be a response. Emma knew she must do something, however small, to unsettle her cousin. She raised her eyes at last and held Joan's glare. And the longer she held it, the more determined she became. A wave of anger swept over her and the wine upon her tongue tasted suddenly bitter. She knew then that she must revenge her lover. If she did nothing, her hatred would consume her.

§§§§

Joan gave a low moan as Thomas lay spent on top of her. One of the few advantages of her marriage to Thomas was that his attempts to produce an heir were both frequent and pleasurable. His love making was in stark contrast to her previous husband, the often rather disappointing Henry. Perhaps it was a combination of factors, the wine, the richly spiced food, but whatever it was, the past hour or so of Thomas had managed to banish for a while all thoughts of ambition from her mind. A considerable feat indeed!

Thomas moved lazily off her and began to nuzzle her breast but ambition rather than lust was now on her mind. Thomas was giving her only half-hearted caresses now and she knew his attention also was moving to other matters.

"You've spent most of the day closeted away with the earl and your comrades," she observed. "Have you concluded your plotting now?"

He seized her breast suddenly - it certainly gained her attention. "Be careful what you say," he whispered, "even here, there may be agents of the king."

She gave him a doubtful grimace. "Even here - in our bedchamber?" She laughed but Thomas did not.

"The time approaches," he said and she laughed again.

"You sound like some ancient prophet!" she said. "Listen to yourself."

"It's others listening I'm concerned with."

"Then you're a fool, Thomas. I can assure you that every man in this building is talking about what's going to happen. There are more plots discussed in the kitchen than there are in the earl's privy chamber! So speak. Tell me what is really going to happen."

"Aye, there are rumours," he acknowledged, "but few are in the know. What I tell you is not to be repeated to anyone - do you understand? Because if this goes wrong, we're dead."

She nodded. "Well?"

"In the spring, or early summer, the earl will give the word and we will march south to take on his enemies: those of the king's counsellors - such as the Herberts and the Woodvilles, especially Lord Rivers-"

"You would strike at the queen's father - he is too close to the king, surely?"

"We shall have a large army - thousands! The king will have to listen to the earl at last."

"So, what is your part in this great scheme?" she asked

"I shall lead the vanguard with Will Conyers and his brother John. It's all arranged and there are others with castles crammed full of fighting men - just as we are, but the earl is waiting for other news."

"What news?"

"Lady Isabel is to marry the Duke of Clarence."

Joan sighed. "That's hardly news! Every kitchen maid knows that!"

"Perhaps - but the king doesn't know it yet. All Warwick is waiting for is a dispensation from the Pope for the marriage to take place."

"So, we must wait in readiness."

"There must be no slip ups, my lady. Yoredale must be locked down tight."

"What of Lady Eleanor? Should we kill her?"

Thomas shook his head. "You have an uncommonly strong lust for blood, my lady. But no, we may yet need her. I'd be happier if I knew where her brother is - he's the member of the family that matters."

"But you said he has no men - he's powerless."

"He has few men, but I'd never describe him as powerless. He will have discovered by now that you and I are at Yoredale and he has reason enough to want to kill us both. That's why we must be vigilant. We'll return to Yoredale tomorrow - the men aren't ready yet. Warwick doesn't want a rabble; he wants an army. I'm determined that my men will stand the tallest in his victory."

37

7th January 1469, at Yoredale Castle

Eleanor bent her knees a little as she landed on the hard floor but her shoulders and head had struck the rock sides several times on the way down. She was bruised all over. She cursed them roundly in her pain - not that it bothered them. They just laughed and slammed down the trapdoor. Worse still, when they left they took the torch with them. She crouched against the base of the wall. Like others before her, no doubt, she explored the tiny space and found nothing to cheer her.

Her memories of this place were all bad. Ned's old retainers, Bagot and Gruffydd, had been incarcerated in the oubliette - the forgotten place. She knew that very well since she was the one who had finally freed them. Time passed slowly and she found there were other occupants of the oubliette: rats, spiders and other tiny creatures that crawled across her in the darkness. It was not very long before the first rats came to visit. No-one had bothered to search her so she still had her small blade and the rats found it a sharp warning - at least while she was awake. She managed to stab one and it scuttled away. Then she heard its squeals as the other scavengers found it, wounded and available.

She was obliged to relieve herself on the floor and already the place had a foul stench to it. The stench of her: she felt filthy; she was filthy. After a while she could not tell how long she had been there: hours - no days, surely. It seemed like weeks. Every so often, the hatch above her opened and a guard tossed in some bread and lowered a leather flask of water on a rope. It obviously amused them to let her drink from the flask and then snatch it up again. Her throat was always dry even soon after she had drunk.

She was no stranger to imprisonment but this time she could see no way out - as Bagot and Gruffydd had found: there was no way out of an oubliette without the help of others. She could not see how Hal or anyone else could get her out as long as Thomas Gate held the castle. Yet she would fight to stay alive. In the crevices and cracks, the rats gathered once more. Good. If they came in numbers she had a better chance of striking one - and that one would keep its fellows away from her for another day.

If Joan Elder thought a spell in the oubliette would break her, then she would be greatly disappointed. Eleanor had survived the worst the Radcliffes could throw at her and Thomas Gate was no Edmund Radcliffe! She had survived before - at a cost - and she would survive again. Did they not know that Eleanor would eat a rat raw if it meant she could live to be revenged upon them all?

§§§§

Father Baston sat on the front bench in his chapel, head in hands. What a fraud he was: not only a faithless priest but also a coward, a man incapable of exacting the revenge he had journeyed all this way to take. He had led others into his scheme, albeit willingly, but still he had let them down. When they were under attack, he had sat there in his hiding place and done nothing to help them. He was the worst sort of priest, cowering beneath his veneer of faith. He looked up at the altar, tasting the salt tears as they ran onto his lips.

Then he heard her laugh and twisted around to see her standing at the gallery above. Lady Joan was back: the devil had returned to Hell. As soon as she had his attention she walked away and he hung his head. Still he danced to her song.

A sudden knock on the chapel door made him gasp. Then he relaxed: if it were Weaver or Lady Joan, they would not have bothered to knock. The door creaked open and Hal walked in. Father Baston glanced up at the empty gallery and stopped Hal just inside the door.

"Have a care!" he whispered. "She's in her chamber - she may hear you."

Hal gently closed the door and leant back against it. He was stern-faced, grim.

"What is it?" asked Father Baston. "We agreed to wait until spring…"

"Spring?" hissed Hal. "You foolish priest! My lord's sister lies in a stinking oubliette in the bowels of this castle! Do you honestly believe I'm going to leave her there till spring?"

Father Baston fell to his knees. "I was too weak… I know I shouldn't have told him…"

Hal seized him by the shoulders and lifted him up. By God, the lad had a strong arm!

"What did you tell to who?" asked Hal. The youth's voice had a hard edge to it now and

Father Baston felt fear loosening his bowels.

"I told Weaver about… Lady Eleanor."

There, he had said it, admitted it. He hoped he would feel better; he didn't.

Hal still held him. "You told Weaver who she was?"

Father Baston felt sick to see the contempt in Hal's eyes.

"But …why?" asked Hal.

Father Baston shook his head. "Weaver beat me - you can still see the bruises. I held out for a long time…I withstood much."

He could feel the tremble of Hal's anger and for a moment he thought the archer was going to crush the life out of him.

"We trusted you, Father," Hal spat at him, "trusted you

with our lives! Pity you didn't have the courage of your mother and bear your pain to the grave. I should've realised what you were when you talked about revenge yet had done nothing about it for months! What else have you told Weaver?"

Father Baston shook his head, unable to speak.

"Did you tell him about John?" Hal demanded.

He shook his head, and was glad he hadn't but he knew he would have done if Weaver had asked. His torturer had been so pleased to hear about Lady Eleanor that he had stopped hitting him.

"I'll give you a reason to endure the pain, Father," murmured Hal. "For if you tell anyone about John, I'll kill you myself!" Hal hurled him to the floor and turned to go.

"Wait!" said Father Baston, "there's something I haven't told you! I haven't had the chance…"

Hal half-turned towards him. "What?" he demanded.

The priest clambered up onto his knees, still quivering.

"Lord Elder has come back," he whispered, still fearful that Joan might hear.

"What? And how long were you going to wait to tell me that?" growled Hal.

"He's not here any longer - he thinks you went to Corve."

Hal sighed. "Is there anything else I should know?"

Father Baston shook his head.

"Well make sure you tell no-one else!"

Hal went out and the priest was left to his fears. What if Weaver came back? What if Weaver did ask about the boy? He sat on the floor for a very long time but the more he pondered, the worse his predicament got. He knew now that death was certain whatever he did. He must act; he must find the knife he intended to use all those months ago - and he must somehow find the courage to use it. He must not betray them all again.

§§§§

Hal hurried away from the chapel, down to the ground floor and took refuge in one of the cellars. There had already been too many times in his life that he had known despair but he could not recall a worse situation that that he found himself in now. His every move was being watched. He left John with Bess, for enough attention had been drawn to the lad as it was. He was powerless to help Lady Eleanor for, even if he got her out of the oubliette, where would they go then? Worst of all, unbearably worse, he rarely even caught a glimpse of Agnes. Whenever she saw him she turned quickly away, shunning his company. He could think of a dozen reasons why, but it still preyed upon him. There was hardly a waking moment he did not think of her and she lingered in his dreams when he slept.

It could not go on - none of it could go on: Lady Eleanor must be rescued, Agnes freed from Sir Walter and John taken to safety - but how? If it wasn't for the boy, he would have taken his chances. The priest was worse than hopeless, he was a walking risk. He should have taken him out at the chapel when he had the chance but he was not a priest killer.

He must think; he must plan. He must do something. Could he, Wulf and the others take the castle? No, there were nearly eighty men in the castle - more than twice the number it was built to house. He could rely on perhaps eight or nine - and it wasn't enough, not nearly enough. But Lord Elder would not find them at Corve and when he did not, he would come back. Hal knew he would come back.

38

14th January 1469, at Salisbury

The Boar in Salisbury's market square was busy and Spearbold struggled to make his way in through the crowded doorway. It was many years since he had visited the town on Warwick's business and he had only a hazy recollection of the place. It was clear there would be no hope of securing lodgings at the Boar. He stifled an angry protest as a burly client lurched into him and half a jug of ale found its way down his cloak. Oh, the joys of being in a thriving town!

"Master Spearbold!" At first Spearbold ignored the shout of his name for he was certain he knew not a soul in Salisbury and assumed that he had misheard.

"Master Spearbold!" When the cry came once more, he peered through the jostling throng to the far side of the room.

"Come over, Spearbold!" He recognised Crabber at once and in the time it took him to traverse the floor he had worked out why Crabber was there.

"Sit down! Sit down," said Crabber with surprising enthusiasm. "Chubb! Get Master Spearbold some ale!" he bellowed.

"This is a happy meeting, Master Crabber," said Spearbold sitting on the stool, which he suspected the unfortunate Chubb had just been obliged to vacate.

"Have you eaten, Spearbold?" asked Crabber. "No, I can see you haven't," he continued before Spearbold could squeeze out a reply. "Chubb, bring some food too."

"I hope I haven't inconvenienced Master Chubb," said Spearbold.

Crabber laughed. "Spearbold, Chubb is my man as I am Lord Scales' man. It's his job to do what I tell him and I pay him well enough for it, I think."

"I suppose then that Lord Scales is in the town."

"Oh, indeed, he is one the judges in the oyer and terminer hearing going on at present," Crabber informed him.

"Aye, I knew there was to be treason trial, but not the details."

"It'll be a swift judgement I should say," advised Crabber, leaning in towards Spearbold. "Hungerford and Courtenay are as good as dead already."

"Who else presides?" asked Spearbold, who had more than a passing interest.

"Well, the Duke of Gloucester holds sway, then Scales, Arundel and a few others - oh, and Stafford - there's a rising star in the courtly firmament, Spearbold, Humphrey Stafford. The rumour is that 'Humph' has taken a fancy to Courtenay's inheritance: the Earldom of Devon. Be interesting to see what happens next, won't it?"

Chubb, a lanky, pale-skinned fellow, brought Spearbold his ale and set it down upon the table with a board of cheese and bread. Crabber took one look at it and seized Chubb's arm.

"Good God, Chubb, it's January! Get the man some hot potage at least, or a beef pie!"

Chubb went off muttering audibly which Spearbold thought was an achievement considering the swell of chatter in the room.

"So, your lord is here in Salisbury?" asked Crabber.

"Aye, he will be, but don't tell the world and his dog," said Spearbold with a nervous look about him. "He'll be here shortly for we hear the king is to attend the trial - but I don't want any of Warwick's men to hear that."

"Hah! No chance of that, my friend. The Earl of Warwick was to serve on the commission too but he's not here - and do you know who else isn't here?" asked Crabber, lowering his voice.

Spearbold shook his head.

"The king's brother!"

"But I though you said Gloucester headed the commission."

"Gloucester's here, of course he is! The other brother - George, the most gracious Duke of Clarence - he was supposed to be here too. From what I've picked up from Lord Scales, Warwick and Clarence have been very friendly of late…"

Spearbold could hardly draw breath. His knowledge of court intrigue was not as sharp as it once had been, so he ventured no opinion and merely soaked up Crabber's torrent of gossip as he dipped a chunk of bread into the steaming bowl of potage that now sat on the board before him.

"I know Lord Scales would be pleased to meet Lord Elder at last," finished Crabber. "After what happened at Sluys, he has much to thank him for."

"Aye, I'm sure that can be arranged," said Spearbold, reflecting over his ale that the meeting with Crabber was just the sort of happy coincidence he needed after the winter he had endured.

"Lord Elder should be here in a day or two," he said.

"Well he'd better make haste or the commission will have finished its business before he gets here!" laughed Crabber.

§§§§

Ned rode into Salisbury town alongside the river and crossed over a stone bridge just below a clutch of mills on the east bank. It had been a long ride from the Corve valley and Ned had been obliged to ask the way several times.

Now that they had arrived he felt a pang of regret for he had driven his small party on at a fair pace. Maighread looked pale and drawn and even Ragwulf had his cloak wrapped tight around him. Their entry into the town brought them to a halt as they encountered the busy flow of traffic.

"There are so many people," said Maighread, "and an appalling stench!"

"Which one?" replied Ned, catching several ripe scents in the air. "I think you're getting a whiff of the slaughterhouse, mingled with a strong smell of fish with just a hint of the fullers' racks."

"Is it the same in every town?"

"My dear lady, this is a good deal less unpleasant than London!"

She grimaced. "Then don't take me there, Ned, I beg you."

"If you don't like it, then you shouldn't have come," Ned told her, unable to keep the weary tone from his voice. Yet he tried to remind himself that Maighread had never left the borders - in fact had rarely ever left Crag Tower. Salisbury was only a little larger than some of the other towns they had passed through but it seemed to unsettle her now that they had reached the end of their journey.

The letter from Felix had arrived on Twelfth Night. It was short and to the point; it told Ned to meet him in Salisbury by 15th January. The king was expected to be in the town. Above all, Felix stressed secrecy. So, Ned's decision was made for him and he had come with his full retinue: which meant both Bear and Ragwulf. Maighread refused to stay behind and Spearbold, he hoped, was already here, doing what he did best: finding things out.

"Where to first then, lord?" asked Ragwulf.

"We'd best find our lodgings," said Ned, steering them south along the main thoroughfare. "Our friend from Bordeaux told us to go to the George Inn."

Maighread came to an abrupt halt and sat silent and still. She stared ahead towards the great stone cathedral spire. Ned leant in and laid a hand upon hers. "You see there are also things of beauty to be found in towns such as this, my love."

She nodded with a wry smile. "Aye, there's beauty where God's hand has been - less so by the hands of men!"

Ned discovered when they reached the George that Spearbold had already secured two chambers for them: a small room for Lady Maighread and a larger one for the men to share.

During the evening, Felix arrived. Ned had seen Felix bloodied, beaten and near to death but he had never seen him look so nervous. Usually the Frenchman's optimism seemed to conquer all fears, but on this occasion he gave Ned only a cursory glance and inclined his head towards the chambers upstairs.

"Wait here," Ned told the others and followed Felix up the stairs. Felix was waiting on the landing and then went into a small chamber adjacent to Maighread's. Ned followed him and closed the door.

Both men sat on the bed and sighed - then both grinned and clasped hands.

Ned shook his head in bewilderment. "I'm the one who's always in trouble Felix, yet…"

"Indeed, Ned," replied Felix, "and you still are! I fear that my troubles arise from yours."

"Why the need for such caution?" asked Ned.

"I am being pursued, Ned, tracked wherever I go."

"Were you followed here?"

"It's possible, though I did all in my power to avoid it."

"Are you safe here?"

"I do a deal of trade in Salisbury, Ned," he explained, "and I find it makes inn doors open faster than goose grease! I'll be safe enough in here - until I walk the streets."

Ned grinned. "You're not exactly difficult to spot," he

said staring at Felix's ebony skin.

"Alas, Ned, I was born with it - I can't shed it!"

"Very well then, tell me what has happened?"

"There has been trouble in the city before this winter but plots are still feared at court and unrest is everywhere it seems - in short there is much mischief!"

"Aye," said Ned, "but what does that mean for you?"

Felix grimaced. "Many are accused of plotting with the old Queen Margaret in France."

"But surely King Edward is secure, now that his differences with Warwick are settled?"

Felix held up a hand. "It is complicated," he said, "Queen Elizabeth's family cause much offence, they seem - and I say this in strict confidence of course - too grasping. There are many stories abroad of their avarice."

"But are such stories true?"

"Well, perhaps not all, but if a man such as Thomas Cook, a previous Mayor of London no less, is not safe from them, then there must be at least a little truth behind the rumours. And the queen's rise has been very swift…"

"Aye, his Grace is very fond of a handsome woman."

"Quite," said Felix.

"But how does all this affect you?"

"I'm being followed I think because I gave help to one of those accused," explained Felix. "John Goldwell."

Ned's heart sank. "Go on…"

"Alderman Goldwell only escaped arrest by a few hours. Finch took him and his family out of the City on The Catherine just in time."

"But who would accuse the Alderman - and of what? He's an honest man, isn't he?"

"Yes he is - well, as honest as any man that lends money - but this isn't about honesty, Ned, it's about treason - or fear of it."

"He's helped me several times - is there anything I can do for him?"

"That's one reason I wanted to see you. I have him in safe keeping in Bristol at present but he can't stay there forever. I need to get him safely away but, since I'm being watched so close, I wondered - because he had helped you in the past - if you could take him in at Corve? Just until we can unravel what is going on.

"You hardly need to ask, Felix! Of course he can come to Corve - I owe him my life - not to mention the obligation I have to his grandson."

"Well, that of course is a complication. Will Lady Eleanor be there?"

"No, but her son is… Still it can't be helped. I owe the Goldwells everything. You can bring them as soon as you wish."

"Not I, for I shall no doubt be found soon enough by the watchers. But I know men who'll convey then to you - men I can trust."

"Holton will make them very welcome," said Ned, though he imagined that several extra guests would not be welcomed so readily by Mistress Mags. "Wait. They're in Bristol, you say? A better plan would be for them to join us on our way back to Corve."

"Is that wise?" asked Felix. "There's a risk and you have your lady with you."

"But I also have Bear and Ragwulf with me. They are match for most."

"Then your offer is gratefully accepted."

"Make the arrangements with Spearbold before you leave."

"I have another favour to ask," said Felix. "And this one is not so easily done."

Ned shrugged. "However great it is, Felix, I can never repay the debt I owe to you and John Goldwell."

"Well, the matter is: someone has stirred the pot and thrown in some new ingredients. As you said at the first, John Goldwell is not involved in any plots but someone wants to bring him down. Now, to be sure, a goldsmith makes enemies but few with the power to intervene in matters of state. Someone has discovered that Goldwell's ship took you to safety - more than once. It would not be a hard trail to follow and that someone has set up John Goldwell - and perhaps me - for a fall."

"Someone?"

"As far as I can establish, this business all started out of the offices of Benjamin Warner."

"A Woodville man?" asked Ned.

"No - and that is exactly the point: it would make sense if he was a Woodville client but he's not. He is Warwick's man."

"So you think Warwick has discovered that John helped me and is now punishing him by setting the treason lawyers after him. I'm not sure Warwick would bother - unless he could see an advantage to it."

"One advantage might be to remove your friends so that he can strike at you."

"I suppose, but I'm hardly much of a threat to him now. In any case what can we do to help poor Goldwell?"

"I'll be blunt, Ned. You'll be seeing the king in the morning, I'd guess. Ask him to help John Goldwell."

"That's not going to be easy - after all, I relied upon others' help to get my pardon. His Grace is not going to be amused at the need to issue my pardon again - let alone if I ask about John. But I'll do my best."

"I pray you are able to help us, Ned. Tis the power of the crown against us - so only the crown, or those near it, can help."

Felix went out first and after a short while Ned followed. Spearbold had arrived in his absence and looked well pleased with himself. Ned said nothing to his companions of what Felix had told him but warned Spearbold to expect a visit from Felix.

"Well, Spearbold, what have you managed to arrange?"

he asked.

"All is prepared, my lord. The king has arrived and will pronounce the verdict in the trial tomorrow. Once the men are sentenced he'll not stay so I've asked if he will see you before that and the elusive letter of pardon will be made ready."

"Excellent. Well done, Spearbold. Let's hope we can conclude our business swiftly."

"I've also arranged for you to meet Lord Scales who wishes to thank you personally," said Spearbold, keeping his voice low.

Ned's smile turned to a frown. "The fewer reminders I have of what happened in Sluys the better," he said. "I may have saved one young woman but only to condemn another."

"Lord Scales might be an …influential friend," said Spearbold.

"Well, clearly, he's the queen's brother," observed Ned.

"Aye, my lord, but it's said that much of the energy to prosecute the likes of the London men, Thomas Cook and …others comes from the queen."

"Ah, I see," said Ned and looked thoughtfully at Spearbold. His man had clearly found out a great deal in his short time in Salisbury.

"Very well then, Spearbold, we will see the king tomorrow."

§§§§

Ned decided to take only Spearbold with him to meet with the king. Maighread would be safer remaining at the George with Ragwulf and Bear. She had been surprisingly quiet since their arrival and he thought he knew why. The serving man at dinner had stared, almost transfixed by her scarred face. In the end he looked away but the damage was done and Maighread's brash confidence was bruised. Ned realised that she was learning for the first time how folk would see her - and, in a town, there were people all around her.

"I hope you can see His Grace before the commission opens today," said Spearbold as they threaded their way through Salisbury's streets towards the market place.

"Why is it so wet underfoot?" complained Ned. "Are these streets or streams?"

"The town has watercourses here and there, my lord - one of its charms."

Ned thought it would be less than charming to meet the king in soaking wet boots, but they pressed on and Spearbold led him to the king's lodgings, which looked almost grand enough for a monarch.

"Fine lodgings," he observed.

"Generously provided by the Bishop of Salisbury, my lord," Spearbold informed him.

Ned was surprised how quickly the king saw him. Last time he seemed to recall a good deal more difficulty in gaining an audience - but years had passed. Now he was ushered into a large solar where King Edward sat at ease on his own.

Ned bowed low. "Your Grace…" he said, still a little wary of how the king might receive him.

"Ned, Ned! How long has it been since I saw you?" King Edward greeted him with warmth - it was how Ned remembered the youthful king. "Stand up man! Your letter of pardon - a second copy - has been signed and sealed. Don't lose this one! I am in your debt again Ned, for my sister's sake."

"Your Grace, my part in that was very small," said Ned.

"Nonsense! If Anthony Woodville concedes it, then it must be so!" Edward laughed.

"I trust your Grace is well… and the queen."

"By God's beard, Ned, my heart still beats but I doubt you came here to reassure yourself upon my health!"

Ned smiled as he recalled their first meeting in the

Shropshire hills when both their fortunes were at a much lower ebb. "Your health is a matter of grave importance to us all, Your Grace, but no - though I'm pleased to see you well - it's true there are some other matters I hoped to bring to your notice."

Ned knew that the king had buried his recent differences with the Earl of Warwick and he had thus agreed with Spearbold that he would not mention Warwick at all.

"Well, out with it, Ned," said the king, "We've to pass sentence this morning."

"Your Grace, on my estates in Yorkshire...men have been raised... I believe, to be used against you."

"Raised by whose order?" asked Edward.

"Sir Thomas Gate, Your Grace. Gate was behind the attack on your sister and I know not what he intends now but I fear he is in league with some others."

"That part of Yorkshire is close to Warwick's domain," the king said thoughtfully. "I'll send word to him. He can look into it, I'm sure."

"Perhaps, Your Grace, I could ... assist the earl - as a gesture of good faith to promote harmony between us."

Edward looked doubtful and Ned guessed why: if he had just salvaged his relationship with his most powerful subject he would not want Ned to cause another rift.

"Your Grace, you have generously returned to me my lands and titles. Let me go to Yoredale and arrest Thomas Gate. His treason, by acting against your sister, is already clear. I shall disband his forces but if I discover that the conspiracy is wider then I shall defer to the Earl of Warwick's judgement on the matter."

Ned had no intention of deferring to Warwick on any matter but he decided it might be rather foolhardy to say so.

Edward considered only briefly. "That sounds a good compromise, Ned. I shan't trouble Warwick with the matter until you've found out how deep the treason runs."

"Thank you, Your Grace."

"But Ned…"

"Your Grace?"

"This is a matter of state - there must be no wanton killings. Gate and any others are to be arrested, not slaughtered!"

"And if they do not consent to being arrested?" prompted Ned.

"Use only what force you must, Ned. These are difficult times and there are some that speak against me. The king's law must be upheld but I don't want any more disorder."

"Aye, my lord. I'll do my best, but I have few men. I don't suppose…"

There was a discreet knock at the door and an armed servant opened it to admit two men.

"Ned - two fellows you must know and trust: Anthony, Lord Scales and, my dearest brother, Dickon of Gloucester."

Ned bowed to the two men. "God give you good day, Your Grace… my lord."

Scales stepped forward and grasped his hand at once. "I am relieved to see you still breathing, Lord Elder, and glad to give you my thanks in person."

Gloucester seemed to view him more cautiously. "Lord Elder," he acknowledged, "I am pleased to meet a hero of Towton."

Lord Scales flinched at the mention of Towton - as well he might, thought Ned, since he had fought for Henry of Lancaster that day and been wounded to boot. He wondered whether young Gloucester's reference was deliberate.

"I am no stranger to the north, or to Yorkshire," said Gloucester. "I know Yoredale very well. I have many fond memories of the time I've spent at Middleham. You have a nephew there, I believe."

"Aye, your Grace, your namesake, Richard. Of course,

I've not seen the lad for years…"

"Well, I can tell you that he's an excellent youth. He spent a little time as my page - albeit a rather young page." Gloucester smiled. It was a boyish, hesitant smile.

"I'm grateful to you, Your Grace," said Ned. "It must have been hard for the lad without his mother."

"Well, I'm sure it would have been but of course his mother, Lady Radcliffe, is with him."

Ned must have shown his astonishment for Gloucester continued: "You did not know your sister was at Middleham, my lord?"

"No, Your Grace," replied Ned, trying to make sense of it, "exile has a way of confusing one's life."

"Indeed," agreed Gloucester.

"She is still there now?" Ned asked.

"I was there but a few weeks ago. So, I believe so."

"I am indebted to you then."

"We must go, Dickon," urged the king, "remember, you're supposed to be in charge of this trial!"

"Indeed, brother," acknowledged Gloucester with a frown.

Scales led them from the room and several men at arms joined them as they descended the stairs. Ned followed them out, leaving a respectful distance between himself and the royal party, only to find the Duke of Gloucester waiting for him on the landing.

"Your Grace?" said Ned.

"A word of advice to you, Lord Elder: don't get too close to Scales. The queen's brood are a faithless lot but … if you need an ally at court - or anywhere else - you may rely on my friendship. . ."

"Thank you, Your Grace," mumbled Ned.

Having delivered his terse message, Gloucester descended the steps swiftly to rejoin the others leaving Ned on the landing to consider what the duke had told him.

He wasn't sure which surprised him most: the revelation

that his sister, Emma, was lodged in Warwick's castle - which that lying Canon Reedman must have known very well - or the disdain that Gloucester had just displayed for the queen and her "brood" as he put it. Could the unity of the House of York really be so fragile?

He cursed the fact that his meeting with the king was so brief that he could not broach the issue of John Goldwell. There would not be another meeting. Gloucester promised friendship but would he pervert the course of justice to free a friend of Ned Elder? Ned thought not. He would have to see whether Scales had any more to offer. One thing was clear to Ned: he might get assistance from either Gloucester or Scales, but he could not be a friend to both.

§§§§

St Thomas's churchyard was dark and still. There was a hint of mist in the air. As they passed close by the church, they were obliged to make a detour around a stack of timber beams and Ned noticed the outline of wooden scaffolding poles encasing the body of the church.

"Rebuilding," observed Spearbold, "I gather the chancel roof fell in."

"Aye," said Ned, wondering idly how Spearbold knew such things. "Do you think he'll come?" He rubbed his hands together briskly.

"Aye," said Spearbold. "He'll come - he wants something."

Ned looked back to where Ragwulf followed twenty paces or so behind them.

"It's freezing out here," said Ned. "When I said 'somewhere quiet,' I foolishly thought you'd arrange somewhere inside!" He stood for a moment, stamping his feet on the cobbles.

"Crabber said that Lord Scales wanted no possibility of witnesses. Here, you'll have your man on watch and he will have his."

"Well. Let's hope he's not going to keep us waiting all night!"

"He's not," said a voice from the shadows.

"My lord?" Ned tried to make out the figure emerging from behind several old yews.

"No need to shout, Ned," said Lord Scales. "It is cold. Let's walk together. Crabber and Spearbold can wait here whilst we take a stroll around the graves. I always find that rather a sobering experience."

He held out his hand and, after a slight hesitation, Ned took it. By doing so Ned knew he was crossing a line, a battle line that had not yet been drawn - and might never be - but a line nonetheless.

"You asked to meet me?" said Ned, as they set off walking very slowly in the darkness.

"I think we should begin by being honest with each other, Ned. We both wanted this meeting, did we not?"

"Aye," agreed Ned. "It seems so. I know why I wanted it but what concerns me is why you did."

"Your name, your reputation as a warrior, wins men over, Ned."

"Perhaps once, but I'm not the soldier I was in my younger days."

"But men don't know that, Ned. They remember their heroes. Take me for example. They remember that I fought a tough tournament against the bastard of Fauconberg a year or two ago but they don't remember my wounds and misery after defeat at Towton. They remember you for Mortimer's Cross, for St Albans - even in defeat - and, most of all, for Towton."

"So, perhaps a few men recall my exploits. How does that help you?"

"I want you on my side," said Scales.

"Your side? I am for the king - there is no other side I will fight for."

"I am for the king too," said Scales, "but I am also for the queen, my sister, and for Lord Rivers, my father. Do you not fight for your family and friends, Ned?"

"Aye," said Ned, his head suddenly crammed with images of Eleanor, Agnes and his young, as yet unseen, son.

"You've been away for some years, Ned. The kingdom has changed in your absence."

"Surely we are at peace now that the House of Lancaster has been expelled."

"The old king still lives on... in the Tower. His queen still plots in France…with the King of France and others. But not only that: we Woodvilles, the new queen's family, are mistrusted, threatened…endangered. You have returned to a much divided kingdom, Ned. We are a kingdom of rebels now. Warwick and the king have buried their differences, it seems, but the earl still seeks to destroy my sister and all of our family."

"Let's assume I accept what you say. What are you proposing?"

"Warwick is your enemy too, is he not?"

"Aye, I believe he still is - though my king tells me a different tale."

"The king is misled by Warwick, but he is not alone. Suddenly this earl is everyman's friend - well I, for one, don't believe it."

Ned stopped pacing and leant his hand upon a tall gravestone. "What is it you want from me?" he asked.

"Your support - if it comes to a struggle with Warwick."

Ned expected as much and knew he had no choice but to agree. He did not deceive himself though: his commitment this night could plunge him into a renewed feud with Warwick. Yet he must do it, for alone he could not hope to free his own people. He needed men. Thus the wheel turned and once more he must make common purpose with the enemy of his enemy.

"Very well," said Ned. "You'll have my support as long

as I'm not required to act against King Edward. That, I will not do."

"Nor would I ask you to, after all, without King Edward, you and I are both dead men."

"I'll want several things in return," said Ned.

Scales grimaced. "I thought you might."

"I need men at arms - a score perhaps - and some archers. Men I can rely upon, mind you."

"I can't give you more than a dozen men - half of them archers."

"What about a dozen men at arms and half a dozen archers?" suggested Ned.

"Very well," said Scales, "but that will have to include some mercenaries."

"I want only good men," said Ned.

"Good men? What is a good man, Ned?"

"You know what I mean: men who will fight."

"I'll give you men who can fight."

"Then that will serve well enough," said Ned. He would have accepted a handful.

"There is one other condition," he said, "and it must be met."

"That sounds ominous," replied Scales. "Go on then, what is it?"

"You spoke of Lancastrian plots. One of the men who stands accused of treason, of collusion with Margaret of Anjou's agents in London - is a merchant called John Goldwell."

"The goldsmith? His flight caused a small panic in the City. What of him?"

"I want all charges against him dropped. He is an innocent man and he has been a good friend to me. He has fled his home and I want his good name restored."

"That's not within my power, Ned. It is a matter for the law."

"It is within your sister's power," said Ned. "She could

wield her influence in his favour. God's blood! The man's wrongly accused in any case - he's someone's pigeon!"

Scales seemed to consider for a moment. "I will do my best for him, Ned."

"So that we are clear," replied Ned, "this condition must be met or I will not support you."

"Very well," agreed Scales, "but it is no small matter, Ned."

"Your hand upon it?" said Ned and they clasped hands. Then they walked back to where Crabber and Spearbold waited, no doubt as cold as statues by now.

"How soon will I have the men?" asked Ned.

"It'll take a week or two at least," said Scales. "Where do you want them?"

"Spearbold," said Ned, "where and when do I want some of Lord Scales' men?"

Spearbold's face creased into one of his deepest frowns as he rapidly calculated distances and destinations. "Stafford, by the end of the month would be helpful, my lord," he replied finally.

"Can you do that?" Ned asked Scales.

"You have a casual manner about you when you ask for mountains to be moved, my lord," said Scales. "But Crabber will do his best, won't you Crabber?" His aide gave a shivering nod.

Lord Scales gave Ned a final embrace and whispered, "Let's pray that you are never required to fulfil your part in our pact, Ned."

"Aye, amen to that," said Ned.

§§§§

Maighread greeted him with a worried look when he entered her chamber at the George Inn. She had already retired to bed but got up to greet him.

"You look as if you've sold your soul, my lord," she

observed grimly.

"Aye, you might well say that. I've done what I had to do: I've made my bargain with Lord Scales. I've no men without patronage and without men I can do nothing. In the end it all turns upon the men who stand with you. Corve has already bled to death for my family and I won't ask it to do so again."

Maighread took his hands in hers. "Oh, you are ice cold, my lord," she exclaimed and massaged his fingers with the palms of her hand. Then she surprised him by wrapping her arms around him and hugging him close to her.

"So, will you go to Yoredale now?" she murmured, still holding him close.

"Back up to Corve and then aye, on to Yoredale with the king's warrant and Anthony Woodville's men."

They stood together for a time and he felt her tremble in his arms.

"It must be very cramped next door for you and the others," she said.

"We can manage," said Ned, "and we'll be gone by tomorrow."

She unfastened his cloak and pulled it off him. "Come," she said, "my bed is still warm."

"We are not wed in the church yet." He found his voice had somehow grown husky.

Maighread smiled. "We will be, Ned and did we not pledge our marriage before witnesses?"

"Some very damp witnesses, I think."

"Damp or dry, they were still witnesses. But our marriage is not lawful until consummated."

"Consummated? That's a big word for a country lass," he said with a grin.

She took him by the hand and drew him to her bed. She was a woman who never failed to surprise him. She regarded him steadily, sensing his reluctance, then she sighed and shook her head.

"Forgive me, Ned. It's too soon, isn't it? I've been foolish."

Not for the first time he studied her face, one cheek red and rough, the other flawlessly smooth and her tragic beauty pierced his heart.

"For the love I bear Amelie, it'll always be too soon but … for the love I bear you, it can never be soon enough. Wasn't it I that proposed we marry, my lady? I just wasn't expecting…"

"Ned, I was married and widowed before I was eleven years old. I kept my shrivelled maidenhead until four years ago when Henry Radcliffe forced me. I know nothing of men and nothing of marriage. I asked your sister's advice."

"I can't see why you'd ask Eleanor's advice about anything," laughed Ned.

"Because she would give me an honest answer. I asked her if any man could possibly love me. She told me that if she had a face like mine, she would throw herself off the highest tower."

"What?" Ned was appalled. "She shouldn't have said that!"

"Why not?" asked Maighread. "At least she didn't look away and pretend my scars weren't there. Eleanor and I came to understand each other - a little late perhaps…but we both like to speak, and hear, plainly.

"My sister speaks a deal too plainly!" he said.

"She said I needed to find a man who could look at me without flinching but that I wasn't going to find that man sitting in Crag Tower."

"My sister's a fool…"

"No, she was right," said Maighread, with her crooked smile. "Do you see a long line of men waiting to lie with me, Ned?"

He didn't know how to answer.

"My scars are not limited to my face, Ned, and I don't want either of us to find out after saying our vows before

God that you can't stand the sight of me or … the feel of me beside you. I think for both our sakes, we should find that out now… tonight."

Ned sat on the bed and took her hand in his. "Blood of Christ, it's been a busy day! You're not the only one with scars, you know," he said drawing her to him to kiss her on the mouth.

She broke the embrace for a moment. "I know, Ned."

He nodded. "Right, then. Are we going to bed or not?"

"Aye," she said. "We are and it feels as if I'm about to jump off the highest tower."

39

17th January at midday, in the market place at Chippenham

Ned hated waiting at the best of times and now more than ever. There was so much to be doing; he was desperate to return to Corve as soon as he could.

"Are you sure this is where Felix said?" he asked Spearbold. The latter nodded wearily for it was not the first time Ned had put the question to him.

"And he definitely said midday?"

Spearbold gave another nod.

"Well where are they then?" he demanded. "We can't wait by the Yelde Hall all day. It's a handsome new building, but I've felt less exposed in the field!"

Maighread laid a calming hand on his arm. "Come. Walk with me and save your anger for your enemies."

He shrugged and she threaded her arm through his and they left the others waiting in the market place.

"They'll be travelling slowly, I expect," she said. "You say there is a boy with them?"

"Aye." Ned sighed and Maighread stopped walking and looked at him.

"What does that mean?" she asked. "I know you, Ned Elder. Tell me about this boy."

"Ah, the boy…Jack is his name," he said. "I'm going to need your help with this…"

Maighread started walking again. "Why do I feel a little anxious now?" she asked. "Go on, tell me."

"Jack is the bastard son of my good friend, Will - my

good, dead friend, Will Coster."

Maighread stopped again. "But, isn't young Will, Eleanor's son, the son of Will Coster?"

"Aye."

"How many bastard sons did he have then?"

"Only two - but two will be enough to bring trouble…"

"Does Eleanor know about Jack?" she asked.

"No, but she will."

"Perhaps she'll not notice the boy too much…"

"I think she might," said Ned, he was already finding the whole idea slightly terrifying.

"Does the boy's mother, Sarah, know about Eleanor?"

"Aye - but not about her son."

"Having them all under the same roof - that sounds as if it might be … difficult," observed Maighread.

They stopped to allow a wagon to pass by them along the street

"Aye, well I did say I thought I'd need your help…"

A voice hailed them from the passing vehicle. "Ned! Ned!"

He looked up to see Alderman John Goldwell framed at the back of the covered wagon which was moving slowly on into the market place. The wheels of the wagon were caked in mud and peat.

"God's Blood!" said Ned, "It's no surprise they're late if they've come all the way from Bristol in that!"

They followed the wagon and soon introductions were made. Sarah Goldwell looked tired and when the alderman presented his grandson, Jack, to Maighread, Ned noticed that she turned rather pale and glared at Ned.

He grinned sheepishly and whispered in her ear. "Don't take me to task, my lady. He's not my bastard son!"

"I don't want to be there when Eleanor meets him and his mother!" she hissed.

"Pity," he said, "I was rather hoping you would be."

She shook her head. "Is there no part of your life that is

simple, Ned Elder?"

He shrugged. "Well, I don't think you'll be travelling any further today," he said to the others. "We'd better find rooms at one of the inns. We'll set off early tomorrow."

§§§§

After Chippenham they made good progress north in the next few days using several roads that Spearbold reckoned would be passable since they were used regularly by both packhorse and wagon. They were fortunate that the mornings turned frosty and hardened up some of the muddier stretches. Even so, on their fourth day they barely covered ten miles as the heavy wagon was stranded more than once in boggy ground.

Maighread, who had found riding arduous on the journey south, travelled in the wagon. Ned was secretly quite pleased since he knew she would take the opportunity to get to know Sarah and Jack a little better. John Goldwell rode Maighread's horse and told Ned all that had happened to them in their flight from London.

"So," he concluded, "here we are penniless and ruined, throwing ourselves upon your charity, Ned."

"Well, relatively penniless," remarked Ned, who had noted the small strongbox inside the wagon.

It took them a week to reach Corve Manor, north of Ludlow, and Ned was glad that Spearbold had sent word to Holton about their impending arrival. All was prepared and they were greeted warmly by the steward and his wife.

Mags lost no time, however, in acquainting Ned with the difficulty of finding sufficient room for the Goldwell entourage, which brought half a dozen more guests.

"We don't have enough bedchambers, my lord - you know that!" she complained. "The boy and his mother and the maid can share one room, the alderman will have another and the apprentices can sleep in the Hall. But even so, I'll have to move out Master Spearbold to...I don't know where!"

"I'm sure it is difficult," Ned said trying to soothe her, "but you need not move Spearbold. Lady Maighread will be sharing my chamber."

"Oh, I'd already worked that out!" she retorted, rolling her eyes at him. "I'm not blind! I was depending on that anyway - as I said, we're still short."

Ned retreated and followed Maighread, who was making her way upstairs grinning.

"I'm sure that you have it all in hand!" he called to Mags.

§§§§

Ned spent a week at Ludlow preparing to go north and he chewing over his options with Spearbold and the others - the small group that Maighread liked to refer to as his 'privy councillors'. In truth they were not so much an inner circle as the entire circle. Spearbold knew where Scales' men were due to meet them at a crossroads just north of Stafford. Ned hoped that they would not be late for the thought of wasting any more days filled him with dread and fear for his boy and his sister. Now he sat alone in his chamber, beginning to contemplate saying farewell to Maighread.

She came silently into the room and stood behind him, putting an arm around his shoulder and resting her face against his neck. He turned to face her and take her in his arms. Then he stood back and looked her up and down.

"What are you wearing?" he asked.

"Master Holton told me it's a brigandine," she said with a grin.

"Did he?"

"Aye, he did. He said there are bits of steel sewn in it - but it's not too heavy."

"And Master Holton just gave this...brigandine to you,

did he?"

"Aye, he did."

"He just came along - when I happened not to be there - and handed it to you."

"Aye," said Maighread, bright-eyed. "Well, I might have asked his advice at Christmas…"

"His advice?"

"How a lady might protect herself…you know, from harm. And he just …made it for me … when we were away in Salisbury."

She smoothed it down. "It fits me well, do you not think?"

"You're not coming with me," said Ned.

"Oh, I think I should."

"You are not coming with me," he repeated.

"I think you'll let me."

"I won't!"

"You will." Her voice was infuriatingly calm.

"Maighread, there's nothing you could say that would persuade me to let you come with me to Yoredale."

"You may need me," she said.

"What I need is three times as many men at arms, not another person to worry about!"

"You won't need me to fight."

"Exactly! So why would I take you then?" he asked.

"Because your son won't know you yet; but he will know, and trust, me."

"He'll know Bear and Ragwulf well enough."

"Aye, but you have too few men; you'll need both of them to fight. I'll keep the boy with me." She drew out the long knife at her side. "And I'll protect the pair of us with this."

"Where in God's name did you get that? No, don't bother to tell me. I'll have Master Holton whipped when I see him next!"

She sheathed the knife and put her arms around his

neck again.

"Do you know how I knew he was your son?" she whispered. "He looks you in the eye, he weighs up the task and then he goes for it with all the fight he's got in that little body. That's him - and that's you. And I may only be an Elder by name, but I am hewn out of the same stone."

"You're still not going with me. You're staying here."

Maighread dropped her arms and knelt down before him. She looked up at him and took his hands in hers

"Listen to me, my lord. I've been starved, I've been raped, I've been beaten, I've had every weapon known to God hurled at me and I've been scourged by fire - twice! Wherever you are going, there is nothing worse that any man can do to me. So don't tell me to stay here and wait. Don't tell me it's too dangerous - for I know as much about danger as anyone alive. Now that I've finally found a man that I love, I'm going to be by his side, no matter what. If I die, then God has willed it and I will die knowing I have loved. But I'll not sit here idly waiting for you to return and not knowing. When you go into Yoredale Castle, I'll be going with you."

"As my lady, you should obey me."

She laughed aloud. "We've not taken our vows in church yet... and I've never been a great one for obedience. Obedience took me from my home and got me shackled to a man thrice my age. I've not been fond of obedience ever since. But you know that well enough - if you love me."

He lifted her up and drew her to him. "Very well, I give up - but you're not going into the castle until it's safe."

She did not answer but simply smiled and kissed him.

PART SIX: THE STORM BREAKS

DEREK BIRKS

40

1st February 1469, at Middleham Castle

Emma walked slowly along the narrow passage that led from her chamber to the south west tower. Her mind was still in turmoil, she had not slept, she was waspish towards her young daughter and she knew she must put an end to it. She had grown fond of Middleham: her chamber in the west range was home now and her children were safe and happy here. But despite that harmony, which she had always craved, she had made up her mind to help her sister.

No matter that they argued and spat insults at each other whenever they met. Still, Eleanor was her sister by blood and Eleanor had always been willing to shed some of that blood to help her. Whatever their differences, Emma could not now abandon her sister to her fate, even though she feared being embroiled in her brother's affairs - for Ned would surely kill them all in the end.

The difficulty was that she could see only one way to help Eleanor: she must enlist the support of the Countess of Warwick. If the countess used her influence, then perhaps Eleanor could be brought to Middleham. Aye, Eleanor could be a trial - more than a handful - but she thought it might be managed without losing her own place there and without danger to her children.

The Earl of Warwick seemed to be very busy through the winter and she had never seen so many men at Middleham. There were enough men and arms to fight a war - did the earl fear an uprising? There were stores enough, even in the heart of these coldest months, to endure a long siege. Every day messengers came or went somewhere. She kept her distance from all such business, which is why she had won the trust of her hosts. But now she would no longer be distant; she would be involved once more. The very thought made her chest tighten as she ascended the spiral stair and she was out of breath by the time she reached the floor above. The countess had some of the new chambers and the walls still smelled of fresh plaster, though perfumed rushes were spread across the threshold and the floors within.

Emma liked Anne Beauchamp. She had been one of the wealthiest heiresses of her age when she was married to the Earl of Warwick and he must have gained a great deal from his wife. Emma found her a kind, if somewhat forthright, woman. Anne must have been in her early forties so the two women were not of an age but they shared many of the tribulations facing all women of a certain rank as their children grew up in a dangerous world. Emma had come to learn that it was not only gentlewomen who worried about their children, which made her gratitude to the countess all the more sincere.

The countess always remained a little aloof but she permitted Emma to kiss her cheek in greeting. Emma's anxiety must have been very obvious for the countess frowned at her at once.

"You bring some troubles with you, my dear," she said. "You wear your cares heavily."

Emma dropped to her knees. "My lady, I come as a poor supplicant…"

Lady Warwick gave her a wry smile. "Well, you'd better out with it before you burst," she said.

So Emma passed on to her all that Canon Reedman had told her, omitting only any mention of Eleanor's previous imprisonment at Middleham and her subsequent escape. She expected a hundred questions - or worse, a flat rejection of involvement. In fact she got neither and Lady Anne regarded her in silence for a time, as if weighing up her options.

"From what I've heard about your sister Eleanor, she will be a trouble wherever she is," she said. "What do you want to happen, that you and your sister will live here the rest of your days in quiet contentment?"

Emma's hopes began to wither as she knelt there on the rushes, inhaling the sweet scent of lavender.

"My sister is a restless spirit, it's true," replied Emma in a trembling voice, "but I don't want her to be a prisoner - and in particular, not... of that woman." She would have said more but she could already feel the tears welling up and she could not revisit the miseries of the past. It was just too painful.

"Get up, dear Emma, you're crushing the lavender," said Lady Warwick. "Sir Thomas Gate is a trusted man of my husband and is therefore above reproach. His new wife, however, does not enjoy the same favour - not with me, nor with my husband. If Sir Thomas agrees then Lady Eleanor might be released into your charge. But you must consider well: what will your 'restless' sister do then?"

"If I could but speak to her, then I believe she would consent to go elsewhere - my brother has a manor in Shropshire. She could certainly go there."

"And what of your brother, who is now restored? Will he try to take back Yoredale Castle?"

"I haven't seen my brother for almost five years, my lady. I'm not privy to his thoughts - nor do I want to be."

"I will speak to the earl about your sister, Emma, but there are several other matters I intended to talk to you about soon - and since we are here..."

"My lady?" Emma thought it sounded rather ominous.

"When you came here, we took you in for charity's sake but now you have lived here for several years. Your daughter is old enough to be cared for by others and your son, Richard, is of an age where he should be broadening his training. He was much praised by the Duke of Gloucester last year. All in all, it's time you had a position reflecting your birth and status."

Where was Lady Warwick heading? Was she going to send her away?

"You are fond of my daughter Anne, I know."

"Aye, my lady. She's a sweet girl."

"Well, not always, but the point is that her sister will soon be married and Anne too must be prepared for a similar match."

"Anne is still quite young, my lady."

"Nonsense, my dear. She's already twelve. I'd been married three years by that age!"

"Lady Isabel's marriage is to be soon then? May I know to whom?"

"No," said Lady Warwick firmly. "There are still matters to be arranged - but her husband will be a young man of great wealth and standing."

"What is it you want me to do, my lady?" asked Emma.

"Anne needs to be prepared for marriage and for running a household. You have experience of both - but more importantly she has asked for you. I want you to join her and help her to assemble a small, but suitable, household of servants who will go with her when she marries. Your son will become her page and you would move chambers so that you are near her."

"And what of my daughter, Alice?"

"The nurse who cares for Alice now will assume more responsibility for her until Alice is old enough to manage without one. Now, how does this position sound to you?"

"My lady, I was born to run a household. I did so for my father from the age of ten and I would be very pleased to attend upon Lady Anne. But…the matter with my sister…"

"The one is not dependent upon the other," said the countess. "We do not hold you accountable for the actions of either your sister or your brother, which is as well for you. You must not act against Sir Thomas Gate, but your cousin Joan… is another matter entirely."

41

4th February 1469 in the morning, at the old mill near Carperby

They arrived by night like thieves, not like bearers of a royal warrant. The night was cold and there was sleet in the air. The abandoned mill was a convenient place to rest but hardly the best site, Ned thought. Not only did it offer precious little shelter, but it carried bitter memories for Maighread. She looked exhausted but uttered no word of complaint.

Scales' men at arms and archers had been waiting for them at the appointed place. They had probably been waiting all day and they were also, he assumed, rather put out to have been loaned to him by Lord Scales. By the time he met them they were cold and impatient. They all looked competent enough but Ned wondered how committed such men would be if it came to a fight. Their spokesman was a tall man at arms who introduced himself as Croft and delivered a message from his master.

"I am to tell you, Lord Elder, that your friend, Lord Scales, is working tirelessly to aid the family you mentioned to him," said Croft in a hushed voice.

"And?" said Ned.

"That's all he said, my lord," said Croft.

"Aye," muttered Ned, "all well and good, I suppose…'tirelessly'?

"That was the very word he used, my lord," said Croft.

"Aye, well thank you, Master Croft, your news is welcome."

Whatever Scales was or wasn't doing to help the Goldwells, it mattered little now. For now Ned was in Yoredale and the real business would soon begin. On the morrow he would pay a visit to Coverham Abbey and have a few strong words with Canon Reedman. He had written a letter for his sister, choosing his words carefully for, once they were written, there could be no going back. He hoped he could trust Reedman to deliver it.

Then he must deal with Thomas Gate. He had been tempted to enter the valley openly, to go to Yoredale Castle and attempt to parley with Gate, but if he did so all he would do was warn him of his presence. In any case he could not see how they might reach any agreement in which Gate surrendered. Nor did he have enough men to make an assault on the castle - the best he could do was isolate it, but he knew that such a course might prompt Warwick to turn up with two dozen men at arms. A pitched battle with Warwick was the one thing King Edward had instructed him to avoid.

His only real option - aside from riding away empty-handed - was to get a man inside the castle - unless of course he already had a woman in there. That was where he was hoping that Emma might play a part. He did not delude himself: there was little chance that she would help him. If she did not, then one of his men was going to need to walk into the castle.

Croft's men were bedding down for the night in the old mill with many a curious glance still directed at Maighread.

"Croft, are all your men here?" he asked, scanning the mill.

"Yes, my lord."

"Did Lord Scales tell you what you would be doing with me here in the wild and frozen north?" he asked.

"No, my lord," said Croft.

"Very well. Men! Listen, please." He tried to make eye contact with as many of the men as possible whilst he explained.

"It's time we talked about the reason we're here. Croft tells me that you're all men from the south, from Lord Scales' estates mostly. If that's the case, then you must not care too much for my harsh northern tones," he said.

There were a few shrugs but it seemed that most of them really didn't care much.

"We are here on the king's business," he continued. "We're here to enforce an arrest warrant issued by His Grace, King Edward, against Sir Thomas Gate - a man who knows no shame; a rebel, a deceiver, and murderer. But, although we have the law on our side, this is not going to be easy. I'm not a great lord. I'm a lord of little importance but I am acting here for the king and I need to arrest this man at Yoredale Castle. I don't think he'll like it much and he'll put up a fight. He has far more men than we do but with luck we can take him by surprise.

"I need to know that when I lead, the men with me are going to follow. I won't ask more of you than I would my own men but I don't expect any less either. I told Lord Scales that I wanted men I could rely upon and he sent me you."

Their response was not exactly overwhelmingly supportive. They looked at each other, said little and then settled down for the night.

"Croft," he said, "post some men for the night watches."

"Aye, lord," he muttered.

Would his words encourage them or cause them to run off during the night? He had no idea but he thought talking to them was a better strategy than ignoring them and waiting for them to draw their own conclusions. If he was not prepared to strip Corve of its young men then he must make do with men who knew nothing of him at all, who owed him no fealty. They were men who, in the end, had simply been bought by his promise of support to Scales.

42

5th February 1469, at Middleham Castle

After her meeting with Lady Warwick, Emma found the days that followed difficult. On one hand she was waiting to hear whether she could visit Eleanor - with all the trepidation that such a visit would bring - and on the other she was anticipating with nervous delight the prospect of at last having a worthwhile role at Middleham. However, before either event occurred, she received an unexpected visit from Canon Reedman.

She could tell at once from his face that he did not bring tidings she would welcome, so she took him down to the chapel where he pretended to take her confession to avoid them being overheard.

"Without giving offence, Canon, I had hoped not to see you for a time," she said.

"Aye, my lady, but there has been a …change."

"A change? What do you mean a change? Is my sister still at Yoredale?"

"Oh, aye, yes she is, I believe, still there."

"Then?" she enquired.

"Your brother, newly restored as Lord Elder, has returned and, in short, he knows you reside here at Middleham and he is not best pleased with me for failing to tell him."

Emma was relieved. She had imagined that Eleanor had committed some heinous act at Yoredale and was about to embarrass her further.

"There's more," said Reedman. "Your brother has come with a royal warrant to receive the surrender of Sir Thomas Gate and his garrison."

"What? Why?" she stammered out. She began to feel queasy. How could that be?

"Sir Thomas is accused of raising men without a royal commission to do so…"

Emma's head was spinning. It just got worse and worse. She didn't understand.

"But Sir Thomas is the Earl of Warwick's man… and the earl is the king's man…"

"Don't ask me, my lady, I'm already up to my neck in this and I never desired any of it. My loyalty to you has cost me much. I shall do well to escape with my mortal soul!"

She attempted to collect her thoughts. "But why have you come here to tell me this now?"

Reedman seemed to hesitate. That was not good. "What?" she demanded.

"Your brother demands to see you."

She gasped, knowing he was going to involve her in his plots and destroy all her hopes for the future.

"He seeks to meet you outside Middleham."

"Well, I didn't expect him to come here where the earl resides!" she hissed. "But I don't want to meet him - and I'm not going to! I'm trying my best to free Lady Eleanor and I don't want him doing anything to upset that."

"He won't accept your refusal, my lady. I fear he will make more trouble…"

"Aye, he's good at making trouble, like my sister. Sweet Christ! Why am I the only one in my family, canon, who seeks a life of peace?"

"What shall I tell him, my lady?" asked Reedman.

"Tell him, I'll not meet him. Tell him I hope to get into Yoredale any day now to visit Lady Eleanor. Tell him… I beg him not to act until I have done that."

"Very well, my lady, but I think he may have expected

such an answer."

"Why do you say that?" she asked.

"Because he said that if you should intend to go to Yoredale, then you should go ... before Sunday and... he gave me this..." He held out a tiny, sealed scroll.

"No," she said firmly. "I'll not take it."

"Don't fret so, my lady. I believe he understands your ...conflicting loyalties," continued Reedman.

"Hah, it'll be the first time he does then!" retorted Emma.

"He said you should take the letter and then it was up to you whether you read the letter or not and whether you act upon its contents. But whether you read it or not, he bade you destroy it."

Emma regarded the letter Reedman still held out to her with the utmost suspicion. But Ned knew her too well: he knew her curiosity would get the better of her, knew she would take it and knew, in the end, she would read it.

"It will only mean trouble, canon," she said with sadness. "Trouble for him, trouble for me and trouble for everyone else too."

She gave a sigh and snatched the scroll from his hand.

"What shall I tell him, my lady?"

"Tell him I wish he was in Hell," she said. "No...don't tell him that. Tell him I'll try to get Eleanor out. And tell him I pray God to keep him safe. Now, please leave me."

§§§§

Emma did not read the letter. Instead she carried it with her, close to her body, so that none should find it by accident. If she could have Eleanor released then the contents of the letter could make no difference to her. But she must go 'before Sunday' - why? It was already Friday - what did Ned plan to do on Sunday? He surely could not have the men to storm the castle.

She could wait no longer for the countess to answer her plea but to press the matter harder would surely be a mistake. By the afternoon she had heard nothing and she began to fret about what her brother was planning to do. By evening she still had not heard from Lady Warwick, but then she was summoned by the earl himself to see him in his privy chamber. She went full of trepidation for he had never before asked to see her in all the time she had been at Middleham.

"Lady Radcliffe," the earl greeted her, using a title she had done her best to forget. He embraced her as if she were a close friend. That worried her from the outset and she hardly knew what to say.

"What a trial our blood relations can sometimes be," he said.

"You mean my sister, my lord?" asked Emma.

He gave her a rueful grin. She had forgotten how charming the man could be - in small doses.

"In fact, I meant your brother," he admitted. "I've said it several times - and meant it every time - I have no quarrel with your sister."

The relief Emma felt was short-lived.

"However," the earl went on, "Joan Elder - now Lady Joan Gate - does have a quarrel with your sister...and I suspect with you too. Joan Elder wronged both of you - I know that. You are important to us here at Middleham and we have come to value you: you are to guide my daughter's household. You have committed your future to us and I, as a good lord, should help your cause, but..."

"But Sir Thomas Gate is Lady Joan's husband and you are his lord also," said Emma.

Warwick nodded. "Indeed, my lady, you understand my dilemma perfectly. The question is: what are we to do about it?"

"And what are... we to do, my lord?" asked Emma, for despite all his talk, she knew that he would not have summoned her if he had not already decided what was going to happen.

"Well, my lady, I've spoken to Sir Thomas and he tells me that Lady Eleanor gained entrance to Yoredale Castle disguised as a mason's wife. Do you know why in all Christendom your sister would have done that?"

"Who knows why my unruly sister does anything, my lord?" replied Emma. "She is… impossible."

"Sir Thomas believes she was plotting to kill his wife," said Warwick. Emma noted that the warm tone of their initial conversation was cooling somewhat. She had better not stray too far from the truth or Warwick would find her out.

She adopted an aggrieved expression. "It's possible with Eleanor, my lord, for, as you've agreed, Lady Joan did my family great harm."

Even discussing it as dispassionately as she could, Emma was beginning to struggle with the emotions it was stirring up. She knew she must not lose control in Warwick's presence or the prospect of a role in Lady Anne's household would vanish as swiftly as it had appeared.

"Even so…I cannot have this squabble disrupting our lives here. Lady Eleanor must accept that… if she is to be freed."

So there it was, thought Emma. Eleanor would be released but only if she promised to be a good girl - but there was little chance of that and… Eleanor was right after all.

"Am I to be held responsible for my sister?" asked Emma.

"I understood that is what you asked for, my lady."

"My lord, Lady Joan murdered my sister-in-law and… others who were dear to us. My sister has good cause to act against her - it is Lady Joan who should be censured - aye, and called to account for her crimes!"

Emma felt the flush in her cheeks and, despite her resolutions to the contrary, Emma knew she was losing control. She had enough reason to hate Joan as much as Eleanor did. She had repressed that hatred to survive but it still lay there, festering inside her.

"My lady!" Warwick's voice was suddenly stern and when he spoke, Emma listened.

"I will not allow my faithful servant, Thomas Gate, to be compromised in any way by this matter. But… he has agreed for you to see your sister and - if you can persuade her to desist in her mischief making - she will be released into our custody at Middleham."

Emma tried not to let her anger show. The earl spoke as if Sir Thomas had free will in the matter but he did as he was told - as she was about to do - for Warwick's power could not be gainsaid. Ned was a fool to oppose the earl for it would only lead to his destruction. If she could save Eleanor at least, then she must do her best. She composed herself.

"Thank you, my lord. When may I go to Yoredale?"

"Sir Thomas will expect you tomorrow morning."

Emma thanked God she was to go before Sunday, whatever Sunday was going to bring, but Warwick had not finished.

"I want this whole unpleasant affair settled by the end of the day. Let us hope your words are persuasive enough to quell your sister's talent for self-destruction or she may not be the only one to suffer!"

43

6th February 1469 early morning, at Yoredale Castle

"Is she presentable?" asked Joan.

Margaret shrugged. "Depends how 'presentable' you want her, my lady. She doesn't stink quite as much and I've put her in clean clothes. I'd say that 'mistress oubliette' has taken her down a bit, but she's still spitting fire."

"Oh, get her in," ordered Joan.

Weaver dragged Eleanor into the chamber. She made a show of struggling but Joan could see that the oubliette had at least made its mark on her. She looked like some child's doll, carved out of wood with scraps of cloth tied to her. Her hair had been ragged to start with, now her face was scratched and one of her ears was torn - the rats were clearly hungry down there. If Weaver hadn't been holding her up, she would surely have been crawling on the floor. Joan grinned.

"Not so confident now, lady?"

Eleanor made an unintelligible croak.

"Hmm. Perhaps Margaret needs to scrub you clean inside as well!"

She stooped a little closer. "Have you been enjoying our…hospitality?" she asked.

Eleanor's response was a gobbet of spittle into Joan's face.

Weaver slapped her hard and let her fall. She looked up, bleeding from the lip but smiling.

"I've been saving that for you, cousin."

Joan turned away, livid that she had been duped so easily. She could have cheerfully killed Thomas for agreeing to the visit; it was not going to go well and it would all be his fault. The best she could hope for was that Lady Emma would be so disgusted with her sister that she would run back to Middleham and forget her forever - but she didn't think that would happen - at least not without a little help.

She turned back to Eleanor. "Your sister is coming to visit you today," she said.

Eleanor's expression remained grim. "I did wonder why you'd bothered to get me out."

"Just listen, cousin - if you will. Your sister thinks that she will take you out of here to Middleham - but she won't, because I would have her killed, before I'd let you go."

"Hah!" Eleanor's eyes flashed at her. "You wouldn't dare - if she has the support of Lady Warwick...of the earl, even."

Joan was beginning to enjoy this encounter. "If two sisters were to quarrel and one should happen to kill the other, no blame could be attached to me or my husband - except perhaps, carelessness. Believe me: you're never going to leave here alive - the only question is whether your sister leaves or not."

Eleanor remained silent.

"Nothing to say now?" asked Joan. "Do you really doubt me? You know I've killed, and if I have to, I'll kill again. I let your sister live once before and now I'm regretting it. She was at my mercy. It's a lesson to us all, isn't it - better to be safe... So, it's in your hands: persuade her to leave you here and she goes free."

Eleanor glared at her and then whispered: "Believe me, cousin: if you harm my sister, I shall cut out your heart."

Joan turned away abruptly. "Weaver, put her in the bed chamber on the ground floor, the damp one near the oubliette... and lock her in."

§§§§

Emma was escorted to Yoredale by none other than Sir Thomas Gate himself. She was astonished and could only assume that this gesture was intended to reassure her. His charm and wit during their ride almost convinced her of his sincerity. She had seen him many times in the years she had lived at Middleham but he had rarely spoken to her. Like many folk there, he distrusted her. She might be called Lady Radcliffe but she was an Elder by blood and Ned Elder's feud with the earl had touched the lives of many of his men.

Listening to Gate's sparkling conversation, it was hard to doubt him. She must remember that he might be Joan Elder's husband but that did not mean he was like her. She resolved to reserve judgement on Thomas until she knew him better. For the majority of their journey she hung upon his every word. Then Yoredale Castle came into view for the first time and she found it a terrifying sight. She pulled up, taking Sir Thomas by surprise.

"My lady?" he turned his mount to go to her. "What is it?"

"Yoredale…" she breathed, still staring at its walls and towers.

"Of course," said Sir Thomas, "it must bring back memories…"

"It does, Sir Thomas, and all of them bad."

He drew alongside her and put his hand reassuringly on hers. "There's nothing for you to fear there now," he said. "You are my guest."

Emma was not reassured. She didn't fear Sir Thomas but, if the man could not yet see what his wife was, then he would probably die not knowing. They rode on and Emma endeavoured to suppress her fears. All the same, when they passed through the familiar gatehouse and into the courtyard, Joan Elder stood waiting to greet them. Emma felt a chill of apprehension and shuddered.

"Dear husband," called Joan cheerfully, "and dear cousin…it's been a long time, Lady Emma, since we last met."

Emma had played over this meeting in her head a hundred times in the past four years: if she ever spoke to Joan again, what would she do? Now Joan faced her as Sir Thomas helped her to dismount and Emma did the last thing she could ever have imagined herself doing. As Sir Thomas held her hand, she let herself sway and leant into him, so that he must either hold her to him or let her fall. She knew he would not let her fall and she gave him the sweetest smile she could muster as he held her.

Disengaging herself from him, she turned to Joan and said. "Isn't your husband the most charming man alive?"

Joan wore a face of stone and mumbled her agreement. Emma knew she had hit her target but almost at once she began to regret her impulse. It was not a clever beginning for she had let Joan force her into a rash and meaningless gesture. Well, let Joan do her worst; she would do nothing whilst Thomas was there.

"Perhaps, we should let Lady Emma see her sister as soon as possible," said Sir Thomas.

"If you please, Thomas," said Joan, "I'll take you to see your sister at once, Lady Emma." Her tone was neutral, her manner formal.

"Thank you, Lady Joan," replied Emma, echoing her formality.

Sir Thomas excused himself then and Emma watched him go with an anxious look as she followed Joan across the courtyard.

She did not know what to expect when she was shown into Eleanor's room but whatever she expected, it was not what she saw. Barely had she had time to take in her sister's woeful appearance, when the door slammed behind her.

"What have they done to you?" whispered Emma, still in shock.

Eleanor shook her head. "The oubliette," she said and began to weep.

The oubliette: aye, it was explanation enough, thought Emma.

"I've come to take you away from here. You'll go to Middleham first but Ned is nearby and you'll soon be able to escape to him, get away, down to Corve. It's all agreed."

Eleanor said nothing but stopped her weeping.

"Warwick himself has arranged it with Sir Thomas," said Emma.

Eleanor shook her head once more and began to chew her lip until it bled.

"Ned? Ned's alive?"

"Aye, he's alive."

"You've seen him? Is he well?" asked Eleanor.

"I've not seen him - but Reedman has."

"Ned is back then," breathed Eleanor.

"Aye sister! You've been mistreated," said Emma, "but it ends here!"

"No," replied Eleanor in a small voice, "I fear, it begins here…"

"Sir Thomas is a good man, Ellie."

"Oh? I don't think Ned would agree. Shall I tell you what that 'good man' Sir Thomas did?"

Eleanor's low voice was scaring her. "Sir Thomas-"

"Sir Thomas was the one who imprisoned Ned to start with!"

"But Ned is free now!" said Emma.

"Very well, but I'll warrant it was not Sir Thomas who freed him. Also Sir Thomas stole away Ned's young ward, Agnes. She was a sweet, orphaned girl. He brought her here where she now whores for Walter Grave!"

"I can't believe that!" retorted Emma.

Eleanor's scarred hands suddenly seized her around the neck. "Well you should believe it because she's here, daily spreading her legs to keep herself alive!"

Emma shook her away and was surprised how weak her sister was. "I'm sure that can't be right. Walter Grave must have taken her himself!"

"Poor fool," said Eleanor. "You're one of them now, aren't you? You do Warwick's bidding as they all do. And to think I was worried for you…"

"You've no need to worry for me - aye, I live at Middleham. They gave me food and a place to stay. It was a dark time for me. But now I'm proud to live in the Neville household. They are not monsters, sister! Why is everything so stark for you? We are all frail, we all do wrong at times - even you!"

"I'm not going with you," said Eleanor.

"Oh, I can see very well that you have a great life here!"

"I'll not go back to Middleham."

"You were a prisoner last time!"

Eleanor nodded. "Aye, and I'd be a prisoner this time too."

"If you stay here, Joan Elder will find a way to kill you," pleaded Emma. "Your only hope is to come with me."

"I came here knowing I might be taking my last step and I haven't done yet what I set out to do. My only hope is to stay close enough to Joan Elder to kill her when she gives me a chance. Just one chance is all I'll need."

Emma sighed and decided to try a different lever. "Reedman told me that Hal and the others are here too. What about them?"

Eleanor stared at her for what seemed a very long time then she asked softly: "What do you know, Emma?"

"I know only what Reedman said, that you are all here."

"And who would you include in that 'all'?"

Emma had no idea what her sister was getting at but humoured her. She had nothing else to do. "I mean: you, Hal, Wulf - he has a girl, I believe, and there are other young men - and a little boy, I think, with the girl. I'm not sure where he fits in. Have I left anyone out?" she asked.

Eleanor came over and gave her a hug. "No," she whispered, "that's everyone."

"But they could leave if they wanted to, couldn't they?" asked Emma.

"Go home, Emma. Home to Middleham and leave me. Please. You can do nothing more to help me. If you want to do something for the others, then just tell Hal that Ned is nearby. That'll be enough - but do it privily. And for God's sake, don't let anyone else see you speaking to Hal."

"But Ellie-"

"Go now, while you still can," said Eleanor with a grim smile.

Emma banged on the door and it was opened almost at once by a large swarthy man.

"What is your name?" asked Emma as he closed the door behind her.

"Weaver, my lady," he replied with a little bow. Emma could not decide whether he was mocking her or not. Perhaps it was her imagination. He locked the door.

"Does it have to be locked?" she asked.

He gave a little chuckle. "Oh, aye, my lady, it does."

44

6th February 1469, in Lady Joan's Chamber at Yoredale Castle

"I don't trust her, Thomas. It's clear she has no love for me and she's throwing herself shamelessly at you."

"Hmm, I must admit that seemed a little out of character," agreed Thomas.

"Hardly!" scoffed Joan. "This a woman who had a bastard child by some young man at arms. Hidden depths there - I'd watch her if I were you."

"Nonsense, but in any case it's quite simple. I've agreed with the earl that Eleanor can go back with her sister to Middleham. Let's be rid of the pair of them, I say. They'll be nothing but trouble. They're a distraction I could do without at present - there are more important matters to deal with."

"Eleanor won't go," said Joan.

"Of course she will - why wouldn't she?"

"Because I told her not to."

"And why would she go along with you - you've said she hates you."

"Because I told her that her sister would not leave here alive if she went."

"You did what?" Thomas said, taking her roughly by the arm. "I told you I've already made an agreement with Warwick - and we don't cross him, Joan."

"Let's see how Lady Emma has fared, shall we?" replied Joan, pulling her arm gently away. "Weaver will be here with her shortly. Although the idea of being... 'rid of both of them' is very appealing."

Thomas looked at her thoughtfully.

Was he was getting to know her well enough yet, she wondered?

"Why don't you leave the sisters to me," she said, "then if I act against your agreement with Warwick you can say I did so without your knowledge?"

Thomas held her gaze. "I don't hide behind women - and I don't let women make my decisions for me," he said. "Whatever Lady Eleanor does, you are to send Lady Emma back to Middleham today - she's under my safe conduct! For the love of God, Joan, this is not the time to argue!"

At that moment there was a loud knock on the door.

"That'll be the ever subtle Weaver, I suppose," he snapped.

§§§§

Emma was still puzzling over what to do about Eleanor when the door opened and Sir Thomas himself ushered her in. At once she picked up the tension in the room between Joan and Sir Thomas.

"Did you find your sister well?" asked Joan

The callous bitch, thought Emma. "I'm sure you both know exactly in what state I found my sister," she said coldly.

"So, will she go back with you this afternoon, then?" asked Sir Thomas.

"No, Sir Thomas, she will not. I fear I could not persuade her."

He seemed genuinely surprised. "Does she understand that she is free to go?" he asked.

"She believes she must stay…"

"If she stays, she'll stay in the oubliette," said Joan, "Surprising she's so keen to stay. She must like us more than we thought, Thomas."

"The oubliette is torture, my lady," said Emma. "And

that is not what the earl wants."

"Well," said Joan with an icy smile, "the earl isn't here - and it's your sister that's refusing to leave…"

Emma could cheerfully have scratched the woman's eyes out, but she daren't let her thoughts turn that way.

"Perhaps you would like to stay here tonight and try again to persuade her on the morrow," suggested Joan.

For a moment Emma thought that she should. Perhaps Eleanor would change her mind. Then it occurred to her that it would be Sunday. What had Ned said about Sunday? Perhaps she should have read his letter.

"No," said Sir Thomas, "I think it best, my dear, that Lady Emma goes back to Middleham today. Her sister may be persuaded by another night or two in the oubliette."

"Very well," conceded Joan. "I'll have Weaver take her down and arrange an escort."

"No," said Sir Thomas sharply. "I'll take the lady down myself."

Joan smiled and nodded to Emma. "Take care, dear cousin."

"And you," replied Emma, looking her in the eye this time, "take very great care indeed."

She followed Sir Thomas down the stairs.

"I'll get Sir Walter Grave to escort you back to Middleham," he said, taking her into the Solar. "You can wait here in comfort for a little, my lady. Sir Walter will come very soon. For my part, I hoped that Lady Eleanor would agree to go with you. I wonder if we shouldn't just throw her over a horse and take her."

Emma could not make him out. "It may come to that, my lord. I can't bear to think of her in that horrible place."

"It is not my doing I assure you," he replied.

"But are you not lord here?" said Emma.

"I'll see what can be done to make her more comfortable," he said. "But we must get you back home. I'll send Sir Walter presently."

"Thank you, Sir Thomas."

Emma waited deep in her own thoughts. Should she have tried harder to move her sister? She did not see how, yet going without her would be a bitter failure. She had half convinced herself to try one more time, when there was a knock at the solar door and the man Weaver poked his head in.

"Ah, you're still here, my lady - thank goodness!"

"What is it?"

"Lady Eleanor's asking for you. I was hoping to catch you before you left. Will you see her, my lady?"

"Of course, of course. Take me to her at once!" Relief filled her heart. God be praised: for once, her sister had come to her senses in time!

"She's still in the same chamber," advised Weaver. She followed him through the Great Chamber and down the spiral stair to the ground floor.

"Watch the steps, my lady," warned Weaver, "we don't want you breaking your neck, do we?"

He gave a little chuckle and she smiled weakly, wishing the fool would get a move on. Eleanor might change her mind yet again if she didn't strike at once.

The door to the chamber was ajar, which Emma thought was odd, but she went straight in.

The chamber was empty. She turned to find Weaver behind her. "Where is she?" she demanded.

"She's back where she belongs," growled Weaver, all trace of his bonhomie gone. "Down in the oubliette, where she'll slowly rot to death - if the rats leave anything of her to rot, that is."

"We'll see what Sir Thomas has to say about that!" she retorted and went to push past him.

But Weaver caught her by the arm.

"Don't touch me!" she said.

"Have you got as much fight as your sister?" he asked, tightening his grip on her arm. Then he pushed her back and punched her hard on the side of the head, neatly throwing her onto the bed as she fell. For an instant she saw him looming over her and then she passed out.

45

6th February 1469 midnight, in the chapel at Yoredale Castle

The priest lay on his low, hard bed in the small cubicle off the chapel. He had not slept and had lost track of time - it must be well after midnight, he thought. A single candle burned nearby, the plucky flame doing all it could to lift his gloom. He never valued luxuries for he never had them. His life had been simple as a young boy in Northumberland - not that he recalled much of his early life. He had lived in a place of worship for as long as he could remember and the church had been good to him - if only it had not sent him back to Crag Tower.

He turned the knife over and over in his hands - feeling the cold steel. It had been a bright blade once but now it was dulled. He ran his finger along the edge and winced. It was sharp enough. He got up, tossed the weapon onto the straw mattress and padded in his bare feet down the two steps into the chapel. He knelt at the altar and began to intone some familiar phrases. After a while his voice faltered and his prayer petered out. He sighed heavily and got to his feet. There was a dim glow of light from the gallery: Lady Joan was still awake too though he doubted that remorse was disturbing her sleep.

"God forgive me," he muttered as he went back into his cell and retrieved the knife. He stared at the candle but left it behind. He walked back to the chapel and shut his eyes tight to allow them to adjust to the darkness. He crossed the floor to the door and opened it. The passage outside was just as dark. To his right was a small room which he thought had once been a nursery but now was occupied by the fearsome Margaret. Ahead was the spiral stair down to the floors below and the rampart above. To his left was the door to Lady Joan's chamber.

He took a pace to the left and then checked himself. Margaret sometimes slept in her mistress's room - it would be wise to find out where she was first. He approached the woman's room with caution: she could be trouble. Before he reached her door, he could hear noise beyond it. He leant his ear to the wooden door and listened. Margaret was not alone and she was very animated; it was not hard to imagine what was going on. Well, if it kept her out of his way then it was a blessing.

Outside Lady Joan's door he hesitated and wiped the sweat from his brow. The knife hilt felt slippery in his hand. He had not thought this far, perhaps he hoped to find an obstacle, a reason to give up and return to his cell. There had been light so she could still be awake but to succeed he would have to take her by surprise. Somewhere a door slammed and he jumped. He could not stand there all night: he must act.

He lifted the door latch and opened the door a little. There was no reaction from within so, after a short pause, he opened the door wider and looked inside. The chamber was quite large and he could not see the head of the bed from the threshold. He took several silent paces into the chamber. An oil lamp burned near the bed but there was no-one in the bed. The covers had been thrown back it appeared. He cast eyes swiftly around the room. Where was she? To the left there was a short flight of steps up to the chapel gallery - she might be up there. He turned to the right where a narrow passage probably led off to a latrine. He peered around the corner of the wall and there in the darkness, sat Joan. He was so surprised he pulled his head back and banged it against a timber beam. He grunted.

"Who's there?" demanded Joan, her voice sharp, annoyed. "Margaret?" she called, "is that you?"

He gulped down a breath, rubbed the side of his head and retreated a few steps. There was a rustle of clothing and Joan hurried along the passage from the latrine. She looked at him, skewering him to the spot with her eyes - eyes that knew no fear.

"Can't woman even piss without a man ogling her? I never took you for that sort of man, Father," she said. A trace of a smile played across her lips. "Did you see enough to whet your appetite? Surely not, it was too dark. Would you like another look?" She raised the front of her linen shift until her bare knees were revealed then lifted it higher to reveal her pale thighs.

He was transfixed where he stood. Sweat dribbled down onto his chin as his eyes tracked the rising hem of the shift. The knife was still in his hand; she had not noticed it yet.

"No!" he shouted and stepped towards her, lifting the knife above his head. A flicker of alarm showed in her face but, as he struck at her breast, she caught his wrist and slowed the blow so that the point of the knife barely touched her. Then she gripped the knife hand in both hers and grappled with him for the weapon.

"Margaret!" she screamed and he redoubled his efforts to drive the blade home. She was so strong, far stronger than he had imagined. She aimed a kick at his groin and he discovered new levels of pain as he doubled over. She wrested the knife from him as Margaret hurried in half-naked, closely followed by Weaver. The priest stared at Margaret's bare breasts until Weaver struck him with something hard and he went down.

§§§§

He came to lying on his bed. Thank the Lord! It was a nightmare, nothing more except …there was a dull ache in his loins and in the doorway stood Weaver. He began to weep then, not for himself but for those he knew he would soon betray, for what they would think of him and how folk would remember him for the rest of their days: Baston, the treacherous priest. He offered a silent prayer to God, for strength or for a quick, painless death. Perhaps Weaver would ask no more questions…

Weaver took out a familiar looking knife. "This is fine blade," he said.

"Then I beg you to make a swift end of me, Weaver," he said.

"You're a keen one, Father; but, if you like, I can make it quick for you… just as soon as you've told me all you know about what Lady Eleanor Elder is doing here."

§§§§§

In the darkness Agnes listened to Walter snoring contentedly in his bed. She could have lain alongside him if she wanted. She didn't want - instead she lay on the wooden floor. But tonight it was not the hard timber boards that kept her awake, but the cries from the chapel. She knew better than to go in there - and besides, she had an idea what was happening and knew that she could not prevent it. So she lay with her woollen shawl wrapped tight around her shoulders. She doubted Walter would want her again that night, hoped he would not.

The cries became more desperate. Surely others could hear them too - though Spearbold had once suggested that her hearing was more sensitive because she was a mute. It made no sense to her, but perhaps he was right. Dear Spearbold - she would never see him again, nor Ned - for Ned must be long dead. And Hal, for a brief few moments, Hal had given her a little hope. But now even that had passed for he must know now what she had become: used and unclean, another man's plaything. Hal could not possibly care for her now.

It was not that Walter was a bad man: he was kind to her and he never struck her any more. If she were to ask for something, he would give it to her… as long as she was in his bed at night. An anguished cry jolted her from her contemplation. Another louder one followed. Walter stirred and turned over in his sleep. She sat up. She was listening to a man being tortured, no: a priest being tortured. She put her hands over her ears but it had already gone quiet. It was not the first time she had heard it. She remembered at Christmas time - that great festival of good will. Well, she hadn't seen much goodwill at Yoredale.

She got up, went to the chamber door and turned to glance at Walter. He seemed settled and his snoring rumbled noisily on, so she opened the door and stepped out into the passage. The small, rear door to the chapel was only a few yards away. She went to stand beside it. No more cries emanated from the chapel. She waited a while, to be certain, and then opened the door. The chapel was dark and appeared to be empty but from the priest's small cell there was a flicker of light. She sighed. Last time she had put a salve on his cuts and bruises. He would probably need her help once again.

She felt her way towards the light and found Father Baston on his bed. She gave a long, silent scream and fell against the wall, shuddering away from the sight of him. He had bled. He had bled a great deal and she knew he must be dead. She recalled then every cry she had heard, each one a new cut, a new wound. She had seen men bleed before - she had even stabbed a man to defend herself and felt the warm blood on her hands. But this was different: this was cold, bleak and final.

She remained in Father Baston's cell, willing herself to look at him. She thought about Hal, about Ned, about Walter Grave and what he might do about the child she was carrying. She believed that Walter loved her in his own way but he deserved to be punished and she decided that it was high time she did something about it. She looked one last time at Father Baston. His eyes were open. She brushed her fingers gently over them and closed them before gripping the hilt of his knife with both hands and drawing it out of his chest.

46

6th February 1469, in the Hall at Yoredale Castle

Hal spent the evening in the Hall, drinking with Wulf and the others. While they exchanged ribald jokes, he brooded over his harsh words with Father Baston. Harsh words - and hollow words too, if truth be told, for Hal had done little better than the priest. When the rush lights burnt out, his friends lay down on the floor to sleep - well, mostly they slept. Wulf and Bess had other things to do before they slept but they were discreet and finally the Hall was quiet.

Only Hal remained awake, still sitting with a jug of ale in his hand whilst all around grunted and sighed in their slumber. This evening he had drunk more than usual and the others noted it. Bess even tried to take this last jug away from him. He still had it though, cradled protectively on his lap. He stared into it a lot but drank no more.

He had seen Lady Emma today - that had been a shock for he was sure that she was supposed to have gone to a nunnery but perhaps he was remembering it wrong. He had caught a brief glimpse of Lady Eleanor too before they shuffled her back into the oubliette. He had almost drawn his sword then - for one moment his hand was on the hilt. But Wulf stopped him with a whispered warning: "She is not the only one at risk here!" That was right enough but how long could he continue to do nothing?

He must have dozed off and when he came to he moved slightly and the jug tilted over, spilling the dregs of the ale onto his breeches. He brushed the liquid away and got up. His legs were stiff; he must have been sitting cross-legged half the night. It was almost Sunday morning. He decided to go for a walk up onto the rampart. Up there the raw night air scoured his cheeks, bringing him roughly awake.

He nodded as he passed one or two sleepy men on guard. Some faces he knew well, a few he had trained during the autumn. He leant on the wall looking hopefully out to the east but dawn was still some way off, he thought. What should he do? He felt a sudden urge to relieve himself and released a stream of warm piss out over the wall. He considered trying to free Eleanor - it would mean killing men - probably some of those he had trained - and then what?

He thought about killing Joan Elder - not a bad place to start for she had slain Lady Amelie who was without question the greatest, kindest lady that had ever lived. The piss slowed to a trickle. He thought of taking John, stealing a horse and fleeing away to Corve through the postern gate. He thought of going to Walter Grave's chamber and dragging Agnes out to freedom - he would kill Walter if need be. He finished relieving himself and walked back the way he had come. He could not do all of those things so he must choose just one or two - but which? Agnes, for one…and John. He might perhaps save both Agnes and John.

Making a decision somehow released him, gave him fresh confidence for what lay ahead. He bounded down the first flight of steps then came to an abrupt halt. He reined in his enthusiasm: he must take great care or he would kill them not save them. This was a time for steady nerves.

He had come down by the northwest tower because the chambers there were vacant. It was typical that, despite the overcrowding, ordinary men at arms or archers like himself would never be housed in the bedchambers. At least it meant there was no-one to see him but when he reached the foot of the steps, intending to cross the courtyard to the east range where Grave's chamber lay, he heard a sound from the ground floor chamber. This was one of the few chambers with bolts on the outside - useful he supposed for housing the odd high ranking prisoner that was not destined to suffer the oubliette.

He put his ear to the door and listened. Nothing. He turned away and then it started again: weeping. Christ's Blood! He'd had enough of weeping! He drew back the bolts and looked in.

"Who's there?" asked a small voice.

"Lady Emma!" he breathed, taken aback. "I thought you were going back to Middleham!"

"So did I. It's Hal, isn't it?"

"I'm surprised you recall me, my lady."

"In the north, your voice still stands out a little," she said.

"Why are you locked in here, my lady?" he asked. His new-found confidence had swiftly abandoned him. Where there had been clarity, there was once more confusion.

"I have no idea," she replied. "I thought Sir Thomas…then Weaver put me in here."

"Weaver? Weaver only does what Lady Joan tells him. I sometimes wonder if Sir Thomas even knows what's going on in his own castle."

"Lady Eleanor said I should tell you something," she said. "She said I should tell you that my…" She stopped and stared at him.

"My lady?"

She fell silent for a moment, shaking her head.

Hal thought she must have lost her wits.

"My lady? How can I help you?" asked Hal.

Emma sighed. "Find me a torch, Hal please. Or a candle - or even a rush light…"

47

7th February 1469 in the early hours, in Joan's Chamber at Yoredale Castle

"Get the boy!" ordered Joan. "Now!"

"My lady," said Margaret, "is that wise? He'll be in the Hall with Wulf's men at arms all around him."

Joan never liked being gainsaid but she glanced at Weaver. "Can you do it?" she asked.

Weaver grinned. "I can do it - if Sir Thomas doesn't mind losing a few of his men at arms."

She glared at him. "I mean can you do it without a pitched battle in the Hall?"

He nodded with easy confidence. "I'll wake up a few lads I can rely on," he said. "If we take them sudden - in their sleep - there'll just be a bit of blood to clear up, that's all."

"Be sure, Weaver," said Margaret.

"Well you'd better come with me and deal with the brat's mother, Bess," he replied.

"Perhaps Margaret's right," said Joan. She could do without a bloody tangle in the Hall. She already had Emma's continued presence to explain to her husband. Thomas was not a weak man; there was only so much he would put up with - and she still needed Thomas.

"Best do it now, my lady," said Weaver. "Better now while they're off guard. Any other time… if we just grab the boy, you can be sure they'll want to make a fight of it. This way, we take them out before they've got a chance."

"I suppose that makes sense, my lady," agreed Margaret,

"but only if it can be done quick, Weaver."

"I can do most things quick," said Weaver, still grinning. "Now's a good time, my lady, just before the dawn. They'll be fast asleep when our knives slice through their gullets."

Joan nodded. "Very well. Do it - and Margaret, make sure that boy gets to me alive! Bring him up here - and watch him! He's a tricky little bastard. In the meantime, I'll go and wake Sir Thomas and tell him what we've discovered. I'm sure he'll see the advantages…"

Margaret went out, closely followed by Weaver. He had her hand on her arse before they were even through the door. Joan shook her head - the man was impossible. She waited a few moments and then left the chamber. She passed by the room that had once been the nursery - before her time when there had still been children here. She had not borne a child - God knows she had tried often enough with Henry and now Thomas. She had kept it as a nursery - in hope - but perhaps she should have the room cleared. She was about to pass on into the gallery when she heard a low moan coming from the nursery. She went very still and then slowly reached under her kirtle to put her hand on the knife sheathed in a velvet garter about her thigh.

The moaning continued and a smile crossed her lips. She left the knife where it was and threw open the door.

"Fuck!" said Margaret. She shoved Weaver off her and scrambled off the small bed, smoothing down her clothing.

"So, I see," said Joan. She stared at Weaver, who stood proudly with his breeches around his ankles.

"I was being quick, my lady," he said.

Did nothing trouble this man? And still he wore that irritating grin, though he wore little else… She found her fists were tight clenched, she was angry with them both but she recognised that it was not just anger. She observed with interest that her arrival had done nothing to lessen Weaver's ardour.

"Leave us, Margaret," she murmured. "Weaver will join

you in the gallery… in a little while."

Margaret smiled at her knowingly. "Aye, my lady, as he said, he's quick at everything - perhaps a little too … quick for you, my lady."

"Get out, Margaret!"

Margaret lingered a little longer while she dressed so Joan pushed her out of the door and slammed it shut. Then she felt Weaver's fingers unlacing her bodice. Well, she could afford a little delay.

§§§§

Joan had found in the past few years that Margaret was right about most things. Her assessment of Weaver's prowess turned out to be no less accurate. Even so, by the time Joan arrived at Thomas's chamber in the north east tower, she could see a faint glow on the eastern horizon. Thomas was still in bed and she shook him roughly awake.

"What? What is it? Joan?" He shook off her hand and sat up. "Good Christ, woman! There are more subtle ways of waking a man - you didn't have to shake me. You could have just got in beside me!"

"I didn't come here for that," she said, feeling a trace of guilt - but only a trace.

"What then?" demanded Sir Thomas. "What is it that won't wait another hour?"

"I've things to tell you," she said.

"Well your tidings had better be worth waking me for, my lady!"

Whilst Thomas dressed himself, Joan told him as quickly as she could all that Weaver had found out and then she paced around the chamber as he took in what she was saying.

"That's all?" he asked when she fell silent.

"Isn't it enough, Thomas?"

"Well, I'd no idea about the boy but the rest is no great surprise. Hal's comrades made little secret of the fact that they had served here before. I didn't think it would matter - after all they are not supposed to be fighting Ned Elder in any case."

"But he'll come here," Joan insisted.

"Aye, probably, and he'll want a reckoning with me, but we've been keeping an eye out for him all winter and we've yet to see him. There are men out there now - even on this bitter night, searching for any sign of him. He's not the 'great lord' men spoke of once. He's finished - he's no men of his own and he's not the warrior he used to be either. Ned Elder's a broken reed, my dear. All the same, perhaps it would be prudent to take a few more precautions."

"And what about his son?" asked Joan.

"Oh, for certain, the boy must be kept… safe. Do we have him yet?"

"Weaver is doing it now."

"Quietly I hope," said Thomas. "I'll go and double the guards - you get hold of the boy."

He took her in his arms and embraced her.

"We've done nothing wrong so far, my dear. Lady Emma can still go back to Middleham today - a few feathers ruffled, but unhurt. We serve the great Earl of Warwick - we've no need to fear the likes of Ned Elder!"

They parted on the landing: he to rouse a few more of the castle garrison from their sleep and she to meet Weaver who should now be on his way back up with the boy.

§§§§

Emma read Ned's letter again, shook her head and then held out the scroll to Hal.

"No, my lady. I won't be able to read it…"

"Aye, of course, no reason why you would," she said. She chewed her lip as she contemplated the collapse of the future that she had been offered: joining Lady Anne's new household and making a new start with her children.

"My lady?"

"Aye, Hal…"

"May I know what it says, my lady?" he asked.

"It's a very few words, Hal, just a sentence or two. Just enough words to kill us all."

"My lady?"

She held the document rolled up tightly in her fist. Perhaps if she squeezed it hard enough, she could squeeze the dread out of it.

"It is Sunday today, isn't it, Hal?"

"Yes, my lady, Sunday."

"Aye, I thought it was…"

"My lady, what does it say?"

"It's your freedom, Hal - or your death warrant. Just now, I'm not sure which."

She suddenly noticed the room was lighter. Dawn. "God save us all," she whispered.

She was trembling. She could still do nothing. She could just ignore the letter and she would save many lives if she did.

"What does it say, my lady?" Hal repeated. He seemed to sense the need for urgency.

She sighed. "He's here, Hal…Ned's here. The note says he'll be at the postern gate by dawn…"

"But …that's now," he replied.

"Aye."

"Then we must go … now, my lady!" He took her arm to hurry her out but she pulled away.

"We should leave him out there, Hal."

"No, my lady. Your brother's a good lord to us all - he'll get us out!"

"If we let him in, then he'll bring death with him."

Hal stared at her for a moment. "No, my lady, death's already here," he said.

48

7th February 1469, in the chapel at Yoredale Castle

Agnes thought it would be easy, but it wasn't. She sat on a bench near the front of the chapel only a few yards away from the altar. Her father had never taken her inside a church though she supposed that there must have been one somewhere near the forest where they lived. She knew the figure near the altar was a man called Jesus Christ because the priest had drummed it into her a hundred times - back when he cared enough to try to 'bring her back to Christ' as he put it.

She put the knife blade against her breast and pressed the point gently. It was going to hurt. The priest had told her she must be good, and for a while she had believed him. She had never quite understood how it worked and now he was dead. If a priest could be killed then there was no hope for her. Yet .. she did not have the will to go through with it. She sighed, got up and left the knife on the bench. Then she trudged towards the chapel door.

Her hand was on the latch when she heard Grave bellow her name. She returned to the bench and snatched up the knife. When Walter Grave peered around the door and saw her, she looked at him and he saw the knife in her hand

"Agnes, no!" he roared. "For pity's sake, Agnes, don't!"

If there was a God, as Father Baston had told her, then why had God chosen to ruin her using a man with her own father's name? Even one of her few warm memories had to be tarnished by this careless God. She stabbed angrily at her breast.

She was surprised how swiftly Grave reached her, drawing the blade from her grasp even as she plunged it at her heart. For an instant they were frozen there: he held the knife and she stared at the cut she had made in her chest. Then he flung away the weapon and picked her up, carrying her to his chamber where he laid her gently on the bed.

She saw the blood on her shift and felt lightheaded which surprised her for she had seen blood before - but perhaps not her own.

"Agnes," he moaned, "why Agnes? I would have given you anything."

She was still conscious as he made a tear in her shift and examined the wound, a deep cut above her right breast. He stroked her face and hair.

"You'll be alright, Agnes. Don't worry," he said.

He ripped off a piece of linen from her shift and pressed it against the wound. He was trying his best to save her; well that would not do at all. She struck him across the face with her hand and threw aside the bloody cloth. A trickle of blood leaked from the cut. How she would love to have shouted at him then but all she could do was scratch at his face and eyes.

He backed away and stared at her, appalled.

"Was it so bad, Agnes?" he asked in a trembling voice. He approached her again warily, his face a mask of desperate concern. "Let me tend to your wound," he pleaded.

She felt weak but not as weak as she had expected. Her eyes flitted down to the wound and she saw with despair that the bleeding had stopped. Where was the knife? She struggled to get up but Walter held her down on the bed.

"You must lie still," he urged her. "The wound will open again!"

She squirmed in his grasp and his hand touched the bloodied breast. She gasped as pain stabbed through her but his hand slipped off and she slid under him onto the floor. By the time he turned to follow she was crawling towards the door. Then she stopped. A pair of legs blocked her path. She looked up: Thomas Gate stood in the doorway

"Walter! What's going on? Agnes, you're hurt. Walter - what have you done to her?" snarled Gate.

"Twas not my doing, my lord," protested Grave. "Agnes cut herself!"

"Why would she do that?" demanded Gate. He lifted Agnes up. "She's covered in blood, man! You've blood on your hands ... I saw you struggling with her."

"I was trying to staunch the wound, my lord. I never meant Agnes harm!"

Gate propped Agnes against the wall outside the chamber. She was aware of the dawn light - perhaps it was not quite the end she'd had in mind.

Gate and Grave were arguing in the room but she was barely listening. Her legs felt shaky so she slid down on the floor. It was so cold. She closed her eyes. Gate was shouting now and she wanted to cover her ears.

"I told you, Walter, not to harm the girl!"

"You gave her to me in the first place!" said Walter, "and I didn't harm her!"

"Then why is she dripping fucking blood then? I warned you - it was the one thing I made clear to you. She was... not... to... be ...hurt!"

It went so quiet then, so suddenly, she thought she had died. But she hadn't because when she opened her eyes Gate stood in front of her.

"You did not deserve this, Agnes," he said softly. He lifted her into her arms. "I'll take you to my chamber for now. You'll be safe there."

Safe? She didn't think so.

§§§§

Hal stood in the Hall and looked about him. Some of the kitchen servants were already up and working. The bakers too had long been about their work. Those that remained in the room comprised Wulf's men, several other men at arms who liked to share a drink with them and a handful of household servants. No major threats here at least.

He bent down to shake his friend awake. "Wulf!" he whispered.

Wulf snapped upright and felt for his sword. Hal put a finger to his lips and led him out of the Hall.

"What is it?" asked Wulf.

"Ned Elder will be outside the postern gate very soon."

"What! He's here in Yoredale? Now?"

"Yes. You need to decide what you want to do, Wulf. Because if I let him in, I'll be bringing the devil in here - you know that."

"Are you going to?"

"Yes, but if you and the others aren't going to stand with me - it'll be a slaughter."

"We broke our oaths to him, Hal."

"No, he released us from our oaths - not the same thing. There's no guilt here."

"I don't know, Hal. Another damned decision to make…"

"What will the others do?"

"That's the problem," said Wulf, "they'll do what I do."

"If Ned Elder gets in here, he'll want to put a few things right."

"He will."

"How many men has he?" asked Wulf.

"Don't know," replied Hal.

"Is my father with him?"

"Don't know that either."

"You're not making this very easy, Hal."

"What does your heart tell you?" asked Hal.

"My guts are telling me to go back into the Hall and go back to sleep!" said Wulf. "Are you sure he's coming, Hal?"

Hal looked him in the eye. "He wrote a note to his sister - and if Lord Ned Elder says he's coming, then he damned well is! I'm going to open the gate, Wulf. Are you with me or not?"

Wulf sighed. "I'll wake the men."

"Softly, mind," said Hal, "and take them all down to the cellars under the Hall for now. Lady Emma is already waiting in the cellar nearest to the postern."

"Aye," agreed Wulf.

"I'll meet you there as soon as I've opened the postern and let them in," said Hal and hurried to the nearby gate.

There were, as always, two men there. As was also usual just before dawn, both men were dozing. Hal was disappointed to find that both were Weaver's men and they barely acknowledged his arrival.

"Morning, whipped boy," murmured one. "Early start?"

Hal knew him well: Reeve - a weasel if ever there was one.

"Bit early to be going to the butts, isn't it?" observed the other, whose name Hal couldn't even recall.

"Open the gate," Hal told them.

"Who says?" asked Reeve.

"Sir Thomas. It's privy business."

"Don't talk shit! Sir Thomas wouldn't trust you with his privy business."

"So?" asked the other. "What do you want?"

"Listen," said Hal, "it matters little to me; but Sir Thomas has a man out there freezing his chestnuts off waiting to come in. Are you going to tell Sir Thomas why he had to wait so long?"

Reeve looked at his fellow guard.

"There were a score or so out there tonight but they'll be coming back in the main gate, not through this little fellow," said Reeve.

Hal could see they doubted him, but did they doubt him enough? He turned to go. "Very well, I'll go back to Sir Thomas and tell…"

Without a word Reeve went to the heavy oak door and slid the iron bolts across. Then he took the ring of keys from the wall and selected the largest to insert it in the great lock. He paused then and looked at Hal.

"You're sure about this?" he asked.

"I am," said Hal, wondering how the pair did not hear his heart thumping out of his chest.

"Right then." Reeve turned the iron key and then hauled the door open. It moved very slowly. "Time some idle turd greased these pins," he muttered. "In Christ's name, give me a hand, Poll!"

Poll leant forward and between them they pulled it open. Reeve took a step through the archway. "Where is this freezing bastard then?" he demanded.

A figure stepped into view. It was not yet fully light but it was light enough for them all to see that this was no man.

49

7th February 1469 just after midnight, in Yoredale Forest

Ned was dozing, only half aware of the men around him. They had moved camp during the night and now waited in one of the thickest parts of Yoredale Forest, less than a mile from Yoredale Castle. Maighread lay beside him and he felt her warmth even through their several layers of clothing. Most of the others there had just come off watch or were already fast asleep. Bear leant against an oak; he looked asleep but Ned knew he wouldn't be.

A movement caught his eye: it was Ragwulf pacing amongst the trees - he was a restless man these days. He wanted to thank Ragwulf for his part in getting his son out, for the pain he had endured from the quarrel with Wulf. But these were not matters he knew how to talk about and he did not think Ragwulf did either.

He heard the hooves before he saw the horse and he was on his feet by the time the rider pulled up in the clearing.

"Well?" said Ned.

"Men, my lord! Horsemen coming fast from the south. Coming to the castle, I think, my lord."

Ned sighed: it was what he had feared.

Ragwulf and Bear joined him.

"Reedman warned us," said Ragwulf, "that there were men out looking for us."

"He didn't tell us there'd be a score of them! I thought a dozen at the most," replied Ned, "and I was hoping to avoid them altogether!"

"We'll have to take them before they get too close to the castle," advised Ragwulf.

"By 'take them' I assume you mean kill them," said Ned.

"Whatever my lord commands," said Ragwulf stiffly.

"We have a royal warrant to act against Sir Thomas Gate. We can arrest him, even kill him if he resists - or if his men resist. What we cannot do is cut down twenty men at arms who are simply riding to the castle. We're no longer outlaws."

"Would you rather fight them when we get inside the castle, my lord?" asked Ragwulf.

"I'd rather not fight them at all!"

"Then what are we doing here, lord? Didn't we come to free your sister, the boy and the others?"

"Aye, but Gate's men must be given a chance," Ned insisted. "Now, rouse the men. I want every man I have in the saddle and ready to ride!"

"Aye, my lord," acknowledged Ragwulf.

"Bear!" Ned said, "Bring in all the scouts except the two watching the road to the east. We'll need every man."

Maighread waited in silence beside Ned, pulling her cloak more tightly around her.

"I'll have to leave you alone," he said. "I can't spare a single man…"

"I know." She smiled. "I'm alright alone, Ned."

"But it's dark in the forest."

She frowned. "Believe me, Ned, there are worse places to be. There's nothing I fear in the darkness. I'll not forgive you though, if you don't come back to me."

Ned embraced her and strapped on his sword. Ragwulf brought up his horse and he swiftly mounted and rode off through the trees, closely followed by all the others.

As they rode he gave clear orders to Bear and Ragwulf. "I want archers ahead of them and behind. If they break we'll need to bring them down. But first we stop them and talk."

He was surprised how quickly they came upon the column of horsemen. First he saw one of his own scouts - a Scales man - who waved at him to slow down.

"They're not far away, my lord - a few hundred yards at most."

Ned took his own group, swelled by others who had been following the column, and halted in the middle of the track.

"I want a warning arrow across their path. After that, no-one looses a shaft unless I order it. But if they make a break, I don't want any of them getting back to Yoredale Castle. Understood?"

There was a ragged chorus of "Aye, lord" from all around him.

"Now, fan out and keep quiet," he ordered.

Ned remained motionless in the centre of the way, listening to the steady rhythm of the hoof beats as they got louder and louder. He closed his eyes and offered up a silent prayer - it couldn't hurt. His eyes flicked open and he motioned to the archer who already had an arrow nocked. He waited and took careful aim and let his shaft fly. It was a close thing: the leading rider's horse reared up and unseated its rider as the arrow sped across its path and embedded itself in a spindly birch. If the archer hit what he intended to, it was no mean feat.

"Halt!" cried Ned, "In the king's name, halt!"

The column slowed and several horsemen gathered around the unhorsed rider. He swiftly remounted, though his mount was still restless. Ned walked his horse slowly towards them, flanked by Ragwulf. His other men at arms and archers moved noisily through the trees on either side of the column and at its rear a giant figure rode across the track and raised his arm.

Excellent, thought Ned, they had accomplished the most difficult part: they had halted the column without any casualties - a good start. He edged forward until he could make out the front riders and pulled up a few yards in front of them. He took off his helmet.

"I am Lord Ned Elder," he announced, "and I have a royal warrant for the arrest of Sir Thomas Gate on a charge of illegal retaining." As he expected, this was greeted by a rumble of discontent.

"Now, I expect that many, perhaps all, of you were recruited by Sir Thomas and you joined him in good faith."

Many cried "Aye!" to that.

"I have no quarrel with you men - and nor does your king - providing that you leave now and make no attempt to go to the aid of Sir Thomas."

"How do we know that you have the king's authority?" challenged one man.

"You may see the warrant for yourself," invited Ned, "for it is here." He held it up for them to see.

"Aye, so you say, but it's too damned dark to read it! What true servants of the king would assault honest men under cover of the night? If you are truly Ned Elder then it's well known in these parts that you were banished and if you're back here, then that makes you an outlaw!"

"You may not be able to read, friend, but perhaps you would recognise the royal seal. See it for yourself - here it is."

The rider came forward and peered at the seal on Ned's warrant. "Well?" said Ned.

"Aye, it could be," conceded the rider.

"Are you from 'these parts'?" asked Ned.

"No, I came down from Cumberland, looking for employ - and I thought I'd found it. Now you tell me I haven't but … Sir Thomas Gate has fed me and my horse all winter."

"Is there any man here who knows the Elder badge?" Ned asked, raising his voice. He knew that the men on both sides would be getting nervous. He needed to end this stand off as soon as he could.

Several answered and rode forward. They looked at the badge he wore and nodded. "Aye," said one.

Ned smiled at him. "And how do you know my badge?" he asked, but even as the words came out he studied the badge the man wore and sighed. "You're Warwick's man…"

"Aye, lord - if lord you are - some of us know your badge because we've fought you, or heard stories of your treason. And…we've ridden with Thomas Gate before, many times. I plain don't believe you - warrant or no warrant."

"But the king-"

"I see no king here… just a band of armed outlaws. There's only one man rules in this vale and that's Richard Neville, Earl of Warwick. Now, you're blocking our path…"

"I no longer have a quarrel with the earl," said Ned.

"Hah! Sir Thomas is the earl's man. Why do you think we're riding round out here in the middle of the night when we'd rather be in our warm beds? Sir Thomas sent us to watch out for you - and now we've found you!"

They drew their swords and Ned realised that he had been wasting his breath for as soon as he identified himself, these men had stopped listening: they had found their quarry.

"No!" he shouted. "There's no need for this!" But it was too late for the column was already breaking up.

"Shit!" roared Ragwulf, backing his horse away.

"God damn you! Loose!" shouted Ned and in moments the air was thick with arrows. Several horsemen fell at once but those nearest him urged their mounts at him.

He exchanged a rueful look with Ragwulf and drew out his sword. It was always his weapon of choice on horseback though he knew others preferred the power of the mace or war hammer. Hardly had he engaged with the first horsemen when a second flight of arrows struck the column. He knew this because his immediate opponent took a shaft through his neck and fell choking from his horse. There would be no more arrows for a while, now that a melee had begun - exactly what he had hoped to avoid.

In broad daylight a melee, even in a tournament, was a dangerous place to be. Here in the half-darkness it was a churning, utterly confused knot of men and horses. You were as likely to be killed by friend as foe as you strained to make out men's badges. Ned pounded his sword against the next man who came at him. The stunned knight rode off into the trees where a pair of Scales' men at arms converged on him and bludgeoned him onto the forest floor. A terrified horse shrieked close by and then the poor beast cantered across his path, shaking its head wildly to dislodge the arrow which had struck its neck.

He must end this swiftly before Gate's men scattered and disappeared into the forest. He drove his mount into the heart of the column, striking to left and right to carve a path through. Behind him Ragwulf finished those he had wounded and cut others down. Ahead he could make out the shape of Bear, his dread axe rose and fell as men were despatched.

His men had been outnumbered but the archers had almost halved the numbers against them. Scales' men at arms were experienced and they wrought havoc in the fight. Amid the shouting and the chaos, Ned tried to judge when to call a halt. He had ordered his men not to allow anyone to escape on horseback - no-one on foot would get back to Yoredale in time to hamper him.

He wheeled away from the fight and shouted: "Yield! Yield if you want to live!"

The fighting continued - men's blood was up and even his own men had little inclination to stop. But time was against him and even now he could see a glimmer of dawn light. He needed it to end - now.

"Yield!" he bellowed once more. "Your last chance! No quarter will be given if you don't lay down your arms now!"

First one, then another threw down their weapons.

"Dismount!" he shouted. The surrendering men did so, but a small, tight group of mounted men punched their way out of the circle of Ned's men.

"Archers!" cried Ned.

The rest of the men had come to a standstill. They turned to watch as the escaping horsemen thundered along the track to Yoredale. Then half a dozen arrows struck the group and every man fell - save one, who was slumped forward in his saddle. His horse trotted on slowly for a few yards and then came to a halt. There the rider tumbled to the forest floor and lay still.

"Ragwulf," said Ned quietly. "Gather all the horses. Leave the men their swords. It'll take them a day and half to walk to Yoredale or Middleham."

He raised his voice. "If anyone wants their mount back, they can come to me at Yoredale in two days' time and it will be returned - as long as they swear to keep the king's peace."

He turned to Ragwulf with a wry smile. "By then we'll have succeeded - or it won't matter anymore."

"My lord," said Ragwulf, "dawn is almost upon us."

50

7th February 1469 at dawn, by the postern gate at Yoredale Castle

"Who in the name of Christ are you?" asked Reeve.

Maighread had the hood of her cloak up to keep out the cold and, though it also served to cover most of her face, Hal knew her at once.

"She ... is the Lady Maighread Elder of Crag Tower," he said.

Maighread had no plan, no clear intention but when dawn approached and Ned did not return, she ran to the castle. Early morning mist drifted around the lower walls. She found the postern gate, though it was smaller than she expected - barely high enough, she decided, for a mounted man to pass through.

"What's all this about?" Reeve asked her. "What are you doing here, lady?"

Good question - she hardly knew that herself. She was just doing what her instincts told her to do - living in the moment. But just now, she would rather be living in a different moment.

Hal looked dumbfounded because of course he had been expecting Ned. She took a deep breath, stepped through the archway and brushed past Reeve. Under her cloak her right hand rested on the hilt of the knife she wore at her side.

"I've come to capture your castle," she announced.

Reeve guffawed at that. "What, on your own? A little ... 'undermanned' aren't you? Still, I suppose you might warm a man up on this cold morn."

He seized her arm to pull her towards him. She pulled her hood down to reveal her face and he took a pace back, releasing her arm.

"Good Christ, woman - if you are a woman!" He gave a nervous laugh and glanced across at Poll.

"You could surrender," suggested Maighread.

Reeve looked back at her in disbelief. Then he stared out of the door beyond her.

"Poll, go out and have a look," he ordered.

"Your last chance to surrender," said Maighread.

"Will you shut your ugly mouth, woman," Reeve snapped back, "or I'll open it wider with my bill!"

Maighread bristled. "What… that bill over there against the wall?" asked Maighread. "The one that's … just out of your reach…"

Reeve glared at her.

Hal had his sword out but not before she had thrust her knife through Reeve's left eye socket and driven it in hard. She didn't intend to stab him in the eye; the knife just seemed to go there. He trembled, whimpered briefly and dropped stone dead at her feet. She gulped and stood still.

Poll walked back in. "Can't see …" He stared down at Reeve's body and, before he could move, Hal clubbed him down with the hilt of his sword.

Maighread stood there, staring at him, still holding the bloody knife in her hand.

"It seems you're in good health, my lady," stammered Hal, peering out of the postern towards the forest edge.

"He is coming, Hal; believe me: he's coming," she said.

"But soon I trust, my lady, for Wulf and me can't hold this gate for a few minutes, never mind take the castle!"

She sheathed her knife and clasped his hand. "He will be here," she said. But she prayed to God she was right.

"Does he bring men?" asked Hal.

"Aye, some," she replied. "Where are the others?"

"They're all below," said Hal. "You'd best go down there with them, my lady, down the steps to your left. And send up Wulf, if you please."

She hurried down the steps without another word and stopped at the bottom, allowing her eyes to adjust to the gloom. Wulf and the others were gathered in the first cellar she came to. "Hal needs some help," she said, "until Lord Elder comes…"

"He's not here yet?" said Wulf.

"He will come," she replied, but even she noticed the tremor in her voice.

Wulf shook his head. He quickly kissed Bess before hurrying up the steps to the postern gate. Maighread looked around the ring of startled faces. Among them was a lady she knew only by Ned's description.

"Lady Emma?" she said. Emma took a step towards her and studied her ravaged face.

"Who are you?" demanded Emma.

"I'm your aunt, Maighread," said Maighread.

Emma nodded slowly. The others bent a knee and said: "My lady," as one.

"John?" enquired Maighread.

Bess stood aside and revealed the boy sitting cross-legged on the floor. Maighread could not help smiling for there was John, unconcerned and concentrating on building a tall column from small fragments of stone that lay on the flags. When he saw her he leapt up and gave her a hug around the legs, then he went back to his little tower.

"Have you met your new nephew, Emma?" she said with a smile.

§§§§

Weaver and Margaret stood in the empty Hall.

"Where are they?" he complained. "They're usually here - so where are they all?"

"Perhaps you shouldn't have wasted some time with

Lady Elder," said Margaret.

Weaver slapped her across the cheek. He liked to think of it as the same as clapping a man on the back - almost a gesture of affection.

"You've lasted with her ladyship for so long, because you know your place," said Weaver. "Don't start forgetting it now."

"What makes you think you're any more important to her than me?" asked Margaret.

"Because I've fucked her and you haven't!" grinned Weaver.

"Well, if it helps you," said Margaret with a smile, "you just go on believing that, my dear."

Weaver glared at her. In his view, most folk - but especially Margaret - would be better off for a regular thrashing with the lash.

"Come on," she said, "let's try the kitchens. Bess works in there."

Weaver nodded and set off through into the butteries and on into the kitchen. He grabbed one of the kitchen drudges he knew well and pulled her close to him.

"Seen Bess or her lad about this morning?" he asked.

The girl's eyes flicked across to the cook as she continued her work. "They're probably in the Hall," she muttered.

"They're not there," said Weaver. "We're in a hurry, so think: have you seen them?"

"No!"

He took hold of her arm and twisted it up behind her back. She squealed and one of the cooks came over. He had a cleaver in his hand.

"Leave her be, Weaver," he said. "She's got work to do - and you've no place in here."

"I've a place anywhere I choose, 'mutton man', and you'd do well to remember that!"

He moved as if to leave but, of course, he couldn't leave

it there: the cook had faced him down in front of others and Weaver couldn't let it become a habit. He shoved the girl against the cook and snatched the cleaver from his hand. Then he reversed it and pounded the blunt end of the head into the cook's face, staving in his cheekbone. He went down with a groan, arms flailing wildly. One arm pulled over a broad iron pan of cooling goose fat. The sticky, glutinous contents of the pan slid down onto the hot coals of the spit roast.

Soon thick black smoke billowed up from the hearth and then the wench screamed. What was the little bitch playing at? He hadn't touched her.

"Oh Holy Mother!" cried Margaret. "She's fallen into the fire!"

"Stupid cow!" said Weaver. He was surprised there was so much smoke so swiftly - but that was goose fat for you.

"Pull her out!" Margaret shouted at him.

He peered through the smoke and saw the girl writhing in the spit hearth. Flames were already racing over her kirtle, the greasy cloth fuelling the fire.

"Get her off there!" shouted Margaret.

The cook was holding his head in his hands and moaning. Others ran in from other parts of the kitchen and circled the fire.

"Too late," said Weaver, and sauntered to the door. "She's already burned too much. Best let her go - it's a kindness."

"We need to put the fire out!" said Margaret.

"Well you get some water from the well if you want - but I'm going after the boy. Let the kitchen folk put out the fire - we haven't time to worry about it!"

Weaver strode out and went back through to the Hall. Margaret followed, tearing her eyes with difficulty from the grisly flames.

"I like a good goose," said Weaver, "but that bastard's going to stink the place out."

"Well you started it!" said Margaret, glancing back towards the kitchen.

"Hey! Let's not start making things up, shall we?" He gave her a stern look. "That could only end badly for you, my dear."

He sniffed the air: it was more than goose fat burning now, he thought.

"Those kitchen dogs can take care of her - if they can get the damned fire out!" He laughed.

"Burning's nothing to laugh at! That poor girl," said Margaret.

"What's one less piece of kitchen grease matter? Just forget the careless bitch, will you?"

"But she'll be scarred for life!"

"Well she won't be getting my business any more if her looks have gone. Now think: where could that pair be at this time of day?"

"I don't know. Bake house? Cellars? They could be anywhere," said Margaret.

"Alright. Let's check the cellars," said Weaver. "We'll start this end at the well and work our way towards the postern. And we'd better hurry - the place is getting busier now. When I find them, they'll wish I hadn't."

They descended the steps from the butteries down to the ground floor where they encountered the kitchen servants trying to bring up pails of water from the well.

"Get out of the way!" roared Weaver, knocking them aside so that much of the water spilled from their pails. They passed the well and entered the dark of the wine cellar.

"Wouldn't mind stopping here for a while, eh Margaret?" He slid an arm around her waist and drew her to him.

"You said we hadn't time!" she retorted and twisted away from him.

"No, we haven't - we all make sacrifices for our lady, eh?

Keep it warm for me though," he said, giving her buttocks a casual squeeze.

"Get us a torch," said Margaret.

"Hah! I've an idea where I can light one!" Weaver called as he headed back out.

51

7th February 1469 at dawn, in Yoredale Castle

Joan had returned to her chamber to dress for the day. It would not look good to be seen about the castle in her night shift - an item which also bore, in its various stains, much evidence of her night's work. The absence of Margaret caused her some inconvenience and she had to kick another idle girl awake to lace up her clothes. She felt lethargic - too little sleep and too much activity, she reflected. She shuddered when she thought of her indiscretion with Weaver; that could have gone badly wrong. There was ever a thin line between boldness and folly.

She felt suddenly flushed and permitted herself a smile, then rinsed her face in a bowl of water.

"Bring me the heavier bodice," she told the girl, "the one with threads of steel through it." Who knew what the day would hold? Prudence, for once, seemed appropriate. The reinforced garment was even heavier than she remembered but once she had it on, she could move well enough. She knew what she must do next and she was not looking forward to it. A few kind words with her cousin, Emma - and it would be a few - to apologise for the misunderstanding. She only hoped the honeyed words wouldn't stick in her throat.

Then on to more important matters: with luck Margaret and Weaver would have the boy in their hands by now. She left her chamber, a smile playing upon her lips as she passed the nursery - after last night perhaps she should rename the room. The gallery beyond was still gloomy - dawn seemed a long time coming this morning. She descended the steps in the north-west tower two at a time and giggled when she stumbled and nearly fell. The bodice was making her a little top-heavy. Steady, lady, steady, she told herself, this is not the moment to throw yourself headlong down the stairs. She reached the foot of the spiral stair intact and stopped abruptly outside the chamber in which Emma was secured - or rather was not now secured since the door stood ajar. She gave a great sigh and slammed it wide open to reveal an empty room.

"Where has the little meddler gone?" she muttered to herself. "And with whose help?"

She realised at once that the postern was only a short walk away and hurried down the few steps from the northwest tower. On the last step she halted and peered through the archway towards the gate. Then she forgot all about Emma and shook her head in disbelief as she watched one of the guards at the gate being stabbed. It was not the stabbing itself that chilled her, but the one who wielded the knife: her aunt, Maighread Elder.

Joan backed away, barely able to stand, feeling at once sick and bewildered - how in all Christendom could Maighread be here, alive? She was dead, burned to cinders at Crag Tower. It could not be her. Joan could not look again, dared not look again. She had seen enough in a glance: that face ... the scars. Maighread had been burned alright but not enough, not nearly enough! Now she looked fierce, monstrous...there was no forgiveness in that ravaged face. Maighread had come for revenge.

Joan ran. She must find Henry! No, not Henry - Henry was dead - but then so was Maighread, wasn't she? She ran along the short passage which took her into the stables and she hurled open one of the tall stable doors into the courtyard. She must find Thomas - that was it, Thomas - or

Weaver. Either would do. She felt the bile rising in her throat and she dropped to her knees on the cobbles, retching hard enough to make her heart bleed. When the convulsions eased, she ran her fingers across her face and shivered. She tried to stand but her knees buckled under her.

"Courage, you fool," she whispered to herself. She looked around the empty courtyard. "No-one else knows…no-one. Must find Weaver. Weaver will kill her for me and this time she'll stay dead."

She clambered to her feet and leant against the stable door way. A groom peered out at her.

"Go away!" she cried. "Go, feed some horses - or whatever else you do…"

The scared groom bolted into one of the stalls and she ignored him. Where would Weaver be? He would have the boy by now. She headed towards the Hall and pulled up sharply. No, the way to the Hall went past the postern and she could not risk seeing Maighread again.

She changed direction and walked unsteadily across the yard towards the steps up to the butteries. The air in the stairwell was smoke-filled. She seized a passing servant heading down the steps with an empty pail.

"What's amiss?" she demanded.

"Fire in the kitchen, my lady," he replied and sped on past her.

What was going on in her home? Lady Emma disappearing, dead women killing her men at arms, now a fire in the kitchen. It was madness. But amidst the madness she glimpsed Weaver coming down the steps towards her, a flaming torch in his hand.

He stared at her; she must look distracted. "My lady?"

"Madness," she muttered and put a hand on his arm. "I need you, Weaver. Where's the boy?"

"We're still searching, my lady, down in the cellars."

"I'll come with you," she said, "I want you with me

wherever I go - is that clear? You're not to leave my side!"

§§§§

"Shit, Hal - we're up to our armpits in it now," said Wulf.

They had dragged the two guards' bodies down the steps towards the cellar but some blood still stained the stone flags by the gate.

"Just hold your nerve, my friend," Hal reassured him.

"Well, what about when someone wants to go down to the cellars? What do we do then?"

"We'll tell them … the steps are…dangerous - which they would be if anyone tried it."

"The relief guards will be along soon," said Wulf. "What do we do with them?"

"We'll do whatever we have to do!" replied Hal.

"What if he doesn't come?" cried Wulf, gripping his friend's arm tightly. "Not at all, not ever…"

"Blood of Christ, keep your voice down!" said Hal. "He'll come."

Then he saw two men approaching from across the far side of the courtyard. Each carried a bill over his shoulder and they took slow steps, in the manner of many a postern gate guard, for they were not relishing the tedious stint that lay ahead.

"The relief's coming!" hissed Wulf.

"I can see them."

"What do we do?" asked Wulf.

Hal laid a hand on his friend's shoulder. "We kill them, Wulf, because if we don't they'll kill those we love. And if we don't hold the gate, Lord Elder can't get in."

The two guards continued their unhurried march towards them.

"We could just get out now," said Wulf, "and join up with Lord Elder in the forest - isn't that what we were going to do anyway?"

"Can't do it, Wulf. There's not enough time. There's Agnes to get out - and Lady Eleanor to free."

"Shit!" Wulf put his hand on his sword.

"Steady. It must be done quietly - but swift."

"I know one of them," said Wulf, "I shared a guard with him last week…he told me about his wife…she's with child."

"Which one?"

"The one on the left…"

The two men came through the archway from the courtyard.

"Alright, I'll take him - you do the other one."

"Could we not just knock them out?"

"They're fighting men, Wulf! We can't afford to spend all day exchanging blows with them!"

"I don't like this, Hal."

"By God Wulf, you've slain a score of men at arms without asking how their widows would feel! You came here to fight - what the hell does it matter who you kill first?"

Their replacements stopped in front of them. They looked puzzled.

"Wasn't Reeve on last night?" asked one.

"Aye," said Wulf.

"He got taken ill …very suddenly," explained Hal. "Come, help me with this gate - I can't shut it." He pointed to the still wide-open gate.

The two men eyed the gate suspiciously and shrugged. "We're not carpenters, we kill for a living!"

Hal gave a sigh. "Yeh, so do we."

He thrust his knife through the nearer man's throat and took the dead weight of his body as he fell. In one swift movement, Wulf drew his sword, drove it through the other guard's midriff and ripped it out again. He was sheathing his sword as his victim was coughing blood onto the stone at his feet.

The two friends exchanged bleak looks.

"I'd better get the others up," said Hal. "It's going to need all of us to hold this damned gate. We should get Lady Eleanor out too."

He shouldered one of the bodies and went down the steps. Wulf began to drag the other out of sight.

§§§§

Maighread watched the rest of the men at arms go up the steps and a moment later another body was brought down. She glanced at the others: Emma rolled her eyes, Bess gasped and John looked up with interest for a moment before continuing his play.

"Stay here for now," said Hal. "We'll keep the gate open for Lord Elder. If… it doesn't go well…I'll send a man down to get you out the postern."

"What about Lady Eleanor?" asked Maighread.

"Yes, my lady, we're getting her out now. I'll bring her in here. Don't worry. And if anyone comes through that cellar door, scream and I'll come."

"We can look after ourselves," said Maighread.

"Indeed, my lady," said Hal, "I've seen your handiwork! But killing one man…"

"I know," she agreed. "May God watch over you, Hal."

"And you, my lady." He gave her a smile and left.

She went over to John by the cellar door and whispered in his ear. "John, if you hear any sound at all from the other side of this door, I want you tell me at once."

He looked at her thoughtfully and then nodded.

52

7th February 1469, in the cellars at Yoredale Castle

Joan and Weaver joined Margaret and made their way along the stone passage that gave access to the storerooms. They searched each one thoroughly but found no-one.

"This is taking too long!" grumbled Joan.

At the end of the passage, they heard voices and stopped. Facing them were two doors, one leading down to the oubliette and the other directly into the final and largest cellar.

"Shit! There are men down in the oubliette," said Weaver. "Sounds like someone's freeing that witless redhead, my lady."

Joan said nothing.

"My lady?" prompted Weaver.

"I forgot to tell you something," whispered Joan, "there was trouble at the postern gate."

"Trouble, my lady?" said Weaver. "What sort of trouble?"

"Fighting…"

"Fighting?"

"There was a woman… and she struck one of the guards. I think there were others…I didn't notice."

"Didn't notice, my lady?"

"In the name of Christ stop repeating what I say!" cried Joan, punching his shoulder with her fist.

"Keep calm, my lady," said Margaret.

Joan's hand flew out and seized her servant around the

neck. "Don't tell me to keep calm, you foolish bitch! You don't know what I saw!"

"My lady!" snapped Weaver. "Was the postern open?"

She nodded.

"How many men?" he asked.

She shook her head. "I don't know…"

"Fuck!" breathed Weaver. "Does Sir Thomas know?"

"I… I don't …I don't know…Never mind that. We just need to find that boy!"

She was clearer now: the boy was the key. If she had the boy, nothing else would matter!

Weaver gave her a strange look.

"Just find the boy," she ground the order out.

"Aye, my lady," said Weaver. "The voices have gone. They could have heard us…"

"Come on! Make haste then!" she urged.

Weaver looked at Margaret. "Are you ready?" he asked.

She lifted her kirtle to the thigh to reveal a knife.

"Getting to be the fashion around here," he muttered. "Best have it in hand, girl. My lady?"

Joan shook her head. She could not remember what had happened to the small blade she usually wore.

Weaver drew out his long knife. "Can you handle anything this long, my lady?"

She did not reply but snatched it from him. He nodded and drew his sword gently from its scabbard. He put his head against the cellar door and listened.

"Just in case," he said softly, "we'll go in fast: me first, then Margaret, then you, my lady."

"Just get on with it!" hissed Joan, gripping the knife firmly in her hand. She could feel the anger building inside her breast now and she would likely stab the first person she saw. If Weaver didn't hurry up, it might be him.

Weaver passed the torch to Margaret then he lifted the latch on the door and pushed hard.

§§§§

In taking Agnes back to his chamber, Thomas had wasted some time, so now he was in a hurry. She had passed out but her wound stopped bleeding so he left her on his bed. He still found it hard to believe what Grave had done. On the steps down from his chamber he began to smell smoke and when he reached the kitchen landing the fire was all too obvious. The kitchen servants were all in a line passing up pails of water and he dared not break the line. Instead he stepped into the kitchen itself: there was a blazing fire in one of the hearths but flames were also licking up the adjacent walls, no doubt thick with grease.

Pail after pail of water was being thrown onto it, though to little apparent effect. The roof beams were not yet alight but the heat was beginning to char them and he was pleased that his men had acted so swiftly.

One of the cooks appeared beside him, face blackened and chest wheezing.

"What happened here?" Gate demanded.

"Weaver happened here!" growled the cook.

"Can you put it out?"

"Aye," said the cook, "but it'll take a while - and there'll be costly damage, my lord. You should have Weaver's neck for it!"

Gate sniffed the smoke. "Looks more like carelessness to me. You had some meat on there…"

The cook gave him a bleak look. "No, my lord, that's not meat. That's one of my kitchen lasses on there…and if you don't take Weaver's neck for this, I'll take his head off myself!"

Gate stared at the man for a moment. "Just put it out and let me know when it's been doused," he said, "and leave Weaver to me."

He struggled down past the bucket line on the steps and crossed the courtyard to the main gate, glad to get some fresh air in his lungs. A swift inspection reassured him that the gate was fully manned and intact. He was pleased to see that the tired guards straightened up as he approached. He went into the guardroom, which was adjacent to the gatehouse. There were men lying everywhere - no wonder it was costing him so much to feed the garrison. He hoped his patron could use all of these men but he supposed the Earl of Warwick knew what he was doing.

"Look sharp!" he called, as he put his head around the door. "We'll be doubling up at the gates and on the walls. Make sure you're ready."

He left them and crossed the yard again this time heading for the postern gate but he slipped in what appeared to be vomit.

"Too many drunken men and whores in this place," he muttered.

As he wiped his boot on the cobbles he happened to look through the arch to the postern gate. What he saw caused him to forget about the state of his boots. The postern gate lay wide open and two of his men at arms were being dragged away. For an instant he considered intervening but he knew it was more important to rouse his men from their beds. He hurried back over the cobbles and noticed a swirl of black smoke drifting down from the first floor. Was the fire worse? Well, if so, the cooks would just have to deal with it on their own for now. He burst into the guard room again.

"I want every man to the postern gate!" he shouted. "We're under attack!"

Only a few of the men moved swiftly - no doubt experienced men at arms. The rest looked bewildered and sat fiddling with scabbards and breastplates.

"The gate is breached! Make haste or it'll be too late!" he urged them. Then he went down to lead the first group across the yard to the postern, now held by several men at arms - all he noted were his own recruits. The men with him looked confused too.

"Where are the attackers, lord?" asked one.

Keep it simple, Thomas told himself. This was not the time for lengthy explanations.

"Those men are traitors. Arrest them!" he ordered. "And if they don't yield, kill them."

He picked out the youth, Hal, and made straight for him. His men followed and a skirmish soon grew up around him. He smiled as he saw the numbers swelling behind him. Hal appeared to be the ringleader - disaffected no doubt. Thomas was relieved to see that although the gate lay open, there were no men coming in. He would make short work of these rebels.

He swayed back to avoid Hal's sword and thrust at him, though with little force. Pity as the youth had only a jack on, no breastplate. A firmer thrust would have done for him, as it was there was blood on the young man's chest and he was stepping back. Not much of a swordsman, this archer. Yet in the cramped space by the small gate the fight became a crush as more of his men tried to join in but could only press their comrades forward. Soon he struggled to move in the press and found himself trapped against a wall, unable to take part in what was fast becoming a raucous pushing match. He watched in vain as men tried to bludgeon each other around the head. Then, above the clamour of the men at arms, the air was filled with the sound of women screaming.

53

7th February 1469, in the cellars at Yoredale Castle

Eleanor came up into the cellar from the oubliette aided by Wulf and when she saw Maighread she hugged her close and clung to her, sobbing into her breast. When her aunt released her Eleanor still felt unsteady and, not trusting her legs to hold her, she sat down heavily on a box next to Emma. She laid her hand on Emma's arm.

"I see you've discovered that all is not quite as you imagined, sister."

"Aye," said Emma.

She was still cool, aloof, but she must feel betrayed too, Eleanor told herself. She looked up at Maighread, her scars seemed somehow more obvious in the flicker of the single torch.

"I am so glad to see you," said Eleanor. "Ned is come then?"

"No, not yet," said Maighread with a grimace. "Just me."

"Just you," said Eleanor, staring at her brigandine, "and dressed for a fight…"

"Well, we still have the postern gate," said Maighread, "but, if that is taken then we'll be trapped in here. Do you know if we can bar the door to the store chambers?"

"No, the bar's on the other side of the door," said Eleanor. "It's to keep anyone from getting through there from the postern gate."

"So the castle garrison could all come thundering

through there any time?" said Maighread.

"Aye," grinned Eleanor. "Anyone got a sword?"

Maighread took out her long knife and brandished it with a flourish. Emma picked up a small knife from the floor. "Hal gave me this," she said and placed it back on the box between them.

They all stared at the door in silence for a while but heard nothing. Then they all looked at each other and laughed.

Eleanor noticed that Maighread's eyes often lighted upon John.

"He looks so sweet, doesn't he?" Eleanor said softly.

Maighread nodded. "His face... a picture of concentration."

John looked up at her suddenly and smiled as if realising that he was the subject of their attention.

"I don't get many smiles from children," said Maighread. She smiled back. John turned away slowly and glanced at the cellar door. Then he stood up and looked back at Maighread.

"My lady," was all he said before the cellar door flew open and he was knocked off his feet. Bess screamed and shied away from Weaver who came through first, sword in hand. Margaret followed him with a blazing torch in one hand and a knife in the other.

"Shit!" growled Eleanor and picked up Emma's knife to spring up at their attackers but after her stay in the oubliette she could only manage to stagger forward and fall onto the floor. She cursed her own weakness and looked up to see six inches of steel burst out of Bess's back.

"Oh, Good Christ!" Eleanor caught Bess as she fell. Weaver slashed down at her but his sword point struck only sparks from the stone flags.

All were screaming now. Emma got up but Weaver clubbed her down with his sword hilt and reached for John.

Margaret lunged at Maighread and caught her full in the

breast. Maighread looked shocked and dropped down onto her back where she lay still.

"Blood of Christ!" roared Eleanor and rolled the lifeless body of Bess aside. She reached up and stabbed Margaret in the calf, forcing her to take a step back and collide with Joan on her way in. Joan. Eleanor fixed her with a fierce glare. It was time she did something about Joan.

Weaver had hold of the boy's arm and was trying to drag him away but John was kicking out at him. Eleanor did not know who to go for first. And where were the men at arms? Could they not hear their cries? Sitting on their arses, no doubt, whilst women did their business for them.

She staggered to her feet. Weaver had the only sword - she was no match for him. He was still grappling with John but he could have killed him already and he hadn't - that was good. Margaret was hurt but only a little and Joan stood beside her, eyes blazing and ready to strike.

Eleanor stepped to the right to put Margaret and Joan between her and Weaver. She could not move well but she could just about stand.

"Come on then, girls," she taunted them, "two of you against little, crippled me - yet you're still scared!"

Margaret rushed her first but Eleanor caught her wrist and ripped her own blade through her stomach and dragged it out. Eleanor's face was next to her victim's as the life faded from her. Eleanor spat in her eyes. "Not good enough, you sullen cow!" she said and pushed her back against Weaver. As he thrust her aside, John slipped from his grasp for a moment, but only for a moment.

Eleanor held her bloodied knife before her and Joan ran at her like a wild animal, carving the air with her long steel blade. They crashed into each other, screaming. Eleanor grunted and Joan cried out as both blades struck home. For a moment they stared at each other before the shock of their wounds hit them. Eleanor gulped in air. It hurt. Joan's contorted mouth was close to hers. They locked eyes and sealed a wordless pact of death. Both wanted to fight but as they drew apart both fell back and felt for the blood they knew they would find.

Eleanor felt dizzy and sat down. She discovered a wet, sticky patch on the front of her kirtle and felt a trickle of liquid running down from her breast. It felt like a lance of fire was lodged in her chest. She must be losing blood in buckets. She looked at Joan and saw that her own blade had inflicted only a slight shoulder wound.

Joan smiled down at her. "A painful way to die…" she said.

"Leave her!" shouted Weaver, "I've got the boy!"

Joan ignored him. She was coming again, but she was not looking at Eleanor. She was staring at Maighread, who lay on the floor. Joan went slowly to her, a step at a time.

"Come, my lady!" implored Weaver, waiting in the cellar doorway with John under his arm.

Eleanor tried to get up. The trickle of blood down her chest quickened. Joan stood over Maighread and then crouched down with her knife poised above her breast.

"This time I'll make sure of you," she said.

PART SEVEN: FATHERS & SONS

DEREK BIRKS

54

7th February 1469, in the forest near Yoredale Castle

"Two men is not so great a loss," said Ragwulf.

"Three!" retorted Ned, urging the mount beneath him to an even more breakneck pace. "One man at arms dead, one archer wounded and another needed to get him back to camp before he bleeds to death! That's a hefty part of Lord Scales' men - and we can't afford such losses!"

He sped on along the winding forest track oblivious to the bare, wiry branches that whipped across his face.

"We'll soon be there, lord," Ragwulf assured him.

"I know. I know this land better than you do," snapped Ned, "Soon, but not soon enough. I said I'd be there at dawn - and dawn is long gone!"

"Aye, lord," said Ragwulf, "I know…"

Ned glanced across at the older man. He looked as pale and drained as Ned felt.

"Be ready!" called Ned and slowed his horse to a trot. The castle towers appeared through the trees ahead and he abandoned the path to veer to the left. Just before dawn the light would have been dim and the castle half asleep. Now there would be fresh men on the ramparts with their eyes peeled and a clear enough morning to see for miles. Speed was now all he had left.

There was no time to see Maighread. She would be worried and she would be more worried as the day went on. She would also be angry that he had not taken her in with him. He smiled grimly - one blessing at least. He stopped at the treeline and waited for his men to draw alongside. Soon one of the scouts he had left watching the castle trotted through the trees to join them.

"Well?" asked Ned.

"No-one's left this morning, my lord, but they seem to have a fire in one of the towers," reported the archer.

"A fire? Now, is that good news or bad, I wonder. Stay here," he ordered the archer, "and if any man attacks us from the wall, give him some trouble."

"Very well, my lord."

"Ragwulf, you lead. Bear, with me."

He turned to address the men. "You all know what to do. If the postern gate's not open, we ride back here. We're not assaulting the castle. Our warrant is for the arrest of Sir Thomas Gate... and any man who resists. Make no mistake, if we get involved in a fight with the whole garrison, we'll die there."

His words were greeted with silence. He was wasting time for their blood was up and they wanted to fight - it was what they did. He sighed and turned to Ragwulf.

"Lead on," he murmured.

Ragwulf set off fast and rode for the castle wall following a well-beaten path. They had hardly cleared the trees when there was a shout from the ramparts - fresh men, alert. Ragwulf's head was bent low as he galloped into the lee of the wall and Ned followed close behind in similar fashion, keeping as close to the rough stonework as his mount would allow.

There was a cry from behind him and he glanced back to see one of the men at arms tumble into the hard ground. Shit! How many more? Ragwulf dismounted by the postern, with Ned hard on his heels. Ned felt the very earth tremble beneath his feet as Bear leapt to the ground beside him. The postern gate was open - but only just. He spotted Hal and Wulf at once but they were being steadily driven out of the gate towards him. He rushed past Ragwulf and thrust himself into the line of men alongside Hal.

"My lord!" shouted Hal. A grin of relief lit up his bloodied face. "Thank God!" There were tears in his eyes.

Ned quickly assessed Hal's position: the gateway was partially blocked by dead and wounded. Hal's few men at arms were being harried by many more of Gate's men. It was a shock when he glimpsed Thomas Gate for the first time - only a few yards away from him urging on his defenders. Ned swallowed hard and it took all his will not to launch himself into the melee. In his younger days, that's what he would have done…but not now. He had learned that much at least.

"Archers! Stay mounted!" he shouted. He glanced around at them and his heart sank: he had forgotten there were only two with him now - well, better two than none.

"Hal!" he bellowed, "fall back your men and get down!"

"But they'll close the gate, my lord!" Hal cried.

Ned shook his head. "Do it now!"

Hal dragged back his men out of the gateway and they took little persuading.

"And get your heads down if you want to keep them!" Ned roared above the din.

Gate's men surged forward to clear the gateway and then looked up at Ned and saw the two archers taking aim.

He noticed Gate diving for cover and then the arrows began to fly, the pair loosing in grim unison. They could hardly miss and man after man was driven backwards by the force of an arrow at the closest possible range.

"I thought we weren't killing the men," said Ragwulf with a bitter grimace.

"Unless they resist…" said Ned.

The defenders scattered, abandoning all thought of closing the gate.

Ned turned to Bear. "Shall we?" he said, "before Gate gets his own archers down here."

He joined Hal in the gateway. "Sorry we're late, Hal," he

said and clapped him on the back. "Take care to mark these men!" he said to Scales' men. "I've not got so many you can kill each other."

Whilst Ned was still talking Bear was already through the gate, battle axe in his giant hands. Ragwulf went with him stride for stride. Ned drew his sword and followed hard after them. Half a dozen men at arms sprang out at them from either side of the doorway but Bear's heavy axe carved them aside with great sweeping, bloodletting blows. The survivors fled into the yard and made for any door that might offer some respite.

"Hal, take two of your men and the two archers up and clear the ramparts - now!" ordered Ned.

"My lord," said Hal, "Lady Maighread and your sisters are with John in the cellar - we couldn't get down to them…"

Ned seized his arm.

"My lord?" said Hal.

"Lady Maighread is in here?" said Ned, "But how?"

"She came at dawn, my lord," said Hal. "She…killed one of the guards…"

She would, thought Ned. "They're in the cellar?"

"Aye, lord, but hurry, for I fear they're in trouble."

"Get to the ramparts," said Ned. "Bear, hold the gate! Ragwulf - with me!"

But Ragwulf was no longer there, nor Wulf. Ned looked for them in vain. Bear pointed down the steps. "Cellar!"

Ned hurried down the steps after them, worried at what he might find.

55

7th February 1469, in the cellars at Yoredale Castle

Maighread came to with Joan's knife hanging over her.

"I'm glad you'll see it coming, you sour bitch," said Joan. "You should have died long ago at Crag."

"But I didn't. A brave knight came to rescue me," breathed Maighread and smiled, thinking about him. A few feet away she saw Eleanor crawling very slowly across the floor towards them. She would not get to her in time.

"Well, your knight isn't here to rescue you now," said Joan.

"My lady, I'm taking the boy!" cried Weaver, "Now!"

"Go on! I'll follow," she told him without a glance back at him.

Maighread looked up at her and smiled. She was still holding her own knife by her side and now she lifted it to press the point up against Joan's stomach.

"If I die, then so do you," Maighread said, in a voice as hard as granite.

"And so will the boy," said Joan.

"He's a tough little boy," breathed Maighread and thrust her knife up. Joan screamed at her and instinctively stabbed down. Maighread tried to turn aside but couldn't and the blade struck her in the ribs. Joan staggered to her feet and clutched at her wound, staring down at the blood welling from between her fingers. She pressed her hand hard against her belly and looked about her. Margaret lay still upon the floor and Weaver had already gone. Eleanor sat up and tried to seize her leg, but her hand was bloody and Joan slipped from her grasp. Eleanor began screaming for help as Joan stumbled to the cellar door and passed unsteadily through it.

Maighread coughed and tasted blood on her lips. Then she started to weep. Eleanor managed to get across to her and held her.

"It's the shock of the blow. You'll be alright," she said, "you're wearing a brigandine."

But Maighread shook her head. She knew that the knife had passed through it, it was a thrust driven by such anger, such torment, that even the armoured jacket could not keep it out.

"What have I done?" said Maighread, her voice scarcely a whisper. "John - they'll kill him."

"I'll go after them. Joan has a belly wound - she's a dead bitch walking," said Eleanor. "If she doesn't know it now, she soon will. Can you manage to get to someone?"

"Aye. How are the others?" asked Maighread.

Eleanor blinked. "Bess is gone. I think Emma's just out cold." She paused for breath and gently took Maighread's knife from her.

"I think I'll need a longer blade," she said with a faint smile. "God be with you, Maighread. Remember me to Ned."

Maighread clutched at her sleeve. "No...you're hurt bad!"

"Aye, I'm a dead bitch walking too but I'm not letting John go without a fight."

Maighread sobbed as Eleanor picked up the torch Margaret had dropped and lurched through the door into the darkness.

She slowly crawled across to Emma. She was still breathing but her head was cut and bleeding a little. Dear Bess had bled out on the dusty cellar floor - a paltry reward for her selfless life of service.

Maighread's breathing was tight but she dragged herself up the cellar steps, taking several short wheezing breaths before she attempted each one. When she reached the top she looked out and understood at once why Hal and Wulf had not come to her aid. They were no longer guarding the postern - instead Thomas Gate stood with a crowd of his men at arms filling the gateway.

She leaned back against the wall, out of sight. She felt weak and the brigandine was now blood soaked down the side. Men were falling at the gate. She pressed her hand against the wound and it hurt so much she almost passed out. Everything seemed blurred. Objects flashed before her eyes. Then Maighread cowered back a little further and fell back down the steps.

§§§§

"Bess?" cried Wulf as he came down the steps two at a time. He almost knocked Maighread over in his haste but swiftly gathered her up and helped her to sit.

"My lady?"

First he saw the blood on her brigandine then, beyond her, he saw the open cellar door and Emma slumped upon the wooden chest.

"Wulf," she said, "Weaver's taken John... and, I'm sorry, Bess is..."

But Wulf had already seen her and gave an anguished cry as he fell to his knees beside her.

"Bess!" he roared.

He must have known at once but he picked up her lifeless body and cradled it.

"Weaver?" he asked.

Maighread nodded and, before she could stop him, he laid Bess down and was gone - through the cellar door.

Ragwulf came in and stood still at first, absorbing the shock of what he saw. Then he crouched beside Maighread. "My lady?"

"Please… don't ask me if I'm alright," she whispered.

Ragwulf went over to examine the others. "She was a good lass, Bess," he said.

"Aye, better than good," murmured Maighread.

"Is Lady Eleanor…?"

"She went after Joan and Weaver. But she's hurt, Ragwulf - she's hurt badly…"

Ragwulf stared at her. She understood his dilemma.

"I'll get help for you," he said. "Your wound must be bound up."

She took his hand. "You'll not! I'll live. Wulf's gone after Weaver too. Now go to him and find Eleanor, before it's too late."

He gave her a grim nod, drew his sword and left her. She removed her hand from the wound and tried to examine it. She reached up under the brigandine and it felt horribly wet with blood. How quickly did you run out of blood, she wondered? Then she smiled for Ned landed heavily beside her at the foot of the steps.

"God's Blood!" he exclaimed when he saw her.

"No. Maighread's blood," she said in a low voice. "I'll complain to Master Holton when we get back to Corve - his brigandine didn't work."

He hugged her to him and she gave a squeak of pain.

"Sorry," he said and kissed her cheek. Then he helped her out of the jacket and looked at her wound. He gave a sigh.

"Does that mean I'm dying?" she groaned.

"No, the bleeding's stopped. But you should be thanking Holton, not cursing him. You took the first blow to the breast and the brigandine held. That would've killed you for certain."

He got up and went to Emma. He lifted her and carried her across to where Maighread sat. Emma groaned and shook her head.

Maighread put her hand on his chest. "She'll be fine

with me," said Maighread, "we'll look after each other."

He swiftly checked both Bess and Margaret then he tore some lengths of cloth from Margaret's linen shirt to bind around Maighread's wound.

"It was Joan," said Maighread. "She's got John. Eleanor went after them… so did Ragwulf… and Wulf."

His head dropped. "There's not enough of us," he breathed, "I need to stop the whole garrison joining the fight or we're all dead. Ragwulf should have stayed with you."

"I told him to go," said Maighread. "He needed to."

"He needed to be here with me," said Ned. "And now I'll have to leave you too."

She smiled. "I know."

He held her again for a moment and then two of Scales' men at arms descended the steps.

"Croft," he told one, "you only have one task now: you're to stay with these ladies and … if it looks very bad, you're to get them out to safety - they can tell you where. Do nothing else - and do not leave them for any reason. Is that clear?"

"Aye, my lord!"

"Good!" He gave Maighread a final smile and then beckoned the other man with him and went back up the steps to the postern gate.

She smiled at Croft. He had a fair face, she thought, but he was a soldier and she could see that he was less than happy to be told to watch over her. She could see the contempt in his eyes: what was this disfigured woman doing here, getting herself wounded and getting in the way of fighting men?

She remembered how she had nagged Ned to let her come. She looked over to where Bess lay and recalled how distraught Wulf was to see his young love butchered thus. And she understood now, too late, why men did not want their women beside them when they fought.

56

7th February 1469, in the cellars at Yoredale Castle

"Weaver!" Joan screeched. She staggered into the next storeroom and found him waiting. She stared at the boy slumped over his shoulder.

"Is he dead?"

"He will be if he fucking bites me again!" barked Weaver. "Come, my lady, we'd best make haste!"

"I need… help, Weaver," she said, gritting her teeth and glancing down at her bloodied belly.

He took a closer look at it. "How deep is it?" he asked.

"How should I know? It feels like a great bill's cut me! Below the bodice."

"We can't stay here, my lady."

"Just help me get to somewhere I can lie down for a while, let the bleeding stop…"

He stared back at her and she knew that there, as he watched her blood seep away, he was considering the depth of his loyalty.

"I'm not dead yet," she growled at him. "Get me to Sir Thomas's chamber - that's nearest."

He put John under his arm and gave her his shoulder to lean on. They struggled into the next store and through the wine cellar to the well. She leant against the brickwork whilst Weaver took a look at the stairwell. The line of dishevelled fire fighters was still there though they moved wearily, slopping water onto the floor. They looked beaten, Joan thought.

"They're not going to stop that fire like that," said Weaver.

"What do I care if the kitchen burns down - we'll build another one!" said Joan.

"Aye, but fire doesn't know where to stop, my lady, and Sir Thomas' chamber is above the kitchen."

"Just get me outside then," she said. "Leave the fire to others!"

He shrugged and took her weight again to guide her out into the yard. To her relief, Thomas was there forming up a troop of men by the gatehouse.

"Thomas!" she cried and stumbled over to him.

"Ned Elder's in the castle!" he announced.

"Then tell him you'll kill his son if he doesn't surrender!" she said with triumph in her voice.

Thomas looked at her with disgust. "I don't kill children! Get them inside, Weaver!" he rasped. "Take them up to the privy chamber. Then call out the rest of the men."

His voice carried only anger - no concern for her grievous wound, no praise for her courage, no word of care.

"I want men everywhere, Weaver - we surely have enough of them!"

"Fewer than we did, my lord," replied Weaver. "Last night's patrol hasn't come in and Lord Elder's got archers…"

"They've got archers - well so have we."

"Aye, my lord," said Weaver with a grin, "but we've got something better than archers too."

Gate looked at him for a moment then nodded. "Very well, prepare what you need."

"When you have time…" cried Joan, "from your men's talk… this standing is… not helping my wound!"

"I'll take my lady up to the privy chamber, my lord, as you say," said Weaver. "She'll be safer there. Then I'll find some men who know what to do."

Gate gave him a curt nod and Weaver half-carried Joan

up the spiral stair. Every wretched step pulled at her stomach wound, tearing her severed muscle and flesh a little more. She grunted but bore the pain, keeping a bloody hand pressed against her belly.

Weaver sat her down in the chair and it felt good to take the weight off her legs. He tossed the lad down at her feet.

"You're losing too much blood," he observed coldly.

"Well, I'm... so... sorry," she ground out the words, "so... damned careless of me. Fetch someone to look at it, then!"

"I am looking at it," he said, "You've not got long. I could say you've been a pleasure to serve, my lady, but you haven't. Though there were some good times..."

"You're a worthless shit, Weaver... to think I let you...."

"Aye, well, my lady, I have to say that fucking you was one of the good times," he said with a grin. "I'll be back, but I reckon you might be dead by then. Do what you want with the boy - I hope he's worth all the blood spilled for him."

She held the knife tight in her hand, tempted to throw it at him - except she still needed it. If she was going to die, then the boy was going to Hell with her - an unnatural boy, whom God had never intended to be born. She would at least have one, final revenge upon Ned Elder.

Then as if her spiteful God was listening to her, she heard him: Ned Elder. At first she thought he was speaking only to her.

§§§§§

Ned returned to the postern where Bear waited, an anxious look on his face - and when Bear looked worried, it was time for all sane men to be terrified.

Bear shook his head. "Too many men, lord. We should get out."

"How many men have we got?"

"Hal, three for him… eight or nine of ours… and two archers. Ragwulf?"

"I don't know," said Ned. "Gate will come at us again - no doubt with plenty of archers. Let's try reason."

He took the warrant the king had given him from a pouch under his breastplate. Wiping the sweat from his eyes, he walked straight out into the courtyard.

At the far end by the main gatehouse, stood Thomas Gate ringed by a dozen men, perhaps more.

"Listen!" shouted Ned. Every man in the courtyard spun around towards him and he held up the document so that all could see it.

"I have here the king's warrant to arrest your lord, Sir Thomas Gate, on charges of treason and sedition! This warrant bears the king's seal. No harm will come to any man who stands down now. But if you raise arms against me, then you are raising arms against King Edward - the fourth of that name, anointed by God and acclaimed by Parliament. Sheathe your swords and lower your bows! Any man that remains in the guard house and does not fight has broken no law and will receive no punishment. Any man who wishes to leave the castle now, may do so freely.

His announcement clearly took Thomas by surprise but he was not a man to be so easily outmanoeuvred and when Ned paused, Thomas stepped forward.

He raised his voice too. "Very good, very well done." He laughed aloud. "This is Ned Elder - once Lord Elder of these parts - you may have heard of him. He's an outlaw now, banished by the king whose name he is so keen to mention. He may have persuaded you with his false words but consider well, my friends. I have recruited you with the full support of the great Earl of Warwick, Richard Neville, whose stronghold at Middleham is only a few miles distant. Where is Ned Elder's king? I assure you that he's not as close as my lord of Warwick. He's swaddled in fur cloaks down in the south somewhere."

"The king has no quarrel with honest men," shouted Ned, "nor have I. Enough blood has already been spilled - and there's no need for any more. Lay down your arms, or leave in peace-"

Gate's bitter voice interrupted him. "Before you leave these walls for the cold, bare lands outside, remember that it isn't the king who has fed you these past winter months, but me. If Ned Elder arrests me, then you'll be turned out to starve! Now, give this outlaw an answer to remember!"

Ned knew he had lost even before he dodged the first arrow. He glanced up to the rampart where Hal stood with his two archers. He gave a signal and then dived back through the archway as more arrows struck the stone work. Then he watched as Hal and his fellows loosed arrow upon arrow down into Thomas's men in the yard. They scrambled under the cover of the gatehouse and occasionally came forward for a frantic exchange of arrows.

He had known all along that Gate's men were unlikely to fear a king who was several hundred miles away - but it was worth trying to avert what would happen now.

"Lord?" enquired Bear.

Ned sighed. "How can I leave my son, my sister Eleanor, Ragwulf and the others? And somewhere here, I'm sure is Agnes."

Bear nodded.

"Do you think he'll come at us across the yard?" Ned asked.

"Too open - come through the chambers in the walls."

"I was afraid of that…" said Ned.

There was a movement by the postern gate but Ned was relieved to see that it was his remaining two archers coming in from their watch outside.

"Thought it sounded as if you needed some help, my lord," said one.

"Aye," acknowledged Ned, "that we do, man. That we do. One of you go up onto the ramparts and tell them all to come back down here."

Bear was right. The key was not the courtyard but the walls for each side of the castle contained a range of chambers within the walls. Even now, he thought, Thomas could be sending his men pouring through the ground floor bake house or the Great Chamber on the first floor in the west range and perhaps also through the buttery and the Hall in the north range. Ned's position would be easily outflanked and he would need every man he had just to defend the postern.

Hal soon came down with his three men at arms and the archers. Ned knew Hal's men well for they had set out with him from this very castle years before. Their fathers, their brothers and their friends - many of them fell in his service. He had invited them, during his exile, to renounce their oaths and they had left Crag Tower with Wulf. Now they found themselves back with Ned Elder and he wondered how they felt about that.

"The best we can try, Hal, is to find those we care for and get them out through the postern gate."

Hal gave him a bleak look.

"I know, I said it was the best we could do…"

"Very well, lord," said Hal, "Let me go for Agnes. I'm not sure where she is but I know where to start."

"Which is?"

"Walter Grave's chamber, two floors up on the south wall between the chapel and the garrison sleeping quarters."

"Where Bagot used to sleep," said Ned.

Hal nodded.

"Eleanor, Ragwulf and Wulf went through the cellars under the north range," said Ned. "I'll go after them and get John. You take your men to the south wall and find Agnes. We'll meet back here. Bear, you'll hold the postern with the rest of the men."

Bear nodded, grim-faced but resolute. "I will hold this gate, lord."

Ned embraced Hal. "Go Hal - and be as swift as you can."

Hal set off to climb the steps in the north-west tower to the second floor, taking his men at arms with him. Ned briefly gripped Bear's hand and set off down to the cellar, leaving Bear to marshal his defences. If he had to rely on any one man to keep that gate open, it would be Bear.

He passed Maighread and paused to kiss her. "Bear is at the top of the steps - he'll hold the postern long enough for us to get out. I'm going to get John and the others."

"Ned?" Emma had come to. Ned stared at his sister for a moment. She had a bloody weal on the side of her head. But she looked older too, much older than he remembered - and somehow more frail, though she was two years younger than he. When had he seen her last? Four years or more.

"Ned?" Emma prompted again but he struggled to find the words to reply.

"The king's brother, Gloucester, told me you were at Middleham," he said.

"I was... I am."

Ned wrestled with this notion for a moment. Why had she gone to Warwick?

"They told me before you were taking holy orders..."

Emma sighed. "Aye, I was, but our Lord had other designs for me. I had a different burden to carry: a daughter."

At last Ned understood... the young man, Garth. He nodded but said nothing.

"The earl and his lady have been... kind to me, Ned."

"Well," he replied, "the earl has been far from kind to me."

They both fell silent. He should have been pleased to see her but instead her presence there called into question everything he had taken as fact: Warwick was his enemy, plain and simple. There could be no mitigation for the trouble he had brought upon the Elders and no single kindness to his sister could change that.

"There will be a reckoning with Warwick, Em. Not now, for he's reconciled to the king and so am I, but sooner or later… I know it. You'd best make sure you're not between us when it happens."

He kissed her on the forehead and went to the cellar door.

"Stay alert, Master Croft - it may be us coming back through the cellars - then again, it may not."

He flashed Maighread a smile full of confidence - a confidence he did not have.

§§§§

Thomas Gate's broad grin faded as he entered the privy chamber. He had never had much love for Joan Elder but to see her slumped in a chair, bloodied and broken, caused him to stand still on the threshold.

She fixed him with a grim stare. Her face was almost white but the skin was stained by smears of dried blood. Her right hand still gripped her knife and the boy lay at her feet. There was blood all over her clothes where her left hand pressed against the wound. At first Thomas thought that John was dead but he soon noticed the gentle rise and fall of the lad's shoulders.

"I'll send you up some help, Joan," he said, but they both knew he would not.

She said nothing. She didn't need to: her bitter eyes spoke eloquently enough.

"Let me take the boy," he said.

She gave a slight shake of the head and glanced down at her wound.

"You're dying," he said. "This is no place for the boy."

She winced as she shifted her position on the chair.

"You know who he is," she muttered. "Ned Elder's heir - the heir to Yoredale and all his other estates…"

"Not necessarily..."

"Aye, necessarily…"

She looked all but done, he thought. Perhaps it was for the best. There was no harm in her knowing now.

"Well, my dear, that rather depends on who you think those estates belong to in the first place."

"Don't play with me, Thomas. I've not the strength for it."

"The Yoredale estates rightly belong to the Radcliffes."

"The Radcliffes are all dead! Unless you mean to let cousin Emma's boy, Richard, have it all - and he's only a Radcliffe by name!"

He smiled at her. "No, that's not quite what I had in mind," he said. "My father was-"

"My lord!" said Weaver from behind him. Blood of Christ! That man could move like a cat when he had a mind to. Thomas noted the look of disgust on Joan's face as Weaver entered the chamber. She clearly resented losing one of her playthings, even at the end.

Gate frowned. "I shall return as soon as I can, my lady," he told her. "And I'll send women to bind your wound."

She shook her head and closed her eyes, shutting him out. So be it, she could take care of the boy and he would deal with Ned Elder.

"All is ready, my lord," said Weaver, with a grin.

"This is not sport, Weaver," Gate chastised him. "Send your men through the first floor rooms: the Hall and the Great Chamber. When they're in position, send the rest to the archway opposite the postern gate. You'll attack the gate from three sides."

"Aye, my lord," said Weaver.

"Retake that gate swiftly, Weaver, and you'll find me a generous lord."

57

7th February 1469, in Thomas Gate's chamber at Yoredale

Agnes lay on Thomas Gate's bed where he had left her. He had ordered her to wait and she was waiting but it seemed to her a very long wait indeed. If she still had the knife she would have used it already. Instead she lay there, her self-inflicted wound no longer weeping blood. The room was getting warmer and her keen sense of smell told her there was a fire below long before wisps of smoke began to drift up through gaps in the floor boards. How there could be a fire in the kitchen she did not understand, for had she not spent hours roasting meat in the two great stone hearths with stone flag surrounds?

Not that the fire worried her unduly - she might as well stay where she was for one death would do as well as another. So, let her burn - she was not a fool but she thought she would succumb to the smoke fumes long before she endured the flames. She felt used, soiled, all her young hopes long ago forgotten. The fire would make her clean again; take her back to her father and her long dead mother. She struggled to recall now what her mother had looked like. Her mother lay in the forest, as did her father, and soon she would join them.

At first she did not notice the voice. Over the years she had learned to shut out distracting noises in the background but something about this sound nagged at her. She could not hear the words, only the timbre of the voice. It was familiar - more than familiar, she knew it. But it was the voice of a dead man.

She flew across the room, wrenched open the door and choked on the smoke that rushed in, not thick but enough to catch in her throat. Ned Elder was alive and once more her world was turned upside down. He had come for her. She could face Ned. He would understand... not like Hal, who she could not look in the eye, for Hal would only ever see her as the whore of Walter Grave. Ned was ever her protector, tall and strong as a great forest oak. She would not feel ashamed to go to Ned.

But how could she get to him? She could hear him, but where was he? He could not be far and must be inside the castle! If Ned was there then he would be fighting Thomas Gate.

All had changed: the fire below was no longer the means of her deliverance, it was her enemy. The smoke crept into her mouth, her throat, her chest: stealing her breath. Her eyes blinked away tears as she considered what to do. Rushing to Ned was the last thing she should do, for if Gate caught her it would only make things more difficult. Yet she could not stay in Gate's chamber because of the fire and, not least, because he would know where she was. She must find somewhere safe to wait out the struggle and hope that her lord would prevail. But where?

She was in the kitchen tower, the north-east. The nearest places were too dangerous: below her was the burning kitchen; next to her on the east wall was one of the garrison dormitories - not ideal - and on the other side, along the north wall, was the Hall and nowhere was more exposed than that. Even so, she must go somewhere.

She slipped through the door and descended the steps through the thickening swirls of smoke. In the stairwell the heat of the fire struck her with such ferocity that she cowered against the curved stone wall. On the landing below she found several women standing with empty pails of water. Their blackened faces, etched by lines of sweat, were silently fixed upon the kitchen door. A sudden flame shot out of the kitchen door, followed by a stumbling figure, all ablaze with fire-laden arms flapping horribly up and down. The cook screamed in agony and the women screamed too as he lurched back into the cauldron of fire. His scream was abruptly cut short. The women dropped their pails and fled down the steps. Agnes remained, shocked, on the landing. All she could smell was burning flesh.

In the end, the heat drove her away and she backed towards the privy chamber which was next to the kitchen and below the men's dormitory. If Gate was occupied elsewhere, she reasoned, it might just be safe. She held her breath and lifted the latch on the chamber door. Quickly she stepped inside, closed the door behind her and let out a sigh of relief.

§§§§

Eleanor felt weary as she plodded through the cellar store rooms. Ahead of her some women screamed. It was ever thus: when were there not women screaming? Joan would scream too when she got her hands on her. The last shrill echoes faded away as she reached the well chamber. It was deserted but there was water all over the stone flags and an upturned leather bucket.

There was no door between the well chamber and the tower steps but the door out to the courtyard was shut so she decided it was a good time to examine her wound. She unlaced her kirtle and tore away some of the linen beneath, revealing her breasts. She brushed her fingers over the old scars. Why was it always her breasts! She explored the knife wound gingerly and found it was still seeping blood. It needed binding up and she had neither the time nor the inclination to do it. She folded the torn strip of linen into a wad and pressed it against the wound for a moment. Then she laced up the kirtle again to hold the small wad in place.

She moved cautiously out into the stairwell where she

could hear voices from the courtyard, muffled by the door. Then it slammed open and several men at arms came in. They saw her at once and she backed away from them through the archway into the well chamber. They followed her in and she thrust her burning torch into the face of the first man in. He screamed and, as he drew back his head, she plunged her knife into his neck. Two more men entered the well chamber, swords drawn. She could not outrun them and backed away until she came up against the wall.

She gave a yelp as she was pushed aside and Wulf hurtled past her into the men at arms. Wulf was the most skilful swordsman she had ever seen - apart from her dear, lost Will. He almost gave butchery a grace - almost. Several lightning fast caresses of his blade felled the two men at arms in a welter of blood. Wulf was in no mood for clemency and she could not blame him. A third man outside the well chamber ran off into the yard and the outside door now stood open.

"Thank you, Wulf," said Eleanor. "More will come, I fear."

"Are you alright, my lady?" he asked.

"I'm fine," she lied. "We must get out of here - up the steps."

"Smoke's coming from up there," he pointed out.

She gasped as two great hands came to rest on her shoulders.

Wulf crouched and spun round ready to strike. Then he grinned and she turned around to find Ragwulf. For a brief moment they simply stared at each other with his hands still upon her shoulders.

"Ragwulf," she found herself saying, stupid cow that she was - she might have found a more original greeting for him.

"My lady," he replied and his familiar gruff tone somehow made her eyes water.

If any other man had touched her she would have

slapped him in the face and told him to take his hands off her, but not this man, not this time. Instead she did something she rarely ever did: she burst into tears and hugged him.

"I didn't think I'd see you again," she sobbed into his shoulder.

"Aye," was all he said, but she felt him trembling too as he held her.

"Father," said Wulf in a low voice.

Ragwulf held her on one arm and clasped his son's hand. "The two folk I love best in all Christendom," he said.

"They killed Bess," mumbled Wulf.

"I know, son," said Ragwulf, "but by God's breath we're going to make them pay a high price."

Eleanor wept some more to see the two men reconciled. "I think I've become a weak and senseless woman," she said.

"Aye, you were never weak before," said Ragwulf. He noticed the blood on her for the first time. "Is the hurt bad?" he asked.

She shook her head. "No. My breasts are used to being hacked about - as you may recall …"

"Let me look," he said.

"Wulf, I do believe your father would seize upon the slightest excuse to fondle my chest."

Wulf turned away in embarrassment and she gave a bitter laugh, which started the wound hurting even more.

She put a hand on Ragwulf's chest. "Come," she said. "You can explore my bloodied dugs later."

Ragwulf went out first and spun back inside cursing, an arrow through his shoulder. He snapped off the shaft angrily and swore a few more times for good measure. Eleanor examined his wound and scoffed. "Hardly worth bothering with; mine's much worse."

"We can't go out that way," said Ragwulf, "we'll get cut

to pieces!"

"We have to go after John," said Eleanor, "whatever it costs. I'm not leaving that boy to her!"

Ragwulf's face clouded with concern. "Aye, but we'll do the lad no good if we're dead!"

As always, what he said made complete sense. She wanted to do as he bade her and stay there. She wanted to tend his wound, then wrap him in her arms and stay there with him forever - but she wasn't going to do any of those things.

She brushed aside a stray tear. "Smoke in the air..." she said. "One of us must get to John... you two could hold here for a while, couldn't you?"

"I'm not letting Weaver go!" said Wulf. "Never..."

"And I'm not letting you go!" Ragwulf told her.

She smiled at him.

"No!" he said firmly.

Time was slipping by whilst they argued. She leant into Ragwulf and whispered softly. "Forgive me... for all I've said and done, for my faults without number... in the past. I love you." Then she ran out through the arch to the stair.

"No, wait!" roared Ragwulf as she slipped from his grasp.

Arrows flew past her, but she wore a broad smile on her face as she scrambled up the steps into the smoke, because whatever happened to her now, she had finally told him.

The smile soon became a grimace as she struggled up through the clouds of smoke onto the searing hot kitchen landing. Her chest ached with every breath and the wound was bleeding badly again after the exertion. She had to escape the smoke and heat for it was draining away the little strength she had left.

She started up the steps to the next landing. Thomas Gate's chamber was up there. Joan might well have gone there. She stopped for a while on the steps to rest, but the cloying smoke seemed to be following her up, slowly choking her. She clambered up the remainder of the stair and stumbled, wheezing, into the minstrels' gallery above the Hall. The air there was clearer and she sat down, leaning her back against the gallery rail to get her breath back. She looked at the wound again, willing it to stop bleeding but every cough caused a little more blood to seep out. If she didn't move, the blood flow would slow; but if she didn't move, she would be leaving John to his fate. Footsteps sounded along the passage and she crawled into an alcove, praying the smoke was thick enough to hide her.

§§§§

Ragwulf and Wulf stared at each other. Neither spoke. No more arrows came. Ragwulf felt helpless - he should have known that she would go. How could he let her go on alone? He had fought his yearning for her for so long and now, at the very moment she declared her love for him, he had let her go. She was sorely wounded and hopelessly outnumbered. She could not succeed alone.

Wulf stood at the archway, keeping an eye on the courtyard. "There are still at least three archers I can see - there may be more."

"Men at arms?" asked Ragwulf.

"Can't see."

"They could keep us here for a week with just a handful of archers," said Ragwulf.

"We could run through as she did?"

"She was a smaller target - besides, they'll be ready for that now."

"So," said Wulf, "we can't get out, we can't go after her. There must be something we can do! I can't just wait here. All I can see is … that hole torn in poor Bess's back! And I want Weaver for that."

"Aye, I know, so do I."

58

7th February 1469, in the west range at Yoredale Castle

Hal led his three comrades from the second floor stairwell, keeping an arrow nocked in his bow. He crossed an open gallery, taking short, quick strides. There was no sudden flurry of arrows from the east range opposite and no sound of movement beyond the next door, which gave access to the nursery. They passed on through to the southwest tower and stood outside Joan Elder's chamber. Hal burst in and there was a scream as several servant girls retreated to the far wall.

"Is she here?" Hal whispered. They shook their heads vigorously but he spent a few more minutes making sure.

"Best stay here," he told them.

He left Joan's chamber and found the chapel door ajar. He stepped lightly over the threshold.

"Father?" he called softly. There was no answer.

Together Hal and the others walked through the chapel to the far door, where Hal paused. He had hoped that Father Baston might have seen Agnes. At the very least he expected to find the priest cowering at his altar, but he was not. Yet where else would a priest be?

By the time they found Father Baston in his cell, Hal had an idea what to expect. By the look of it, the priest had sold what he knew dearly. So, Lady Joan and probably by now, Thomas Gate, knew all Father Baston had to tell them. He sighed and patted the priest's chest and there, sticking to the blood on his vestments, Hal saw a long, fine thread of gold. He touched it, mesmerised by it. He squeezed his thumb and finger together to pick up the gleaming strand of hair.

Then, without a word, Hal took up his bow, left the cell and returned to the small door that led from the rear of the chapel to the passage by Grave's chamber. For a moment he paused in front of it and took a breath. He glanced back to his comrades.

"Wait here," he said and, ignoring their horrified warnings, he wrenched open the door.

"Agnes!" Her name echoed along the passage and a startled face appeared briefly at the far end by the garrison's sleeping quarters. In three paces Hal was at Grave's door. The door was ajar and he pushed it open. Grave was sitting against the wall, half-dressed and wholly dead. Someone had thrust a sword through his bare chest and a pool of congealed blood had formed between his legs. Of Agnes, there was no sign but he noticed spots of blood on the bed.

"Hal!" A chorus of voices implored him from the chapel door.

He stepped out into the passage and drew quickly back in as a shaft flew past his face. He put an arrow to his bow and eased himself into the doorway, slowly drawing back on the bow. Then he edged his head and shoulder over the threshold so he could see the passage end. He stood motionless, only a slight tremor in the muscles of his right arm betraying the strain of the bow. There was only so long he could hold, even an archer of his experience. Sweat began to form on his brow and the anger rose in him: this delay might be hurting Agnes for all he knew. Then a head, shoulders and bow came into view and Hal let fly at once.

"Come!" he called to his friends and they hurried to join him. He stepped out into the passage and went to the fallen archer. At twenty paces, he only had to hit something to kill - in fact his aim was true and only the goose feathers now protruded from his victim's chest.

"Shit!" he muttered, shaking his head. It was a raw youth who, only a few days before, Hal had been training at the butts.

They walked into the dormitory, weapons at the ready, but the room was empty.

"The garrison must be spread all over the castle," said Hal. "They only left this poor sod to watch the stair."

Hal peered down the spiral stairwell. They were in the south-east tower now, diagonally opposite where they had started at the postern gate. There was plenty of noise from below but he had no need to investigate there. He looked down from a narrow window facing out into the yard. Smoke was drifting across beneath them, obscuring his view until a sudden breath of wind cleared it. Then he glimpsed a tight knot of men moving cautiously across the yard towards the postern. He looked more closely and then beckoned his comrades to see. Each in turn glanced down and then looked at his fellows, ashen-faced. "God have mercy!" breathed one.

"We have to warn Bear!" said Hal, but at that moment they heard footsteps at the far end of the east range passage ahead of them. Several men at arms hurried out of the kitchen tower where the fire was. It also housed Thomas Gate's chamber. Seeing them, the men at arms faltered and came to a halt twenty feet away. For a short while the two groups stood and looked at each other. Until this morning all had eaten at the same table and had drunk ale together on cold winter evenings crowded around the Hall fire.

Hal took a pace towards them. "Let us by, lads," he said. "We're just looking for Agnes. No-one need get hurt here."

"Don't think we can, Hal," the leading man answered. "A line's been drawn and... we've all had to choose."

"You heard Lord Elder," pleaded Hal, "he has an arrest warrant from the king. Thomas Gate is raising men without the king's consent."

"Aye, but we are those men, Hal - you too. What

happens to us? We heard Gate too: the Earl of Warwick's backing him - who's backing you?"

Hal could feel the apprehension amongst his own comrades.

"Have you seen Agnes?" asked Hal. They shook their heads.

"Will you let us past to search for her?" he asked.

"Can't see how we can, Hal…"

"I'm sorry," said Hal. There were very few reasons he could have found to kill men who had lived and trained with him but Agnes was one such reason. He would find her no matter how many men tried to stop him. Swiftly his hand snatched an arrow from his bag and, in the blink of an eye, he nocked, drew and loosed it. The man he had just been talking to was driven back along the passage and dead by the time he hit the floor.

Wordlessly, Hal dropped the bow, dragged out his sword and knife and walked resolutely along the passage. After the briefest moment of hesitation, his comrades followed. He stepped over the dead man, whose companions fell back a few paces. Hal willed them to run, but they didn't, so he launched himself at them with fire in his heart. His anger flowed as he cut at arms and thrust at ribs and groin. He felt nothing but misery as he parried a heavy blow at his shoulder and drove his dagger into his opponent's throat.

He was not a great swordsman but at close quarters that often meant little. When the grisly grind of the struggle ceased, all their adversaries lay bleeding. Hal had received a cut to his leg but he found to his horror that two of his comrades had been struck down. One leant against the wall weeping with pain, his face battered in around cheek bone and eye socket. The other sat on the floor contemplating the rivulets of blood which poured from his torn stomach. Only one other man, Will Wright, was still standing.

"Go on," said Will, "I'll stay with them. You can pick us

up on your way back."

Hal did not move.

"Go!" urged Will, with a harsh edge to his voice. "Go, unless you want all this to be for nothing?"

Hal nodded and hurried through the door at the end of the passage into the north-east tower. Thomas Gate's chamber was on his right and he kicked the door open. The chamber was empty but for the smoke drifting up through the timber floor boards. He put his hand on the floor and pulled it away again sharply: the boards were red hot. The burning kitchen was directly below but he was surprised the fire had not been contained by its stone-vaulted hearth. The whole underside of the chamber floor must already be charred for it to feel so hot. Blood and fire... what next?

"Where are you, Agnes?" he muttered aloud.

Then he remembered Bear. Shit! He needed to warn him, tell him what he had seen in the yard! He dashed out of Gate's chamber and ran through the smoke across to the minstrels' gallery and there, below him in the Hall, he saw more men, equipped like those he had spotted in the courtyard. His bow lay twenty yards away in the east range where he had left it - yet he must be swift. There was only one swift path to the postern gate and that was through the Hall.

He started down the tower steps, feeling his way through the thick, oily smoke filling the kitchen stairwell. On the landing below, the smoke was denser still and the flames were hungrily consuming the ceiling beams. By the time he leapt past the blazing kitchen doorway, his eyes stung and tears streamed down his cheeks. He pushed on through into the butteries where the smoke was thinner and paused to wipe his face. He peered out into the Hall. In the far corner a clutch of men stood with their backs to him. There were about half a dozen of them, some still preparing their weapons for the attack on the postern gate. If he waited another moment, it would be too late. He sighed and drew his sword.

"An Elder, an Elder!" he shouted at the top of his voice and charged across the Hall. They swung around in alarm and scattered. There was a burst of flame and smoke. Something small and hot singed his ear on its way past and then he was upon them. He slashed his sword from side to side with clumsy strokes, carving his way out of the Hall door. No power, no artistry, just sheer terror. He passed through the door and met Bear on the way up the steps from the postern.

"Hand guns!" cried Hal, ducking behind the wall as another shot was fired from behind him.

"I heard," replied Bear, who seemed to take the news with calm indifference.

"They'll be coming through from the yard too!" said Hal.

"Get down!" Bear bellowed at his defenders, but it was too late.

The morning air was shattered by a succession of explosions not only from the direction of the Hall but also from the archway into the courtyard. Bear and the other men dived for cover but then a third group of hand gunners opened up from the adjacent north-west tower. Bear's men were trapped in the crossfire. Gouts of flame speared towards them carrying lead shot that at such close range was mortally effective. One man at arms, struck twice, was tossed back screaming into the wooden gate. A bewildered archer lay watching his life blood gush out from the artery in his shattered thigh.

The firing ceased but the sound of the gunfire still echoed in the narrow, walled space near the postern gate. Hal peered out but could see little. The smoke hung in the air and the acrid smell of burned black powder scoured his nostrils. After a few minutes, the air began to clear and Hal saw two of the archers change position, eager to get a sight of their opponents to inflict a little revenge.

"Wait!" Bear roared at them from the shelter of the Hall stairwell.

It was quiet but they could all hear the subtle sounds of the hand gunners reloading and shuffling into position.

Bear cursed. "Stay down!" he ordered but the two archers, unused to Bear, ignored his warning and stood ready with their arrows nocked at their bows.

"Get down!" cried Hal.

The archers glanced across to him and nodded but they stayed where they were. Hal understood for he was an archer: they wanted to make the hand gunners pay. They knew they could fire half a dozen arrows in the time it took a hand gunner to load and fire once. True enough, when the hand gunners edged out from behind the shelter of the walls, both archers let fly and two gunners fell. Then the rest of the gunners fired and lead balls exploded into the gate entrance to tear the archers apart. Their cries were pitiful but so terrible were their wounds that they died quickly.

"Now!" said Bear. He tore up the steps and hacked into the hand gunners in the Hall who were reloading. Hal could only watch as Bear's angry arm swept his axe in a merciless flurry of strokes. There were four gunners loading and they did not stand a chance against Bear. Hal followed him and stumbled over a fallen hand gun with a severed hand still gripping its stock. By the time Hal reached the rest he was only able to put one dying survivor out of his misery. Bear was already on his way back to the gate, absently wiping away the blood that had sprayed onto his face.

"We can't hold the postern gate, can we?" said Hal, following close behind him.

Bear shook his head and then ducked back as another irregular volley came from the gunners at the archway. In the lull that followed, the other survivors scrambled over to join them.

"The only way out is through the cellars," said Hal. He

could see that Bear was reluctant to leave the gate.

"We still have men," said Bear, looking around at the men at arms.

"We can do nothing here but die," Hal told him.

Bear shrugged. "Then I hold the gate till I die."

"Brave, but pointless," said Hal, "if you die at the gate then you'll die for nothing because you'll still lose the gate! Your lord needs his men elsewhere. Ned's lady is below - and his sister. Would you leave them defenceless? Now, come."

Even then he had to pull at Bear to get the man mountain to move and he grumbled as they descended the steps to the cellar where Croft was still waiting. The latter looked very relieved to see them.

Lady Maighread looked up as they entered.

"Come, my lady," said Hal, "we must go."

"I'm not leaving this castle without Ned," she said.

"No, my lady," said Hal, "neither are we."

Lady Maighread helped Emma up and they linked arms to support each other.

Hal began to have second thoughts: was he doing the right thing? Their way out of the castle, the postern gate, was lost. All he could do was try to get those who were left safely to Lord Elder - then let him decide. The cellar would take them into the darkness of the store rooms where they might be safe - or they might be trapped. Then there was the fire to consider, they would be heading nearer to it... but nowhere was safe.

"Come," he said, leading them through the cellar door.

He tried to sound calm but in his head a plaintive voice was imploring Agnes, wherever she was, to stay safe until he found her.

59

7th February 1469, in the cellars at Yoredale Castle

Ned needed no torch in the cellars for he knew them well enough to find his way by touch alone. Soon Gate would decide to send men to search back through them. Ned's plans lay in ruins. He had underestimated Gate - he should have known that such a bold fighting man would inspire other men to follow him.

He passed through the wine cellar with more caution and then stopped to listen at the doorway to the well chamber. He heard voices and, easing the door open a crack, he was relieved to see Ragwulf and Wulf by the well. He swung open the door and both men looked around in surprise, their swords half-drawn before they recognised him.

"By God, you gave me shock, lord!" said Ragwulf. "That's the only way I thought was clear!"

"Aye, well it still is. Have you seen Lady Eleanor or the boy?" asked Ned.

"Lady Eleanor ran upstairs after Joan and the lad," replied Ragwulf, "but the damned archers have got us penned in here now. Your sister's hurt, my lord."

"Aye, I know. So are you, it seems," said Ned.

Ragwulf shrugged.

"So, what are our choices?" asked Ned.

"We can't go up now for the fire, can't go out for the archers, and there's not much to gain by going back," said Ragwulf. "We've just been looking at that chamber door opposite."

"It's just another store chamber," said Ned.

"In your day, lord, but there's so many men here now it's used as an armoury and weapon store," said Wulf.

"As I recall, you can pass through it to the main gatehouse," said Ragwulf, "and there's another stair not far beyond the gatehouse."

"So, we could reach Eleanor," concluded Ned, "if we could get up the steps at the other end of the east range…"

"Aye, 'if,'" said Ragwulf. "But there'll be plenty of men at the main gate…"

"It's our only hope," said Wulf.

"I'll go first, lord," said Ragwulf, "I've already got one arrow in me."

"So? How many are you looking for?" replied Ned. "I'll go first this time. Let me get the door open and I'll wave you over."

"There could be men in the weapon store," said Wulf.

"Then I'll invite them to join us!" retorted Ned. "Now, be ready to move fast!"

Ned moved to the archway and took a deep breath. He was about to launch himself across the opening to the door when there was a fusillade of bangs from somewhere else in the castle.

"What in God's name was that?" he whispered.

"Go! Go now!" shouted Ragwulf. So Ned did. Like Ragwulf, he realised that others would have been distracted too. He crossed to the door in two bounds and wrenched up the latch. The door was stiff and he had to put his shoulder to it to force it open. The noise he made alerted the archers in the yard but their belated arrows struck the wall harmlessly in the empty stairwell. Ragwulf and his son then hurled themselves through after him and Ragwulf slammed the door shut.

Ned looked at Ragwulf. "Tell me that wasn't hand gunners we just heard!"

"At least half a dozen, I'd say, maybe more…" said Ragwulf. "Came from behind us… the postern gate."

"Blood of Christ!" Ned felt as if he'd taken a lead shot himself - deep in the pit of his stomach.

"My lord, you've got the most experienced soldier in the land at the postern," said Ragwulf. "Trust him. If Bear can't hold it, then no-one can."

"I know," said Ned, but he found it hard to ignore the fact that the woman he regarded as his wife must now be a good deal less safe than he had envisaged.

He examined the store room. The door at the far end which gave access to the gatehouse was closed and he walked over to block it with a few barrels. A single torch burned on a wall bracket by the door but since it was a long, windowless chamber and piled high with barrels, boxes and arms, the light was still very dim.

"Damn me, but it's smoky in here!" he observed. "Thank God stone doesn't burn."

"The stone won't have to burn," said Ragwulf, glancing up at the ceiling where some of the joist were already charred and smoking. "Any time now those beams will catch light. Look at this place: timber racks, barrels. Aye, there's plenty to burn here."

"We can put the fire out later!" said Wulf. "We've other tasks first!"

"Aye, Wulf," said his father slowly, "but what do you think is in all those barrels stacked against the wall?"

Wulf studied the barrels for a moment and his head dropped. "Black powder," he murmured.

"Aye, and enough to turn half the castle into a heap of rubble!" said Ragwulf.

"How in God's name did Gate get so much powder?" demanded Ned.

"It's been coming in ever since I've been here," said Wulf. "Some say it comes from the Warwick's garrison at Calais but I think they mix it nearer here - perhaps at

Middleham."

"Well, I don't think we'd make it to the well to douse it with water," said Ragwulf. "Could we move it?"

Ned shook his head. "We haven't time. We'll just have to pray the fighting's done before it needs moving…"

As if to emphasise his point there was a loud crash as something, or someone, thudded against the door by which they had just come in.

"Come on," he said, "we need to get after Eleanor." He drew his sword and went to the other door.

Wulf swiftly dragged aside the barrels Ned had stacked in front of it. Ragwulf sheathed his sword and rummaged amongst the stack of weapons. He picked out a long bill.

"I think I'll try this," he said. "It's going to be rough out there…"

"Keep to the side," said Ned, "in case of an archer."

He swung open the door. There was no archer but a hand gunner, who stood barely ten feet away and appeared as surprised as Ned was. Ned stared at the hand gun with only one thought and his answer came at once in a blast of smoke and fire.

60

7th February 1469, in the privy chamber at Yoredale Castle

Agnes shut the door to the privy chamber and stopped open-mouthed. Lady Joan sat with her back towards the narrow loopholes in the outer wall: from there she could see the two doors into the room. She stared at Agnes, a look of contempt on her grey, blood-smeared face. When Agnes tore her gaze from the face, she was horrified at what else she saw. Joan had one bloody hand clamped to her waist but the other held a long blade and its point rested on the neck of the small boy, John. The boy whose wounds she had salved after his whipping… the boy with Hal. John looked at Agnes with a miserable expression on his face.

"You…" said Lady Joan. She sounded weary but not cowed and the hand that held the knife did not tremble. The lady looked like death, thought Agnes, but she still had some strength left. Agnes took a step towards her.

"You're Walter Grave's little bitch, aren't you," said Joan. "We're all whores to them, you know, but you might be of some use to me. They promised to send me someone. They won't… but you're something of a healer aren't you?"

Agnes gave a slow nod.

"Well, come here and look at my wound then."

Agnes hesitated.

"Come," insisted Joan, "or I'll cut the boy!"

Agnes hurried over to her and gently tried to remove Joan's hand to examine the wound.

"Be very careful, girl," said Joan, and pressed the knife

harder into John's flesh, pricking the soft skin on the side of his neck. Agnes swallowed hard as she saw a small speck of blood appear.

Joan lifted her hand from her belly and winced as Agnes examined it. She was losing blood slowly but steadily through a long tear in her stomach. Agnes tried pressing hard on the site of the wound and kept her hand there for as long as she could. When she released the pressure, blood began oozing out again almost at once. She had seen few such wounds. Her experience was limited to setting broken bones, applying salves or mixing pain-relieving potions. Yet even her inexperienced eye told her that Joan was certain to die and, though she could not say it, Joan read it in her face at once.

"You're no use! I need a surgeon… I know, or I'm dead. I know that. Now you know it too, but it'll do you no good. I have nothing left to lose and I'll kill this boy without a care. And, if by some carelessness on God's part, Ned Elder should somehow triumph, you two will be my hostages. I'm sure Ned hasn't forgotten you, my dear. Sit here, by the boy, at my feet."

Agnes crouched down beside John on the floor. Joan's knife, she noticed, remained on John. The lad would certainly run if the point wasn't actually on him - boys were like that.

"Do you know who this little boy is?" Joan asked her suddenly.

Agnes shook her head.

"He's Ned Elder's son, isn't that just perfect? I can't tell you how much it means to me to have this boy here… under my knife."

Agnes searched the boy's face and smiled: the likeness was obvious once you knew. Her eyes met his and he smiled back. She took his hand to offer him encouragement.

"Take care," murmured Joan.

A sudden, staccato burst of noise made them all jump. Joan's knife cut into John's neck and he yelped. Agnes squeezed his hand.

"That will be our gunners," said Joan, with a defiant smile, "and Ned Elder will have no answer to that. It might be over sooner than I thought. There might yet be a way out for me. We'll just have to wait it out together, won't we?"

Agnes looked up at Joan, trying to assess how swiftly she was weakening - you could only lose so much blood, she thought. Joan would begin to lose her grip on the knife and when that happened she must be ready to snatch John away. For the first time in many months, she felt alive with purpose. Here was hope of redemption... and to think she had almost thrown her life away.

The door she had entered by swung open abruptly and Lady Eleanor Elder stood in the doorway. Agnes felt Joan tense and the knife pricked John again. The boy trembled and gripped her hand more tightly. Lady Eleanor took in the scene without a word. Then she gave Agnes an almost imperceptible nod and darted out as swiftly as she had appeared.

"You want to scream, girl, don't you?" said Joan softly. "Oh, but of course... you can't, can you?"

But Agnes did not want to scream; she had hope and she was not alone.

§§§§

Hal reached the wine cellar and stopped. What was he to do? He had nine men at arms, one archer and Bear - not exactly an army. They could not simply wander around the castle with the two injured ladies. Through the next door was the well chamber and, beyond that, the kitchen afire. The wine cellar, though, was defensible and as good a place as any for them to wait.

Bear was looking at him, waiting. "Did you bar the cellar

door?" he asked him.

Bear nodded.

"My ladies," he said, "we must leave you here - it'll be safer and Croft will stay with you."

"But where are the others?" asked Lady Maighread.

"I don't know, my lady," he confessed, "but I'll find them."

Bear gave him a doubtful look and then lifted down two barrels for the women to sit on.

"When we've gone, put a hogshead against the door," Hal told Croft.

Then he opened the door through to the well chamber. It was empty. The floor was damp and the air smoky. The spiral stairwell outside it was so choked with smoke Hal couldn't see out into the yard. He bent down and picked up a broken arrow shaft. The traces of blood on it were barely dry.

Just as he took another step towards the courtyard, several men at arms appeared through the smoky haze. It took each group of men a moment to decide whether they had found friend or foe. Most hesitated or, like Hal, took a pace back in surprise. Bear did neither: he cleaved his axe down the face and chest of the first man - not a deep wound, but terrifying to see, let alone feel. The man screamed until Bear crushed his throat with a blow from the end of the axe head.

There was a hiatus of horror and then every man attacked at once and in the small chamber it was chaos. Blows fell upon Hal so fast he could hardly parry them all and he was soon driven back to the well. By then the room was choked with men, crushed together in bloody discord.

The desperate combatants grappled toe to toe. Most drew knives, wrestling for a chance to stab their opponents somewhere vital, but others fought with any means. One of Scales' men at arms butted his helmet into the face of an adversary and then seized the man's head to smash it against the wall half a dozen times. Hal felt a dagger graze his thigh and reached down to prise the weapon aside as he tried to bring his own knife to bear. An archer's arm was his one advantage in a struggle from which only the strongest would emerge. He grabbed his opponent by the throat and levered his head back. Then he stabbed - three swift stabs into the groin - until the poor man slid down in agony. Hal thought he was finished but the fellow, still sobbing with pain, managed to plunge his knife through Hal's calf. Hal cried out and cursed his folly as Bear kicked the wounded man in the neck until he lay still.

Then, with shocking suddenness, it was over. Hal leant against the brickwork around the well shaft, breathing hard and trying to take stock. The floor was littered with bodies. There was blood everywhere. Four of the garrison lay dead or dying at their feet but his last archer, Ruskin, had taken two wounds and was bleeding profusely. Dere, one of Lord Scales' men at arms, dragged him back to the wine cellar.

"Did any of them get out?" Hal asked Bear. The big man spread his hands and shrugged. It was too hard to tell in the smoke. It was a miracle they had not struck down each other.

"Well, I think we can assume they know we're here now," said Hal.

Bear nodded and casually wiped his axe blade on a dead man's sleeve. Hal tore off a strip of cloth and sat on the floor to bind up his leg. The blade had cut badly enough to make him limp and it would slow him down - but only a little.

"How many out there, do you think?" he asked Bear.

"Too many," replied Bear.

They edged out of the archway where the heat from the fire felt stronger and the smoke still billowed out. Hal tried to catch a glimpse of the courtyard but could make out little and soon his eyes stung too much so he pulled back.

"Shit! Where did Lord Elder go?" he muttered.

61

7th February 1469, in the weapon store at Yoredale Castle

Ned felt the lance of heat singe his side as the hot piece of metal shot past him. Then in a breath the hand gunner was dead, near cut in half by Wulf's swift sword.

"Quick! Outside!" said Ned. "Make for the tower steps and then up to the privy chamber."

He led them out into the yard where they found at least a score of men at arms waiting for them, no doubt alerted by the roar of the hand gun.

"Oh, shit!" said Wulf and launched himself into the throng. Ned watched them fall back, before the youth's mortal blade. Ned dared not hold back for he knew that this tiny moment of surprise was all they would have.

"An Elder, an Elder!" he shouted as he carved his way towards the tower steps alongside Wulf. Ragwulf followed and swept the curved bill blade around in an arc, cutting two men at arms and forcing the others back. But despite his efforts, the crowd of men closed in around them. Ned fought in his own private rage, hacking down men whose faces he neither saw nor cared to see. These men stood between him and his son, between him and his sister… and he would kill every one if he had to. He had offered them quarter and they had spurned it; well, now they would pay for it.

At first Ned thought they would make it but the press of men around them was growing and they were left with no space in which to wield their swords. All they could do was defend themselves whilst Ragwulf kept men from their backs by swinging his lethal bill from side to side. Then Ned noticed Thomas Gate in the yard, barely twenty feet away from him and leaning on his sword as if he had not a care in the world. Gate waved back his men at arms and pointed to his archers.

Gate smiled across at him. "Give it up, Ned!" he shouted. "You've lost! There's no reason any more men should die... and I do have your son."

It was a blow, though Ned had never even seen his son, let alone held him or spoken to him. The awful possibility occurred to him that he would never do any of those things. But was Gate telling him the truth? He attempted to edge his way towards the tower, which was still a few yards away.

"We might get you as far as the steps, lord," said Ragwulf, "after that, it'll be just you… but you'd have a chance of getting the lad, then getting back to the postern."

Ned knew that such a plan would not include escape for Ragwulf or his son - was one man's son worth more than another's?

As he hesitated, a roar came from the gate near the well chamber and out of the black smoke erupted Hal, Bear and the rest of his men at arms. They charged Gate's archers, throwing them into confusion. Ned had never been so pleased to see Bear and the raging warrior did not disappoint him, wreaking death wherever he went. Those who were quick enough to turn and face the fearsome Bear died just as swiftly as those who didn't. The rest tried to flee across the yard and as they did so, Ragwulf went forward to slash his bill across their backs and cut several to shreds. None of Gate's archers escaped alive.

Now Hal's men joined Ragwulf and formed a common line before the east range. Gate himself drew back to the stables opposite with his remaining men at arms. Ned thanked God for their small victory but knew that Bear's very presence in the yard meant that he had lost the postern gate - their way out. On the other hand, they were standing right in front of the main gate.

"We won't have long, lord," whispered Ragwulf, "but time perhaps to get up the stairs and down again?"

Ned gave him a nod. "Aye, you'd better come with me."

Ragwulf gave his bill to Hal and drew his sword. "Hold the line here, lad," he said with a dour smile.

Ned darted towards the steps and Ragwulf followed. Ned took a final glance back to see that Hal, Wulf and the others had shuffled over to form a screen of men in front of the tower entrance.

They hurried up the spiral stair but halfway up a sword crashed against Ned's helm, knocking him back. Ragwulf did well to catch him before he tumbled down the steps but the damage was done: the stairwell was a blur before his eyes.

"Blood of Christ!" raged Ned. His head felt hot and bruised as if he had stuffed it into a bread oven and banged it from side to side. He should have known Gate had men above the gatehouse. They came on down and Ragwulf could only parry the repeated thrusts aside with Ned sitting crumpled upon one of the lower steps.

"Two men, I think, lord!" cried Ragwulf, but a familiar voice from above them yelled: "only one now!"

Even in his befuddled state, Ned rejoiced to hear his sister's voice.

The man at arms on the steps half-turned to look behind him. Ragwulf seized the chance and lunged up at him only to strike the wall. Nevertheless, the knight swayed back and then fell, rolling down past Ragwulf to come to rest at Ned's feet, choking noisily on his own blood. Ragwulf looked down at him, shook his head and removed Eleanor's knife from the back of his neck. Then he put an arm round Ned's shoulder and helped him up to the landing.

There Eleanor awaited them, standing over the body of

the other man at arms. Ned was mightily relieved to find that his vision was clearing as Eleanor hugged him. Then she embraced Ragwulf in a rather different kind of embrace which involved a lengthy kiss on the lips.

"I missed something… somewhere, didn't I?" said Ned.

Eleanor gave him a wry smile. "For a time, brother, I thought we were all going to miss it."

"Did you find John?" asked Ragwulf.

Eleanor's expression hardened. "Aye, but Joan has him in the privy chamber… Agnes too, Ned."

Ned sighed. "We have only a few moments - men are going to die down there to give us this brief chance. We must use it well."

"I'll go in," said Eleanor, "for she already knows I'm up here. You two wait by this door whilst I go in the other. Don't come in unless I call you - if I do, come with all speed…"

"We'll be ready," said Ned.

"What are you going to do?" asked Ragwulf.

"Oh, I'll think of something," she replied and kissed him on the cheek.

"How's the wound?" he asked her.

"It only bleeds when I move. Yours?"

"It's but an inconvenience."

"Liar."

"Take care, my lady," he said softly and held out the knife hilt to her. She took it, gripping his hand for a long moment before concealing the blade under her kirtle. Then she walked unsteadily along the smoke-filled passage.

"I think she's hurt more than she lets on," said Ned.

"I know she is," said Ragwulf.

They moved along a short passage a few paces to wait at the other door to the privy chamber but then they heard footsteps coming down the stair from the second floor. They exchanged a glance and returned to the stairwell, poised to strike.

A face peered cautiously down around the central pillar of the spiral and they breathed a sigh of relief.

"Come down, Will," said Ragwulf, "and keep on going to the bottom. They could do with another man down there."

Will Wright gave a wave and headed down the steps. Ned and Ragwulf once more crossed into the passage and approached the door of the privy chamber.

§§§§

Dense smoke was drifting across the courtyard and Hal, who had been keeping an eye on the door to the well chamber, suddenly realised he couldn't see it - yet it was only a dozen or so yards away. A pall of smoke swirled around the kitchen tower. The wind had freshened a little and turned northerly to drive the fire back along the east range.

"What is it?" asked Wulf.

"Lady Maighread and Lady Emma are still in the wine cellar," said Hal, "and the only way to get to them is the way we came out by the well. As long as I could see that doorway, I'd know if anyone passed through there."

"So, what do we do?" asked Wulf.

"There's nothing we can do. They'll be safer where they are - for now."

"Gate's got no archers," said Wulf.

"Neither have we," returned Hal.

"We have you, Hal," said Will Wright coming out of the tower. "I rescued these," he added, handing Hal his bow and arrow bag.

"What of our comrades?" he asked.

Will shook his head. "I stayed with them…"

Hal nodded and then weighed the arrow bag in his hand - it was almost empty.

"I'll save my few arrows," he said, "they've got hand

gunners remember, and it won't be long before Gate uses them."

"They'll likely be short of powder by now," said Wulf.

"Says the man who knows nothing about hand guns," replied Hal.

"Well they must be," said Wulf. "And they have to go through us to get to the powder store."

"There are more arrows in there too," said Hal.

"Aye," said Wulf, "and some bills too - easier to keep them at arms' length if we're fighting out here."

"Will," said Hal, "go into the arms store and see what you can find? If only we had more men."

Will stepped carefully over the corpse of the hand gunner in the doorway and disappeared into the powder store.

A moment later Hal's heart sank, for several hand gunners appeared at the arch from the postern gate.

"Shit!" muttered Wulf.

"Take cover!" shouted Hal and dived down onto the cobbles, hoping the others were quick enough to fall flat or close enough to the doorways to dart inside. The guns spat smoke and flame across the courtyard and shots of lead ricocheted around the stone walls. The noise was deafening and Hal covered his ears, waiting for the echoes to fade. When he looked around he was astonished to find that no-one was hit.

He quickly strung his bow and nocked an arrow. He was not short of targets and let fly. He managed to loose two more arrows and, unlike the gunners, he did not miss. The rest of the gunners stepped back through the arch to continue reloading.

Then, out of the corner of his eye, Hal noticed a sudden movement to his left: it was Weaver hurrying from the stables through the door at the west end of the yard with one or two others following. They were going to come through the ground floor rooms in the south range: the bake house and the brew house - and there was no-one there to stop them!

"Hal!" cried Will Wright.

"Not now!" retorted Hal.

Hal released his last arrow. With Weaver going through the south range and the hand gunners firing from the arch, Gate and his men at arms started walking slowly towards them across the yard. The noose was closing around their necks.

"Hal!" cried Will again.

"What? What is it?" he demanded."

"You should look at the weapon store!" cried Will.

"What, now?"

"Aye, now!"

Hal hurried to the store and Will pointed to the far wall.

"Oh, sweet Jesus," breathed Hal, for the wall adjacent to the kitchen, lined from floor to ceiling with rack upon rack of powder barrels, was engulfed in flame. Hal stared at the smouldering barrels in disbelief. Then another small fusillade outside forced him to go back out into the yard once more.

He ran to Bear. "The powder store's alight!" he hissed.

Bear reacted with trace of a frown.

"Lord Elder, Ragwulf, all of them…they're all up in the east range…" said Hal.

"Get them out," growled Bear. "We'll hold the tower steps."

"I'll bring them all back down to join you," said Hal, "but watch your backs, Weaver's heading through the south range!"

Hal headed for the tower steps and Wulf followed. "Go!" said Wulf. "I'll take care of Weaver."

Hal ran into the tower. He was dimly aware of a figure on his right and glanced around. It wasn't Weaver but a hand gunner who must have been sent on ahead. For an instant Hal froze, unsure whether to turn and fight or hasten up to warn the others. He knew Wulf was behind him so he went on, mounting the first two steps. Then there was a sudden crash as the hand gun fired below him. Too late, he ducked and the shot struck the central pillar of the spiral stair, scattering tiny chips of stone into his face.

§§§§

Wulf saw the hand gunner a split second before he fired up the steps. He leant into the cover of the arch wall and then ran at the gunner who threw down his gun to draw out his sword. Wulf heard footsteps coming through the south range to his right, perhaps only yards away. The gunner had barely got his sword out when Wulf's blade plunged into his chest. He wore no armour, just a padded leather jack, and the sword sliced easily through it. He dragged out his blade and let the gunner fall.

The sharp head of a bill poked out of the passage to the south range. A long bill was hardly a weapon for close work, thought Wulf, as he let the sharp point brush past him, seized the wooden shaft and pulled it hard. The oncoming man fell headlong and Wulf brought his sword swinging down across the man's back, near cutting him in half. His scream was short-lived.

Wulf waited for the next man to appear but no-one did. He was expecting Weaver but Weaver was canny, clever. He had sent his fellows first, taking no risks. Wulf glanced quickly back to the steps, feeling he was being watched. There was his father, a grim, proud smile on his face. Ragwulf said nothing but gave him a curt nod of approval. Wulf smiled back at him and turned back to the south range.

He stepped over the fallen bill man and went carefully along the passage, expecting another man at arms to appear before him at any moment. He reached the end of the passage and stepped into the first chamber, which was a large grain store. He glanced around the room at the sacks of meal and flour... It was still winter and stores were low, even so some sacks were still piled high. Weaver stepped into the doorway from the brew house.

Wulf nodded. This man was all he cared about now.

"All alone?" said Weaver. "Now, is that wise, boy?"

"I'm going to kill you," said Wulf, "for my Bess."

"Ah, Bess… a pretty lass," replied Weaver, "but not worth much blood, surely. She was a wench like any other, I'd say."

Wulf took a pace towards him. Weaver had not yet drawn his sword - how could he be so confident? Wulf took another step. Weaver did not move.

"You grow careless, Weaver," he said.

"Aye, but not as careless as you, lad." Weaver grinned and Wulf suddenly worked it out. He whirled around to face the pile of sacks in the corner, but too late. A knife struck him as he moved and slit him under the ribs. He gasped but his sword carried on swinging and almost decapitated his assailant. The damage was done though for now Weaver had his sword out and swung it hard down at Wulf's shoulder. He blocked it, the blade held an inch from his body, then he forced Weaver back. Time was on Weaver's side for they both knew that Wulf was bleeding badly.

Weaver stood off him, inviting him to make the next move, knowing he must before he bled too much. Wulf shut out the pain of the wound - cursing himself for his carelessness. His wound was but a scratch compared to the foul, gaping chasm that Weaver had put through his love's breast. He was breathing hard, yet he had barely exerted himself. His sword point was on the stone flags and the weapon felt heavy in his hand.

Weaver noticed it too. "Like a rest?" he asked. "Don't worry: you'll be getting a very long one soon."

Wulf tried to clear his mind. Thinking of Bess now was

only clouding his judgement. He was hurt, that's all.

"I've been hurt before," he said to Weaver.

"I haven't," replied Weaver. "Never a scratch on me."

"Aye, you get others to bleed for you," said Wulf. Then he realised that Weaver was just delaying him with his words, letting his blood flow out until he was too weak to fight. Wulf moved as swiftly as he could and at his best he was lightning fast. He gave no hint nor warning but brought his sword blade up to cut at Weaver's groin. His aim was astray but he cut Weaver's thigh, slicing up through his elbow as he tried to parry. Weaver did not even cry out. He gave a grunt of pain and briefly glanced at his arm where blood dripped.

"You've a scratch now," said Wulf.

Weaver said nothing but now he was losing blood so they both had reason for haste. Wulf backed away towards the door, encouraging Weaver to come fully into the chamber, which he had to do.

"Do your worst," said Weaver. "It won't be enough."

He crossed the floor in two strides and hacked at Wulf's midriff. Wulf went forward to meet him and the two wounded men slashed and cut at each other, sparing nothing. They twisted and turned to avoid the other's sword and strike a killing blow with their own. Wulf's blade rattled on Weaver's breastplate, carved through his gambeson, sliced his leg open and cut his shoulder blade, but Weaver cut him badly in return.

Neither let up. Neither seemed to notice as the pitiless steel mutilated their bodies. Neither used knife or buckler - just their swords. Both were tiring, bleeding from wounds that would never heal, yet their will forced them on until the end came in a flurry of scything strokes. Weaver's sword evaded Wulf's breastplate and plunged through his side and, as it punched through muscle and lung, Wulf's own sword completed a final, bloody arc, cutting into Weaver's neck, slicing through windpipe and artery.

The two men let go of their swords and stood for an instant longer. Wulf saw the gush of blood from Weaver's throat and smiled. Weaver buckled to his knees and leant against Wulf. Wulf backed away to let him fall. Weaver's blade was still lodged in his chest and a sudden wave of excruciating pain hit him. He coughed up some blood and spat it out - that hurt even more and he felt faint. He looked down at the offending weapon. He tried to lift his arms. The left one no longer obeyed but he gripped the blade in his right hand and slowly, inch by inch, pulled it out. Blood poured from the gaping wound and he leant back against the wall. His breath came in short gulps of blood and air.

He tried to walk with the aid of Weaver's sword but at the door he slid to the floor, weeping with pain. He sat then upon the threshold with his hand on the wound and watched the blood pump out between his fingers until the agony ended. He felt nothing, heard nothing and lay with but one last thought in his head: Bess.

62

7th February 1469, in the east range at Yoredale Castle

Eleanor took a deep breath and opened the door to the privy chamber. The chamber was smoke-filled now and flames were creeping up around the edges of the floor, reaching for the thick woollen wall hangings. In all other respects, the scene had not changed at all. Joan, a little paler perhaps than before, sat with Agnes and John at her feet, the knife point still resting on John's neck.

"You again?" said Joan. "Not dead yet then, bitch?"

Eleanor slowly unlaced her kirtle a little to reveal her bleeding breast and took several staggering steps towards Joan.

"It won't be long for either of us," she murmured. "Why not let the girl and the boy go? We can just sit here together and see who dies first…"

"Get out," said Joan. She sounded weary now.

Eleanor spoke almost in a whisper. "You don't mean that: you'd love to take me with you. But killing a child? Surely even you wouldn't go that far?"

Joan gave a slow shake of the head. "You forget: I thought I'd already killed him while he was still squirming inside his mother's belly."

Eleanor's jaw tightened and every instinct she possessed urged her to spring forward and plunge her knife into Joan Elder's throat. But she did not. She did though take another pace forward because she needed to get closer.

"Stay there," warned Joan.

"You're getting weaker," breathed Eleanor.

"Not weak enough to fall to you," murmured Joan. She scratched the knife slowly across John's skin. "It's so soft. It won't take much to cut him open… from ear to ear."

Eleanor bit her bottom lip and glanced at Agnes. The girl met her eyes; she looked alert, ready. Eleanor looked again at Joan. She could not see how to free the lad unless Joan let fall the knife and those flint eyes told her that Joan would kill the boy long before she reached such a point of weakness.

A shot very close by made them all jump and Agnes struck like a bird of prey. She clamped both her hands around Joan's knife hand.

"Run, John!" cried Eleanor, and he did, darting over to her as Agnes grappled with Joan and dragged her onto the floor.

"Ned!" cried Eleanor. "Ragwulf!"

But Ned did not come, nor Ragwulf. Eleanor pushed the boy behind her towards the door. If they did not come, she would have to finish this with Agnes.

§§§§

Ned stood with his ear against the door of the privy chamber but could hear no sound through it. He wanted to be ready - the instant Eleanor called for him, he would be through that door, sword in hand. The shots outside worried him and he began to wonder whether there would be anyone left when they got back down to the yard. Ragwulf too stood nearby, ashen-faced. Poor man, his love was up here and his son in the yard - and both in mortal peril.

Smoke funnelled along the range and filled the small passage. It was getting harder to breathe. Then footsteps sounded once more on the spiral stair close by.

"Stay here," Ned whispered, "I'll go." He backed away

and Ragwulf moved up to the door.

Ned was relieved to see Hal coming up the steps, but the youth's face bore a worried frown. There was a deafening roar, a spurt of flame and Hal screamed. The explosion of sound reverberated around the stairwell and rocked Ned back against the wall. His head crashed into the wall and he shuddered with pain. He staggered backwards, let fall his sword and tore off his helm. Thunder rolled inside his head. Lightning flashes stabbed his temples rekindling his old wound. He dropped onto his knees and his eyes fell upon Hal. Brave, loyal Hal with his face a mask of blood.

"Lord..." breathed Hal and tried to rise. Ned wanted to comfort him, but he could not speak. His head still rang and his vision was blurred. Ragwulf appeared beside him and then went down to Hal.

Ned clambered to his feet and leant against the wall at the top of the steps. Somewhere a gunner would be reloading.

"Get him!" he slurred at Ragwulf, but he did not need telling. Hal was trying to crawl up the steps and Ragwulf vaulted past him into the smoke, sword in hand. There was a stifled cry and a moment later Ragwulf re-appeared.

"Weaver..." muttered Hal.

"One thing at a time, lad," said Ragwulf. "Wulf's accounted for that one at least."

The echoes hammering in Ned's skull began to subside and in some shattered recess of his mind he knew he should be doing something. The stairwell and passage were murky with smoke. Soon Ragwulf was at the top of the steps once more with Hal hanging onto his shoulder. Ned staggered towards them to help but Ragwulf suddenly stood very still, eyes fixed upon a point behind Ned.

Eleanor! Ned suddenly remembered what he should be doing and turned back towards the passage. Then he stared across to the door of the privy chamber where, on the threshold and wreathed in smoke, a small boy stood in the open doorway.

§§§§

"Ned!" Eleanor cried again but the door remained firmly shut. Good Christ! Where were they? Agnes was still wrestling with Joan for the knife. Joan was weakening fast and Agnes would soon get the better of her but Eleanor did not want to leave it to chance. She took John's hand and pulled him to the door, but he glared at her and tugged against her, shouting "No!" and pointing back to Agnes.

Eleanor gasped with pain - the boy did not know it but he was tearing open her wound and she could feel the blood trickling down her breast.

"Come, John!" she pleaded with him. "Don't worry. I'll help Agnes, as soon as I get you out."

She took him to the door and wrenched it open. There was no-one there and all that came in was a little more smoke. She stood John in the doorway. "Don't move!" she told him. "I'll help Agnes."

She reached for her knife but it seemed now a great effort. She held it tightly and went back into the chamber. Time seemed not to pass as Eleanor approached the two women struggling on the floor to gain control of the knife. It was still in Joan's hands but they were slick with blood and Agnes suddenly lost her grip. Then Agnes made a lunge for the hilt but clasped only the blade. Joan sliced it through her fingers and reached for the seat of the chair to drag herself up. Agnes' bloody hands tore at her clothes to drag her back.

Eleanor took another step towards them but her legs gave way under her and she fell onto her knees. She felt faint but willed herself to crawl forward. Before she knew it, John was kneeling beside her, hugging her and trying to lift her. She shook her head.

"Go, John… please," she said, her eyes still fixed upon

Joan Elder. But the boy would not leave her.

She saw Agnes reach up for Joan's knife again. Joan stabbed down at her.

"Go, John!" pleaded Eleanor. "If you have any love for me, go. Your father's outside." At least she hoped he was. To her relief, John began to back away towards the door.

Joan got to her knees. Good Christ! Where did the woman find the strength? Her blood was all over the floor. Eleanor edged towards her, also on her knees, taking short, shallow breaths to ease the pain. Blood dripped from her wound onto the floor but she ignored it. Had she not faced death before and overcome it? All she would need was one clear strike.

They slithered towards each other until they were only half a yard apart, grim faces stained with blood, hands squeezing their weapons tight. The floor beneath them rumbled strangely but neither woman so much as blinked and in that instant both lunged forward with their knives.

§§§§

Ned's instinct was to rush forward at once and scoop the lad up but his legs felt like two great blocks of masonry. He could only drag himself a pace nearer the door and felt unsteady as if the floor itself was moving, shuddering. Then the building growled at him and Ragwulf shouted from the stairs.

There was a sheet of light and a wave of searing heat. The boy flew towards him and caught him full in the chest. Together they were tossed back down the steps into Ragwulf and Hal. The four sprawled down the spiral stair in a tangle of bodies. Chunks of stone as large as a man's head crashed into the walls all around. Shards of wood and plaster speared at them out of the smoke. An angry blast of sound swept over them - a deafening, shrieking howl that crackled like the wrath of God and seemed to last forever.

And when it did end, the final echoes spawned a storm of grit and splinters. Fragments of stone and timber fell like rain and Ned seemed to hear every tiny sound until each piece came to rest. Then, when only dust was left to fall, there came silence - an eerie, empty silence.

63

7th February 1469, in the wine cellar at Yoredale Castle

The large barrel upon which Maighread was seated began to vibrate. She glanced across to Emma and could see that she felt it too. Croft, who had been squatting on the floor, began to get slowly to his feet when a sudden blast of noise shook the whole cellar. One of the wooden racks collapsed and a hogshead of wine crashed to the floor and burst open, sending a red tide washing across the floor. Maighread snatched her feet up and sat still, waiting. There was a crack of timber and an entire row of tuns rolled off the end of a splintered rack. The first one caught Croft on the shoulder and knocked him off balance. The next two followed him onto the floor and disintegrated all over him.

Maighread and Emma both leant forward to go to him but the next shockwave threw them off the barrels. The torch too was swept to the floor and extinguished. All was pitch black. There was a crash as something large and heavy thudded into the door from the well chamber. Wood splinters flew through the dust-filled air. One embedded itself in Maighread's scarred cheek and she shrieked more in shock than pain.

The roar reverberated around the cellar and then gradually subsided, leaving them with a deathly stillness. In the darkness Maighread explored the contours of her face, found the large splinter and drew it out with a trembling hand.

"Emma?" she said.

"Aye, I'm alright," came the reply at once.

"Master Croft?"

There was no answer. Maighread had seen him go down. She felt around her with her hands. She was lying in an inch or so of wine. Her fingers scraped on sharp pieces of stone and wood.

"Emma, come towards my voice," she said and after a few moments she could hear Emma splashing across the floor. A hand brushed her arm and she gripped it tightly in hers.

"Let's find Croft," she said.

When she moved onto her knees, she felt her wound open up again. Her clothes were drenched with wine; perhaps it would dull the pain. She put her knee down on a stone fragment, wincing as it cut into her. "Oh, sweet Jesus," she muttered.

They found Croft lying against the wall under the pile of barrels. Maighread ran her fingers lightly over him, seeking any wounds or broken bones. It was all she could do in the dark.

"If he's alive, then he's out cold," she said.

"Let's try to sit him up," said Emma.

They removed the remains of the barrels from him. Maighread looked up for a moment.

"Sweet Mary, I hope there are no more barrels to fall," she whispered.

Croft was a tall, broad-shouldered man and they struggled to lift him. By the time they had him sitting up, Maighread's ribs felt very sore again. She was also wheezing badly, overcome by the dusty air and the stench of the wine.

"Can you die from inhaling too much wine, do you think?" asked Emma.

"I can think of worse deaths," replied Maighread. "Can you walk?" she asked.

"Aye."

"Then see if you can get to the door and open it. We

may be able to get out if the well chamber's still in one piece."

"I'll try," said Emma.

Maighread listened to her move around the cellar.

"I've found the door!" announced Emma. There was a pause and more scrabbling. "Mother of God! There's a timber the size of Bear blocking it," she cried. "There's no way out here."

"Try the other door, back the way we came," said Maighread. "If you could go back the other way to the cellar near the postern, you could bring help."

Emma crawled back past her but made no reply.

Soon after, Maighread heard the creak of the door opening.

"Emma?"

"Aye, we could go through but... does not Gate hold that side of the castle? Are you sure you want to ask for his help?"

Maighread gave a bleak sigh. "We may have to," she conceded.

"We'll have to feel our way and we can't carry Croft," said Emma.

"Something has happened," Maighread said, "beyond Gate, beyond Ned - as if... God has raised His hand. Who knows who lives now and who does not?"

"We can't stay here."

"You go then," said Maighread.

She heard Emma move and suddenly a hand gripped hers.

"Come," said Emma. "We'll both go."

§§§§

Ned opened his eyes to a world of dust and smoke and shut them again. He dared not move. No-one else seemed to be moving. Perhaps he should wait a little to see if the building was still sound. He waited and then, gingerly, he tried to move his limbs a little and found that none were broken. For once, his head did not hurt - and that could only be God's work. The dust was still settling on and around him.

The boy raised his head, black hair turned white with stone dust. He expected the lad would start wailing soon but he was mistaken, for John simply gave him a grim smile and patted him on the shoulder. The simple gesture sent a spear of emotion through Ned's very heart, a feeling beyond his understanding. He was a father and it changed him in a heartbeat.

They were halfway down the stairs under a pile of rubble. Ned tried to get up but stopped when he heard Ragwulf groan beneath him. He squinted down the stairwell at Hal. To his relief he saw that Hal was still moving. He was surprised how bright it was in the stairwell but when he looked up to the privy chamber, he realised why. The privy chamber had gone and with it Joan, Agnes… Eleanor.

There was movement at the foot of the stairs and Bear's face appeared above the pile of rubble in the doorway. "Lord?" he enquired.

"Aye," answered Ned, his hoarse voice barely audible. "Help Ragwulf and Hal - and have a care…"

Ned stood John up on the step above him and gently extricated himself from the pile of debris. Bear and another man at arms were carefully digging out Ragwulf and Hal. John started to climb the steps to the top.

"Wait!" breathed Ned.

The boy carried on walking.

"Wait!" Ned said again, louder.

John paused and waited for his father to reach him. Ned held out his hand and the boy stared at him. Then he took Ned's hand and they mounted the remaining steps together.

Beyond the steps there was nothing: no stone passage, no privy chamber doorway and no privy chamber - just a large expanse of fallen masonry. Here and there, ugly spars of timber pointed skywards. Guardroom, main gate, powder store and kitchen were all reduced to a sea of rubble overflowing the few stunted walls that remained.

Ned looked in vain for any sign of life: a moving arm or a trailing leg. Nothing moved. He listened for the cry of someone trapped beneath the rubble. No cries came but he did hear horses. He swung around to look across the courtyard. The stables on the west range were untouched by the explosion and from there emerged Thomas Gate and several others. They rode through the archway and out of sight. They would be leaving by the postern gate and there was nothing he could do about it - nor at that moment did he care.

Bear clambered up to him.

"Ragwulf and Hal?" Ned enquired.

"Both will live, my lord," replied Bear, "but Ragwulf's leg is broken."

Ned gripped his arm and nodded. "We must find the others," he said.

He realised that John was clinging to his leg and bent down to pick him up. Then he followed Bear down to the yard to face the carnage. Many of Gate's men had been crushed under the falling east range and gatehouse. The great portcullis hung from one chain at a perilous angle a few feet off the ground. If the chain broke it would crash down to add to the carnage. Most of the kitchen tower had disappeared and its charred interior lay open, the breeze brushing burnt fragments out to drift down on to the remains of the east range.

Ned put John down and cast his eyes over the shell of the kitchen tower.

He clutched Bear's shoulder. "Where is Lady Maighread?" he demanded.

Bear nodded. "In wine cellar. Should be safe."

"Wait here," he told John and stumbled across the

debris to the doorway at the foot of the kitchen tower - or rather the place where the doorway had once been. The stairwell had gone and the well chamber lay open. The well itself had been demolished and the door to the wine cellar splintered and battered by fallen masonry. Safe, thought Ned, nowhere was safe.

"Maighread!" he yelled. "Maighread! Emma!"

He paused to listen, but there was nothing. John tugged at his arm.

"Not now, John!" he snapped. "I told you to wait across the yard!"

John let go and wandered away over the stone-strewn cobbles. Ned hammered on the door until the whole doorway began to shake.

"Peace, lord!" warned Bear. Ned stopped and turned away. He wasn't thinking straight - and he must, if they were to save as many as they could. He heaved in a few deep breaths, which hurt his dust-coated chest but helped clear his befuddled head.

He stepped out into the yard again and regarded the survivors. Bear and at least seven or eight of his men at arms were still standing. Hal, remarkably, was moving quite well as he tried to make Ragwulf comfortable. Ned turned to Bear.

"Do what you can for Ragwulf's leg and then get everyone else searching the rubble for survivors. Tell them to be careful! I'll go into the cellars from the other end. I'll shout if I need you."

He looked around for John and began to panic when he could not immediately see him. Bear pointed across the yard to where John was searching amongst the corpses that had already been recovered. Ned called out to him but the boy ignored him.

"What in God's name is he doing there?" muttered Ned and trudged after him.

John glanced down at every body and then wandered off

into the south range.

"It's not safe, John!" he cried.

The boy moved faster than he and it took him several minutes to catch up with him. He found him in a store room, kneeling in a pool of blood.

"Wulf," said John in a quiet, broken voice. It was the first time Ned saw his son cry. He felt like weeping too as he looked down at Ragwulf's son lying against the door frame, his body ripped asunder by bloody wounds.

He thought of Ragwulf, for Ned was just beginning to grasp what it might be like to lose a son. John looked up at him and Ned put an arm around his shoulder.

"Wulf was my friend," sobbed John.

"Weep for him then, lad, and then wipe away your tears for he was the bravest of young men and should be remembered with love... and honour, not tears."

"Aye," said John.

He knelt beside the boy. "I'm your father, John," he whispered.

"I know," said the boy, looking him in the eye. "I know."

Ned felt like a stranger - but then he supposed that to John he was.

He bent down and gathered up Wulf's body into his arms.

"Come," he said and John followed him out into the yard.

Ragwulf grimaced as Bear braced his broken leg with timber spars and bound them up tight. Ned carried Wulf to his father and laid the body down beside him.

Ragwulf's face was already grey and he stared at the corpse.

"I knew - somehow, I knew," he muttered as he laid a gentle hand on his son's head.

"No man had a better son," said Ned.

"I wish only that I had died with him... or with her.

Now I've neither one of them."

"We've not found her yet," said Ned, "she may still live."

Ragwulf looked up at him. "You don't believe that, lord."

"I won't believe she's dead till I see her, nor Agnes," said Ned. "But, if she's alive now, she won't be much longer."

Ragwulf nodded then staggered to his feet. "Give me a moment with Wulf and I'll join you."

"Take as long as you want," said Ned, "we can search."

"He'll still be here to mourn in a few hours. I'm going to look for the woman I love," he said savagely, "and you should do the same!"

Ned left him and headed for the arch at the far corner of the yard. Before he had taken many steps, a tiny hand clutched at his. He gripped the boy's hand tightly and continued across the yard and out to the postern gate. It was wide open and nearby lay the bodies of his men. It was a brutal sight for the lad, but wherever he looked, he would see death - best that he became accustomed to it.

They descended the steps to the cellar where a lone torch was burning its last. John suddenly broke away from him and threw himself sobbing onto the body of the girl, Bess. Ned tried to pull the boy off but he clung to her cold corpse. Slowly Ned grasped who and what the girl must have been to his son - perhaps the boy had seen enough death for one day.

He went to the door that led through to the other store chambers, but it was barred from the other side. Of course it was. Bear and Hal would have secured the door at their backs.

He banged on it but there was no response. "Maighread!" he shouted.

John looked up at the sound of her name.

He kept shouting, "Emma! Maighread!" until his voice

cracked.

He cursed himself for bringing Maighread to Yoredale. He should have argued with her and left her at Corve - bound and gagged if need be, but still safe.

"She's a brave lady," said John suddenly.

Ned saw that the boy still sat beside Bess but his attention was now focussed on the cellar door.

"Lady Maighread or Bess?" Ned asked him.

John gave him a stern look. "Both!" he retorted as if he were talking to a halfwit.

"Aye," agreed Ned, "both."

"Lady Maighread's quite safe," he said to reassure the boy.

"No she's not!" said John, his tone dismissive, scornful.

"No… she's not," said Ned, staring at the barred door. He would need to learn how to talk to his son for it did not seem that easy.

Then the cellar door opened and there stood Maighread and Emma. They staggered into the chamber and Ned rushed forward to help them. John ran to Maighread and hugged her legs.

"You are a welcome sight," said Maighread, in a hoarse whisper, "my two fine warriors…"

"We weren't sure who we'd find here," said Emma.

"Nor were we," said Ned, wrapping his arms around the two women.

§§§§

Ragwulf stood in the yard. All was quiet, save the occasional cracking of a burnt timber in the kitchen tower and the rumble of stones that Bear was moving aside as he led the search. Death was ever quiet. He cast a final look down at his son and then across to Bear. The big man was staring at him, willing him to come. Well, no-one argued with Bear. He tried to walk and gave a grunt of pain. His leg moved about as well as the strips of timber that braced it.

He limped over to the ruined east range. Somewhere under all that stone were Eleanor and Agnes - and Joan Elder, of course. Eleanor was tough, tougher than most men - but could she still be alive, could any of them? He sat for a time on a chunk of fallen masonry and considered. He tried to work it out: where would she have been, which way might she have fallen, or been thrown? If she had been cast out of the chamber she would have been seen already, so she must lie under the debris. Perhaps it was better that she lay there. It had aged him to gaze upon his son's tortured corpse and he could not bear the thought of her beautiful face crushed and bloodied. It would be better to remember her at her glorious best - that was the Eleanor he loved.

64

7th February 1469, at Yoredale Castle

They searched all morning - everyone searched, even Maighread, despite her wound. Bear had tended to it again after he had retrieved the dazed Master Croft from the wine cellar. Maighread would not countenance sitting and watching while there was a slim chance that someone still lived. John knelt beside her, moving small stones aside with a grim expression on his face. The same stern look was on Ned's face a few yards away.

Ragwulf, she soon realised, was now organising the search, directing each of them - including his lord - to search here or there. She sensed a coolness between Ragwulf and Ned - and no words were said between them. Worst of all though, was watching Hal scrabbling in the rubble with his bare hands, tears rolling down his scratched and bruised face.

As time passed and no sign of life was found, a cold dread began to seep unbidden into her heart. Then, amongst the gritty stone and ash, her fingers touched something soft - a piece of cloth, and inside it, a woman's bare arm.

She screamed - at first incoherent, shocked but full of sudden hope. "Here!" she cried out, not sure whether she was touching living flesh or dead. Everyone rushed to the spot and began heaving stones aside.

"Careful!" shouted Ned, pulling some folk away and then lifting Maighread up. He took one look at the freckled arm.

"It's Agnes," he said.

Maighread felt him trembling beside her as Hal worked to free the thin, pale arm.

"Agnes!" cried Hal. "We've found you. Hold on!"

She watched Bear and Hal anxiously as, between them, they worked to clear the debris around Agnes. Too many careless boots might crush the life out of her.

She was lying on her chest, they discovered as they cleared around her. Her legs, her back, her shoulders - then her golden hair, twisted and tangled with only a little blood upon it. There was not a mark or a wound on her. Ned's tense body relaxed as Bear gently lifted her and turned her over and all the while Hal spoke softly to her as a lover would. Then Hal stopped talking and they all stared at her. Her face was bruised, cut and blood-stained and under her chin was the ragged gash in her throat that had killed her.

Maighread looked away, burying her face in Ned's chest. Emma led John quickly away and Hal fell upon Agnes' frail body, crushing it to his breast.

"What a miserable end," murmured Ned as he held Maighread close. "Cursed be Thomas Gate for taking her from me and bringing her here to die such a death."

For a while depression engulfed them all as they sat amid the desolation. Then Maighread glanced at Ragwulf, who was still casting his eyes over the remains.

"Come," she said to Ned, "we've not finished yet."

He nodded. He went over to Ragwulf and held out his hand to help him up. "Come on, old friend," he said, "we've still work to do before we can rest."

Ragwulf met his gaze, then nodded and took his outstretched arm to get to his feet once more. Starting where Agnes was found, together they lifted aside great roof timbers and stones. Maighread began to weep then for she thought that no-one could survive under such weight - the breath would surely be crushed from them utterly. Yet the two men continued searching there whilst the others excavated a few yards away. She was about to leave them to go to John when she glimpsed a flash of blue in the dust.

"Hold, Ned!" she cried and bent down onto her knees. She was unlikely to forget Joan Elder's blue kirtle too easily. She tugged at the material, and Ned bent to help her. Bear levered up a great half-charred timber and part of Joan's kirtle was revealed.

"Wait!" snapped Ned. "Leave her be! Joan Elder can lie there. Let the crows tear at her flesh and rend her wretched eyes!"

"But she may be alive," said Maighread.

"Good! Then I'll sit and watch her die."

"Then you'll be damned for it!" retorted Maighread, and she did not want her man damned.

"I'd have thought that you - of all folk - would want her dead… punished."

"God will punish her - she'll be forever damned for what she has done," she said.

He looked at her uncomprehendingly. "She has killed those I loved…and near killed you, my love - left you for dead, burned and scarred. She deserves only the worst death I can conceive."

She noticed that the others had backed away, leaving the pair of them arguing over the body. She gripped his hand and dragged him away. Then she took his dusty, angry face in both her hands forcing him to look at her.

"Would you give your soul to watch her die?" she asked softly. "I have only you left now. I want a man who is whole, a man who values life, not death."

He returned her intense gaze, but said nothing.

"Look at me!" she insisted. "Look upon a face scarred by death, but still alive - and still able to love!"

He nodded then and held her but she did not stop there. It was better that her bitter words were said now.

"All the fallen must be treated the same, buried and prayers said. Let God decide what happens then."

"Very well," he conceded. "Let there be an end to this

feud and let God give His judgement when He wills."

She looked back across the east range, now bathed in sunshine, and saw Joan move.

"Oh, Lady Mary in Heaven!" breathed Maighread, "what have I done? I thought she was dead…"

Ned's mercy was short-lived and his hand flew to his sword hilt. But Ragwulf had seen the movement too and began hobbling over the ground towards her, his knife already in his hand. Maighread and Ned followed Ragwulf but, before any of them reached her, she began to raise herself up. Maighread stared at her in fascination, noticing for the first time a knife hilt protruding from the side of her neck. As she got nearer she could see congealed blood and dirt below the wound. Joan looked stone dead but she must have the strength of an ox.

Ragwulf was barely two yards from her when she was suddenly thrown forward and a blood-covered arm thrust itself up from beneath her into the sunlight. A desperate, ragged voice screamed in triumph. "Blood of Christ! Must I crawl out of this wretched hole on my own?"

Everyone moved at once. Maighread ran with Ned but Ragwulf was already there, scrambling over the rubble and tossing Joan's lifeless body aside. He grasped the bloody hand in his and pressed it to his lips. Maighread and Ned began to scrape away the ash and stone, but Ragwulf seemed unwilling to let go of the hand.

"Good Christ, get me out, Ragwulf," cried Eleanor. "You can kiss me later!"

They cleared the debris from her and found her trapped against the base of the wall that once separated the weapon store from the gatehouse.

"Ellie," murmured Ned.

It must have been the first time he had seen her face for five long years, thought Maighread. She was spent though and must have used the last of her indomitable spirit to get free. She barely flinched when Ragwulf lifted her up into his arms. He carried her across to the bake house and laid her down gently on a long table.

"Bear!" he roared, but Bear was already close by and Emma too. Bear pushed Ragwulf aside and Emma hurried to examine her sister's wounds.

Eleanor reached out for Ragwulf's hand. "Stay close to me," she whispered. "Stay close…"

65

8th February 1469, in the yard at Yoredale Castle

"It was Sunday yesterday," said Emma absently. "How did I forget that?"

"We all forgot that," said Ned. "Are you sure this is what you want, sis?"

"Aye, Ned - if the earl will still have me. And are you sure about what you want?"

"Aye, Maighread has persuaded me. I want to live long enough to raise sons with her-"

"Just sons?" asked Maighread, leaning into his shoulder.

"Well, perhaps a daughter or two," he added, but even when he said the words, his thoughts strayed to Agnes, calling up her image in his mind.

"You're ready to go, then?" he said. "Croft seems fit enough to ride with you - and he seems to want to see you safely away. You've young Will Wright with you too - just in case. Remember, Thomas Gate is still out there somewhere."

Emma nodded and then embraced them all. Ned lifted her up onto her mount.

"So," she said, "in two days, then."

"If the earl is willing to come," said Ned.

"I think he will, Ned," said Emma, "I think he will, but in any event I shall be there."

Croft led them out of the postern gate and she gave Ned a last small wave of her hand as she disappeared from view.

"I must be a fool to let her go," he said to Maighread.

"She wants to go back to Middleham. It holds no fears for her. Her children are there and she must go back to them."

"But what if Gate is there? He's Warwick's client! He might even be on his way back here now with a score of Warwick's men!"

"Gate has no quarrel with Emma - or at least she believes he does not."

"Perhaps," he acknowledged.

"If Gate returns, you can deal with him then. But now, go," she said. "Go and do what a good lord must - and I'll be your good lady."

So he busied himself with all that had to be done: graves were dug for the dead who were now laid out in the Great Hall. Since the priest, Father Baston, was amongst them, Emma would go to Coverham Abbey on her way to Middleham and arrange for Canon Reedman to come tomorrow to say the words.

The castle was finished: its main gatehouse in ruins along with the kitchens and the entire east range and wall. In the Hall Ned had torn down Thomas Gate's red banner and was glad of its demise. It reminded him of the Radcliffe banner. This castle had never felt like his home - it was the Radcliffe family's seat and he could not forget that. It was a place of death for him and, when he left in two days' time, he vowed he would never return to it. Eleanor and Ragwulf would stay there until she recovered enough to make the journey to Corve.

Men and women from the estate had wandered up to Yoredale Castle amazed and he had put their labour to good use. He did not tell them yet that he would be leaving for good - that could wait a day. He thought they would be glad to see him go.

66

10th February 1469, on a high moor west of Middleham Castle

They had dismounted. Now they waited.

Ned thought it must nearly be noon, but there was no sign of Warwick. There were others though - more than he had expected, far more. Mostly young men and women with small children, desperate for a new place, a new beginning - well he shared that with them. He had offered them tenancies and hard work, nothing more. He had seen for himself how few tenants were left at Corve Manor - the product of his older brother stripping away the men of the estate a decade before. He could hardly blame him - had he not done the same himself in Yoredale? He had overseen the slaughter of a generation of Yoredale men and those who waited here for him were those too young to fight before. How desperate must they be to risk trusting him with their lives again?

"My lord!" Hal rode in. "Riders, coming up the valley."

"How many?" asked Ned.

"A score or more."

"Well that makes sense; I told him to come alone…"

"Would you?" asked Ragwulf.

"No," he conceded, "I wouldn't - and I won't. Bear! Stay here and keep a watch out. Hal - go up on the highest ground. Ragwulf stay with Eleanor in the wagon. Maighread and I will go to meet him."

"You're certainly not going without me," cried Eleanor, clambering down from the wagon which had been commandeered for the sole purpose of conveying her more comfortably. "After all I've been through? I'll see this to the end!"

Ragwulf shook his head. "She won't be satisfied until she makes an end of herself," he said, spreading his arms wide in frustration.

Ned was about to argue with his sister but Maighread laid a hand on his arm and he thought better of it for he was not prepared to argue with both of them. He slowly shook his head.

"She's your responsibility now," he growled at Ragwulf, who simply grinned and shrugged his shoulders.

"She does as she wills," said Ragwulf but he lifted her carefully onto his horse and she rewarded him with a tearful smile.

"Aye," said Ned, "and don't we know it!"

They picked their way up a short slope which took them onto the high moor overlooking the Cover valley - the place Ned had agreed to meet Emma.

They waited and could see that the Earl of Warwick's party was already on its way up to them. When they were about fifty paces away, Emma came on with Warwick and one other beside them: Reedman. Ned recognised the earl at once though it was several years since he had seen him. At the mere sight of him, he could feel the hostility rising within him, but he suppressed it. He had renounced the feud with Warwick - all that remained to be seen was whether Warwick was prepared to do the same.

The earl pulled up his horse a few feet from Ned but remained mounted.

"I don't much like being summoned," he said.

"It was… an invitation," said Ned.

"It didn't seem so. And why do we have to meet up here on this God-forsaken moor?"

"I wanted to be sure you came up alone," said Ned.

"And why is the Canon here? Are we to take vows?"

"He will bear witness to what is said - for you, as well as me."

Warwick grimaced with evident distaste. "Aye, well, now… you have me here, what do you want?"

"I want peace," said Ned.

"Do you, by God - you want peace."

"You've made your peace with King Edward," said Ned, "why not with me?"

"You've cost me a great deal over the years, Ned Elder - and not least in the past few days if I am to believe what I'm told."

"His Grace sent me north to root out the traitor, Sir Thomas Gate."

"And so you killed his lady and most of his men at arms. You destroyed his castle and God knows what else. Did the royal warrant allow for all that, I wonder?"

"You could argue I destroyed my own castle. Gate was a traitor, raising men who would be rebels!"

"Rebels? If you listen to the queen and her overbearing kin, there are rebels wherever you look!"

"Thomas Gate was your client," Ned pointed out.

"Indeed, he was my client - and most of Christendom probably knows that, what of it?"

"If he was planning a rebellion…"

"… Then I must know of it?" said Warwick, with an iron smile. "What do you really want, Ned?"

"I want an end to this blood between us. I'm done with feuds. I'm going to Corve Manor in the Welsh marches and my sister, Lady Eleanor, will follow when she's recovered from her wounds. Any from the Yoredale estates who want to join me will be free to do so. No reprisals - against anyone. Lady Emma will take up her position in your daughter's household - as already agreed - but she will also administer the Yoredale estates until her son Richard comes of age. He will then inherit the estate."

"Is that all?" asked Warwick.

"No, it is not. Do you have Thomas Gate?"

"Why would I?"

"Thomas Gate will not be forgiven. He must be attainted as a traitor and murderer. If he is not found, he must be declared an outlaw. For your part, you will agree not to harbour him or give him aid."

"Oh, will I?" Warwick was teasing him, he knew, but he did not rise.

"You will," said Ned, "or I shall tell the king that Thomas Gate acted entirely upon your orders."

Warwick breathed a heavy sigh. "His Grace would not believe you."

"He could not ignore it," said Ned, "and you have many enemies at court, my lord, only too pleased to support a campaign against you."

"I have the power to crush you into the dirt."

"Yet… in all these years you haven't been able to do so," observed Ned.

"How do you suppose threatening me is likely to heal the wounds between us?" asked Warwick.

"Because what I ask is easy for you to give."

Warwick's eyes briefly met his and in that instant Ned saw something - perhaps a glimpse of his future, perhaps nothing. Then Warwick nodded.

"Very well, I agree to your terms. Thomas Gate, when he is caught, will be despatched. Gate will be no more. You have my word on that and, if my word is good enough for the king, then it will certainly suffice for you - and this canon here."

"Agreed," said Ned. He eased his mount forward and Warwick did the same. The two men then clasped hands to seal their agreement.

"Good," concluded Warwick. "I'm a busy man. Are you coming, my lady?" He addressed his brusque question to Emma but he did not wait for her. Instead he waved Canon Reedman aside and cantered his horse back the way he had come.

Emma embraced her brother and sister.

"We may not meet again for an age," she said. "I've made my choice and I'm part of the Neville household now. Leave me to it, Ned. I won't need rescuing again."

He nodded and watched her set off after the earl. He watched her until she passed out of sight along the track that led down off the moor towards Coverham.

He looked to Maighread. "God's blood, my love, but I hope I've done the right thing."

"You've done what your king has done; you've put an end to strife," she said with a smile. "Now, you can take me home to Corve where we will hold a fine, and long overdue, wedding."

"No," said Eleanor, "two… long overdue weddings!"

Ragwulf took her back down to the wagon but Ned remained for a moment with Maighread looking out over the valley.

"There is also the matter of a certain prominent London alderman waiting for us at Corve," said Ned, "and his grandson, Jack."

"Aye, I'm looking forward to witnessing how you manage that when Eleanor arrives," Maighread said.

"Well, perhaps marriage will mellow my sister a little."

She gave him a doubtful smile and they rode down off the moor together.

67

12th February 1469, in the privy chamber at Middleham Castle

Warwick sat at the great oak table in his privy chamber. At his left hand was Benjamin Warner and before him stood Sir Thomas Gate, nervously shifting from one foot to the other.

"You're a brave man, Thomas, coming here," said the earl.

"Brave or not, I've always been your man, my lord," replied Thomas, "and I remain your man still."

"But you'll be an outlaw now, Thomas."

"You could change that easily, my lord, by just a stroke of your pen."

"I could end it easily with just a stroke of my sword too! You've made many mistakes, costly mistakes, Thomas - you and your reckless wife. Men, arms, powder - all squandered to no purpose. You bragged that you would kill Ned Elder and when you failed, you flaunted power in my name before I was ready for you to do so."

"You spoke of spring - well, it's almost spring..."

"Almost, Thomas? There is no 'almost' when it comes to unseating a king…"

"But, my lord!" protested Gate.

"I was not ready - and I'm still not ready!" growled Warwick. "At the moment I'm waiting for the pope, but there's always something that a plan can snag on. I must take care. The queen has spies everywhere..."

"So what is to be my fate then, my lord?"

Warwick could see that Gate was trembling.

"I gave Ned Elder my word that you would be despatched - my word, my hand upon it, Thomas. Thus, Sir Thomas Gate has to die, I'm afraid."

Gate fell upon his knees. "I beg you my lord, for the love and service I've always given you!"

Warwick could not resist a sly smile at Warner.

"Oh, get up Thomas, or I might change my mind. Gate must die, but you'll live - at least a little longer. I need you as a soldier, a leader of men - and men on their knees rarely make good leaders, so get up!"

"My lord, I'm grateful…"

"Save your gratitude. I'm despatching you north to Sir John Conyers. But, if you fail again, I shall kill you myself. Gate is - as of now - a dead outlaw. He no longer exists. You, Thomas, are going to be reborn - not an experience every man has in life. But of course, it's not the first time you've been reborn, is it?"

"My lord?"

Warwick smiled and Gate looked wary, as well he might.

The earl glanced at the lawyer. "Warner has chosen a name for you. Warner?"

"Robert, my lord," announced Warner.

"Robert?" said Gate.

"Sound familiar to you, Gate?" said Warner. "The name your mother gave you… Robert… when she bore you… up in some grubby hovel in Redesdale."

Gate's face was like stone. "Redesdale?" he said, his voice barely a whisper.

"Well, were you not born there?" asked Warner.

"Good Christ! How do you know that?" demanded Gate.

"It's his business to know," snapped Warwick, "so that he can tell me. You'd be very surprised how much Warner knows."

"How much exactly does he… do you, know about

me?" asked Gate.

"I know you were born in Redesdale and I know who your father was and I know why you've taken such a close interest in the Yoredale estates. Is that enough?"

Gate said nothing.

Warwick was enjoying himself so he decided to push Gate a little further. "Very well, I know that your father was Lord Robert Radcliffe - spreading the excess seed of his youth rather widely, it seems!"

"Even he didn't know about me," said Gate defiantly.

"No, probably not, but if he did, he certainly didn't care. But you, Thomas… you harbour a few… ambitions hidden away," said the earl. "Well, for now, they'd best stay hidden. After all, Radcliffe already has a legitimate heir."

"I've always served you loyally, my lord."

"Which you will continue to do, but you'll call yourself…" He glanced at Warner.

"'Robin of Redesdale'," said Warner.

"Just so, 'Robin of Redesdale,' and, when the time comes, you'll lead a rebellion in the north… for me. After that, Robin, we might consider your own ambitions."

§§§§§ §§§§§ §§§§§ §§§§§

Author's Note: Rebels & Brothers

Readers of the first two books of the Rebels & Brothers series, Feud and A Traitor's Fate, will recall that they ended with many "loose ends." At the end of this book the central storyline, as always, has been brought to a conclusion but other, as yet minor, storylines remain in the air.

We have left Ned to marry Maighread and his troubled sister, Eleanor, to find happiness and peace with Ragwulf. Emma has a future mapped out for her in Anne Neville's household. But yes, you are right: it's all an illusion of peace, as the final chapter reveals. You'll have to wait for the final book to discover how it all ends. Who will still be standing when the story comes to an end? Will there be tears of joy or misery for the Elder family?

To find out more about the series and future developments as they occur, or to contact me, you can go to my website: **www.derekbirks.com**.

I also have an occasional blog:
www.dodgingarrows.wordpress.com.
You can follow me on Twitter as **@Feud_writer.**
My Facebook page is:
www.facebook.com/feudwriter.

Thank you very much for reading my stories about the Elder family and I certainly hope that you have enjoyed them. As a self-published writer, I must market my own work and one thing that helps me enormously is the response from readers. Please feel free to get in touch by using the contact form on my website. If you have enjoyed my work then you might like to give it a favourable mention either in the shape of an **Amazon** or **Goodreads** review or on another site of your choice.

Either way, many thanks for reading.
Derek Birks
August 2014

Historical Notes

The Wars of the Roses

Everyone knows about the Wars of the Roses – or do they? The range of historical opinion is so broad and varied on this whole period that I could not hope to do more than follow a consistent thread of narrative through it. Besides adhering to an accurate chronology of the events, I have also tried to set the events between the Elders and Warwick within an appropriate late fifteenth century context. In this book the Earl of Warwick continues to have a very prominent role in national politics but we are also beginning to see the rise of King Edward's new in-laws, the Woodvilles. [see below]

Whenever the story encounters an actual person I have attempted to create a character who would at least be recognisable to students of the period. Since this story uses Richard Neville and his wife, Anne as well as Anthony Woodville and Margaret of York as important named characters I have endeavoured to make them as believable as possible, though of course their actions in this story are completely fictitious.

The North of England in 1468

In 1468 when the story begins, the north of England is in a bad way. The Lancastrian rebellion of 1463-4 has passed but there are still men who have little or no commitment to the new king, Edward of York. Their loyalties are more closely attached to local men of power. With the temporary decline of great families such as the Percies and the Cliffords, the power of the rival Neville family has never been greater. There is also scope for disaffection in the north with poverty, heavy taxation and an absence of royal authority.

People
Richard Neville, Earl of Warwick
The earl has a strong affinity around him and his home castle of Middleham in Yorkshire is a pivotal position of power in the north. In 1468 he continues to support his king but there are signs that he is becoming increasingly disenchanted with his lot. It is not just that Edward's marriage to a widowed gentlewoman has wrecked his own plans for the king's marriage, but that the king seems to be paying more attention to some of his new relations, such as the queen's father, Earl Rivers and her brother, Anthony Woodville, Lord Scales.

There is no evidence that Warwick fomented revolt in the summer of 1468 but he was certainly hostile to the king during those months. As is clearly stated in the book, Warwick made his peace with King Edward towards the end of the year and the king had frequently shown his willingness to take such reconciliations at face value. There is plenty of evidence, however, to show that Warwick was behind a revolt later in the summer of 1469 and such a revolt could not have been spontaneous. What is described in the book must have been happening at some point between summer 1468 and spring 1469. It was not of course being carried out by Thomas Gate, who is fictional, but another mentioned in the book, Sir John Conyers, was certainly involved.

Not a great deal is known for certain about Warwick's wife, Anne, Countess of Warwick, beyond a basic framework of dates. It does appear to be the case though that she took an interest in the lives of local women and did attend some childbirths. Childbirth at this time was an event where women supported each other and men were excluded - thus it is not surprising that some ladies like Anne felt a particular responsibility for what happened in this realm where women ruled.

Warwick and Anne also had two daughters to arrange

marriages for and since the queen's numerous sisters had used up quite a few eligible peers Warwick decided that his best option would be to marry at least one of his daughters to a brother of the king - one of the Dukes of Clarence and Gloucester. However, Edward made it abundantly clear that he was not in favour of this. Nevertheless, in the very last chapter of this book we learn that Warwick is waiting for news before he takes any further action. The news he is waiting for will be a Papal Dispensation - applied for behind Edward's back - allowing Warwick's daughter, Isabel, to marry George, Duke of Clarence. In Book 4 we shall see how this all turns out for Warwick - and everyone else!

Princess Margaret of York - Duchess of Burgundy

Princess Margaret has a cameo role in this book. She did arrive in Sluys in Burgundy at the time and date described in the book and she was escorted there by Anthony Woodville, Lord Rivers. The French were very keen to sabotage the marriage of an English princess to their Burgundian enemy and attempted to do so by the influence of the Earl of Warwick who was keen on a French alliance. When the marriage was clearly going ahead, there was a French attempt to attack the ship carrying Margaret to Burgundy. I am not aware of any attempt to assassinate her upon her arrival at Sluys, but it does not seem so far-fetched.

Anthony Woodville, Lord Scales

Anthony Woodville, the queen's brother, was given the task of escorting Margaret of York by ship to Burgundy for her marriage to the new Duke Charles. He is an interesting character, much valued by King Edward - a man of many talents and interests. His alliance with Ned is of course fictional, but in the political climate of 1468/1469 the Woodvilles had to watch their backs. Many other men with influence distrusted or envied their meteoric rise to prominence. The king's brothers, George, Duke of Clarence, and Richard, Duke of Gloucester, were also suspicious of them as is shown by young Gloucester's warning to Ned.

During the summer and autumn of 1468 there was much concern at court about the possibility of a Lancastrian revival. The old king, Henry VI, was safely in the Tower, but his queen, Margaret of Anjou, was in France hoping to entice the wily King Louis XI of France to support her. Fear of Lancastrian spies in London was fuelled by a few arrests resulting in the use of torture - less common than one might think! This led to further arrests but there was little substance to these fears. The fictional Goldwell family is caught up in this madness and forced to flee from London, but more of that anon…

Places
Bruges & Sluys
Bruges was a major trade centre in the fifteenth century and its trade came from Spain and the Mediterranean in the south as well as the Baltic in the north. It specialised in luxury goods such as amber jewellery and it had excellent finishing trades in the cloth industry. Much of its raw wool came from England. But by 1468 Bruges as a port could no longer accommodate ocean going vessels. With the silting up of the river Zwin, only flat bottomed boats could bring goods in and out of Bruges. For a time the small port of Damme, further upriver, received shipping but then it too became a victim of the silted up river. By 1468 therefore it was Sluys which was the conduit through which Bruges trade passed and even then, as is described in the book, Sluys was already in decline. All the goods mentioned would have been found there, as well as the bell tower, warehouses and the docks. The Golden Ship is a fictional tavern but there would have several such places on the waterfront and

others in the small town.

Sluys [now Sluis] lies just across the present day Dutch border from Belgium. It is a delightful town but has suffered from its position, being heavily destroyed in both World Wars -not to mention in previous centuries.

Male Castle

There is a castle at Male near Bruges today but it is not the castle that was there in 1468. Castles in the area did take heavy punishment in the earlier struggle between Ghent and the Count of Flanders. They were frequently destroyed and rebuilt, hence the number of ruined castles available at the time!

Other Place References

Yoredale is the old name for the valley of the river Ure, now called Wensleydale, an area once much more heavily forested than it is now. Ned's original home, Elder Hall, if it had existed, would lie near the river Ure and Yoredale Castle would be further east and higher up the northern slope of Wensleydale. Yoredale Castle is fictional but some of its features are reminiscent of one or two castles in Yorkshire. The village of Carperby, mentioned in the book, is genuine and the description reflects what little is known about its layout, though I doubt anyone called Ragwulf lived there!

Nearby is the giant Neville stronghold at Middleham. It is a ruin now but it is still possible to get a measure of the majesty of this palatial residence. The events described there fit the layout of the buildings as they would have been at the time.

Crag Tower, situated on a promontory over the North Tyne valley, is also fictional but is typical of the kind of small fortified castle in the northern border regions.

London references include actual medieval street names and places, though of course Alderman Goldwell and everything about him is fictional.

Celebration of Christmas

In this book there are a number of references to activities that occurred at Christmas. Christmas Day was a quarter day and this meant the day that rents must be paid by tenants to their lord of the manor. Being in the middle of winter, it could represent a bit of a low ebb in the spirits of ordinary people so some sort of celebration was desirable. Wealthy lords might keep plenty of meat available for a lavish banquet but most people only shared the less desirable remains of it. Mince pies actually did contain minced meat - well, offal at least. Hence the term "humble pie."

During the Christmas period there were a number of festivals such as St Stephen's day, the "Massacre of the Innocents" and a tradition of a "Lord of Misrule"- usually chosen by servants. He represented a period when traditional roles were reversed and one of the low born "ruled". The fictional Weaver's activities are, I fear, only a little exaggerated and mayhem did sometimes occur... Several mummers plays have survived from this period - albeit mostly in fragments - and lords of large households could commission such plays which usually had quasi-religious themes, as mentioned in the book.

Coverham Abbey and the Praemonstratensian Monks - the White Canons

Coverham Abbey did exist but remains now only in a few ruined fragments. The order took a more pragmatic approach to their worship than some other orders and believed in going out into the community to fulfil pastoral roles in parish churches. The abbey itself plays a less prominent role in this book than in A Traitor's Fate but the role of the fictional Canon Reedman is of course very important.

About the Author

Derek was born in Hampshire in England but spent his teenage years in Auckland, New Zealand, where he still has strong family ties.

For many years he taught history in a secondary school in Berkshire but took early retirement several years ago to concentrate on his writing. Apart from writing, he spends his time gardening, travelling, walking and taking part in archaeological digs at a Roman villa.

Derek is interested in a wide range of historical themes but his particular favourite is the late Medieval period. He writes action-packed fiction which is rooted in accurate history.

His debut historical novel, Feud, is set in the period of the Wars of the Roses and is the first of a series entitled Rebels & Brothers which follows the fortunes of the fictional Elder family.

The sequel to Feud, A Traitor's Fate, was published in November 2013 and Book 3, Kingdom of Rebels, in September 2014. The final book of the series will be published in the summer of 2015.

Printed in Great Britain
by Amazon